HER PURSUERS
INCREASED THEIR PACE

Abandoning all pretense at oblivion, Jen tried to run, but her skirts tangled in her parasol, almost tripping her. As she lurched to one side, she heard the punctuated belch of a blow gun, and felt the wind of a tiny projectile brush past her left ear. A sudden wave of nausea swept her.

I wasn't trained for this, I'm not ready for this, they're supposed to be tailing me, not killing me! For an instant her body froze, and then she gathered her skirts in both hands and began to run, weaving a frantic, erratic path through the narrow street—her parasol unfurled behind her like a lacy shield— dodging projectiles. She was keenly aware of every tiny, failed missile that whizzed past or impacted against the panels of her impromptu buckler.

And still she kept running, the whole while repeating; *why did I think this would be fun, why did I think this was a game?*

ANVIL
OF THE
SUN

ANVIL
OF THE
SUN

The First Book of the Cloak and Dagger

ANNE LESLEY GROELL

A ROC BOOK

ROC
Published by the Penguin Group
Penguin Books USA Inc., 375 Hudson Street,
New York, New York 10014, U.S.A.
Penguin Books Ltd, 27 Wrights Lane,
London W8 5TZ, England
Penguin Books Australia Ltd, Ringwood,
Victoria, Australia
Penguin Books Canada Ltd, 10 Alcorn Avenue,
Toronto, Ontario, Canada M4V 3B2
Penguin Books (N.Z.) Ltd, 182–190 Wairau Road,
Auckland 10, New Zealand

Penguin Books Ltd, Registered Offices:
Harmondsworth, Middlesex, England

First published by Roc, an imprint of Dutton Signet,
a division of Penguin Books USA Inc.

First Printing, September, 1996
10 9 8 7 6 5 4 3 2 1

To my parents,
for all the best reasons

ACKNOWLEDGMENTS

To all the kindred spirits who have made this possible, in all its various incarnations. To my parents, for funding the trip that gave me the idea. To Jen and Thibault, for being too bloody-minded to let me go. To Mel, for being the first line of my editorial defense; and to Miriam, for being the second. To Darrin, for providing me with invaluable insight into the male psyche; and to Derek, for letting me steal his name. To Team Spectra, in both past and present incarnations—Tom, Jennifer, Mark, Ev, and Andrew—for overwhelming enthusiasm and support. To Lizzie, for always being there; and to Carol, for keeping me (??) sane. To all those other friends and colleagues too numerous to mention—you know who you are, kids (and Sarah, don't think I've forgotten!)—for listening to me obsess, suffering through excuses, or simply joining me in a really good laugh.

And most particularly, to Kay, Amy, and Jenni, for quite literally making a dream come true. My eternal gratitude and thanks.

PROLOGUE

"I have a job for the Hawk." The old man's voice was level; it was a statement more than a question.

"Indeed," his companion responded, equally noncommittal, folding her hands in her lap and regarding him across the studied clutter of his desk.

Under the lambent glow of the magelights, the room took on a faintly yellowish cast, as if viewed through faded vellum, and the books and ledgers stacked haphazardly on the shelves made it look more like the offices of some rundown shipping firm than the headquarters of one of the most powerful Guilds on all of Varia. But then, the effect was probably a deliberate one—for this, of all Guilds, specialized in concealment, and the keenness of the old man's mind was in no way reflected by the chaos in his office.

No, they all wore their requisite masks, and the woman seated across from him was no exception. Neither young nor old, she had lines that could be called character on her face, and a certain trace of silvering in her hair; yet there was, nonetheless, a taut erectness to her carriage, a vague hint of steeliness in her eye, that spoke of a body never quite at rest. Her dark hair was bound up in a rough braid, her scuffed riding leathers a suitable complement to the worn tawdriness of the room—her boots still dusty from the journey—and yet there was a certain elegant refinement to her, an air that spoke of breeding far beyond her setting. Maybe it was the unconscious tilt to her chin, the knowing and slightly cynical arch to her brows, that fostered this impression, or maybe it was simply the measured confidence in her level grey eyes.

No matter; the sight, as always, gave the old man pleasure. He had known Viera Radineaux—or Vera, as she was more commonly called—for nearly twenty years and had yet to see her looking less than suited to her environment, be it drawing room or hovel.

"Well?" he said, arching an eyebrow. "What of it? Is the Hawk interested in a commission?"

His companion grinned, crossing her legs like a drover, and settled back more comfortably in her chair. "Details, Owen. Details," she chided. "When? And where?"

"As to where," he responded, "Ashkharon. Apparently there is a certain First Minister who has reached the end of his usefulness . . ."

"Bollocks!" she exclaimed, glancing involuntarily at the steadily glowing magelights. "Not another bloody government job?"

"Ah, but this is an eminently proper one, my dear, and infinitely suited to your high moral character." She snorted. "Come, aren't you even remotely curious?"

"Very well, Owen, since you won't let me leave until I've heard your proposition, get on with it."

"How very magnanimous of you, Vera." He smiled, laying one gnarled hand gently against his breast and bowing. Then, in a more businesslike tone, he added, "As it happens, some of the Ashkharon residents are less than contented with the burgeoning policies of their revered leader and so have decided to take matters into their own hands. A sizeable rebel faction has grown up, and now they are looking for someone to implement a little judicial . . . weeding . . . in the ranks of the government—specifically, First Minister Guy Istarbion."

"Istarbion, eh?"

"You've heard of him?"

"In passing. So what is he accused of?"

"You are aware of the conditions in the Ashkharon glass manufactories?" Owen asked, by way of answer.

Vera shrugged. "That they are horrendous, of course, but the work is dangerous and the workers duly compensated. Besides, surely this is the province of the Glass Guild?"

"Who are firmly in the pocket of our revered Istarbion," the old man answered.

"And are skimming the workers' profits into the hands of the government?" Vera nodded. "Yes, I begin to see. But where, specifically, does the Hawk come in?"

"By request only, I assure you."

She grinned. "They asked for me?"

Owen arched a brow. "They asked for the Hawk," he reminded her, pointedly.

"Vera, Hawk, what difference?" She waved a hand

airily. "But why? What about this job is particularly suited to the Hawk's . . . unique temperament?"

"Perhaps because they believe themselves to be in the right?" The old man smiled. "And besides, when one is the best, one has a certain reputation to maintain."

"Ah, reputation, is it? The almost magic words. Owen, my love, has anyone ever told you that flattery will get you everywhere?"

He chuckled, but they both knew he was right. Viera Radineaux was the best, and the Hawk had soared uncontested since she first walked into this office nineteen years ago and signed her name rebelliously to the Guild registry. She had started as the best, and she remained the best: oddity enough in a profession where reputation—not to mention faces—altered by the day.

She raised an eyebrow, and he suddenly found himself wondering how many weapons she carried concealed about her person today. There were no visible bulges beneath the lean, close-fitting leathers, but he had never seen the Hawk less than prepared. There would be a garroting cord knotted into her braid, at least three daggers resting in slim, invisible sheaths, darts of some sort tucked into linings or cuffs, and doubtless some other surprises known only to the Hawk herself.

But then, that was the whole purpose of the Hestian Guild. Assassins, bodyguards, and spies, they were the unofficial police force of the whole Varian consortium.

"So they want the Hawk, eh?" she said. "Very well, tease me some more. When is this mission to materialize?"

"As soon as possible, I imagine."

"I see." Her fingers drummed against the arms of her chair, an unconscious rhythm, flashing silver off the lean brown digits; he wondered what forms of liquid or powdered death lay within the rounded hollows of those seemingly innocuous rings. "At least three weeks' travel by sea," she muttered, "two weeks for the job, three weeks back. . . . Tarnation, Owen, I can't possibly. Jen arrives in six weeks, and I promised to meet her."

"That young hoyden you adopted several years back? Where's she been?"

"Incarcerated at some dreadful finishing school in Haarkonis, and doubtless setting the place on its ear." She sounded unaccountably proud of the latter part.

The old man smiled. "So why send her?"

"Duty. It was Genevra's last request before her death, and you should never refuse family. She wanted her daughter to have the chance to become a lady, you see, away from her aunt's evil influence." Her voice was self-deprecating, but her eyes twinkled.

Owen arched an eyebrow. "And what does her daughter want?"

"To be a member of the Guild, I'm afraid."

"You've been training her?"

"In a mild sort of way."

"She must be good, then."

"She is. But we have a bargain, Jen and I. I shall not petition the Guild for her admission until she has had every chance to make herself a good match in society—including, so help me, a Season."

The Guildmaster chuckled dryly. "Led by yourself, I take it?"

"I know. It's quite a horrendous proposition, is it not?"

"On the contrary. I think you should be rather good."

"No, I assure you, it will be dreadful. Such functions are the very reason I abandoned the aristocracy in the first place. But I have no choice. With both my brother and his wife dead, I'm the only family Jenifleur has. I don't suppose," she added wistfully, "that you could find me some kind of society job for the duration? Just to entertain me?"

"And have Dom So-and-So falling dead on his ballroom floor?" He smiled. "I'll see what I can locate."

"Bless you, Owen. I knew there was a reason I loved you."

"But not enough to take the Ashkharon job?" he demanded, and she frowned.

"Owen, I promised. Can't someone else do it?"

"Such as?"

"The Dragon?"

"No. Requires too much subtlety, I'm afraid."

"The Stiletto, then."

He shook his head. "You see, they asked for you quite specifically; I rather think they'll rescind the offer without you."

"Great flying green elephants, I can't just abandon the girl, Owen!" she exclaimed and glanced again at the magelights, more consciously this time.

The old man just chuckled and shook a gnarled finger

in her face. "Nonsense, Vera, you can't catch me off guard like that. Besides, I just had them recoded."

She relaxed with a grin. The golden globes of mage-light were turned on and off by special phrases, coded into their makeup by the mages who recharged them. Owen DeVeris' tendency to key his to the most ridiculous expressions he could imagine had led to her own wildly inventive pattern of cursing; she was forever trying to turn them off.

"And no one else top-rank is available?" she continued, returning to the subject at hand.

He sighed and reached behind him, almost unconsciously pulling a ledger from the mess. Glancing ruefully at its cover, he blew a smattering of dust off its surface, then opened the heavy bindings. The thick pages creaked weightily as he turned them, and he frowned over the crabbed black writing. "I thought I . . . Yes, there, you see? The Jaguar is out, the Fox is down south, and the Hound and the Falcon are somewhere in Nordevaria."

"And the Kestrel?"

"See for yourself." He passed the ledger across the desk and she perused the stiff pages in silence for a moment. "You see, my dear, you're not only the best, you're the best currently available."

"Owen, I specifically asked for this time free because of Jen."

"Yes, I realize that, but I've no choice. Ashkharon must be served. Bright blue blazes, from all you've said, the girl sounds perfectly capable of taking care of herself! She must be, what—sixteen, seventeen, by now?"

Vera shrugged. "Eighteen."

"Eighteen? Well, whatever are you worrying about? It's a good job, Vera, and very well paying. If all goes smoothly, you can be in and out in eight weeks—only a fortnight late for the reunion with your beloved niece, not to mention several thousand marks richer."

"Don't be sarcastic, Owen," she snapped, and then her grey eyes sharpened. "Precisely how many thousand are we talking about?"

"Three," the old man answered slyly.

"Indeed. The *true* magic word." Viera's nimble fingers fidgeted almost invisibly with the knife in her wrist sheath as she considered, but Owen's trained ears could hear the faint, rhythmic clicking of the lock as she slid it back and forth. Silently, he counted. Out, in. Out, in. Out. In.

Out.

She paused, cocking her head. "Well, I suppose the money will help with the wretched Season, but . . . Blazes, Owen, you're being most insistent. What's the Guild's secret agenda?"

"Secret agenda?"

"Don't play innocent. The Guild *always* has a secret agenda." She sighed and pushed the knife back home. "Never mind. The pay is generous, a king's ransom. I'll have my neighbor's grandson look after Jen until I get back from Ashkharon. He's always good at keeping that girl out of trouble."

"Bless you, Vera. I'll have the mages send your response."

She gave a martyred sigh. "Yes. So who's my contact, DeVeris?"

"The rebel leader, a young man named Jason Andorian. You're to take Captain Black's trader to Nhuras, and someone named Iaon Pehndon—one of Andorian's men—will meet you on the docks and give you whatever other information you need."

"And he'll know me by the red rose I carry, no doubt," she said dryly, but couldn't help the faint stiffening of anticipation that went through her, washing the edges of reality with a razor-sharp glimmer. Much as she loved her niece, there was nothing like the thrill of the chase and the satisfaction of a job well done. Jen could survive for two weeks without her.

"Ashkharon, eh?" she added with a grin. "Blast it, Owen, the place is a ruddy desert!"

"So we must be sure to wine and dine you properly before you leave. Join me for dinner?"

"Dinner? With you?" She laughed.

The room was abruptly plunged into blackness.

"What the . . . Curse it, Owen, you set me up! I'm going to get you for this, you old curmudgeon."

"And sacrifice a dinner at Menot's at the Guild's expense?" His voice, laced with a certain subtle humor, drifted invisibly across the room.

Her laughing imprecations trailed into silence.

"Thirty thousand jellyfish in a jar," her companion said smugly, offering her his arm and escorting her from the room as the lights wafted on once again.

1

Jenifleur Radineaux stood on the deck of the *Oceanic Queen* with the wind in her hair, watching the verdant curve of Hestia swelling over the horizon. Beneath her feet, the bow cut a clean line through the steely waves, tossing up clouds of foam which dappled her cheeks with a salt-spray sting, while above, the great sails belled and creaked, catching the wind. Rollers as translucent as milky green glass crested and fell, the indefinable margin between wave and foam as luminous as if lit from within.

"Going home, Domina?"

The voice was soft and uncultivated yet oddly fluid, as if the leaping sea had acquired a tongue. Abandoning her thoughts with the barest of sighs, Jen turned to smile at the young red-haired sailor who had been lurking shyly in her shadow since she boarded, slipping her the occasional awkward grin as if unsure how to deal with the exalted lady who strode the boards of his ship as confidently as any seaman. The rest of the crew had all but adopted her, tidying her cabin and bringing her meals, making sure she lacked for nothing the ship's poor stores could afford— their rough humor unrestrained—but he alone had stood apart, vulnerable in his youth and more than half infatuated.

"Yes, I suppose I am." She laughed, her open expression encouraging him forward, and tossed back her windswept hair, suddenly aware of the light touch of her hat abandoned between her shoulder blades. What would her mother say if she could see her now, her fashionable skirts in tangles about her legs and her cheeks glowing with the sea and sun, leaning her elbows on the deck railing and grinning at a common tar as if they were lifelong companions? *She'd be rolling in her grave, that's what,* Jen decided. No, it was undoubtedly a good thing that

Genevra Radineaux was safely dead and thus spared the spectacle of her only child forsaking every value that had given her narrow life any meaning.

The sailor's eyes were a lucent green, the very color of the breaking waves, and crinkled at the corners as if a lifetime of laughter and ocean voyages had made them unable to open further.

"Excited?" he said.

She considered this, one side of her mouth rising in a half-smile that brought the faintest trace of a dimple to her cheek. "Not sure," she answered frankly.

Beneath rough-cut gingery hair, his brow furrowed in confusion. "Why not?"

"Because," she grinned, turning briefly to survey the gentle green shores of her homeland. There stretched the white strand beaches of Nova Castria, and there the ramshackle sprawl of weathered buildings that made up the town and wharf, now but a vague brown smear on the horizon. A brief band of emerald fields behind it, and then the shadowy bulk of the forest loomed, where Aunt Vera made her home and in which Jen had spent the happiest years of her childhood, relegated to her aunt's practical and beloved care when the exigencies of living had sent Genevra into yet another nervous decline.

Surreptitiously, her fingers caressed the stiff folds of Vera's letter, secreted in an inner pocket. Interspersed among the innocuous phrases, as if her aunt had merely doodled idly in the margins, were the Guild glyphs that read: *Urgent mission, Ashkharon. Assassination of First Minister by rebels. Money too good; Owen too persuasive. Rejoin in three weeks. Thibault to preside. No trouble! Love, Hawk.*

Jen stifled a grin, aware that her companion was still awaiting an answer. "You know I was in Haarkonis?" she said.

He nodded, his eyes somewhat awed. "At school, right?" He whistled. "They say the Princess herself went there . . ."

"Yes, I've been finished by the best." She snorted. "But if you ask me, it's all a load of bloody nonsense. They only train you for one thing: to snare a society husband. And now after two years of interminable coaching, I shall

doubtless be launched into that indignity of all indignities—
a Ceylonde Season."

"But . . . don't you want a Season?" He sounded vaguely
scandalized, and she chuckled.

"Gracious, no! Do you have any idea, Van—it is Van,
isn't it?—how dreadfully dreary it is to be paraded about
before society like some choice side of beef? 'A tremen-
dous fortune, my dear, but distressingly tough . . .' " She
lowered her voice, donning her most outrageous accents
and screwing a mock monocle into her eye, gratified to
hear her companion's light, liquid laughter. "No," she
added, "I should be delighted to abandon the whole
prospect altogether."

"Then why don't you?"

"Because my aunt shall insist."

"And is your aunt so keen on society, then?"

Jen laughed, tickled by the thought of the redoubtable
Vera as a society maven. "Not in the least. She shall hate
it as much as I. But she promised my mother, and my aunt
is an honorable woman; she believes in keeping her
word."

Her companion considered this. "So there's no gain-
saying her?"

Jen shook her head mischievously, feeling a certain
perverse pride in the denial. "Not once she's made up her
mind," she answered, though what she really meant was,
Not when she's one of the finest assassins in the Guild.
But of course she couldn't say that, for the Hawk's identity was a strict secret, never discussed outside the family—and sometimes not even within it. Vera was the
proverbial black sheep, the Radineauxs' closet skeleton.
Jen had been eight years old before she realized exactly
what her mysterious aunt did for a living—and only then
because Vera had sat her newly acquired houseguest
down and patiently explained it.

After that, there was no going back. Jen was fascinated
by her aunt's life, and her one goal was to follow in her
path—which made such nonsense as Ceylonde Seasons
seem all the more ridiculous. The thought of having to
prostitute herself for a bunch of pale young fops—nine
out of ten of whom she could outmatch in a duel—made
her want to laugh. But at least her aunt's absence would
delay the inevitable, and Thibault would be around to

amuse her. She smiled again at the thought of Vera's injunction: *No trouble!* Dear Vera. Didn't she realize that
trouble was Jen's favorite pastime, and Thibault her favorite companion? It was her nature to drive him to distraction!

"So if you don't care for a fine husband, what do you
desire?" her companion asked, the last of his shyness disappearing in a rash of unfeigned curiosity.

Jenifleur just grinned. The true answer would shock
him, as would the presence of the sharp stiletto concealed
beneath her elegant skirts. So instead she merely smiled
and said, "Freedom," and cast her eye once more toward
Hestia.

As the huge ship approached the harbor, tacking through
the shallows with a ponderous grace, Thibault Lescevre
swallowed against a suddenly rebellious stomach and
shifted on his feet, the weathered boards of the pier creaking heavily under his boots. He hadn't seen Jen in four
years—far too long an absence in his opinion, and one
likely to do more harm than good. When he had left for
his apprenticeship in Gavrone, she had been a coltish adolescent, with her hair in untidy pigtails and her face alight
with mischief, always seeking to lead him into some hare-
brained adventure or other. But now she was eighteen and
a lady, fresh from one of the most prestigious schools on
Varia, and he wondered what she should be like—or if he
should even know her.

"What do you think, mates?" He addressed Vera's
horses, who snorted softly and gave him a dubious look.
"Quite. My point exactly."

Softly, he cursed the letter from Vera which had summoned him, even as he secretly delighted in it. For much
as he wanted to see Jen again, he found himself oddly terrified—and wondered for the umpteenth time what a lady
could possibly want with a carpenter's apprentice, and the
grandson of the village witch?

It had all been so different when they were young. Isolated in a deserted stretch of wood and at each other's
mercy for companionship, they had often found their two-
year age difference—or even their inherent definitions of
acceptable risk—to be more of an obstacle than the artificial mores of class or social conscience. And to be honest,

even those hadn't weighed all that heavily, for where Jenny led, Thibault followed—not blindly, like a dog, but still with a kind of innate loyalty and common sense, looking after her. And although there were times when he felt he had spent his life cleaning up after her disasters, that was often the only way to deal with her—and probably the reason why her mother had had so many nervous collapses. Once Jen got an idea in her head, there was no shaking her. One could only trail along and try to minimize the damage.

Throughout the years of their association, he'd caught her as she tumbled out of trees, fished her from streams and rivers, plucked her off towers and crags, and dusted her off when she'd been pitched from the backs of untamed horses.

"Remember the bull incident?" he said out loud, his deft fingers scratching the ears of the right-hand horse.

But then, Thibault realized, he probably had his own inherent need to be protective. His parents had died when he was but an infant, and his earliest recollections were of his grandmother's tiny cottage in the forest. Once, Sylvaine Lescevre had owned a small house in the heart of Nova Castria, plying a quiet trade as an herbalist and healer, but slowly the reports of her homespun remedies had led the townsfolk to dub her a witch, crediting her with powers she did not possess. Soon they had begun to flock to her with requests for love-philters and curses—things which the haughty mages considered beneath their dignity to provide or for which they charged even more exorbitant prices than they did for sending messages or recharging the ubiquitous globes of magelight—and shortly before his parents' death, she had fled to the forest in despair. There, surrounded by her beloved herbs and potions, she had finally gained some measure of solace, for only the truly committed sought her out, and then usually for the services she could genuinely provide: the soothing of discomfort and the healing of ills.

But while he loved his wise, gentle granny, it was a lonely life for a small boy. Their nearest neighbor was the childless and oft-absent Viera Radineaux—and though she was kind and her vast house and grounds served as a kind of overblown playground for the young Thibault, it was simply not the same as having a companion.

Until the day Vera had summoned him to her garden and had told him soberly of her niece's arrival.

He had been a bit surprised, for in their ten years of association he hadn't even realized she *possessed* a niece, but he soon had it sorted out. As it happened, Vera's estranged brother, Favienne, had died, and his wife had collapsed, leaving their eight-year-old daughter a virtual orphan. And while sending the child to Vera had offended every last one of Genevra's sensibilities, at least the redoubtable Hawk was family—and besides, she'd had nowhere left to turn.

So Jen had arrived for an indefinite visit, and her appearance had been nothing short of a revelation. Far from being the pale, bereaved wraith Thibault had expected, Jenifleur Radineaux had descended on his life like a veritable force of nature. Indifferent to her father's death—for she had rarely seen him, being raised instead by an army of servants and nannies—she considered her sojourn at her mysterious aunt's to be the height of adventure, and he would never forget his first sight of that bright, vibrant face cocked curiously in his direction, measuring him with a pair of mischievous hazel eyes beneath the shining waves of her thick, chestnut hair.

There had been an undeniable challenge in that gaze, and he often wondered if he had spent his life trying to measure up to it.

"What do you think?" he asked, stroking the forelock of the horse on his left, so it wouldn't feel left out. "Eh?"

He had seen her on and off throughout the years as Genevra's health rose and fell, and then Sylvaine had died, forcing him to earn his keep in Gavrone. He had wondered idly, as he left, if he should ever see her again, but then fate—or Vera—had intervened, and here he stood.

He should have known he wouldn't get off so easily.

He chuckled faintly and turned his eyes to the horizon. Her ship was close enough now that he could see the sailors swarming over the rigging like demented monkeys, preparing for the docking. Shouted commands drifted faintly back to the wharf as he watched the ship spin and settle, the sails deflating. Deckhands armed with thick lines spilled over the rails, securing the vessel to the moorings. Any minute now, the gangplank would be lowered and she would descend.

With a rueful chuckle for his foolish panic, he quickly checked the traces on the wagon and gave Vera's two matched bays a final, reassuring pat, but they merely rolled their eyes and snorted, expressing their liberal contempt for being hitched to such a conveyance.

"Well, I only hope Jenny doesn't agree with you, lads," he told them. Then, jamming his hands deeply into his pockets for lack of anything better to do with them, he sauntered off to meet her ship.

He recognized Jen immediately: a slim, elegant figure in bottle green, with a wide-brimmed, floppy hat tied beneath her chin, directing a mass of sailors as to the disposition of her trunks. Her face was lost in shadows, but the hair that spilled from beneath her hat brim was unmistakable—the glossy chestnut curls wind tossed yet still managing to appear artfully disarrayed. She descended the gangplank without hesitation, her eyes picking him out unerringly, and waved a cheerful hand in his direction.

After a minute, he raised his own in return.

"Ahoy there, sailor!" she called, and Thibault grinned— for despite her appearance, her impudent greeting reeked of Jen-ness, and he found himself relaxing.

"Ahoy there, yourself," he returned as she approached, tripping across the pier with her usual fluid grace. "It's good to have you back, Jenny."

"And it's good to be back. But . . . Great flying catfish, Thib, Vera said you'd grown, but I had no idea you'd become such a monster!" And reaching up, her hat falling abandoned down her back, she dropped a quick kiss on the point of his jaw—as high as she could reach.

He grinned down at her, savoring the sight. She was tall for a woman and as beautiful as ever, her skin clear and shining and her eyes the same luminous hazel, like mossy agates, with a ring of liquid gold around the pupils. And she could have passed for a lady of fashion in the highest salons in all Varia but for her voice, which was just the faintest shade too deep, too throaty, to fit with her air of refinement.

He would have known her anywhere.

"You haven't changed, Jenny," he drawled, then added, "At least not where it matters."

She threw back her head and laughed—a behavior which would no doubt have scandalized the fair instructors at her academy. "Good," she said decisively, adding, "You got a letter from Vera, I suppose? Do you know what she said in mine?"

"I shudder."

She linked her arm with his, the top of her head barely brushing his shoulder. "She distinctly advised me," she informed him, "to stay out of trouble."

It was a decided invitation. He groaned and was about to say something more when one of the sailors interrupted, calling, "Where do you want your trunks, Domina?"

"Cursed if I know," she answered, grinning at the redheaded lad who proudly shouldered the first of what promised to be a substantial array of luggage. "You did bring the carriage, didn't you, Thib? Because I've got seven of them."

He exchanged a knowing look with waiting sailors and went to fetch the wagon.

2

The voyage to Ashkharon was a delight, and pleasantly unencumbered by thoughts of Jen. Having made her decision, Vera had promptly dispatched messages to Thibault and her niece, then dismissed the matter from her mind. As Owen had said, the girl was eighteen—more than capable of looking after herself, with a little judicious supervision—and Vera had a job to do.

So leaving the Guild headquarters and Ceylonde, she had retreated only briefly to Nova Castria, assembling a wardrobe and an identity before catching the public stage to Grometiere. There, rattling along the dusty and pitted road toward Hestia's southern coast, she had found herself sharing the tatty, unsprung quarters with a merchant and his wife, two portly and florid specimens of the prosperous middle class. Magnanimously disemboweling their capacious lunch basket, they regaled her with food and conversation, and she passed a delightful afternoon licking savory chicken juice from her fingers and discussing everything from the sugar trade to the king's gout.

Helmuth Rosa owned a series of warehouses in both Ceylonde and Grometiere, and when she told him of her impending journey with Captain Black, he held forth volubly. "Delightful man, Black, delightful! I've had any number of dealings with him, my dear, and have yet to find him anything less than a gentleman. No, you should have no worries traveling with Black." And he patted her hand in an avuncular manner, all but ignoring the fact that she was, at most, three years his junior.

She expressed her gratitude—reflecting with some amusement that her carefully cultivated air of unworldliness must, indeed, be working—and smiled as Elsa asked solicitously whether she should be traveling alone and, if so, how far. So she outlined her voyage to Ashkharon, her emotions decorously restrained as she spoke of her father's fictitious death and the mythical teaching position she had been offered in Nhuras, tutoring the sons of the ruling classes.

"What a remarkable opportunity, my dear," Elsa exclaimed warmly, squeezing her hand. "Though I am so sorry to hear about your father."

"Thank you, but it was a long illness," Vera responded decorously. "We had been expecting the end for a while, and thankfully it came quietly. But the job was a salvation, and I have so wanted to travel." And she let a vaguely optimistic note creep into her voice.

"Of course, my dear," Elsa assured her. "It's quite proper to be excited. Imagine, Helmuth, Ashkharon! I'm sure it shall seem most exotic."

"So I've heard. But . . . Pardon me, aren't you a little warm, Elsa, my dear?" And lifting his prodigious weight from the worn upholstery, Helmuth grunted slightly as he eased down the rippled glass pane of the tiny window. Immediately, a stream of dry, dusty air swirled in through the narrow opening, carrying with it the rhythmic pounding of hoofbeats and the driver's atonal whistling. "I hope this doesn't bother you?" he said to Vera as he resumed his seat, and when she shook her head, he continued, "Yes, Ashkharon is indeed rumored to be unique. Most say it is quite different from anything we are used to in Hestia."

"And the camels spit most frightfully! Or . . . so I've heard," Elsa added, seemingly embarrassed by her sudden enthusiasm.

"Then I shall be sure to stay well clear of them." Vera laughed. "And thank you for the advice."

Elsa colored prettily. "But you shall be met in Nhuras?" she insisted in a motherly tone.

"Indeed I shall," Vera assured her, to which Helmuth added, "And as for the journey, she'll be with Black, my dear, and perfectly safe!"

Vera masked a grin and fingered her weapons, wondering what the kindly couple would think if they knew they were traveling with the infamous Hawk.

When night fell, Helmuth dimmed the magelights in the coach and folded his large hands across his watch-chain, his head lolling back against the seat as he filled the vehicle with his loud, prodigious snores. And by morning they had arrived in Grometiere.

A warm breeze was blowing across the pier as they left the coach, carrying with it the scents of spice and horses, the wharf buzzing with eager voices as crates, barrels, beasts, and bolts of shining silk were loaded and unloaded from the capacious holds of the great seagoing ships. Beyond their furled sails, the sea stretched out in cerulean perfection, its faintly rippled surface marred only by the dories and small fishing vessels which scudded about like heedless bugs in the shadows of their much larger cousins. Warehouses like the Rosas' burgeoned with trade, and to one unused to travel, it would seem that the whole of the world was arrayed within their walls.

To Vera, it was like coming home.

Kharman Black met her on the docks and was every bit as charming as her companion had portrayed him—though she did find herself wondering if Helmuth's vigorous commendations were not, at least in part, designed to reassure her. For the captain had a marked piratical strain, from the breadth of his burly shoulders to the munificent fullness of his bushy black beard. All he needed was an eye patch to complete the image, but that would have been a shame, for those twinkling black orbs needed no disguise.

"Malle Varis," he boomed in a cheerful voice, hefting her trunk to his shoulder with one hand and gesturing her forward with the other. "Welcome to the *Belapharion Traveler*."

"Leonie, please," she responded, taking his proffered arm, "and thank you. I'm delighted to be aboard." And she followed him up the gangplank with a smile.

"Is this your first voyage to Ashkharon?" he asked as he led her to her cabin, his teeth gleaming in the midst of his dark beard. And when she nodded her assent, elaborating the lie, he grinned and added, "Then you're in for quite a treat . . . Leonie."

His eyebrows courted her.

She smiled, baiting the hook. "Indeed?"

"Indeed. The country is a marvel, and the voyage like none on Varia."

"You speak from experience?"

"Vast experience. I've been up and down the Belapharion all my life, and I wouldn't change it for the world."

She raised a teasing eyebrow. "Then I look forward to partaking of it."

"Ah. And if I may be so bold, you strike me as a born traveler, Malle Varis."

"As I have always hoped to be." She laughed. "Captain Black."

Inevitably, they became lovers, and Kharman Black was in all ways the perfect companion. Knowledgeable and proficient, he dedicated himself to her enjoyment during the three weeks of the voyage: imparting tales of the lands they skirted, guiding her hands on the ship's great wheel, strolling on the deck with her at sunset when the light faded behind the islands in a wash of tropical color and the sea glowed persimmon, entertaining her in the sumptuous luxury of his cabin until the sun crept once more over the horizon. He tempted her with exotic foods and taught her to navigate by the stars as they sat up in the rigging at night, the balmy Belapharion breezes sweeping across them like a caress. And later still, his own touches would arouse her, his hands gentle and skillful for all they were rough with sea and rigging.

Consummate actress that she was, she played the innocent and delighted in the teaching—for, like Kharman Black, this was her favorite voyage. The clear sapphire of the water, stitched with darting flecks of brightly colored fish, never failed to delight her, as did the exotic sights and smells of the islands and ports. She lounged on the sunlit decks and rejoiced in the leaping dolphins until he teased her about heathen teachers, for she soon became as dark as any seaman. *Sometime,* she thought, *I want Jenny to see this*—one of the few thoughts she had of her niece during the voyage.

They sailed around the horn of Venetzia and circled the islands of Konasta with their white sands and their whiter houses, set like jewels within the deep blue sweep of sea and sky. And then the bulk of Mepharsta loomed, curving the tip of the Belapharion into a foreign pocket, with the coastal sweep of Ashkharon to the east and the northern coast of Suhravaria flowing away to the west.

She had a brief night to bid farewell to Kharman Black in private, and then they were docking at Nhuras, the golden domes of the Mages Quarter swelling over the wharf in exotic splendor, the air redolent with the dusty smells of dung and camels.

·

"It has been a most pleasant voyage, dear lady," Black said softly as she disembarked. "Enjoy your stay in Ashkharon. And should you, for any reason, find yourself in need of passage back—or simply a little company—do not hesitate to contact me. I am usually somewhere around Ashkharon at this time of year, and I will do whatever I can to aid you. For I do confess, Leonie," and his dark eyes twinkled, "I have my doubts seeing you as a teacher."

But she just grinned and said, "My thanks for your offer, Captain, but I assure you I shall be quite all right."

He raised an amused eyebrow. "No doubt you shall. And now you had best depart, my dear, for I think I see your escort waiting and it wouldn't do to scandalize him from the very first day."

She laughed and offered him a formal hand. "Indeed. Well, thank you for everything, Captain. It has been most . . . enlightening."

He chuckled at her sly tone and pumped her hand enthusiastically, masking a hidden caress. Then, hefting her trunk once more to his shoulder, he ushered her from the ship.

As her feet touched the wharf, the man Black had identified as her escort detached himself from the crowd and came forward. He had a lean, narrow, almost ascetic face, with a hawklike nose and deep-set grey eyes beneath a shock of iron hair. His lips were curved in a slight welcoming smile, and despite his almost unyielding features, there was a kind of magnetic intensity to him; Vera could understand the sway he held in the rebel alliance.

"Leonie Varis, I presume?" he said, his voice deep and resonant. "I'm Iaon Pehndon. Welcome to Ashkharon."

Somewhere in the desert to the southeast of Nhuras, near a remote oasis settlement by the name of Dheimos, Neros Fazaquhian paced his makeshift laboratory with a kind of nervous excitement. He had been skeptical—not to mention reluctant—when Iaon Pehndon had first dispatched him to the heart of the Anvil in search of rumor and supposition, but he hadn't been in much of a position to object at the time. The gambling debts which had driven him to drink, drowning his troubles in the harsh white spirits of the Ghedrin berry, had slowly taken their toll on his work in the glass factories of Nhuras.

Once one of their leading researchers—and the discoverer of, among other things, the much sought-after lapisglass, whose rarity and deep indigo color had made it the height of elegance among the fashionable set—Fazaquhian had flown too high and fallen too deep. By the time Pehndon found him, desperately trying to eke out a living in the gutters, he would have done anything for a handout—even drying himself out and going to work in the heart of the Anvil, one of the deadliest and most inhospitable deserts in all of Ashkharon. Scores of men, it was rumored, had wandered onto the Anvil never to return, hammered into death by the unrelenting sun.

No, the Anvil would have been Fazaquhian's last choice of residence, but one could not afford to ignore Iaon Pehndon, nor the vast sums of money he had thrown Neros' way. It was quite a staggering quantity of cash; one that could cancel all his debts, with interest, and enable him to start again. So what if that start was in far-off Dheimos, his work crew composed of convicts and criminals? At least he had his pride again, and a tiny lab.

And the oily black substance that one of Pehndon's spies had found leaking from the sand, puddling in noxious hollows beneath the burning sun. Black stuff which burned with a light and heat rivaling the magelights. Black stuff which, if properly exploited, could drive the supercilious mages out of business forever and bring Ashkharon to the forefront of the Varian economy.

With Iaon Pehndon, presumably, at its head.

But no matter. Pehndon had saved him, and Fazaquhian would honor that debt as long as there was breath in his body. And if that meant spending his life trying to siphon the black stuff out of the desert, working on ways to control its burn, then that was what Fazaquhian would do, what he had done since Pehndon first offered him the position.

And now, after weeks and months of distilling and redistilling in his tiny adobe lab, he had finally found a formula which burned clear and steady, without the noxious, sputtering black fumes which had clouded his efforts for so long.

Maybe, at last, it was time for more money and new rewards. Maybe it was time to write to Iaon Pehndon.

3

Jen relaxed against the high seat back of the wagon and watched the familiar scenery unfolding before her: the verdant meadows scattered with purple and yellow wildflowers, the tangy scent of the summer grass tickling her nose, the whispers of crickets and birdcalls, and the silent brush of butterfly wings, muted beneath the muffled beat of hooves on the rutted and dusty track. It felt good to be home, in Hestia, traveling down the old, well-remembered lanes with Vera's matched bays trotting smartly before her and Thibault's large, competent hands resting firmly on the reins, just as they had in so many homecomings past.

Dear Thibault. How nervous he had looked when she'd first arrived, as if two years of finishing school had changed her! It was, rather, she who had changed the academy in Haarkonis, and she wondered how many of the instructors were, even now, heaving great sighs of relief to see her gone.

Well, it was mutual, she thought, glancing over at the solid bulk of her old companion and contemplating the wondrous prospect of two weeks without supervision.

"So, tell me, Thib, wherever did you manage to come up with such a charming conveyance?" she teased and was delighted to see his eyes swing toward her with a trace of his old humor.

"What's the matter, don't you like it?" he asked in his slow, deliberate drawl.

"Gracious, I love it. It's wonderfully rustic, but I was just wondering what happened to the carriage. Has Vera abandoned it at last?"

"No, I just knew you'd have far too much luggage for its humble proportions, so I borrowed the wagon from Philippe. You remember Philippe, don't you?" he added slyly. "He owned . . ."

"The bull, yes. Don't remind me."

He chuckled at that, his brown eyes dancing, and absently tossed back a lock of mouse-colored hair. "So how was Haarkonis?"

"Amusing, in its way. And Gavrone? Vera says you've been a carpenter's apprentice."

He shrugged laconically. "It's a living."

"With your size, I'm surprised the blacksmiths didn't take you."

"Rouhtia's too far away," he answered, and she laughed in sudden comprehension.

"Fooled them with that big, dumb peasant act of yours, eh?" she said, and saw the confirmation in his dancing eyes. She could see where the smiths would avoid him: he cultivated an air of quiet somnolence, like a sleepy sloth, that kept everyone from guessing his true abilities. His stolid peasant's body and lower-class speech combined to form the perfect defense. She would have even been fooled herself, if she hadn't known him better. But his soft, unthreatening speech masked a formidable intelligence, and that big, ungainly body could move with a catlike speed and silence. "Well, you don't fool me, my lad," she informed him. "I've seen you train. So . . ."

"Is that a threat?" he countered cheerfully, then added, "You're still training?"

She raised an eyebrow. "Of course. Aren't you?"

He shrugged. "When I have time," he said, which of course meant that he was working as intensely as she; she knew him too well to be fooled by his offhand airs. The time they had spent learning the assassin's arts under Vera had been special for them both, and a dream Jen had yet to relinquish. Nonetheless, she wondered if he even remembered their ancient promise to go into partnership when she finally entered the Guild. She would trust Thibault with her life, but he had undoubtedly grown up and moved beyond such childish bonds.

"Ah, the times we used to have," she sighed. "Remember the day I raced you up the cliffs?"

"And persisted in diving off the waterfall after? Yes, I remember quite clearly."

"Nonsense." She grinned at his dry tone. "It was perfectly safe. You dove off it yourself, as I recall."

"Only because it was the only way of getting you out of that pool afterward."

"Hmph! As if you really thought I was drowning," she responded scornfully. "Admit it, Thib, you wanted to take that dive as much as I did!"

He chuckled. "Ah, for the joys of selective memory." He was silent for a moment, then added, "When was the last time you were home?"

"About six months ago, on winter break. And Vera firmly promised she'd be here to meet me this time around."

"Well, you know Vera. Always in demand."

"Oh, I'm not complaining," she countered airily. "At least this way I get to see you again." And she turned to smile at him, taking a certain pleasure in seeing the once childish features smoothed into a harmonious if unspectacular adulthood. "So how long since you've been back, and how on Varia did you manage to get away this time?"

"Two years, and lied like fury. I said my sister was desperately ill and needed me, that we were unsure how long she might survive."

"Poor Thib, we profligate Radineauxs are corrupting you already! Well, I shall try to languish properly, to give some credence to your story."

"No, you won't," he countered promptly, and she grinned.

"You're right, I probably won't. You know me too well, Thibault."

They lapsed into a comfortable silence as the road meandered into the woods, the thickness of oak and pine immediately arching a silent and sun-dappled canopy over their heads. The light filtered greenly through the branches, and every now and then a rabbit or grouse would scuttle across their path, making Jen long—in an abstract and lazy kind of way—for the familiar heft of her bow; it had been a while since she had tried herself out against a living target.

Thibault drove in silence, his hands steady and even on the reins, and eventually she tilted her head back and adjusted her hat brim over her eyes, dozing until the grey stone bulk of Vera's manor came into sight, its grounds and gardens hewn in a niche from the forest.

"You staying at Sylvaine's?" she asked.

Her companion nodded. "I opened the house last week.

Min and Jacques are still looking after your aunt's place, though. They'll fix your meals and get whatever you need."

"But you are coming over for dinner, aren't you?" she pleaded. "It's silly for me to dine all by myself, and I'd love the company."

"Apart from shooting myself a rabbit"—he grinned—"I was rather hoping you'd say that. It would save me a considerable amount of trouble."

"Not to mention gracing you with my wondrous presence . . ."

"Well, there is that, too. Now," and he pulled the wagon to a halt, "let me see about getting these trunks of yours unloaded so I can return the wagon to Philippe."

"It is delightful to have Thibault back and running things," she remarked later to Min, as that worthy woman bustled about, getting their dinner. "He's so stable, his very presence seems to keep me from disaster!"

Min laughed. "Likely an illusion, Domina. I can recall one or two occasions when not even young Thibault could stem the tide."

"True enough," Jen admitted, not in the least repentant. Then, "There he is," she exclaimed, flying up to meet him as he entered through the kitchen, dropping an affectionate kiss on Min's wrinkled cheek.

Some of the constraint which had vanished on their journey seemed to have appeared again between them as he settled himself across the table, awkwardly unfolding the linen napkin onto his lap. She suspected him of wearing his finest clothing, and for all the times they had spent together in childhood, she was suddenly aware that they had never shared Vera's formal dining room, had never sat across from each other at the polished expanse of this vast table, watching the dim magelight of the chandelier dripping over china, crystal, and silver. In retrospect, she couldn't blame him for being intimidated; the dark-paneled walls and grim ancestral pictures were a bit off-putting, and she resolved in future to have Min serve the meals in the familiar warmth of the kitchen, with the rough pottery dishes and chipped mugs of her childhood. The kitchen in which—she realized with a shock—he'd also never eaten.

Can we really have been so snobbish? she thought. She could barely count the number of times she had shared

meals with Thibault in Sylvaine's cozy cottage, the times
she had lurked, giggling, with Thibault in his tiny sleeping loft above the store room. But maybe that was simply
because Sylvaine had been more of a mother to the two
than the remote, if more exciting, Vera.

"I miss Sylvaine," she said later, as they sat before the
fire in the living room—another room in which, she realized, Thibault had spent very little time. But the soft
couches there were more inviting, as were the shelves of
lovingly stacked leather-bound books, their gold-etched
spines glimmering in the dancing light. She and Thibault
had shared many a lesson from these volumes. And there
was the locked cabinet of weapons which they had spent
so much of their childhood striving to unlock—or rather,
which she had striven to unlock while he had stood about
seeking to dissuade her, citing scores of legitimate reasons why it might not be the wisest of ideas.

"I miss her, too," Thibault responded softly. "It's odd
to be home without her. The cottage seems so empty without all her herbs and potions."

"I can imagine. Do you know, I always used to want
her to make me a potion so I could be as bold and courageous as Vera?"

"You?" he chuckled. "I always wished she'd make you
a potion to render you *less* so!"

She grinned. "Poor Thib. I led you quite a dance, didn't
I? But then I was more than half boast and bluster in those
days."

"I wish I'd known that then," he said ruefully, his big
body perched awkwardly on the edge of one of the armchairs.

"Oh, come now, Thib," she chided, leaning back
against the sofa cushions, her skirts in a lazy froth about
her ankles and her stockinged feet resting casually on the
low table between them. She poked at his knee with one
outstretched toe. "You're making me feel positively wanton! Relax a little; the chair won't eat you."

He grinned self-consciously and settled back, the wide
seat accepting his bulk without a creak. "So was the bull
incident all bluff and bluster?" he demanded—his own
subtle form of revenge.

Despite herself, she shivered. She had been twelve at
the time, and in retrospect she couldn't remember what

had led her to the conclusion that it would be a good idea
to climb the tree in Philippe's meadow and throw conkers
at his new bull. And after once more failing to dissuade
her, Thibault hadn't even stayed to watch but had gone
running straight for Vera. At the time, she had considered
his desertion to be the ultimate act of cowardice and betrayal, and so she had contented herself by throwing
conkers and calling taunts across the field on her own.

The bull wasn't likely to ignore her, nor did he. With a
mighty snort like some earth-shaking giant, he came
charging straight at her, smashing against the tree trunk
with a force that rattled conkers down like hail on the
ground. Half dislodged and clinging upside down to a
branch, Jen squeezed her eyes shut and called on every
power she knew to save her, but the bull shook her loose
on the second pass. She fell heavily to the ground like
some overripe fruit, wheezing, as the enraged animal
paused and turned, then lowered his head to the ground
and charged again, intent on flattening his small tor-
mentor.

Paralyzed with fear, she watched him come, his red
eyes glowing with mindless hate. And then Vera arrived,
led by a frantic Thibault; the silver flash of her aunt's
dagger caught the beast in the throat, inches from the petrified Jen. He stumbled and collapsed, pinning her beneath his bulk, nearly drowning her in a rush of hot,
metallic blood.

It took Vera two days to calm the hysterical child, and
from that day forward she made her niece carry a dagger
and taught her how to use it.

"Well, at least it got Vera to teach me the assassin's
art," she bluffed even now, and Thibault grinned.

"Still the same old Jen. How did they ever control you
in that fancy school of yours?"

"They didn't. And between the kitchen raids and the
midnight excursions I would have gotten into the most
dreadful trouble—if they'd ever caught me!"

"Which, of course, they didn't. And now you shall have
a Season and undoubtedly marry some rich lordling, and
then it will be his problem. So," he added, almost wistfully, "how did it feel to be in the center of Haarkonis society, with all the eligible Firsts dying of love for you?"

"All the married Firsts, you mean," she answered with

a grin. "They made the much more suitable companions; far fewer commitments, if you know what I mean . . ."

Thibault's face froze, and Jenifleur's eyes widened.

"Great leaping polliwogs," she exclaimed, "I do believe I've shocked you, Thib! Come now, surely you've had enough rolls in the so-called hay to know what I'm talking about. It's the fun of sex without any expectations. A passel of us rented this house in the woods, and we used to sneak off for assignations. . . ." Thibault's face had gone progressively redder as she spoke, and she broke off in consternation. "Surely you can't . . ." she began, then started to laugh, flushing slightly herself. "Blazes, I can't believe I'm telling you this!"

He looked as if he couldn't quite believe it either. "But didn't you . . . I mean, weren't you . . ." he stammered nonetheless, and she grinned.

"Wasn't I what?"

"Well . . . in love with any of them?" he blurted.

She stared at him for a long moment, then began to chuckle, throwing back her head and sending hearty peals of laughter tinkling off the clustered globes of magelight. "Tarnation, Thibault, but I do believe you're a romantic! Yes, to answer your question, I thought they were all absolute darlings and was completely infatuated with them for the week or so the obsession lasted. And then another would come along, and . . . Oh, dear, now I really *have* shocked you! But honestly, Thibault, I have no interest in marriage and commitment—not for a very long time, at least—and this silly Season was only Mother's idea, and . . . I think I'll stop talking now, before I get myself into further trouble." She grinned. "Forgive me?"

He looked a bit shaken. "Of course."

"Good." She yawned suddenly, loudly, and glanced at the clock. "And now I think I'll go to bed; it's late. You're welcome to stay if you want; you know where the guest rooms are." And rising, she shook out her skirts and stooped to drop a brief kiss on his forehead. "Good night, Thibault," she said before padding softly from the room.

"Good night," he replied and sat before the fire for a long time in silence before rising to return to Sylvaine's quiet cottage.

4

The sun was streaming in through the windows, dust motes spinning and dancing in the broad beams, as Iaon Pehndon folded his morning paper with a faint half-smile and took another sip of his thick, bitter coffee. Then, with infinite precision, he placed the tiny cup back in the saucer and looked up from the remains of his breakfast.

It was a beautiful morning, representing the fulfillment of all his schemes, for he had done it; he had actually bagged the Hawk! The cursed Guild could be such sanctimonious prigs at times, considering themselves the unofficial police force of Varia when in reality they were just a bunch of meddling bastards who didn't even have the decency to be bought off properly. No, they had to consider such nonsensical things as values and morals, weighing each assignment by their own set of incomprehensible standards, and if they didn't like the motives of their client, they were perfectly liable—at any point—to refuse the job and pocket the payment. It was their own way of discouraging the corrupt, but the whole concept irritated Pehndon beyond belief. What gave them the right to judge, as if they were in some way superior? What made their standards absolute?

But if you didn't work within the Guild's exacting framework, then you were forced to hire the outlawed and all-but-illegal rogues, which instantly gave your operation a less-than-savory character.

And that was the last thing Iaon Pehndon wanted. He had worked for years to lay this particular trap, expertly manipulating all the players into their requisite positions as soon as he had realized the import of the rumors drifting up from Dheimos. It had cost him years of effort and planning—not to mention considerable personal expense—to craft a background that not even the Guild would question.

But by all that was precious, he had done it, and now he was finally in a position to reap the rewards.

The final player was in place, and landing her had been nothing short of genius. Of all the moralistic prigs in the Guild, the Hawk was the worst—and yet here she was, her presence all but sanctioning his actions with the Guild seal of approval. Oh, he would have to be careful, now that she was here, that she didn't discover his true motivations, but after all the time and money he had invested, it was inconceivable that he should fail now.

He felt a certain frisson of satisfaction at the thought and took a final fastidious bite of the sweet, flaky pastry, redolent of nuts and honey, as he remembered his first sight of the infamous assassin. She didn't look like much: a hard-bitten, almost middle-aged woman, no doubt grown bored and careless over the years. A woman who had let herself become distracted by the dubious charms of that scruffy ship's captain, for he could tell by the synchrony of their bodies as they parted that the two had been lovers. Foolish, really.

But no matter; she was his now. The Hawk was his.

"Come, Malle Varis," he had told her in his smoothest, most charming tones. "I'm sure you want some time to settle in from your voyage. Let me show you where you'll be staying, and tomorrow I can introduce you to your . . . charges, if that's quite acceptable." And he had smiled conspiratorially, wondering what she would think when he introduced her to *his* rebel base.

"My thanks, Mal Pehndon," she had said. "A short rest would be pleasant, but I do look forward to meeting my students on the morrow."

"They will be quite a handful, I warn you."

"Nonetheless"—and she had actually laughed—"I shall watch them like the proverbial Hawk!"

Iaon Pehndon had to smile. It was more than perfect. In two weeks, that idiot Istarbion would be dead, the rebel alliance eliminated, and his own faction of the government—under the innocent and gullible Alphonse Jhakharta—firmly in power.

He chased the cloying sweetness from his mouth with the last mouthful of coffee and rose, laying his napkin carefully across his empty plate as he prepared to face his day.

* * *

Vera awoke to the sound of a water-seller hawking his wares beneath her window, his melodious voice rolling like a benediction through the hot, heavy air. She smiled and stretched, flexing her naked body beneath the sheet, then pushed aside the mosquito netting and rose. She had several hours before she was due to meet Iaon Pehndon and the infamous Jason Andorian, and she planned to spend every minute of it reacquainting herself with her environment.

Donning a light robe, she rang for wash-water and breakfast, consuming the tart juice and flaky roll at the table on her tiny balcony, watching the exotic bustle below as merchants and tradesmen wheeled carts and barrels to the hotel's door. Behind her, the air stirred in the gauzelike curtains, making them billow from the open windows like the robes of the native desert-dwellers.

Breakfast finished, she splashed herself with the cool wash-water—already growing tepid in the heat—and dressed, gathering her hair back in a neat braid and tying her purse about her waist before adding a few strategic daggers and darts into hidden sheaths and pockets. Then, quitting the hotel, she set out for the irresistible lure of the open-air market.

The Nhuras bazaar stretched almost half a mile square, the vendors hawking their wares beneath a dizzying rainbow of tents and awnings. The hubbub of wheedling voices blended with the bleating of sheep and goats and the noisy clamor of chickens as livestock were bought and traded, and above all wafted the plaintive wail of desert music. The place was a cacophony of sound and chaos, the smells of dung and incense mingling with the tantalizing odors of frying meats and spices into a heady mix that flowed and drifted over the gathering like a living being.

Childlike, Vera wandered the aisles, fingering scarves and bolts of cloth in savage, gold-stitched colors, hefting knives and daggers, pinching fingerfuls of fragrant teas, laughingly fending off offers.

"Only twenty marks, Domina . . ."

"A special bargain for a beautiful lady . . ."

"Guaranteed to cure all ills . . ."

"You look like a woman in need of clear sight."

Vera paused, the savory meat pie she had purchased halfway to her mouth, and looked down at the speaker in bemusement. Sitting cross-legged on a mat at her feet, the mage grinned back at her, revealing a horrendous mouthful of chipped, stained teeth. His skin was dark as burnt honey, marred by the mottled, shiny scar smeared across half his face. Above a beaky nose, his single remaining eye was dark and infinitely deep, as if it hid a wealth of secret knowledge. His head was wrapped in a tatty turban of maroon and gold, his robes frayed and faded to a kind of colorless darkness, and the grizzled half beard that spouted from the unburned portion of his chin was badly in need of a washing.

Arrayed before him on a piece of lurid cloth was a jumbled assortment of trinkets, charms, and promised potions.

She didn't know what had made her stop—maybe that oddly knowing look in his eye, or the incongruity of his sly words. So, "What kind of inducement is that?" she laughed, lowering the pie.

"A true one," he said fulsomely. "You are a searcher, are you not?"

Her eyes sharpened. "Of a sort. Why?"

"Searchers are always in need of clear sight. Especially when there are those who seek to confuse them."

She arched an eyebrow. "And who is seeking to confuse me?"

But he just winked and tapped a gnarled finger against the side of his nose, adding, "Fortune-telling costs extra."

"Well, then, what do you have that doesn't cost extra?"

"A very special charm for a very special lady. A protection from illusion. Wear it and your eyes will always see truth." And he uncoiled an amulet from the pile, its elegant, exotic lines striking a familiar chord. It took her a moment to realize where she had seen its twin—resting half hidden in the folds of Iaon Pehndon's garments. The principle was a familiar one: in a land of magic and mages, illusions were far too easy to purchase, simple disguises for the everyday. There were illusions to change your face, your sex, to make you disappear. But what, she wondered, did Iaon Pehndon want with such a toy? What stock did Pehndon have in the disguises of illusion?

"The truth, eh?" she said speculatively, suddenly determined to have one—if only to rattle Iaon Pehndon. "How much?"

"For you, beautiful lady, thirty marks."

"Thirty?" She laughed. "You must think my eyes are clouded indeed!"

"Twenty-five, then," he amended, as she made to turn away. "And only because your beauty blinds me to good business." And he crossed his hands earnestly over his breast, revealing the one he had, until now, successfully hidden in his sleeve. With a certain horrified sympathy, she saw that it was scarred and fused into a formless mass.

"Well, fortunately it hasn't blinded me," she countered nonetheless. "I'll give you six."

"Six? You shame me, Domina! The work and sweat I have put into this crafting . . . Does my labor mean so little to you?"

"I am about thirty years too old and thirty thousand marks too poor to be a Domina." She grinned. "As well you know. Ten."

He looked offended. "You wound me. Twenty, at least."

"Very well, fifteen. It's dreadfully generous of me, because the going market rate is eleven, but I'll give you the extra four because I like you."

He grinned suddenly and offered her the charm. "A pleasure," he said, bowing, as she slipped the cord around her neck. "And if you ever need any other magical favors, just asks for Absalom."

"Absalom, eh? So tell me, what is a mage like you doing hawking your wares in the market like a common tradesman rather than in the lofty splendor of the Mages Quarter?"

He shrugged and gestured with the useless hand. "The mages like perfection, Domina. I am too . . . flawed . . . for their tastes. But my power is real, and shall be at your service if you need it. You know where to find me," he added, and his lips once more split into a crooked grin.

"My thanks; I'll remember that. And Absalom?"

"Yes?"

"The pleasure is mine."

The weight of the amulet hung heavy between her breasts as she left the stall and wandered toward the outskirts of the market, where the sound of a magically amplified voice began to make itself heard above the acquisitive clamor: a public speaker with a trained mage, no doubt. Curiously, she drew closer, straining to make out the words.

The speaker's voice was impassioned, his ringing words denouncing poverty and injustice, catching the attention of a few fringe marketgoers.

"Who is that?" she called, as a woman hurried past her.

"Jason Andorian, of course," came the surprised answer, and Vera grinned, delighted at the chance to see her prospective employer in action. She hastened after the woman, following her into a wide square flanked by the palatial edifices of what could only be the government buildings. Majestic and ostentatious, the white stone facades soared high above the square, the smooth, even panes of their windows reflecting the hard sunlight like a myriad of mirrors. And at the top of a set of broad marble steps leading up to one of the grandest buildings, a dark-haired young man, surrounded by a cadre of cloaked, hooded figures, held court from behind a makeshift, red-draped podium.

The ragged mass clustered before him was too thick for Vera to penetrate, so she contented herself with hovering at the rear of the crowd, beside the woman she had followed to the square. From this distance, she could see no more of him than a rough impression of features, but his vitality and magnetism came through as clearly as the earnest conviction of his words, ringing in every impassioned phrase.

"What do we work and strive for?" he demanded. "Who tends our hurts and eases our cares? Not our government; not Guy Istarbion!

"Look about you, at these munificent buildings. Look at the weight and wealth of windows. Who provides them? Who heats and blows the perfect panes? We do, my friends. And at what cost? Look at the price of that labor, at the casualties of the government-sponsored glassworks!"

And he gestured to the men who flanked him, who threw back their hoods and cloaks to reveal the ghastliest collection of scars Vera had ever seen. Each had the same slick, mottled texture as the marks which defaced Absalom, but these were worse. Infinitely worse. Legs and arms were missing or fused into shapeless lumps, faces half eaten away, bodies twisted and contorted, drawn into unnatural positions by swathes of unbending scars.

"This—*this*—is the legacy of Ashkharon! Our revered ministers seek profit, seek to cut costs. Cheaper, more affordable glass is their dream. Yet for every mark their customers save, someone is paying the difference. And who is that, my friends? Look about you. Careless management, pressure to meet deadlines, shoddy equipment too infrequently replaced. It is we, the people of Ashkharon, who are paying the price, with our arms and legs and fingers—with our very bodies! Every one of these people"—and Jason swept his hand across his gathered deformed—"was marred by an accident that could have been prevented if the government had cared a fraction more for its workers than for its profits! How many of you have lost friends or lovers to ruptured vats of molten glass—vats which could have been replaced with minimal care and attention? How many?"

Under the answering roar, Vera turned to her companion. "Effective, isn't he?"

The woman nodded, her eyes glowing with something suspiciously close to reverence beneath the clouded anger. "Jason Andorian will be our savior," she said harshly. "Mark my words."

"And Guy Istarbion?"

The woman hawked and spat. "Istarbion can die horribly and slowly, for all I care. My brother died in those factories."

"I'm sorry to hear it."

"As were his wife and children. And who's going to feed them now? There'll be no bread on that table, believe me, unless Rico goes to work in the factories—and him only thirteen."

"You mean they take them that young?"

"Younger, if they can. Children are cheap and convenient. Smaller bodies for smaller spaces, if you know what I mean."

"But . . . that's horrendous!" Her outrage was only half a sham.

"Blame Istarbion; it's his system that destroys us. He devours the profits we make of our labors, and never a mark do we see. It all goes to his servants and his fancy houses, but it is our lives he uses as his coin."

Vera could almost hear the echo of Jason's words in the woman's voice: words oft heard and memorized. But the bitterness was all her own.

"And if Istarbion dies?" she said. "What then?"

Her companion smiled, a feral grin. "Then maybe we shall all be saved."

"These indignities cannot continue," Andorian cried into the silence, as if in counterpoint to her words. "It is time to end this rule of injustice and inequality! Stand with me, and we will destroy this government's hold over Ashkharon! Stand with me, and we shall be free!"

Vera nodded grimly, her lips echoing the woman's smile. Something told her she was going to enjoy this job.

5

"And this is the headquarters of the rebel alliance," Iaon Pehndon said as Vera looked around. They had met earlier at the hotel, and Pehndon's face had tightened almost imperceptibly at the sight of Vera's amulet resting prominently on her breast. His reaction—or rather the lack thereof—had sent a vague ripple of unease through her, for it struck her that he was entirely too good at concealment for someone who supposedly had nothing to hide. But then, maybe his innate secrecy was just part of his makeup as second-in-command of the rebel faction.

So, "It seems like everyone has one of these," she joked, indicating her trinket, and he smiled thinly.

"All the more reason to purchase one, I suppose."

They lunched in the hotel's airy, glass-walled conservatory, the blades of the ceiling fan slowly stirring the leaves of the potted plants and whispering through the green-scented air—their conversation skating desultorily around nothing—and then Pehndon escorted her into the back alleys of Nhuras.

Skirting the bustling docks, they wove through streets progressively more rutted and run-down, where ragged laundry hung on sagging ropes between the glassless windows. Babies wailed in the heat, their piercing cries an unpleasant counterpoint to the tired, weary voices of their dams. The streets resounded with the hard anger of arguing couples and the sordid sounds of sex-for-hire. The denizens of the slums, their eyes bruised and numb, went about their business in indifferent silence, oblivious to the stink of rotting waste in the gutters and the lean, oily bodies of the rats which scuttled across their feet. Rats which, Vera suspected, made up a goodly portion of their diets.

And above and behind the soot-smeared tenements the

vast smokestacks of the glass factories vomited out black
gouts of steam from the heat of the coal-burning fires.

"So this is where the workers live?" she said, angrier
than ever at Istarbion, and narrowly missed tripping over
a Dreamsmoke addict, his face slack and vacant as he
slumped, oblivious, in a puddle of his own filth.

Pehndon shrugged. "Better than some places. At least
here they have a roof over their heads," and she could
almost hear the echo of Istarbion's indifference in his sarcastic words.

Slowly they wound out toward the coast, the fresh salt-
scent of the Belapharion gradually replacing the ineffable
stink of the slums. The streets grew wider, the tenements
replaced by warehouses—some occupied but most empty
and abandoned, lying too far from the docks to be of
any use.

It was to one of these that Pehndon led her, and from the
outside it appeared as deserted as its neighbors. The windows were caked with years of soot, and the huge loading
door, its green paint faded and flaking, was secured with
weathered chains and an ancient padlock, almost rusted
shut. But around the side, a smaller door eased open on
well-oiled hinges, revealing a cavernous room and a
flurry of activity. The worn floor had been neatly swept
and sanded, and a handful of desks were scattered about,
occupied by studious clerks and writers. In one corner, a
clutter of stained and faded sofas formed an ersatz meeting room, while a huge tin samovar resting on a refur-
bished table scented the air with the tantalizing smell of
fresh-brewed coffee.

At the far side of the warehouse, a run of steps climbed
the wall, leading to a small glassed-in office, yellow with
reflected magelight.

"Jason," Iaon Pehndon called.

All heads turned, startled by the authoritative ring of
his voice, and at the top of the stairs a small door opened
and a dark head poked through.

"Up here," a familiar voice returned. Without the magical amplification of his pet mage, his tone sounded somewhat pale and unremarkable, lacking the passionate verve
she had heard in the square, but the timbre was unmistakable.

"After you," Iaon Pehndon said, and gestured Vera up the stairs.

She didn't know quite what she had expected of the rebel leader up close, but somehow she found herself oddly disappointed. Maybe it was simply that after seeing his performance in the square, almost anything would have seemed an anticlimax. Certainly there was nothing overtly wrong with him. Physically, he was as good-looking as her distant glimpse of him had promised, with thick, dark hair, coppery skin, and chocolate-brown eyes. So what if some of the fire was lacking? He was, after all, on his own territory, in his own office, with only one person to win to his cause—and she already half converted.

"Jason," Pehndon said, somewhat pointedly, "allow me to introduce Leonie Varis—otherwise known as the Hawk."

The rebel leader seemed to marshal his thoughts, suddenly extending his hand and flashing her a charming grin; she could feel his charisma flicking on like a globe of magelight at the appropriate command.

"Malle Varis, my pleasure."

"Please, call me Leonie," she said as his warm, confident hand enfolded hers. She sensed a kind of wicked delight from him, as if he were enjoying his coup immensely.

"And I'm Jason. It's my pleasure to welcome you to Ashkharon, and—needless to say—I'm delighted to be working with the infamous Hawk."

"As I am with you," she responded. "I saw your speech in the square this morning—a very effective performance."

He looked momentarily flustered, then shrugged somewhat self-consciously. "I'm glad you liked it," he said blandly, and she grinned. Could the famed rebel leader be just the slightest bit shy? Somehow, that thought endeared him to her more than all the rousing speeches in Varia.

"We, ah, need to talk a little strategy now, do we not?" Pehndon said smoothly, cutting into the conversation and ushering everyone to a seat. "Leonie, as you know, we hired you to assassinate First Minister Guy Istarbion. Do you think you will be able to go ahead with that assignment?"

Shifting her eyes from Jason's, she crossed her legs and assumed her most businesslike demeanor, her gaze sweeping Pehndon. "Well, as you are no doubt aware, it is Guild policy never to make a final decision on any assignment without appropriate research. It is our own way of protecting against abuses in the system. But while I will have to spend the next few days gathering my data, I think I can say with reasonable certainty that both I and the Guild are leaning strongly toward your position. In fact," and she grinned at the rebel leader, "it was largely your speech this morning which cemented it."

He looked disproportionately pleased and even went so far as to wink at his dour second. "Indeed?"

"Most certainly. I had heard of the poor conditions in the factories, of course, but until today I hadn't realized the extent of those indignities. The burns and the deformities, the living conditions of the workers . . . Iaon walked me through the back alleys today. To be honest, there's much of value in your request." She paused, then added, "The people hold you in quite high esteem, you know."

"Yes." His face tightened slightly, and he averted his gaze for an instant. Then looking up, he added, "Thank you."

"But while we appreciate your concerns," Pehndon said, "there is some matter of timing, which was why we were so hasty in contacting the Guild and why we insisted on getting you down here as quickly as possible. Do you think ten days would be sufficient for you to make a decision?"

"I don't believe that would be a problem. Why?"

"Well," the rebel leader interjected, "if we're going to do this, we need to make it as public as possible, to generate the maximum . . . impact. And in ten days' time, Guy Istarbion holds his annual ball—and gives his annual speech—which will be magecast to the public in Government Square."

"Where you saw Jason speak this morning," Pehndon added. "With the whole city watching—not to mention any other regions of Ashkharon who want to have their mages tune in to the event—it will create a statement like no other. It will show, definitively, that we are no longer prepared to deal with Istarbion's ineffectual rule!"

Pehndon sounded as angry as she had ever heard him, and Vera smiled. "That sounds reasonable. But how will I get near him, in the event I do choose to take the assignment?"

Pehndon allowed a faint half-smile to creep across his lips. "We have agents in the government," he said, and the pale yellow of the magelight flowing off his features made him appear almost feral. "They will get you passes for the ball."

"And why don't they perform the elimination as well?" Vera demanded.

"Because," came the answer, "they are not Guild-trained assassins."

"We expect the best," Jason added. "A special flair that only the Guild can deliver."

Vera nodded and settled back in her rickety chair. "Granted, we are the finest. So what particular effects are you looking for? What kind of death did you have in mind?"

"An effective one," Jason grinned.

"We want a death that will remain in the minds of its viewers for years to come," Pehndon elaborated. "Preferably with a minimum of mess—there will be many richly dressed viewers present, and we don't want to get blood on anyone's hem—but visually compelling nonetheless. Do you have any poisons that would suit?"

Vera frowned and drummed her ringed fingers against the chair. "Several. There is one in particular, though, that might be most effective. Quick and relatively painless, but quite spectacular while it lasts. Providing you don't mind a little twitching and foaming . . ."

"Not in the least."

"How will it be delivered?" asked Jason, somewhat hesitantly. "In a drink, or . . ."

She smiled reassuringly at him. "A dart, I think, should do the trick."

"A dart?"

Before either of them could react, she drew a dart and blowpipe out of her hidden stores and sent a miniature missile zapping into the wall behind Jason's head, the wind of its passing trailing a tiny breeze across his cheek.

There was a moment of silence. The rebel leader swallowed convulsively, then began to grin. "You know, I almost believe this is going to work?"

Pehndon didn't even crack a smile. "She hasn't agreed to take the job yet," he said and rose, crossing to the wall. Touching only the base of the spine, he extracted the dart

fastidiously from the wood and examined it, turning the
tiny sliver dispassionately between his fingers.

"A little subtle, I think," he stated, clearly more cold-
blooded than his companion. "Such a small missile might
go unnoticed in the drama, and we can't have anyone sus-
pecting this death was from natural causes."

"When they see the effects of the poison, they won't,"
Vera countered matter-of-factly. "But I can use a larger
delivery missile, if you'd rather."

"I would."

"Very well. Shall we say I give you your final answer
in a week? That still gives us three days for planning."

"Most acceptable. We remain in your debt, Malle
Varis."

"That remains to be seen. And now," Vera rose, the
blowpipe disappearing almost invisibly from her grasp. "I
must go. Jason, it has been a pleasure to meet you."

"Likewise." He grinned, bowing over her hand, and she
once more felt the undeniable magnetism of his presence.
"Please don't hesitate to contact me if you have any questions or if there is anything I can help you with. I hope to
be working with you in future, Leonie."

She smiled again, detaching herself from his hand.
"That's as time will tell. I'll be in touch with you, Iaon,"
she added as she let herself out of the room.

The last thing she saw as she descended the stairs was
Iaon Pehndon and Jason Andorian smiling rather triumphantly at each other across the narrow desk, and she
wondered why she got the sudden impression that it was
Pehndon rather than Andorian who sat at its head.

"Grahme? Grahme!" Alphonse Jhakharta stuck his head
out the door and bellowed irritably for his assistant.

It was proving to be an absolutely intolerable day.

The lofty stonework of the government buildings, designed to be imposing, had long since proved to be completely unsuited to the desert climate. The offices sizzled
like oversized ovens, while the labyrinthine corridors
were nothing short of claustrophobic. Even the more palatial of the ministerial suites could have doubled as green-
houses on a really bad day.

They might, Jhakharta thought peevishly, have simply
built a large pottery kiln and saved on the expense.

Moreover, with ten days to Istarbion's gala, the First Minister was being his usual insufferable self, expecting everyone to attend to his business while he sat back in luxurious indolence on the green-grassed and peacocked splendor of his estate.

It was, quite honestly, enough to make you sick.

First there were the speeches to pen, and a dozen busy writers and scribes sat scribbling in the back corner of one of the larger offices. Then there were the invitations to send out, a veritable multiplicity of them, to all the influential families in Nhuras. And someone—usually Pehndon, for Istarbion couldn't be bothered—always had some new addition to the list.

And Jhakharta should know; it was his job to see that everyone got the tiresome things on time.

It was hardly an auspicious moment for his aide to go missing—again.

"Grahme!" he called a second time. "Where is that man?" He hailed a passing flunky. "You don't happen to know where Grahme Tortaluk is, do you?"

The aide looked up. "He had to go out, I think he said."

"Out? He's always out," Alphonse exclaimed pettishly. "What is he, moonlighting for the opposition?"

The man shrugged and, scowling, Jhakharta retreated to his sweltering office. There was no help for it now; he'd have to write out those additional invitations Pehndon had requested himself. There were about fifteen of them—a tedious exercise.

Istarbion wouldn't have to do this, he thought as he touched quill to ink and tried to force his hand into its most exacting copperplate. *Istarbion wouldn't have to lower himself to doing the menial work of clerks and scribes.* Of course, if he were being honest with himself, he would have to admit that most of his pique with Istarbion sprang from envy, pure and simple. He would have given most of what he possessed to be in Istarbion's position, pampered in luxury and idleness and isolated in a tranquil sea of greenery which daily cost a small fortune in water to maintain.

In fact, that was most of the reason for Pehndon's attraction. "Stick with me," Pehndon had told him, "and you'll be living like a First Minister inside six months."

"And what of Istarbion?" he had demanded.

But Pehndon had just smiled and shrugged, saying, "Guy can take care of himself."

Jhakharta grinned in memory. He had been a bit surprised when Iaon had first approached him, for even from the start Pehndon had been a bright, ambitious star who moved far beyond Jhakharta's stolid orbit. But there must have been a reason for Pehndon's choice, he assured himself. Pehndon had a plan; Pehndon had genius. Pehndon looked to the future.

And Pehndon had needed him.

Certainly, he had never regretted his choice to hitch his wagon to Pehndon's star, for the infamous Iaon had been as good as his word. From the very first he had provided well for his new ally. The weekly bags of gold proved a pleasant supplement to Jhakharta's government stipend; they were the rewards, Pehndon told him, of some top-secret project he had going in the heart of the Anvil, and Alphonse had often seen the thick missives that arrived from Dheimos. The details were irrelevant to him, though; he didn't care what happened in the desert. All that mattered was that the weekly bags of gold kept arriving on schedule.

He smiled, looking down to where even now the latest bag lay hidden beneath a tumble of papers, and patted the desk drawer fondly. Then, picking up his quill again, he penned the last address:

Malle Leonie Varis
Hotel Arrhyndon
Carteris Street
West Quarter
Nhuras

and threw the whole stack of invitations on the delivery pile.

He had done his work for the day. Tortaluk could take care of the rest—when he returned.

6

"Ahoy there, sailor!"

Coming through the woods two mornings after Jen's arrival, Thibault was hailed by her cheerful voice drifting distantly to his ears. Puzzled, he looked around, eventually catching sight of her perched among the chimney pots, clad only in a loose, sleeveless blouse and a pair of cut-off breeches.

She waved a long brown arm, calling, "Looking for anyone in particular?"

"Yes, you. Can we talk?"

"Providing you remember how to get up here."

"Of course. Up the main stairs, down the second-floor corridor to the left and then up through the tower."

He could see her grin even from the ground. "No such luck. I've blocked the door from out here. Either you come up properly, or you don't come up at all."

"Jenny . . ."

"Look out below," she added, tossing the rope and grapple down over the edge of the roof. It landed with a soft thud on the grass at his feet. "Now you have to come up," she added, "because you've got my only route down."

He resigned himself to the inevitable with a smile, coiling up the rope and hefting the grapple experimentally. It had been a while since he had used one—they didn't really approve of him scaling the workshop walls in Gavrone—and the weight felt somehow alien in his hands. But gamely, he let out a section of the rope and whirled it above his head a few times before tossing the hook into the air.

His first cast fell distressingly short, skittering down the walls with a stony rattle that would have summoned guards from far and wide had it been for real. He flushed; but somehow the very act of making the failed toss had restored the knowledge to his brain and fingers and, as if he had unlocked some secret door, he felt his awkwardness and self-consciousness vanish.

His second toss fell clean and true, the grapple soaring in a perfect arc over the crenelated wall of the lower roof and catching hold with no more than a muted clink.

"Beautiful!" Jen applauded, and he gave her a slight bow before grasping the rope and strolling up the vertical wall as easily as if it had been a garden path.

"You've been practicing, haven't you?" Jen accused, as he crested the wall. A fifteen-foot gap of stone separated them, in the form of a flat deck which ran around the circumference of the house; above, the upper roof sloped to a shallow peak. Halfway up the pitch, her feet braced against a chimney pot for balance, his nemesis grinned back at him.

"No," he responded levelly, "but I imagine it's something like riding a horse; once you learn, you never forget."

"Except that you look entirely too smug," she said as he detached the grapple from the cornice and dropped it at his feet. "I don't know if I believe you."

"And what reason do I have to lie?" He grinned and nodded at the tower door. "You weren't kidding about blocking it, were you?" A scatter of lumber and sturdy nails hinted at her industriousness; the door was firmly barred by a latticework of boards.

"What reason do I have to lie?" She echoed his words pertly, and he laughed. "So, are you joining me or not?"

He clambered up beside her and leaned his elbows against the rough tiles as he looked out over the treetops. He had forgotten how beautiful the view was from up here. Before him, he could see the tiny clearing that held his granny's cottage and, beyond that, the barest hint of the docks of Nova Castria and the distant sparkle of the sea. To his left, the mountains shadowed the horizon, and behind him rose the steep cliffs in which he and Jen had lost themselves as children.

"Well?" she said. "What news?"

Brushing a wayward lock of hair from his eyes, he looked back at her, marveling again at how lovely she had become. Her naked limbs were slim and strong, displaying an unconscious grace even in repose, and her loosely braided hair shone with coppery highlights. She looked like some kind of magnificent panther with those gold-flecked eyes, a dance of mischief never far from their luminous depths.

"Thib?" she prompted, and he shook himself out of his reverie.

"Sorry. You said?"

"What news did you come up here to give me?" Her eyes measured him knowingly, and he flushed. Then, remembering his news, his face sobered.

"What?" She sat up abruptly, her pose instantly flowing to taut alertness.

He sighed and shifted, clasping his hands about his knees. "I think Vera's in trouble, Jen."

"How so?" Her voice was sharp.

"I was in town this morning, shopping for supplies, when Desmond approached me." Desmond di Negri was the local mage. "Apparently someone named DeVeris wants to talk to us."

"Owen DeVeris? The head of the Guild? But what can he want?"

Thibault shook his head. "I don't know." He pulled a folded paper from his pocket and handed it to her. "But this is the message he left with Desmond."

She unfolded it with deft fingers, her brow furrowing as she perused the sparse lines. "He wants to speak to us at two this afternoon, if it's convenient. That sounds unthreatening enough. Blazes, Thib, what makes you think it's about Vera? She's not even due back for another two weeks! Besides, she's the Hawk—and Owen could just as easily have other business with us."

"Such as?"

"Well, perhaps Vera has decided to forgo this silly Season. Maybe this is Owen's invitation to join the Guild." Her eyes twinkled. "Now wouldn't that be delightful?"

He shrugged, unconvinced, and knew she could see it in his face.

"Come on, Thib," she wheedled. "Why must you always be the pessimist?"

Because someone has to be, he wanted to tell her.

"Look, it's probably nothing," she continued. "After all, it's hardly an ominous summons. Owen may just want to talk to me without Vera present, to gauge my commitment to the Guild."

"Then why summon me as well?"

"Because he knows you're staying with me in Vera's absence? Besides, Vera trained you too, Thib; maybe he wants us both."

"But I'm apprenticed in Gavrone."

She snorted. "And don't tell me you wouldn't give that up in an instant if you got an offer from the Guild!"

He was silent.

"Well?"

"That's your dream, Jenny, not mine," he answered quietly, at last.

"You mean . . . you'd rather just be a carpenter?" She looked incredulous. "What about me? What about our promise?"

His heart gave a slight bump. "I didn't know you'd remembered. But who's to say you'll join the Guild?" He couldn't force himself to meet her eyes. "You're a beautiful woman, Jen. You'll undoubtedly find yourself some rich husband, and . . ."

She stamped her foot against the tiles; he could almost feel the anger sparking off her. "Curse it, Thibault, will you drop this marriage business? How many times do I have to tell you that I am *not interested*? I am joining the Guild—Season or no—and that is final! Now, are you with me or not?"

The silence stretched taut between them. "I . . . don't know," he said eventually.

"Why not?"

Because I'm in love with you, Jenny, and always have been. Because you'll never feel the same for me, and I don't want to spend my life living in your shadow, being noticed only when it suits you.

"Well?" she repeated. "You don't believe me, do you? But I'll show you, Thibault! I will join the Guild, and when I do, I'll ask you again. And then you had cursed well better give me an honest answer!" Startled, he looked up and met her flashing eyes. "Deal?"

"Deal," he answered, for lack of anything better to say.

"Good. Then we'd better start getting ready for our journey. We'll take Vera's horses." And running lightly down the slope of the roof, she picked up the discarded grapple and secured it to the cornice, dropping the rope to the ground. Then, swinging lightly over the edge of the roof, she grinned at him briefly and disappeared.

So who's been practicing now? he thought ruefully. Casting a brief, regretful glance at the boarded-up doorway, he followed her down the side of the house.

They tethered their horses outside the local tavern and continued on foot to Desmond's Magerie, and Jen found herself shocked at how much the town appeared to have altered in her absence. Without the childhood glamour it had once held through association with her aunt, it now seemed small and somewhat squalid, a far cry from the quaint and elegant villages of Haarkonis. Here were the unmistakable signs of living, the shabbiness of quiet decay. The small warehouses of the docks were badly in need of repair, their windows dusty and cracked when they weren't replaced entirely by rags or squares of oiled paper. Nor were the houses and shops much better, each of them showing the ravages of poverty—the result of a local economy far too dependent on the uncertain bounty of the sea.

Suddenly she wondered how it must appear to Thibault, for this was ostensibly his home, and these his people. She wasn't often aware of the social differences between them, for whatever faults Jen might possess—and she would admit to many—snobbery was not among them. Instead, she treated people on a rigorous system of merit, unconsciously adopted from her aunt. The deserving she revered, despite their class. For the undeserving, she had nothing but contempt. Her long-standing affection for Thibault, and her innate trust in him, had raised him immeasurably in her estimation—and reminders of their inequity never failed to annoy her.

Yet for all her talk of Thibault and their escapades at school, she knew her comrades had assumed he was the son of the local squire and she had never corrected that impression. Not out of shame, she often told herself, but more to avoid unnecessary complications—for they simply would not have understood.

Looking over at his stolid, rough-cut features, she felt a sudden wave of embarrassment—not for him and his background but rather for herself: for the blue, aristocratic blood running through her veins, for her Ceylonde Season and tenure in Haarkonis, for her ostentatious house and the size of Vera's manor. What need had she, or even Vera, for thirty rooms when Thibault and Sylvaine had gotten away with two—and small ones at that?

Equally embarrassing was Desmond's Magerie, its pristine, perfectly manicured front mocking its tatty neighbors. In yet another glaring inequity, it was all too clear who held the wealth and power in Nova Castria, and who held it in every other city and village throughout Varia. The mages had the world in a veritable chokehold. While the Guilds had developed to feed a specialized market, it was theoretically possible for everyone to be a carpenter or an assassin; the mages alone provided a service that no one else could replicate.

It simply wasn't fair. Apart from the ostentatious Magerie, Desmond di Negri had a manor outside the town even larger than Vera's, and wore robes of only the most expensive silk imported from his native Mepharsta. And short of living in the dark or by weak, unreliable candle-light, every citizen in Nova Castria supported his costly habits.

"Ah, Domina Radineaux, Suh Lescevre," he said in his mellifluous voice, the exaggerated accents of Eshevaria lilting in his words, "I have been expecting you. You are expecting a communication from Ceylonde, no?"

"Yes," Jen said tightly, disliking him as much for his phony solicitousness as his affected tones. Even his name—di Negri—was a fake, given him by the local population in lieu of his unpronounceable birth name: a tribute to his dark skin and, Jen suspected, darker heart. He couldn't even accord Thibault the courtesy of a "Mal," his assiduous correctness relegating Jen's companion to the rank of "Suh"—servant class and lowest of the low.

And solicitous or not, he would be draining her purse on this visit, and they both knew it.

"So, how much?" she asked.

"For a channel to Ceylonde? Five marks, Domina. Ten for a secured one." And he held out a hand.

"And what if I said Suh Lescevre would be paying?" Jen snapped, without reaching for her purse.

"Twenty bits. Forty secured."

"Do you think that's entirely fair?"

The mage just shrugged. "Higher income, higher price," he said, and Jen had to admit it made a certain, insidious sense. The mages didn't charge selectively; they robbed all equally.

She handed over the ten marks.

"Ah, very good. A secured channel." Desmond rubbed his palms together and uncovered the large ball of clear crystal from its silk wrappings. Briefly, he checked the clock. "You contact—DeVeris, was it not?—should be expecting our call by now. Let me just code the link." And, with his usual arrogance, he spoke the words that opened the Guild's public channel, doubtless determined during his previous contact.

Jen wondered idly if he knew what really lay on the other side of that linkage.

Nonetheless, a few seconds later, the milky glow of the crystal cleared and focused into an image of what Jen assumed was one of the Ceylonde mages, likely one in the Guild's employ. Although, were it not for his position, she would have found it impossible to tell, for he lacked an ounce of what she had come to regard as the mages' native ostentation. His beard was short and grey, his eyes a piercing hazel, and his robes a simple academic black. She felt an instant affinity for him that she had never felt for Desmond.

The two mages exchanged a few brief words, and then the former's image was replaced by that of Owen DeVeris.

Jen had never met the Guildmaster in the flesh, but there was something open and honest about the hawk-nosed face that she found immediately attractive.

"Domina Radineaux?" he inquired as Desmond bowed faintly and quit the room, leaving Jen and Thibault to the privacy of the crystal.

"Yes, Mal DeVeris. I'm Jen Radineaux, and this is Thibault Lescevre. I'm sure Aunt Vera has mentioned him?"

He nodded, looking somewhat bemused.

"Mal DeVeris?" she prompted. "What can I do for you?"

"My apologies, Domina, but I had no idea you would look so much like your aunt. Did you know she was as young as you when I first met her?"

"So I've heard. But meaning no disrespect, Mal DeVeris,

I'm sure you didn't contact me to talk of my aunt's appearance."

"No. On the contrary," and his face sobered, "it was rather the opposite that brought me."

"Excuse me?"

Behind her, she could feel Thibault tense, and she flashed him a quick look that said, as clearly as words: *You'd better not say I told you so!* In response, she felt his hands coming up to grip her shoulders, and she leaned into the reassuring warmth.

In the globe, the Guildmaster said, "I regret to tell you that there's been an incident."

Her face tightened. "What sort of incident?"

"A most regrettable one. Jen, I'm afraid your aunt's been taken."

7

Although she had a week, it took Vera less than four days to make her decision. After two days of wandering the slums and a third touring the infamous glass manufactories—quizzing anyone who would speak to her—she had a pretty fair picture built up. She had seen the vermin-infested hovels of the poor, viewed the thin broth and maggoty bread that passed for food, smelled the stink of unwashed bodies and spoiled meat rising with the sickly sweet odor of Dreamsmoke from the small, overcrowded rooms. She had walked the factory floors, felt the hot, unbreathable air pressing on her like a blanket, seen the shimmering waves of heat rising from the furnaces and vats of molten glass. Stripped down and sweating, unable to break frequently enough for water, the workers toiled in untenable conditions. She had witnessed five collapse within an hour.

By her calculations, Istarbion was pocketing something on the order of twenty thousand marks a year in profits—profits which should have gone to bettering the life of the population he was exploiting.

She had left a note for Pehndon at their prearranged drop point, accepting the assignment, and had even stopped by the warehouse in search of Jason, but neither he nor Pehndon was present, nor did the scores of busy workers have any idea when they might return. So she retreated instead to the hotel, where she found the invitation for Istarbion's gala awaiting her.

"Efficient," she said, when she met Pehndon later for dinner.

He just shrugged. "I figured if you didn't want it, you could always destroy it. What is that phrase: 'Better safe than sorry'? I'm glad you're taking the job, Leonie."

"As am I. So, do you think there's any way of getting

me into the building before the grand event? I'd love to get the lay of the place, and you did say you had government contacts."

"Yes, but unfortunately not of that caliber. The gala is being held on Istarbion's private estate and will be managed entirely by a cadre of his handpicked servants. He simply does not let anyone else in on a regular basis, not even his colleagues. Or so I've been told." Pehndon looked disgusted.

Vera grinned. "No trouble, then; I'm used to improvising. But you wouldn't happen to know of a good dressmaker, would you?"

By the night of the gala, all was in readiness. Succumbing to the lures of the open-air market, Vera had purchased a bolt of bronze silk, which she had made up into a truly stunning creation. With a neckline cut low enough to be arresting, the gown flared from a sculpted bodice to a flow of shimmering skirt—its fullness hiding the twin daggers resting in slim ankle-sheaths and the pouch of tiny, needlelike darts strapped to one calf. Onyx earrings and a string of onyx beads completed the ensemble, while the two delivery darts reposed in plain view, stuck crosswise into the bun at the crown of her head, their pinions intermingled with a spray of glossy black feathers. The remainder of her hair, tortured into an artful froth of curls, was loosely gathered from her face by the invisible loop of her garroting cord, while the removal of one of the whalebone struts of her bodice had provided a handy resting place for her blowpipe.

Behind the jet facade of one of her several rings, the poison of choice reposed.

Invitation in hand, with a set of flints and a bottle of the extremely rare and enormously expensive fire-oil hidden beneath the false bottom of her handbag in case of emergency, Vera descended the hotel steps to her hired landau—an elegant vehicle pulled by a set of matched blacks, which boasted a tuft of golden plumes erupting from the top of their gilded harnesses. Decorously, they trotted to Istarbion's vast estate outside the city.

The setting was everything she had expected, and more. There was something almost obscene about the lush carpet of greenery which arose just inside the white stone pillars of the gates, perfuming the air with a delicate fragrance that was everything the desert was not. Lanterns of magelight winked off the branches of flowering trees, twinkling like fireflies through the violet sky, and on the shadowed lawn, peacocks strutted in fading splendor while carriages and landaus by the dozens discharged their glittering passengers at the wide stone porticoes of the sprawling manor.

Unlike the locked and heavily guarded gates, the doors of the house were thrown invitingly open and a wash of laughter and music emerged, the luminous glow of the magelights flowing like a tide over the shallow stone steps.

Disembarking, Vera paid her driver, with an injunction to return for her later, and entered the house. Here, the profits of the glassworks manifested themselves in gilded furniture, crystal chandeliers, and polished expanses of parquet floors, on which an array of richly clad guests perambulated, sampling delicate hors d'oeuvres from the silver platters of liveried servants and sipping champagne from delicate flutes with stems of indigo lapis-glass.

Lightly armored guards, resplendent in breastplates and crested helmets—their uniforms a striking meld of red and black—hovered in strategic doorways like attendant statues, their swords sheathed covertly at their sides.

Accepting a crabmeat roll but declining the champagne, Vera drifted through the open rooms, surveying the crowd. From the sheer multitude of indistinguishable faces, she could see how Iaon and Jason would be willing to risk an appearance, courtesy of their government contacts. With this many bodies in evidence, no one would be likely to notice a few members of the opposition.

The chambers were all uniformly lavish, and the room where Istarbion was to give his address featured a small stage, on which was mounted a cloth-draped podium, its scarlet folds likely the progenitor of the one Jason had employed. Circulating unobtrusively, Vera tried to determine the best locations from which to propagate her deed. There was one shadowed corner, partially hidden behind a column, which looked promising, but it was never her method to rely on only one locale—and especially not in such a public place.

She was in the midst of her survey when she spotted

Jason across the room, resplendent in a vest of blue-green silk over a gathered green shirt and tailored black trousers. Catching his eye, she smiled and waved, only to be rewarded by a polite if somewhat blank stare.

Good, Andorian, she thought. *A very credible job. Would have fooled even me, if I hadn't known better.* She was on her way to talk to him, to ask if he had any suggestions, when his gaze suddenly shifted from her face to some point over her left shoulder. Abruptly he turned and vanished into the crowd, and she whirled to see Iaon Pehndon approaching from the rear.

"What's the matter, don't you conspirators speak in public?" she teased as he reached her.

"What do you mean?" He looked as blank as Jason had.

"Never mind. What do you have for me?"

"Good news." He became brisk. "Jason bribed one of the guards. There's an upper room that opens onto this hall. Used to be a minstrels' gallery in the days before magecasts became so popular." And indeed, she could hear the strains of the orchestra in the distant ballroom, resonating through the various mage-crystals in the chamber with a clarity that negated the need for in-room entertainment.

"A gallery?" she demanded. "Where?"

"No, don't look up now." Pehndon took her by the elbow, leading her away from the wall at an angle. "I feel some need of refreshment, don't you?" And he indicated one of the ubiquitous waiters, standing in the shadow of Istarbion's podium.

"Indeed." She smiled. And when they had refreshed themselves, she cast her eye discreetly up from their new vantage point and spotted the narrow opening which overlooked the podium.

"Perfect. Can you get me up there?"

"I think we can manage that." He raised an eyebrow. "Have you got the . . . instruments?"

"Really, Mal Pehndon," she returned coquettishly, patting her hair and allowing one of the darts to slide unobtrusively from its sheath. "What do you take me for?"

His eyes widened slightly, and with another casual flick of her wrist she resheathed the weapon in her coiffure.

"I'll have to keep the room dark to avoid detection,"

she continued, "so I'll need to get up there early to let my eyes adjust and familiarize myself with the distances."

"Distances?"

She mimed a blowpipe.

"You'll be shooting the guests?"

Pehndon sounded horrified, and she grinned. "Purely benignly, I assure you. So whenever you're ready . . ."

"The speech should be starting in an hour."

"Fine. Come find me in half an hour, then. In the meantime . . . which one's Istarbion?"

"Guess." Pehndon's voice brimmed with contempt.

She scanned the crowd, her eyes falling unerringly on an ostentatious little puff-pigeon, obviously gone soft and lax from years of rich living. His head was half bald and shining in the magelight, his pudgy, moist fingers adorned with a multiplicity of rings as he held forth from a spot she was somehow convinced was the exact center of the room.

"The short, fat, egotistical one, I presume?" she said, and was rewarded by Pehndon's answering chuckle.

"Yes, that's our Guy. No last-minute twinges of conscience?"

"Not in the least," she responded and, taking his arm, allowed him to escort her from the chamber.

From his position at its center, Guy Istarbion surveyed the hall with something approaching satisfaction. All was going perfectly—as usual. The house looked beautiful, and his guest were all impeccably dressed, though none quite so lavishly as himself. There was even one deucedly handsome woman in bronze—likely some ministerial mistress, for hers was a new face—whom he decided he simply **had** to meet. She was really quite phenomenally striking.

He scanned the room—surreptitiously, of course, so as not to interrupt Minister Malmud's pompous monologue; it wouldn't do to make any enemies tonight—but he couldn't see the woman in question. Come to that, the last time he had spotted her she'd been leaving the room on the arm of Iaon Pehndon. Not that he thought she was Pehndon's mistress; Pehndon would, he suspected, not know one end of a mistress from the other. A thoroughly cold fish, that one, with no appreciation of life's finer pleasures.

But ambitious; no denying that. There were times when he suspected Pehndon of jockeying for the First, but how could a man possibly aspire to the position without a taste for the advantages it conferred? No, the choice of his successor was entirely in Istarbion's hands, and he had chosen another. Oh, to be sure, Jhakharta didn't know of his decision, nor could he even say he fully *liked* the man, but in Jhakharta he recognized a fellow sybarite. The luxuries of table and bed were certainly no strangers to *him*. The man would make an exemplary First.

With his eyes still fixed earnestly on Malmud's—nodding sagely at appropriate intervals—Istarbion reached out a hand, seemingly blindly, to pluck several tidbits off the tray of a passing waiter.

Still, he reflected as he consumed them, turning his mind back to more pleasant subjects, if that delightful woman was so tight with Pehndon, then surely she could appreciate some other ministerial charms. It would certainly be a pleasant diversion from his existing stable of servile women, and there was a particularly sumptuous upstairs bedroom awaiting just such an opportunity.

Now if only he could release himself from Malmud's clutches.

Scanning the room again, one ear still half-tuned to his companion's blather, he located his second standing by the podium. The man had obviously been seized by a grasping Potential Mistress (P.M.s, as he called them), and was looking decidedly uncomfortable as the glittering, avaricious female backed him into a tight physical—and no doubt verbal—corner.

Istarbion couldn't blame him for his reluctance; the woman was not at all to his tastes either.

He watched as Jhakharta, flushing slightly, inserted a finger into his collar as if to loosen its constricting grasp, then jumped and brushed something irritably from his cheek. Deciding it was time to rescue them both, Istarbion cut smoothly into Malmud's oration and excused himself with his usual urbanity, saying, "Your pardon, but I believe Minister Jhakharta has need of me; it is likely time to begin my speech," and made good his escape.

Jhakharta looked nothing short of grateful as his superior approached, for, taking the hint, his companion disappeared, leaving the two together.

"Blazes, Guy, you have just saved me from the most dreadful harpy imaginable!" he said, rubbing his cheek, and Istarbion smiled somewhat smugly.

"I know. You owe me, don't you?"

"I suppose so," his second responded pettishly. "You ought to talk to your gardener, though, Guy. There's a plague of insects in this place. One just bit me, and it stings like the dickens!"

"Well, stop rubbing it; you're only making it worse. Now, about that favor you owe me . . ."

"Yes?"

"There's a woman here, dressed in bronze with black feathers in her hair. Go find her; I want to speak to her."

Jhakharta's face pinched disgustedly, but all he said was, "It's almost time for your speech."

"Well, after the speech, then. Don't be such an idiot, Alphonse." Over his second's shoulder, he saw another guest jump and squeak, brushing at her cheek. "For now, get the mages and let's begin the broadcast."

"Yes, of course."

"And Alphonse?"

"Yes?"

"Don't act so petulant; it looks bad for the public."

As his second withdrew, Istarbion took a deep, calming breath and began to ready himself for the moment. It was time for his annual words, the yearly platitudes pronounced via magecast to appease the unwashed masses and dim the fires of that rabble-rouser Andorian. Not that he cared a whit what the man thought—or even what the masses thought, behind their silly sheeplike faces. All he cared was that the money kept coming in and his own comfort remained assured. But he had to admit that Andorian's tendency to keep shoving maimed workers in his face had become a decided annoyance.

From the corner of his eye he noticed the flickering of the magelights which summoned the crowds and caught Jhakharta's signal that it was time to begin. Accordingly, he mounted the platform and crossed to the podium, its draperies matching his scarlet and black attire, and was gratified by the sudden hush which settled over his audience.

He let the silence grow for a minute as the room continued to fill and was about to open his mouth and begin his speech—fed to him by the tiny mage audio link resting below his right ear—when he felt a sudden stinging bite on his neck. *I'll have to talk to the blasted gardener after all,* he thought irritably, then froze as he felt a numbing lethargy invade his limbs and a body that would no longer obey him.

Betrayal! his mind shrilled, and his eyes, as if by design, flew straight to the door where Pehndon waited, a smug, triumphant expression on his face, *Traitor!* his eyes screamed out, but Pehndon just smiled. He wanted to move, cry out—*anything*—but he couldn't.

And by then it was too late, for the dart had hit, tufting like an obscene growth from his neck. And as the first spastic tremors of motion reinvaded Istarbion's limbs and pain sang like silver-hot wires through his nerves, Pehndon was gone, slipping unnoticed from the room.

8

In the darkened recess of the minstrels' gallery, Vera felt the deadly dart of Istarbion's death leave her hand and knew she had succeeded. It had been amusing, earlier, firing her tiny, blunted missiles into the crowd, seeing them jump and curse as if bitten by a swarm of invisible insects. She had missed her target only once and that had been on her first try, as she worked to get a sense of elevation and distance. Accuracy was critical, for when the moment arrived she would have only one chance—at most, two—to get it right.

But she was confident of her success. She was the Hawk, after all, the Guild's foremost assassin. When Istarbion mounted the podium, she would first fire the tiny, almost invisible thorn carrying temporary paralysis, both to confirm the distance and to prevent him from making any sudden movements when she went for the trickier, free-thrown dart. It wouldn't do to have him twitch out of reach, to have the missile and its deadly cargo fly wide. She had only two darts—and she intended to use only one. That way, the minute she had visually confirmed the hit, she could slide out the door and down the stairs, mingling seamlessly with the crowd before the shock of Istarbion's convulsions had fully worn off. With any luck, he would still be alive by the time she reached the ballroom.

At least that was the plan.

Certainly, it seemed as if it was going perfectly when she put away her blunted test missiles and took a deep breath before drawing out a slender spine and dipping it briefly into a solution concealed in one of her rings. Then loading it, she fired and saw Istarbion's tiny flinch as the missile connected, saw him freeze as the temporary potion took effect.

Seized by the deadly calm that infected her during a job,

as if time moved like treacle and herself a vibrant eddy within it, she smoothly stowed both needles and blowpipe before reaching for one of the darts in her hair. Sliding it forth from its sheath, she hinged open her jet ring—black for the color of death—and dipped the glittering point in the viscous, verdant solution. Immediately, the poison clung and hardened on the tip of the dart, forming a deadly coat. Hinging the ring shut again, she poised for the throw.

Istarbion still hadn't moved. From start to finish, barely three seconds had elapsed. She still had a good seven—an eternity—before the effects of the first potion would dissipate.

The instant the dart left her hand, she knew she would need no other. As if the first tiny missile had guided her throw, she could feel the feathered shaft fly clean and true, its point burrowing deep into Istarbion's neck. She counted briefly to three to be sure that he wouldn't dislodge it, then turned away the minute the convulsions started, gliding silently for the door. She had done her job. Istarbion was dead—or would be in a minute—and in two weeks she would be three thousand marks richer and reunited with her niece. With a faint smile, she pulled open the door . . .

Only to see Pehndon framed in the doorway, his face subtly triumphant.

She jumped slightly, not expecting the company, then said, "It's done. Let me pass."

"I don't think so, Leonie." His smile widened as he moved into her path, firmly blocking her escape.

She felt a sudden frisson of fear, all the more terrifying because it was such an unfamiliar emotion. But, "What is this?" she managed nonetheless, her voice relatively steady.

"A setup," Pehndon answered. "Congratulations, Leonie. You are now the property of the Ashkharon government."

"But . . ."

Behind him, Jason materialized from the shadows, an identically smug smile curving his lips. He had, she noticed, changed from his blue-green vest and was now wearing black and scarlet—an ironic echo of Istarbion.

"Well, that was fast," she snapped. "What is this, your betrayal garb?"

He looked momentarily blank. It was Pehndon who responded. "In a sense. Thank you for being so gullible, Leonie, so moralistic. You have done me a great service. Guards!"

His voice, echoing down the long corridor, was almost immediately answered by the tramp of running feet and the clink of armor, the whisper of unsheathed weapons.

Stunned and furious, she could barely react as Pehndon grabbed her arms and twisted them painfully behind her back.

"I've got her, boys! I've caught the bitch who killed Istarbion!"

There was no time to fight. Before she knew what was happening, the guards had surrounded her, cuffing her hands and hobbling her ankles. One even snapped a metal collar around her neck, its edges digging sharply into her throat, while yet another stuffed an unsavory gag, rancid with dirt and stale sweat, into her mouth.

"Take her downstairs and secure us a room," Pehndon ordered. "I want to talk to her."

Her eyes sparked hatred, but he merely smiled—alone in his triumph, for Jason had disappeared. Yet as the guards dragged her backwards down the dimly lit hall, her last sight was of Andorian, rematerializing from the shadows, with one hand on Pehndon's shoulder, to wave an ironic good-bye.

Odd, how in two minutes your world could crumble and be reborn. One moment Jhakharta was the lowest of the low, procurer of whores for his exalted master, and the next that master was in convulsions, his heels drumming the podium, green spittle frothing from his mouth as his body voided itself in a rush of stench and fluid.

And then, in the midst of the screams and the horror, Pehndon had appeared, breathless and trailing a pack of guards, who held within their grasp the manacled form of the very woman his master had insisted he procure. "The minstrels' gallery. Upstairs," Pehndon was saying. "I caught her!"

Seeing Pehndon's flushed face, Jhakharta felt slightly sick, the man's former words echoing through his mind: *Stick with me, and in six months you'll be living like a First Minister.* Suddenly he knew what had happened to Istarbion, why Iaon had been so quick to the rescue.

Pehndon had masterminded the whole bloody thing.

In the chaos, he managed to get Iaon alone for a few minutes, backing him into a deserted corner. Swallowing against the urge to vomit, he said, "This was your doing, wasn't it? You set this all up!"

"In a sense." The hectic flush had faded from Iaon's cheeks; he looked his usual implacable self.

"But . . ."

"I told you Guy could take care of himself. Don't pretend to be upset, Alphonse."

"Upset? Why shouldn't I be upset? You killed the First Minister!"

"So?"

"Well . . . where do I fit in?"

Pehndon just smiled. "You wanted to be the First Minister, didn't you? And you couldn't very well do that with Istarbion still alive."

"But . . ."

"Honestly, Alphonse," Pehndon's voice was testy, "don't be such an idiot! Do you really think Istarbion had picked *me* as his successor?"

"You mean . . . ?"

"Yes. I think you'll find that Istarbion has named you as the next First."

"But . . . I didn't even like him! Why did he pick me?"

Pehndon shrugged. "Maybe your toadying was more convincing than you realized. I don't know; I don't pretend to understand Istarbion. But I don't break my promises, Alphonse."

"You mean you don't want the position?"

"Me?" Pehndon sounded horrified. "What would *I* do as First? No, I'm perfectly content to let you have all the public glory and run things myself in private."

"Run what?"

Pehndon raised an eyebrow. "Frankly, Alphonse, do you really care?"

"No." Suddenly Jhakharta began to grin. "First, huh? And none of this will rub off on me?"

"Not if you play it right. Follow my lead, and we'll both come out as pure as bloody virgins! Now, go and act suitably bereaved. I have an assassin to interview."

"Who are you?" were her first, snarled words as Pehndon, alone with her as last in a windowless downstairs chamber, finally removed her gag.

In answer, he merely smiled, lowering himself into the

room's other chair, and stretched his legs out before him, crossing his ankles. How helpless she looked, shackled upright in her chair, her hair in shambles and a purpling bruise across her cheek where one of the guards had struck her. The noble Hawk humbled at last, her pinions clipped. How fitting.

And it was he, Iaon Pehndon, who had brought her down.

"I'm a member of the Ashkharon government, my dear," he answered. "A legitimate Minister."

"A spy?"

"Openly in league with the opposition?" He chuckled, shaking his head. "You disappoint me, Leonie; I had thought you far smarter than that. What about Andorian?"

"I don't know," she snapped. "What about him?"

"Leonie, Leonie, use that Guild-trained head of yours. Andorian's presence at your arrest means what?"

"That you bought him off?" Her lip, he noticed, had been split and was starting to swell, lending a gratifying thickness to her speech.

"Clever—and closer—but still not correct. No, Leonie, I'll tell you the truth, since you're unlikely to guess it. To buy someone off means they have to exist in the first place, and the exalted Jason Andorian never did."

"What?"

"A fabrication, that's all he was. An elaborate construct to stir up public sentiment against Istarbion. Created," and he bowed faintly, "by your own humble servant."

"But . . . the Guild knew of Andorian; everyone's heard of Andorian!"

"Well, they'd have to, wouldn't they, if this was to work? There's no point in having an unbelievable construct."

"So the entire rebel faction . . ."

"Is a fake, yes. All under my control. Good. I'm beginning to think you finally get the picture."

"And the workers, the causes?"

"Inconsequential. Except for the fact that it caught the Guild's attention."

She spat with disturbing accuracy, hawking a gob of phlegm and blood that narrowly missed the tips of his boots. "You make me sick, Pehndon!"

He just smiled and moved his feet. "Likewise inconsequential. Come, Leonie, aren't you even curious why you got involved?"

"Because I was a fool. Because you wanted the Guild's approval as your seal of legitimacy."

"Very good. Care to continue, or shall I?"

"I'll take a stab at it." Her voice cracked. "You needed Istarbion out of the way, but your personal motivations weren't enough. You needed public support, so you created the rebel alliance to discredit Istarbion."

"And?"

"And?" Her brow furrowed, then cleared, fury replacing incomprehension. "And then you bring in the Guild to return the fake alliance to obscurity. Jason publicly admits he hired an assassin, is put to trial and either discredited or killed, thus breaking the back of the 'rebel' alliance. Leaving you to step in and take its place."

"Excellent. The Guild trains its creatures well. Yes, my dear, you will be going on trial—a very public trial."

"And what if I tell them the truth?"

Pehndon waved his hand negligently. "Who would believe you? A fake rebel alliance? In Ashkharon? No, it's been too well acted—and for too long. Both you and the Guild are duty-bound to admit that Jason hired you."

"And what if I say that you did? The Guild knows you were involved, after all . . ."

"And never even bothered to check if I was a member of the opposition, did they?" He chuckled. "Ironic, really. But I knew they wouldn't; they'd be too caught up in redressing all the dreadful wrongs, as indeed they were."

"Which still doesn't answer my question," his prisoner responded tightly. "What if I named you?"

"Then I would simply use your initial excuse, that I was a spy in the midst of the rebel alliance and therefore privy to their plans."

"And won't that look a little too convenient when you suddenly rise to prominence as the next First Minister?"

He waggled a finger. "Ah, but I won't be the next First Minister. Istarbion's already picked his successor. And why would I have hatched such an elaborate plot just to raise Alphonse Jhakharta to power?"

"Because you own this Alphonse Jhakharta?" she spat.

"Well, obviously, but no one else will know that. And when it comes to the test, it will be your word against Jhakharta's—and whom do you think the courts are most likely to believe?"

"You bastard!"

"Yes, I've got you in quite a tidy little noose, don't I?"

"The Guild won't let you get away with this!" she flared, and he chuckled.

"Actually, I rather think the Guild will have no choice."

She was silent for a long moment, then finally asked, "Why? What did Istarbion do to deserve this?"

"Oh, not Istarbion," he answered airily. "Istarbion's only problem was that he thought too small. He lacked vision."

"And you?"

"And I"—he chuckled—"have discovered something in the desert. Something in the heart of the Anvil that has the capacity to make Ashkharon a household name, to give it more power than the mages. And I will be the one controlling it."

"What is it, then, this great discovery?"

But he merely grinned and leaned back in his chair. "Ah, no, my dear. I shan't tell you. I need to preserve some of my secrets, after all. But suffice it to say that after you are dead and gone, there won't be a schoolchild on Varia who doesn't know the name of Iaon Pehndon!"

9

As soon as Vander had severed the connection on the crystal, blanking Jen's angry face from sight, Owen DeVeris lowered his face into his hands and sat in silence for a long, bitter moment, thinking of all that might have been. By all that was precious, it was hard: hard to know that Vera was in trouble, that he was miles away and unable to help her; harder still to face her irate niece. He hadn't expected Jen to look so much like the young Vera and it threw him badly, summoning memories he would prefer not to handle. Not now, with his best assassin gone, not when he felt as old and powerless as the day he had first retired from active duty.

Like many assassins, Owen had devoted his life to the Guild, and when time and age had taken the inevitable edge off his performance, he had found himself unmarried and childless, alone. It was not a contingency he had prepared for. Assassins were not supposed to live past forty; they were certainly not supposed to retire and find a whole other lifetime stretching out before them. For Owen, taking over the Guildmastership had been one form of salvation; Vera had been another. The young aristocrat had entered his office at the very moment when he was feeling the absence of a child most keenly, and something in her fiery rebelliousness had struck an answering chord within him. She had mellowed and firmed over the years, it was true, yet she still contained that core of molten steel, all too ready to shoot hot sparks.

She had become the daughter he'd never had, and he had guided her career like a father, taking pleasure in her triumphs and finding life afresh through her eyes. Though he had, in time, become attached to all his protégées—feeling like the patriarch of a large extended family—Vera Radineaux had been his first recruit as Guildmaster and she remained his finest. The other faces had come and gone, each not without its own particular heartbreak, but Vera had been his favorite. He was even grooming her to take over the Guildmastership when he retired a second time. To lose her now would be insupportable.

How had this happened? Who had been careless, who had let the Hawk get caught? *Please,* he thought, *don't let it have been me.* He was sixty-five, and though a life spent living on the edge had aged him prematurely—silvering his hair and crimping his once deft fingers—he had never felt old until now. He'd have gone after her himself if he were ten years younger, if he could have still held a dagger in his swollen, arthritic grip.

But the biggest tragedy of all was that, apart from sending another assassin after her covertly, there was nothing he could do to help her. Officially, his hands were tied. The Hestian Guild occupied a shadowy nether region midway between legitimacy and unlawfulness. Technically, what they did was illegal: murder. And yet if they didn't do it, someone else would, and eventually everyone realized that if death was going to become a commodity, then at least it should be a regulated one. And so the Guild was born. Their codes were strictly moral, their kills clean and painless—their penalties on non-Guild operatives torturously severe—and yet, in many ways, they simply did not exist.

Of course, everyone knew of the Guild, knew how to contract their services, though there were no official headquarters located anywhere in Ceylonde. Rather, there was Ceylonde University. Ostensibly serving as the cover for the Guild's activities, it had grown since its humble inception to become one of the finest and most genuine institutes of higher learning in all of Varia. Its training curriculum of diplomacy, political theory, and the martial arts had soon increased to cover as diverse a range of topics as possible, and in time the scholars became almost indistinguishable from the fledgling assassins as they sauntered along the flagstone walkways like somber crows in their black academic robes.

For those who were determined and had sufficient cash to offer, there were always ways around the facade, and yet those who had found it weren't about to turn evidence for fear of getting implicated and those who hadn't could never locate the proper channels. For the Guild was discretion itself, its members operating under strictly maintained code names whose secrecy, Owen suspected, extended even to their fellow assassins. (Everyone knew of the Hawk; only Owen and a select group of friends knew of Viera Radineaux.) Moreover, it was Guild policy never to acknowledge their assassins in public. All missions took place without Guild contact; from the moment of assignment to the completion of the job, the Guild members were on their own. That way, the Guild could disclaim all knowledge. As Guildmaster, Owen alone knew what jobs were extant and which operatives had been assigned, but until the job was done, he had no knowledge of the details. And should an assassin be captured, the Guild automatically denied all connection—and therein lay Owen's dilemma.

He could no longer intervene on the Hawk's behalf because, officially, she no longer existed. Despite the fact that he knew her and loved her—that his heart ached with her loss—Vera had been divorced from the Guild.

No matter that most governments on Varia turned a blind eye to the Guild's activities. No matter that they were the primary procurers of Guild services. No government on Varia could fail to condemn a captured assassin.

It was a cursed chancy life.

There were, of course, many reasons to join the Guild. For some it was a love of danger or adventure, a desire to travel or extend the boundaries of their world. For others—Owen included—it was the financial stability: a Guild assassin, even of the lowest ranks, could earn more in a year than another could ever hope to earn in a lifetime of alternate employment.

In Vera's case, he imagined, it was simple rebellion— and a desire to prove herself something other than a drawing-room ornament.

Yet now the unthinkable had happened. After twenty years, the Hawk had been taken.

"Owen?"

Raising his head from his hands, he looked into Vander's worried face. The mage, he suspected, knew almost as much about Guild business as he did, from sheer extrapolation. But no matter; he would trust the man with his life—in fact, he had, on several occasions.

He ran gnarled fingers through his hair, feeling the old, familiar twinges from his swollen joints. Great gadflies of beneficence, but he felt old. Old and infinitely tired. "I'm sorry, Van," he said, circumspect to the end. "It's always hard to lose . . . a friend."

Vander's sharp eyes softened. "I understand. Can I get you something? A cup of tea, perhaps?"

"No. No, thank you." Owen sighed, mentally reviewing his ledgers "I should get back to my office." Already he was compiling a list of his top operatives, trying to determine whom to send after Vera. He had promised Jen that much at least—and he owed it to her aunt.

He was about to stand when the ball gave off a soft, annoying cheep, indicating an incoming call. He looked over at Vander, who said, "Shall I?"

"Yes, I suppose you'd better. It's probably for me anyway." And he gathered himself into a semblance of his usual order.

Vander made one or two passes over the ball, muttering, then the picture swirled and became clear. In the crystal, the cheerful face of Derek Verhoeven grinned back at him.

"Hey, Van, where's . . . Oh, there he is. Hi, Owen!" The figure waved and smiled; rolling his eyes, Vander retreated diplomatically from the room.

Owen returned the smile with genuine pleasure, feeling his mood swing toward a kind of guarded optimism. The Hound and the Falcon—who better? So, "Hello, Derek. Anything to report?" he said, and the Hound's eyes twinkled.

"The head of House Ferittan is dead. Are we reprieved? Can we come home now?"

Like his namesake, there was a kind of puppyish quality to the Hound; at any minute you expected him to get up and start frisking. Owen almost hated to destroy his pleasure. "Not just yet, I'm afraid. I need you to . . ." Then pausing, his eyes sharpening, he stared intently over the Hound's left shoulder. Behind the man were not the grey stone dwellings of Nordevaria with their narrow windows overlooking the thick stands of northern woods but rather a wide, sun-drenched portico with a series of staggered terraces falling off below it, and in the distance the cerulean glints of what could only be the Belapharion.

"Wait a minute," he said sharply. "Where are you? That's not Nordevaria . . ."

The Hound looked sheepish. "I know, but there was a change of plans. We're in Venetzia."

"Venetzia? But . . ."

"Would you believe," Derek elaborated, "that the little rat had a Venetzian mistress? Certainly gives a new meaning to those 'business trips' of his!"

"And you had to follow him down there? You couldn't just have finished the job in Nordevaria?" Owen sighed gustily, then added, "So, how much did this set the Guild back?"

"One hundred and fifty marks for passage . . ."

"Ah."

"Apiece," Derek added, with an apologetic grin.

There was a moment of silence.

"I think there's something wrong with Owen," the Hound said whimsically, turning to address someone behind him. "I just told him about the detour and he's not even upset!"

There was an invisible mutter from the Falcon, which sounded suspiciously to Owen like "Well, at least he's finally being reasonable," and he smiled despite himself.

"Actually, for once I think your bumbling may have been merited," he said, though he couldn't help the aggrieved note that crept into his voice as he added, "But did you *have* to take the luxury cruise? For three hundred marks . . ."

"What, did you want us to lose our quarry?" Derek interrupted cheerfully, not in the least put out.

"No, but couldn't you have at least gone steerage? Or even second class?"

"Second class? On the *Varian Queen*?"

"I . . . Oh, never mind. Is Mark there?"

The Hound chuckled. "Why does everyone always want my brother?" Then, turning, he yelled in a voice loud enough to make Owen wince, "Mark!"

Owen could hear the faint, irritable answer in the background. "What?"

"I told you DeVeris wouldn't listen to me. So drop that book and get over here."

"I'm on vacation," the voice grumbled.

"Not anymore, you're not," Owen informed them, and Derek grinned.

A moment later, Mark Verhoeven's sharp, uneven features filled the crystal.

"Well, what is it, Owen?" he said dryly. "What was so vital that my brother couldn't handle it?"

Unlike his big, boyish brother, whose blue eyes could widen ingenuously at will, Mark Verhoeven was cunning personified, from the point of his sharp nose to the glint in his steely eyes. A good foot shorter than his sibling, the Falcon was the brains of the operation—the long-distance flier, as he liked to call it—and the physical dissimilarities between the brothers were matched only by the strength of the bond between them. Where Mark schemed, Derek acted—often impetuously, but still there were few who could match the Hound for sheer tenacity once he had picked up a trail. And where Mark's rat-sharp face was often greeted by suspicion, Derek's bluff, hail-well-met charm earned him an almost universal welcome. So while Mark struck from heights and shadows, Derek worked the open crowds, the weaknesses of each perfectly complemented by the strengths of the other. Derek would die for Mark without question and Mark for Derek; fortunately for Owen, the choice had never arisen.

Seeing their interplay, the Guildmaster sometimes regretted that Vera had never taken a partner, but he knew the Hawk was too self-sufficient to give up control for long.

"He says we can't go home yet," Derek complained.

"Why not?"

"Because you're already halfway to where I need you to be," Owen answered, adding, "We have a situation. The Hawk's been taken."

"The Hawk?" Derek's eyes widened. Mark was too well trained to react, but Owen could tell he was shocked nonetheless. "But she's . . ."

"The Hawk, yes, which leads me to believe something has gone dreadfully awry—more than just a simple mistake. She's in Ashkharon, being held at the government prison in Nhuras; I don't know what name she's going under. But I need someone to go down there and examine the situation, see if it's possible to get her out, and personally I can't think of anyone better for the job than you two."

"Always delighted to help," Mark said. "But, not meaning to sound cold, who's paying?"

"I am," the Guildmaster answered firmly. "My own private funds. A thousand marks for information, two thousand to spring the Hawk." And when they paused, he added, "Apiece."

Mark nodded. "Agreed."

"Good. Ground rules, first. This is no ordinary assignment—as well you know. Guild silence will *not* apply. Be circumspect about contacting me, but keep in touch. I want to know everything that transpires!"

"Understood."

"Fine. How soon can you leave?"

"Today, if need be."

"Then do it. But please for my sake . . ."

"Yes?"

"Go third class."

10

Jen was ominously silent on the ride home, and Thibault could almost hear the wheels of trouble spinning inside her head. She was planning something, he could tell, but getting information from Jen when she was feeling recalcitrant was no easy task; he might as well have tried to squeeze blood from a stone. All his efforts were met with a steely reticence, so he eventually gave up and left her in peace, mulling over his own probable responses.

He had a dreadful feeling he knew exactly what she was going to say.

But when they arrived back at Vera's, Jen merely vaulted from her saddle and flung him the reins, saying only, "Would you mind? I have work to do," and disappeared inside.

With a sigh, Thibault dismounted in a more conventional manner, gathering both sets of reins in one hand and turning to the horses. "She's done it again, lads," he said ruefully, but they merely snorted, unimpressed, and with a faint chuckle he turned and led them to the barn. There was no help for it; he would have to wait until he had the creatures settled to find out what Jen was up to. So stripping off saddles and bridles, he haltered each horse outside its box and scattered fresh straw before leading them inside. Then, he added water to their troughs and grain to their mangers and gave both beasts a rubdown before blanketing them for the night. They leaned against him blissfully, their eyes rolling happily, and dribbled doughy mouthfuls of water and oats down his back and arms.

By the time he was finished, he stank like a stable hand and was dappled with a crust of dried horse fodder. *Fine garb for confrontation,* he thought. He longed to go home and drench himself under the pump in Sylvaine's backyard, but he didn't dare leave Jen alone for any longer than he had.

So he merely brushed the worst of the damage from his hair and clothing and hoped she would be too distracted to notice.

Min was in the kitchen when he entered through the back door—he still hadn't conditioned himself to use the grand front entrance—and she beckoned him inside, wrinkling her nose at his odor.

"Did she make you wash them horses again?" she scolded. "Jacques could have done it . . ."

"Nonsense, it's no trouble," he reassured her, adding, "Where is she?"

Min snorted and poked a finger at the ceiling. "Went tearing up the stairs, she did, like the granddaddy of all curses was after her." Thibault groaned, and the old lady shot him a piercing look. "What is it?"

"Vera's in trouble, love," he told her, and winced as she paled, clutching at a chairback.

"Not serious?"

"I don't know," he responded honestly and patted her hand. "I'll tell you all I know later, I promise. Meanwhile, I have to find Jen—and quickly."

She nodded in comprehension, and he passed from the homey warmth of the kitchen into the vast, formal chambers that comprised the rest of the house. His booted footsteps echoed through the lonely rooms, their urgent beat making the crystal chandeliers sway and tinkle faintly in his wake. The seductive, polished curves of the furniture, the brocaded sofas and glints of silver from sideboards and tables never failed to intimidate him, for he felt as out of place as a prince in a pigpen. But swallowing against his residual unease, he passed through dining room, sitting room, and drawing room before taking the red-carpeted stairs two at a time.

He had spent little of his childhood in this house, and the warren of rooms that stretched off the long upstairs hallway never failed to confound him. Jen was here somewhere, he knew; he could hear a rustle of activity and the slam of closing drawers, but the corridor bounced and swallowed the sound so that it was impossible to localize.

He paused on the landing, calling, "Jenny? Are you there?"

"In here," she responded, and one of the doors halfway along the corridor sprang open as if kicked. "Come in."

He hesitated for a moment, the thought of confronting her in her bedroom sending a wash of conflicting emotions through him, then steeled himself and entered.

The room was as large as Sylvaine's cottage, open and airy, with a wall of wide windows leading out onto a generous balcony. On one wall, a mahogany armoire was thrown open to reveal a froth of gowns; on another, a mahogany desk reposed, its rolltop thrown open to reveal a wealth of cubbyholes and a half-penned missive in Jen's bold, spiky writing. Characteristically, she had left the inkpot open, the pen stuck into its top at a precarious angle with the ink drying around its nib. Between two of the windows was a slender dressing table, topped by a silvered mirror which caught Thibault's tentative face in the doorway and reflected it back at him.

He hadn't seen his image in ages, and he found himself vaguely embarrassed by the sight of the broad, workhorse shoulders topped by a homely, peasant face, with spiky, damp hair that had obviously been chewed on by horses. His only consolation was that Jen hadn't changed out of her riding clothes either and was steaming about her room like a heedless dervish, her boots leaving dusty tracks on the elegant carpet.

"Oh, do stop gawking, Thibault, and sit down," she scolded, breezing past him from bed to wardrobe and back. "I promise I won't eat you."

The bed, its slender cherrywood frame rising to a froth of white canopy, was wide and generous, its feathered mattress topped by a comforter that would have been sprigged with pale green were it not half hidden beneath a welter of clothes dredged from drawers and wardrobe. The sight of it brought a faint flush to his cheeks.

"What are you doing?" he asked, to cover his confusion.

"Packing. What does it look like I'm doing? Now either sit down or get out," she added, pushing at him firmly. "You're in my way." And crossing the room, she snatched something off the desk, setting the open inkpot to swaying precariously.

He was across the room in three huge strides, catching it before it fell. Removing pen from pot, he stoppered it firmly, then turned to see Jen grinning at him. "What?" he demanded, somewhat self-consciously.

She chuckled, patting his hand, which still clutched the inkpot. "I'd forgotten how fast you were. Thanks, Thib. I'm sorry for yelling at you."

He sighed and pulled out the desk chair, lowering himself gingerly onto its brocaded seat before restoring the inkpot to its rightful place. Then, picking up an ink-stained

rag from the clutter on the desktop, he absently proceeded
to wipe the pen clean.

"Apology accepted. What are you packing for?"

"Ashkharon," she responded, confirming his worst suspicions.

"But, Jen, that's . . ."

"Only reasonable," she returned, planting her hands on
her hips and regarding him with flashing eyes. "Vera's
my only family, Thib. She practically raised me. I can't
just abandon her."

"Jen, please . . ."

"What?"

"Let the Guild handle it?" he pleaded.

"The Guild can't handle it. I wasn't raised by an assassin for nothing. I know Guild policy, and I know that once
assassins are captured, they are disowned. There is nothing the Guild can do."

"Officially," he persisted. "But you heard Owen. They
can send someone after her secretly, which is what he
promised to do. You saw his face, Jen; he won't abandon
the Hawk."

"Oh, do stop fiddling with that pen," she snapped.
"You're going to reduce it to a nub!"

Sheepishly he put it down, realizing that he had been
nervously polishing it to a sheen beyond mere cleanliness,
and tried to clasp his hands quietly in his lap.

"Jen . . ."

"No, you are *not* going to dissuade me, Thibault. I am
going after her!"

Unaware that he had picked up the dirty ink rag and
was twisting it fretfully between his fingers, he countered,
"To do what?"

"Break her out if she's still alive. Get revenge if she's not."

"By yourself? Without Guild sanction?"

"If need be."

Her voice was infinitely cold, and he exhaled gustily.
"The Guild has a word for that, you know."

"Rogue. Yes, I've heard it. But quite frankly, Thibault,
I don't care. I haven't got time to formally join the Guild,
and this is Vera we're talking about! What would you do
if someone had taken Sylvaine?"

He was silent, and she took that for an answer.

"You see? I have to go! Someone's got to answer for

this, and I don't trust the Guild to do it. They have their hands tied. I do not."

He shifted his gaze from the pile of clothes to her determined face—her chin was set in that familiar stubborn look of old—and sighed yet again. He knew that expression all too well; it signaled the end of the battle. Once she'd gotten that look, he had never been able to shift her—and he didn't see why that should change now.

Reluctantly he stood and headed for the door.

"Where are you going?" she asked sharply, halting him with one hand extended toward his chest.

"To pack," he answered.

She stared at him. "But . . . I thought you didn't want to be an assassin!"

"I don't, but someone has to go along and keep you out of trouble."

There was a moment of silence, and then she flew at him, throwing her arms around his neck and planting a resounding kiss on his cheek. "Oh, thank you, thank you, Thibault! I knew I could depend on you! You won't regret this, I promise!"

Flushing faintly, exhilarated by the feel of her lithe body against his, he tightened his arms around her in a brief hug before detaching himself and adding dryly, "I certainly hope not."

She laughed delightedly. "No, it'll be fine; you'll see. I'll be as good as gold. Oh, Thibault, I knew you wouldn't let me down!" Then abruptly turning businesslike, she added, "There's a stage in the morning from Nova Castria to Grometiere. Jacques can drive us into town this evening; we'll stay overnight at the Leaping Mackerel and catch the coach on the morrow."

"And passage?"

"We'll worry about that when we get to Grometiere. There are bound to be ships this time of year." And diving under the bed, she pulled out a small trunk, unlocking it and spilling a jumble of knives and vials, sheaths and darts across the covers. "Get your kit, Thib. We're Ashkharon-bound!"

Shaking his head, a faint grin playing about the corners of his mouth, Thibault quit the room, wondering just what he'd gotten himself into this time.

* * *

In the heart of Anvil, Neros Fazaquhian sat outside his tent, a flap of cloth projecting over his head as he tried to ward off the worst of the sun, scribbling calculations and figures in a battered notebook. To his right stood the makeshift walls of the lab: it was too hot to inhabit at this time of day, with the wrath of the noonday sun burning overhead. Scattered to his left was the flurry of the workers' tents—for there was neither the money nor the materials to build more permanent structures—and beyond that loomed the vast and improbable conglomeration of tubes and towers that the mages had erected to siphon his fortune from the desert.

A fortune, he suspected, that was soon to be realized, transforming the sneering condescension of his former colleagues into a new respect. Neros Fazaquhian, creator of lapis-glass and ... what would they call it? Black-naphtha, perhaps, after the legendary mages' fire which burned through stone and steel. Yes, he rather liked that: black-naphtha.

Aware that the ink was drying on his pen, he tapped off the residual flakes and ran a fold of his trailing sleeve across his brow. Of necessity, he had taken to wearing the robes of a desert-dweller—for any other type of garb was impossible in this climate. The stubby ponytail of his greying hair was covered by a flowing headcloth, once white but now, like his robes, stained to a kind of colorless tan by dust and sand. The only modern touch in the whole ensemble was the pair of wire-rimmed spectacles perched on his nose, the round lenses of lapis-glass washing the world in a deep, soothing glow. Now, beneath a ultramarine sky, the sand rippled violet, creased by indigo shadows, and shimmering waves of heat obscured the horizon, making the palms of the distant oasis wave like undersea fronds.

With a sigh, he turned back to his scribing—not an easy task with the ink continually drying on the tip of his pen. But then, that was the trouble with this blasted climate: anything with an ounce of moisture was sucked dry within seconds, himself included.

Almost absently, he uncorked the waterskin at his side and took a swallow, the liquid flowing like a benison across his mouth and tongue. He couldn't help thinking that a year ago he would have sneered at the thought of letting something so plebeian as water cross his lips. Another thirst had gripped him then, gripped him and wrung him dry. No, desert climate aside, the warm, flat taste of the liquid reminded him of the depth of his good fortune, and the debt he owed to Pehndon.

Dipping his pen back in the inkpot, he managed another few figures before he looked up to see the caravan approaching: a thin, straggling line, civilization's only foray into the heart of the inferno. Haughty noses pinched shut, the camels swayed in a fluid gait as if they rocked on a sandy sea, the bundles of their cargo describing a dizzy arc against the sky. Food and papers, books and journals—the beasts bore the necessary accoutrements to keep him alive and working

Not that he was complaining, of course. He was extremely lucky. He had to remind himself of that constantly.

Even the Anvil was better than the gutter.

He kept writing, letting the excitement of his discoveries—the mathematical precision of his formulae—distract him from the raging heat and the creeping progress of the camels, until he was finally interrupted by the cocky, insolent tones of his foreman.

"Boss?" The man materialized above him, casting him into shadow, and the lenses of his glasses abruptly went black.

"What is it, Razife?" he said wearily, tipping his head back and sliding the spectacles up to his brow, the white heat of the sky searing his eyes. Against it, the burly bulk of his foreman loomed in stark silhouette, edged with razor light. A former cutthroat and thief, Razife ruled his crew with an intimidating mix of camaraderie and terror. Sometimes Fazaquhian wondered how he himself made it through each night with such a ragged assemblage of criminals. He perpetually expected to wake in a pool of his own blood and was somehow surprised when it failed to happen.

Still, he supposed, he wouldn't be paying their salaries if he were dead.

"Well, what is it?" he repeated impatiently, when Razife didn't answer.

The man extended a letter in silence; Fazaquhian hadn't seen it for the glare. Eagerly he took it and ripped open the seal, recognizing Pehndon's tight, precise hand. At

last it began, his return to fame and glory! He couldn't
wait to see what Pehndon had said about his discovery.
But as he perused the close lines, he felt his face freeze in
disappointment and disbelief.

"Anything the matter?"

Shaking his head and gathering his scattered thoughts,
Fazaquhian looked up at his foreman, relieved that the shadows obscured the vicious scar running from the man's nose
to his chin. "No, nothing whatsoever," he said, as calmly as
he was able. "You'll need a second, though; we're getting
another work crew soon."

"What?" Razife sounded as blank as the desert.

"Which part didn't you get?" Neros snapped, and saw
the foreman shrug.

"You want me to choose?"

"You know the men. Besides, I don't think I'd have
much of a choice anyway, would I?"

He could sense more than see the man's grin tugging at
his scar, and resigned himself to having Razife's massive
companion, Nasur, as his second.

"Thanks, Boss."

He waved an impatient hand. "Well? What are you
lurking about for? Off with you. Go!"

Razife chuckled and departed, leaving Fazaquhian to
stew over Pehndon's other news. Oh, Pehndon was delighted about his progress, no doubt of that. The thirty
new workers—convicts, Neros reminded himself—were
proof of that, as was the promised sum of two hundred
marks, which he knew he would find in his bags: reward
for a job well done. But, by all that was precious, he
wanted to shout his triumph to the eternal skies and yet
Pehndon advised him to wait. Ordered him, really.

It is too soon to reveal these secrets, Pehndon had writ-
ten. *Presently, Neros, when everything is in place. Our
moment is imminent, but it is not now.*

In place? What could possibly need to be in place? The
discovery had been made! The innocuous phrases sent a
white-hot bolt of anger through him, which he restrained
only with the greatest difficulty. But Pehndon had asked
him, and he owed the man.

If Pehndon wanted him to wait, then he would—however reluctantly.

11

The government was in a state of shock; there was no other way to describe it. Of course, Grahme had been present at the gala, had seen Istarbion twitch and collapse, the dart tufting from his neck, his lips flecked with a greenish foam. And in the aftermath, with Istarbion crumpled on the floor—the stupefied guards collecting his mortal remains—he had turned and met Andorian's gaze. Jason had looked as horrified as the rest; moments later, he had turned and melted from the room, leaving his spy to the tender mercies of Alphonse Jhakharta.

Not that Grahme blamed him. Better that the rebel leader *not* be found on the site of such an obvious assassination; it would look far too contrived. But still he regretted the lack of anyone intelligent to talk to. Jhakharta, his nominal boss, had a dazed, bovine look on his face, like a poleaxed steer. And then that Pehndon character had come racing downstairs, babbling about having caught the assassin, and even Jhakharta had disappeared. Knowing he would get no more coherent information for the night—and that he couldn't risk going to Jason on a whim, for fear too many absences might be noticed and his true status discovered—he went home instead, biding his time until everyone sorted out the confusion.

Unbeknownst to his employers, Grahme Tortaluk had been a member of the opposition for ten years, and it had been at Jason's suggestion that he entered the civil service in the first place, securing himself a position from which he might gather some valuable information for his allies. He had agreed not only because his respect for Jason bordered on the fanatical—he would do almost anything for Andorian; in his opinion, the man could do no wrong, nor was he alone in that assessment—but also because it offered him the chance to be part of an organization he believed in with his heart and soul.

Very few people apart from Jason knew of the distaff branch of Grahme's family: of the uncle who smoked away his livelihood in a haze of Dreamsmoke, forcing his children to earn their keep in the factories. And while Grahme had tried to sneak his cousins money on occasion, his meager income was never enough, and Uncle Theron always found out. How a man who passed his days in a fog of unreality could possess such a keen nose for cash remained a mystery, but it was a reality nonetheless. All his cousins' pay eventually found its way into Theron's pockets—and from thence to his lungs and brain—even Ricard's paltry compensation when he lost his hand to the vats.

So Grahme had searched out the dynamic, almost legendary, Andorian and had earned himself a place in the operation, breezing through Jason's rigorous selection process as if he had been born to it. And unlike most heroes, he had found the rebel leader to be even more dynamic in person that he had been at a distance. So when Jason suggested his infiltration of the government, he jumped at the chance to prove himself. By diligence and hard work—and a not inconsiderable amount of acting ability—he worked himself up through the civil ranks until he became a ministerial aide, and there he stuck firmly.

It was merely his bad fortune, he told himself, that the Minister he had been assigned to was the self-involved and ineffectual Alphonse Jhakharta. The man seemed affiliated with few important decisions, his ambitions pertaining only to the furthering of his own career, so in desperation Grahme had turned to the other aides, fostering friendships that might earn him the information he needed. And then he had discovered the first bag of gold, lurking beneath a pile of papers in Jhakharta's bottom drawer.

Its presence had exhilarated him, for he believed he had finally found a plot worthy of his attention, but after months of waiting he was still no nearer an answer. He had no idea who was sending the bribes—if bribes they were, for they would appear as if by magic at the start of every week and would be gone the next day—and he never saw any evidence of Jhakharta's changing his apparent indifference to most government policies. It puzzled him excessively, and he had been on the verge of dismissing the whole thing as an aberration when Istarbion died and he had arrived at work the next morning to find the office in a kind of controlled chaos, with flunkies more junior than himself emptying files and cabinets, transporting brimming boxes of papers and oddments down the twisting hallways.

"What in tarnation is going on?" he demanded, as one passed.

"Moving day," came the answer. "Congratulations, Grahme. You've been promoted."

"Promoted?" he began, but the aide was gone, and his boxes with him. So instead he was forced to seek out Jhakharta, whom he discovered in his office, sitting behind a bare desk amid the blank walls and smiling with a catlike smugness.

"Ah, Grahme, come in," the man purred, waving him to the upholstered seat that, along with Jhakharta's desk and chair, was the sole piece of furniture left in the chamber. "I'm sorry for the confusion, but, as you may have guessed, we're changing quarters."

Grahme looked up at the empty walls, at the discolored patches of paint, unbleached by the sun, where once Jhakharta's paintings and mementos had hung. Now there were only the trailing ghosts of picture wires, twisting from the moldings like severed umbilicals. "So I gathered," he said dryly. "But for what reason?"

Jhakharta chuckled, the catlike smile enlarging to a decidedly feral grin. "Would you believe that ass Istarbion picked *me* as his successor?"

"You? But . . . Why?" The words were out of his mouth before Grahme realized their import. Fortunately Jhakharta chose to misinterpret them.

"I know. Amazing, isn't it? Considering we didn't even like one another . . ." He let his voice trail off, shaking his head, then added, "Congratulations, Tortaluk. You're now aide to the First Minister."

It took all of Grahme's considerable acting ability to keep from whooping. *What a location I'll be in to gather information now,* he thought. *Jason will be ecstatic!* Then, remembering his position, he added, "Congratulations yourself, sir. A well-deserved promotion."

"Thank you, Grahme. Can't say I'm entirely adjusted to it, though. It's been quite a couple of days."

"Indeed, sir. So when did you find out?"

"Last night, unofficially, when the executors read his will. The public announcement will be made later this morning."

"That's truly wonderful, sir. Congratulations again." Then he added, as casually as he was able, "So, what happened after I left the gala? Didn't I hear Pehndon say he had caught the presumed assassin?"

"Presumed, nothing." Jhakharta snorted. "She did it, all right; she admitted as much when Iaon questioned her. She'll stand trial in two weeks."

"A nice coup for Pehndon. Does he have any idea why she did it?"

Jhakharta shot him a look that doubted of his sanity. "Isn't it obvious?" he said. "Andorian hired her."

Grahme's heart gave a panicked bump. With supreme effort, he responded, "You know that for a fact?"

"She admitted it, yes." Jhakharta chortled. "You can bet the hunt will be on for Andorian once *that* news becomes public!"

"And when will that be?"

"Well, officially, not until the end of the trial; we have to give *some* semblance of justice, at least. But the hints will go out this morning, when the announcement of my succession is made."

"Ah." Grahme swallowed. "You won't be needing my help with the boxes, then, will you?"

Jhakharta blinked at the apparent change of subject. "Not particularly. Why?"

Grahme forced a smile. "Because I haven't had a chance to eat yet and, if you don't need me, I thought I'd get a bite. Once the announcement's made, I doubt I'll have another free moment all day."

Jhakharta's suspicions melted like butter beneath the implied flattery. "Indeed. Good thinking. Take an hour, Tortaluk. Get yourself a sufficiently hearty breakfast."

"Thank you, sir." Inclining his head, Grahme rose and sauntered casually from the room. He was barely out of sight of the government complex before he started running.

Jason could hear the commotion even behind the glass and wood panels of his office door. He raised his head from where it lay on the worn, pitted surface of his desk, his mind chasing circles around the implications of last night's assassination, and sighed. This was a weakness, an uncertainty, that he would never show to any of his followers, and he would gladly trade his position now to any of the multiplicity of idiots who raved about the glories of command. Glories, indeed! What they patently failed to realize was that a leader could never be off, could never show fear or hesitation, no matter how strongly he might be feeling it.

At this moment, Jason would have given his whole organization for the chance to be normal. Istarbion's assassination had shaken him, filling him with an unspecified dread. It seemed far too convenient, coming at a time that could destroy him utterly, just when he had gained so much. By all that was precious, he was close, so close to the coup that would bring the government down forever. With an almost intuitive finger on the pulse of his people, he could feel it. He had worked for years, using Istarbion as a rallying point. A random choice, though; he might as well have used a statue or a moth. He knew as well as anyone that Istarbion was merely a symptom, not the disease—and now Istarbion was dead.

Well, he reflected, *at least no one can pin this on me. I wasn't even remotely responsible. In fact, it was the last thing I wanted!* Still, with all of his posturing about Istarbion—a necessity, for the illiterate and uneducated needed something to rally around, someone to hate, however spurious—he wondered if some poor sod hadn't taken his words to heart and eliminated the monster. Now wouldn't that be ironic? Tragically, killingly ironic.

The thought of fighting his whole battle again from scratch made him want to howl.

But instead he rose, crossed to the door, and flung it open, looking down from his tiny landing to the floor below, his outward demeanor reflecting no trace of his inner conflict. "Well, what is it?" he called, his voice crisp with its usual command.

As expected, his words silenced the babble in an instant, and a sea of faces turned quietly upward, indulgent smiles on their lips and a wealth of relief in their eyes, as if the solution to all their problems had just materialized. *I'm only a man like the rest of you,* he wanted to cry. *I don't have the magic answer!* But instead he merely said authoritatively, "What's happened?"

A breathless Tortaluk detached himself from the crowd.

"I'm sorry, Jason. No one followed me, I promise, but I had to come straight off!"

As if his agent's words had been a release, the murmur of speculative, worried voices once again washed over the floor—although more muted this time. And yet, for Jason, the words provided an odd relief. A confirmation of his nebulous suspicions, indicating that something was indeed amiss, sent a wave of resolution through him, stiffening his flagging spirits. "I suppose you'd better come up, then," he answered, a faint smile playing about his lips—reassuring his followers by its very nonchalance.

Grahme looked as relieved as the rest as he trooped up the stairs, grinning as Jason waved him into his office and closed the door behind them. Then, settling himself across the desk, Andorian measured his first and best informant.

"Well, Grahme? What ails the government?"

"Good things and bad, I'm afraid."

"As usual. Never one without the other, eh? Best give me the good news first."

"Very well. Congratulations, Andorian, you now have an ear in the First Minister's chamber."

"I do? How?"

"That imbecile Alphonse was Istarbion's choice for successor, if you can believe. It will be officially announced this morning."

"But . . . That's wonderful, Grahme! This will be a great opportunity for you, for us. Now"—he grinned—"what's the bad news?"

Tortaluk's face sobered. "About Istarbion's assassination: you're being held accountable."

"What?"

"Unofficially, until after the trial, but yes, you're being blamed."

"But I would never . . . I'm against assassinations on policy, Grahme! I've never found it a solution; you know that."

"Yes, but does everyone? You've been rather vocal about Istarbion, lately."

"As a tool, Grahme!"

"Yes, I know. But as I said before . . ."

"How many others?" Jason sighed. "That is, indeed, the question. So what evidence do they think they have against me?"

Grahme winced. "The worst. The admission of the assassin herself."

"She's lying!"

His companion just shrugged. "Perhaps. I haven't spoken to her myself or seen the evidence, so I can't judge. But I did catch a glimpse of her last night, Jason, and she's Guild. What reason would she have to lie?"

"Guild? How do you know she's Guild?"

"Too good, too confident. You saw that shot; that was a professional hit."

He nodded, adding, "Then why did she let herself get caught?"

Tortaluk's face crumpled. "I don't know."

"Nor do I, but I have a feeling that Jhakharta's involved. Are you certain he was ignorant of this promotion?"

"Quite certain; he's not a good enough actor to feign *that* much surprise!"

Jason chuckled. "Respect: ain't it wonderful?" Then, more seriously, he added, "But someone did know, Grahme."

"How?"

"The bribes." Jason steepled his fingers, tapping them lightly against his lips. "Someone was banking on getting Jhakharta in power—and seeking to profit by it." He looked up suddenly. "I want you to find out who that is, Grahme. Then maybe we can find out who's behind this—and what precisely is going on!"

"Anything you say, Jason. But . . . be careful, won't you? They're going to be hunting for you soon."

The rebel leader gave a little bark of laughter. "But not *officially*—at least not until the travesty of their trial is done. And until then, I'd like to see anyone try to stop me!" He grinned suddenly, ferally. "The government's a bloody fool if they think I'm going to retire without a fight. I fully intend to spend the next several weeks making a public spectacle of myself, trying to recoup whatever losses I can. We'll come out of this ahead yet, Grahme. You'll see!"

His agent smiled. "If anyone can do it, Jason, it's you," he said, and the rebel leader grinned.

At the moment, he was rather inclined to agree.

12

Admittedly, Jen felt a little guilty about the way she had treated Thibault, snapping at him so abruptly, as if this whole mess were his fault—as if he were uncaring of Vera's future—but she couldn't help herself; she was in the grip of an unreasoning panic. She needed to go to Ashkharon, that much was certain, but Thibault's confession that he hadn't wanted the Guild had shaken her. Through all the years of her childhood, through all her plans of the future, it simply hadn't occurred to her that he wouldn't be present.

She had spent too many years seeing him as her wiser half; she was no longer certain she could take over those functions for herself.

But while grousing at Thibault was hardly the way of winning him to her cause, fear was an emotion she rigorously denied, masking it beneath a guise of anger as if, by renaming it, she could change its very nature. It never quite worked, but it was reflexive nonetheless, bred into her by years of striving to live up to Vera's example. She could only hope that Thibault understood, that he had agreed to accompany her out of friendship and not out of some obscure form of pity.

It was thus with a certain embarrassment that she found herself trying to be deliberately charming, as if that could offset her previous bad temper.

"So, Thib," she cajoled as they clattered along, their trunks strapped firmly to the carriage roof and Jacques perched on the driver's box like a bundle of old sticks, "aren't you even remotely excited about seeing the world? Just think: a cruise through the Belapharion!" And she shook his elbow excitedly, as if she could impart an eagerness of motion to the rest of his stolid frame.

He turned and gave her his slow, lazy smile, a hint of

indulgence lingering about its corners. "Yes, I suppose it should be interesting," he drawled, and she flung his arm away in disgust.

"Stop it, Thib. You can't pull that peasant routine on me!"

He chuckled. "No, but it might work on others. Which reminds me—what is our disguise to be?"

"Disguise?"

"Well, you can't very well go marching into Ashkharon as Jen Radineaux, can you? Apart from exposing Vera's identity, what do you think it will do to your status in the Guild? That is, if they even consent to let you in after this little escapade."

"Nonsense," she bluffed. "Why shouldn't they let me in? It's not like I'm really going rogue. I'm just doing my family duty."

"Semantics." Thibault snorted. "Still, even you should know that operatives never use their real names."

"Oh. I hadn't thought of that," she said, then brightened, adding. "See? Isn't it good I have you along?"

Thibault stared at her, then suddenly began to laugh. "You're impossible, Jen," he said, when he could speak. "I'm not going to be that easy to persuade!"

She just grinned. "Well, it was worth a try. So, what do you have in mind for our disguises?"

"An obvious ruse: I'd suggest going as mistress and suhdabhar."

Jen considered this. Granted it was unusual for a single lady to have a male body servant, but neither was it unheard of. It would merely label her as a rich eccentric, which would complement her image perfectly; Jen planned to be plenty eccentric in Ashkharon. So, "Brilliant," she said. "And what shall I call you, O suhdabhar?"

He grinned. "How about Tomas? That sounds sufficiently familiar. And you?"

She wrinkled her nose. "I don't know; I'll have to think on it, devise a name I'm comfortable with. Until then . . ."

The carriage shuddered to a stop, distracting her. Through the window, she saw the sign for the Leaping Mackerel swaying and creaking gently in the breeze.

Thibault tapped her arm lightly to get her attention. "Remember, keep up the charade. No mischief."

"Here? But ... Thibault, they know you here. You grew up in Nova Castria!"

"Nonetheless. I doubt many of them would understand our true relationship, nor do I think any of them would see anything odd in my pledging my life to your service."

Jen felt a surge of optimism at his words. "Very well. I shall try to be sufficiently haughty and condescending. Satisfied?"

"Infinitely. And now, Domina"—he descended from the carriage, extending his hand—"your residence awaits."

She grinned and accepted his aid, swinging lightly from the conveyance before composing her face into a suitably haughty expression, which pinched her cheeks and made her want to laugh with the ridiculousness of it all. Ascending the inn steps, she stood on the worn porch and watched Thibault unload their trunks, untying the taut bindings and sliding the boxes easily to his shoulders, ignoring any offers of help from the frail Jacques. She felt an absurd burst of pride as she watched him, the muscles bunching and shifting under his homespun shirt, but there was a certain wistfulness too. They were doing it; they were actually leaving Hestia. She longed to bid Jacques farewell, to assure him she would take care of his precious Vera, but she knew it would be out of keeping with her new persona. So she merely waved a plaintive goodbye as he climbed back onto the box and turned Vera's horses to the manor, clucking them into motion.

As the twilight swallowed him from sight, she felt a wash of homesickness flood her and was abruptly conscious of the magnitude of the step she was taking. Vera was gone, lost somewhere in far-off Ashkharon, and she was stepping off the edge of the familiar and into an unknown abyss. From here, she could no longer predict what course her future might take.

Somehow, she had always assumed this moment would be different—filled with excitement, with Vera and the Guild two steps behind her, ready to support her if she stumbled. But now, with the chasm looming before her, she felt abruptly bereft. It was only Thibault's presence that kept her from despair and, even so, this had been her idea, not his. It was up to her to carry the burden and the blame. Looking out at the dusky swell of the ocean, the familiar salt breeze caressing her cheeks, she felt the betraying prickle of tears in her eyes and might have let one or two drop had Thibault not brushed by her as if by accident, en route to the door, whispering, "I gave Jacques your love and told him you were too blasted stubborn *not* to bring Vera back alive!"

The teasing confidence of his tone restored her, as did the knowledge that he had understood enough to know how much leaving Jacques without a good-bye had hurt her—and all her old assurance flooded back with a smile.

"Thank you, Thib—I mean, Tomas. Now get those trunks inside!"

Tugging at his forelock, he shouldered their baggage and, with a wink, gestured her into their lodging.

Because of her status, she was accorded the largest of the guest chambers, while Thibault was relegated to a tiny room under the eaves, and in the morning they caught the stage to Grometiere, well supplied by a brimming basket of provisions that the resourceful Thib had seen fit to procure from the innkeeper.

The journey started out pleasantly enough. They had the coach to themselves, and Thibault stretched out his long legs across the conveyance, his feet resting on the far seat and the open basket balanced on his knees as they consumed their breakfast and talked desultorily about nothing. But Jen hadn't expected the sheer tedium of the journey. The coach rattled along the dusty roads, tossing them about like dice in a gambler's cup, the horses eating up the miles at a steady, bone-crunching gallop that made Jen's joints ache for lack of activity. Once about every three hours they would stop long enough to post the horses and take care of some necessary business, and then they would be off again, flying into the waning day.

Sometime around twilight—after she had tried every conceivable position to relieve her cramped limbs, including an unsuccessful bout of pacing the tiny coach—she exclaimed, "Are they planning to keep this up all night?"

"I should think so," responded Thibault, who, annoyingly, seemed perfectly content to sit motionless for hours, his legs propped on the far seat and his nose buried in a book. "You should try to get some sleep, you know. We'll be arriving in Grometiere early."

"I know." Her voice was sour.

"I can move my feet," he offered. "You can curl up on the opposite seat, and . . ."

She shook her head. "No need."

"Why?"

"I don't want to disturb you. Besides, you're all the pillow I require." And grinning, she curled her feet beneath her and leaned her cheek against his shoulder, her eyes drifting shut. "You mind?" she added in a mumble and could feel him shake his head.

"No. Lights low," he commanded and, beneath her closed eyelids, she could sense the magelights dim.

After a while, the rocking of the coach and the steady rhythm of his breathing—the faint shift of his muscles as he turned the pages of his book—lulled her into an uneasy slumber, although she woke each time the coach stopped, and once crawled from its depths in a bleary stupor to relieve her swelling bladder. She wasn't sure when Thibault abandoned his book and turned out the lights, or when he fell asleep, but she did remember waking once to a darkened coach with the light of the stars winking comfortably through the open window and Thibault's arm draped loosely about her shoulders, his chest rising and falling with the faint, rhythmic rasp of his snores.

Sleeping with the boys again, Jen? she thought and suppressed the urge to giggle. Poor innocent Thibault slept more decorously than most of her conquests—a point in his favor. But then, she couldn't remember the last time she had slept this decorously in male company, either.

When she woke again it was morning, and Thibault was rubbing sleep from his eyes like a big, languid bear.

She sat up and stretched. "Sleep well?"

"Mmm. Smell the sea? We must be nearing Grometiere."

She tilted her nose to the window, delighting in the perfumed softness of the Belapharion. In Nova Castria, the sea was cold and grey, the plaintive cries of the gulls only adding to the stark desolation of the scene. But here there was a warmth and, as the coach pulled toward the shore, a seductive glitter, languid and inviting. Hestia still, but a foreign Hestia, gateway to another world. She felt her excitement burgeon.

"You take care of the luggage," she instructed. "I'll see to securing us passage."

Half an hour later, she reported back in defeat. Not that Thibault was surprised; as far as he could tell, there wasn't a single passenger vessel moored at the bustling wharf. It was as if every disreputable trader and pirate king had pulled up to the quay, with tattered sails and barnacled hulls, their holds stinking of sweat and horses— not one of them would support her claim of being a lady bred.

"I'm afraid you're going to have to handle this," she told him.

He regarded her with bemusement. "Not that I mind, but are you sure you wouldn't rather wait? At least until a more reputable ship arrives?"

"Which could be how long? A week? Two? No, Vera can't wait, and neither can I. Besides, I'm tougher than I look. Now go!" And she gave him a tiny shove.

He cast a last, doubtful glance in her direction, then hunched his shoulders, a lazy swagger appearing in his walk as he moved toward the docks, his eyes skimming the ships. "Excuse me, mate," he called to an idle sailor, "but can you tell me where . . . my sister and I might find passage?"

The man surveyed him. "Depends on where you're passing."

"Ashkharon."

"That ruddy desert?" The sailor snorted, jerking a thumb over his shoulder. "Try Granville, the *Crow's Nest.* He's Ashkharon-bound."

"Thanks."

The sailor shook his head. "Ashkharon. Hmph. I wish you luck."

"Your sister?" demanded Jen with a grin, when the man had departed.

Thibault just shrugged, a brief memory of her chestnut head resting against his shoulder heating his cheeks. There had been times last night when, he could swear, he had read the same passage ten times over without gaining an inkling of its meaning, distracted by the scent of her hair and the soft warmth of her breath against his sleeve. "It's all I could think of," he said defensively, adding,

"Besides, you're not about to play the lady with this bunch, are you?"

"I doubt they'd care. Or believe me," she answered.

"Quite," he said; but nonetheless, he felt his heart sink when he finally located the *Crow's Nest,* the name painted in flaking letters on the swell of the battered hull. Of all the ships moored at Grometiere, it seemed the most disreputable: dingy and unkempt, the deck rails broken in several places with raw planks nailed crookedly across the gaps. But when he shot Jen a last apprehensive glance, she kicked him surreptitiously in the ankle, urging him forward.

With an obvious shrug, he lowered their trunks, calling, "Ahoy, there. Who's Granville?"

"I'm Captain Granville." Thin-faced and dour, the man poked his head over one of the unbroken rails. "What do you want?"

"Passage for me and my sister. We hear you're Ashkharon-bound. We can pay."

Granville scowled. "Let's see it."

Thibault flashed his purse, opening it briefly to reveal a quantity of Jen's marks.

"Hmph," Granville snorted. "That your sister?" And he jerked his thumb in Jen's direction.

"That's her."

"Awful grand, ain't she?"

Thibault grinned and tapped the side of his nose with one conspiratorial finger. "Likes to think herself a lady, she does."

"Fine togs."

"Mistress's castoffs."

Granville grunted. Through the corner of his eye, Thibault could see Jen's face looking pinched and red in what the captain obviously assumed was outrage but which he more correctly identified as badly suppressed mirth.

"What's in Ashkharon?" Granville demanded.

"New jobs," Thibault responded. "She got us fired. Refused to oblige the master, you know. Felt herself above such hanky-panky." He let a disgusted note creep into his voice and could feel Jen tremble beside him. "Our uncle promised us work in Ashkharon. Have you two cabins?"

"Two?"

"You think she'd share with *me*?" Thibault retorted and Jen spluttered, hastily turning her spurt of laughter into a disdainful cough.

"Mmm." Granville's sharp eyes measured them. "One hundred fifty marks for the pair of you."

Jen choked, in genuine outrage this time.

"One hundred," Thibault countered hastily.

The captain nodded. "Very well. Bring your trunks up and we'll get you settled."

He disappeared.

"Brilliant, Thib!" Jen applauded, when he had gone.

He rolled his eyes. "I only hope you know what you're doing," he muttered as he shouldered their luggage.

She just grinned. "Don't worry, we'll be fine. Trust me."

"That's what you always say," he countered darkly, and she forgot her disguise in a burst of hearty laughter as she followed him onto the vessel.

"Well?" Derek said brightly, looking over the ships moored in the Piavolan harbor with a hopeful eye. There was a wide variety to choose from in Venetzia's largest port city. "How about that one?"

Mark cast him a sour look. "And how much do you think passage on *that* would cost us? You heard Owen: third class, he said, and third class we're going. There— the *Reggan Sprite* looks about right."

And ignoring his brother's plaintive sigh, the Falcon headed purposefully for the gangplank.

13

Vera didn't know what she had expected from her trial, but it certainly wasn't this: not this empty, echoing chamber, the walls a dark severity of polished panels, and ringing her was a semicircle of dour, accusing faces pinched between the black of their judicial robes and the white of their curled perukes. The only touch of color—not to mention life—in that grim place was the scarlet mantle of judgment draped over every set of shoulders, as if each judicial neck had spilled forth a fount of heart's blood. Certainly that vibrant, ruddy hue bore more animation than the stone-carved faces, hard and inflexible as fresh-quarried granite, their eyes cold lenses of depthless obsidian.

A public trial, Pehndon had said. *A very public trial.* And yet surrounding her were no more than fifteen faces: twelve judges, Pehndon, a companion, and a shapeless puddle of robes that may or may not have been a person. There was no audience, no one to witness her confession, no crowd of eager or bloodthirsty faces waiting to drink in every detail of the assassination. But maybe that bundle of rags was a mage, broadcasting her every word to the assembled masses.

Please, she thought, *let it be a mage. Let there be someone out there to hear my words.* She couldn't, in all good conscience, let Pehndon get away with his nefarious scheme. She had to speak. Not to mention that this might be her only chance to save herself from the hangman's rope. To be sure, he had warned her about the futility of protest, the firmness of the net which bound her, but she wouldn't have been the Hawk if she hadn't tried to push her limits, just a little. There must be some detail he had missed, some loophole which would save her; if she protested long enough, surely she would find it.

Never mind that she hadn't located it yet, through all the endless hours in her cell, her mind spinning over her fate in disbelief. If there was any justice in the world, she would discover it.

She still couldn't credit that it had come to this: her body draped in ragged and filthy castoffs, hands manacled and legs hobbled by chains, a metal collar about her neck, imprisoned in the dock, with some of the mages' most potent spells warding against her escape. What had happened? How had she allowed Pehndon and Jason to deceive her? Were her once reliable instincts dead or was she simply getting old?

Owen would kill her for this, she thought with a wince of sympathy for the old man's pain. Owen DeVeris was like a father to her, had been since her own family had disowned her; he would be heartbroken if she died. Yet she knew there was nothing he could do to save her, and her bluff to Pehndon had been just that. As far as the Guild was concerned, she was dead already—and would remain so until she threw off the aegis of this charge. If she somehow escaped, returned to the Guild with her name and reputation intact, they would take her back. But until then she was on her own; the most she could hope for was a clandestine attempt to release her, and even that was doubtful. For how could even the Guild's second-best assassin penetrate the fastness of the Nhuras prison, with its stone-thick walls and iron-gated doors, its windows the narrowest of barred slits barely admitting light and air let alone any more substantial aid?

No, it was a dismal place, that much was certain, and they had tossed her into it without delay. No sooner had she been hustled in chains into the city than they had thrown her into a windowless anteroom, locking three unarmed guards and Pehndon in with her. The burly brutes proceeded to strip and search her around the chains, their thick, callused fingers lingering lasciviously on her exposed flesh, held back from violence only by the icy grey censure of Pehndon's regard. Nonetheless, she could feel the hot, fetid breath of their desires against her cheek, the relentless twitch of prurience reined in. Without Pehndon, she would have been lost, and it sickened her to be indebted to her betrayer in such a fashion.

The bronze gown they cut from her body with one of

her many knives, unstrapping darts and daggers from her
limbs, their rough, thick fingers probing every crack and
crevice in search of hidden weapons, regardless of the involuntary gasps of pain that such searches promoted.
They even pried open her jaws, one guard peeling her lips
back like a horse while another ran a rancid finger inside
her mouth, tugging roughly on her teeth in quest for poison-
filled fakes. She gagged against the taste and tried to spit.
Pehndon decorously turned his head as they cuffed her.

Unbelievably, they found everything, even down to the
garroting cord in her hair. Her fingers were stripped of
rings, the gown was sliced into shreds to reveal the host of
weapons she had sewn into hems and cuffs, the dart twin
to the one embedded in Istarbion's throat was plucked
from her hair. They left her defenseless—or so they believed—and the pile of weapons they had accumulated
when they were finished was nothing short of astounding.

Naked, she had been unchained and thrust from thence
into a narrow cell, the floor matted with filthy straw, rats
chittering around the ripe and open sewage hole in one
corner. The uncompromising metal of the bed was capped
only by a thin and lumpy pallet, directly in line with the
razor-sharp chill of the evening air which funneled
through the high, narrow, grated window. There was no
magelight. Curled around herself on the coverless mattress, she shivered under the invading fingers of the
breeze, for like all desert climates, Ashkharon's nighttime
cool seemed to take a certain subtle revenge for the blistering heat of the day.

After two hours, they threw her a rough blanket that
rasped like sandpaper on her skin and a beaker of stale
water, which she gulped down gratefully between cracked
and swollen lips. Later she wondered if the liquid hadn't
been drugged, given the speed with which the blackness
claimed her afterward.

In the morning, with the sun lancing a thin, blinding
beam into her cell, driving the rats from the narrow highway of bleached stone and straw, it was the heat that
awoke her, sweating from the solid walls and searing
every bit of moisture from the air. Gasping for breath, her
body thick and heavy with the need for water, she threw
off the blanket and pounded against the iron door.

After several hours, they brought her a pail of water

and a bowl of thin gruel, which she devoured with alacrity despite the fact that it was as bland and tasteless as watery glue. Dinner was a hunk of moldy bread and cheese, and then darkness fell and the insufferable swelter of her cell was chased off by the evening chill. The rats re-emerged, scuttling through the straw in search of crumbs. She wrapped herself in her blanket and tried to sleep, the only thing to distract her the nebulous swirl of her thoughts and plans.

The next morning, they threw her a musty, threadbare shirt of a warm shit-brown and a pair of pants of a non-descript color, which she was convinced, both from their size and from the copious quantity of badly mended tears, had last belonged to a rather round and energetic dwarf. They rode high on her ankles and slid from her hips, for there was no belt; when she was rechained and dragged to her trial, they were secured around her waist with a ragged piece of twine.

Which was how she now sat in the dock, feeling the pain of her bruised cheek and split lip, staring back at the twelve implacable faces of her judges.

"Leonie Varis," one of them said to her, "you stand before this court accused of the murder of former First Minister Guy Istarbion. How do you plead?"

Her tongue moved to frame the words of denial. Doubtless they would never believe her innocence, but she couldn't bear to give in so readily. Yet even as the words swelled her mouth, a wracking wave of pain swamped her, leaving her pale and gasping.

"Ah, I forgot to say," added the judge somewhat smugly, "do not attempt to lie to us. We have you under a truth spell. Do you know what that is?"

She managed to nod as the last of the agony drained from her limbs. She had been under truth spells before, as part of the Guild training, but never ones with such dire consequences. Still, she was glad again of the thoroughness of the Guild tuition, for few were aware of the limitations of such spells or of the many levels that comprised the truth. So, gathering her thoughts into the appropriate order, she said, "Not guilty" and felt only the merest twinge of discomfort at the words.

A ripple of disbelief washed through the assembled

judges, bouncing off the paneled walls and making the shapeless bundle of cloth shift restlessly in its seat.

"Your name is Leonie Varis, is it not?"

"Yes." No twinges there. For the moment she *was* Leonie Varis, and Viera Radineaux was buried without a trace.

"And you say that you didn't kill First Minister Istarbion?"

She shook her head. "No. Merely that I am not guilty of his murder."

Another mutter of dissension. "How can that be? We have evidence against you. Not only were you found upstairs, in a highly restricted area to which only a bribe could have gotten you, but a replica of the murder weapon was found on your person, and the murder poison was contained in one of your rings."

"They could have been planted." It was a simple statement, neither truth nor falsehood.

One of the judges chuckled. "Are you really trying to tell me that, at some time during your brief transfer from Istarbion's estate to the Nhuras prison, someone took the time to stitch a multiplicity of weapons into your gown? For they really were quite elaborately concealed; I understand it took the wardens some time to discover them all."

"Besides," another added, "we know the poison you had is the one that performed the deed."

"And how do you know that?"

"Because we tried it," came the answer, cool and unemotional, and Vera masked a grin. No doubt they had; on one of her guards, she hoped.

"Moreover, we know someone was shooting darts into the crowd for a time before the assassination. We have a number of witnesses to that effect; we could bring them in, if necessary. A dart and blowpipe were found on your person, and we know that you disappeared for a considerable time before the assassination."

"And how do you know that?"

"Because I was looking for you," exclaimed Pehndon's companion, jumping to his feet with an irate expression.

"What?"

"Yes, I was trying to find you for Istarbion. He wanted . . . to talk to you."

"Istarbion? To me?"

"Yes, apparently he wanted to sleep with you." The words came out in an accusatory rush. "So if you had merely waited another hour, you could have done anything you wanted to him in private, with no witnesses to the deed. Ironically enough, he was going to play right into your hands!"

"Minister, please," one of the judges responded, and the man subsided with a scowl. "We're running this trial." Then, returning to Vera, he added, "So, you did loose the bolt which killed him?"

"I never denied that."

"Then you are . . ."

"Not guilty," she insisted. "I was a tool: no more, no less. Is a dagger held liable for its actions?"

"A dagger has no morals; a dagger cannot think. You were not forced into this."

"Ah, but a sufficient amount of cash can sway even the most incorruptible of morals."

"So you were hired?"

"Yes. And for quite a handsome sum, I might add."

"Are you Guild?" She could hear the eagerness in their voices, the expectation. Would they be the ones to catch the infamous Guild? Pehndon, too, sat up, his ears almost pricking with anticipation.

"No," she replied, and saw her betrayer start, but it was no less than the truth. From the moment of her capture, she had ceased to belong.

"And who hired you?"

"Iaon Pehndon," she said maliciously.

The outcome was noisy and spectacular.

"What?"

"How can that be?"

"Pehndon?"

"Are you sure the spell is working?"

All eyes turned toward the bundle of cloth, which shrugged and grunted.

"Iaon, is this true?"

Pehndon's brows lowered. "Not in the least," he declared emphatically.

"Are you sure it wasn't Andorian?" they demanded.

"No." Her denial was as emphatic as Pehndon's. "There is no Jason Andorian. Pehndon owns Jason Andorian, just as he owns First Minister Alphonse Jhakharta."

They were startled by that. "How do you know he's First Minister?"

"Because Pehndon told me, just like he told me all the rest. There is no Andorian, no rebel alliance. It's all a construct, created by Pehndon for his own nefarious amusement!"

"Iaon?" they asked again.

Pehndon shook his head, a bemused smile playing about his lips. "A patent falsehood, Your Honors. Listen to her! The rebel alliance a construct? We've all felt Jason Andorian's influence; how could something like that possibly be a construct?"

"And Jhakharta is not under your pay?"

"Ask him yourself," came the laughing answer.

"First Minister?"

"Most emphatically not!" Pehndon's companion retorted, and Vera masked a groan. By all that was precious, *that* was Jhakharta?

"She's simply striking out at me," Pehndon added reasonably. "I caught her, after all; it's only natural she should feel a little . . . hostile."

"You lie!"

"Impossible," the judges assured her. "Everyone in this courtroom is under a truth spell, Malle Varis. Minister Pehndon is incapable of lying."

"Then what about me? Aren't I supposed to be incapable of lying? Yet Pehndon just accused me of the same thing!"

They were silent, unsure of how to acknowledge that.

"I'm telling you, he set me up," she persisted. "He admitted it!"

"My dear young lady," Pehndon countered, "what reason could I possibly have to set you up?"

"Yes," one of the judges added. "What reason could he have to hatch such an elaborate plot?"

"Because he found something in the desert, in the heart of the Anvil. Something that would make him rich."

"On the Anvil?" A ripple of amusement ran through the assembled judges. "Malle Varis, you must be imagining things. The Anvil is the most inhospitable desert in all Ashkharon; it won't even support life, let alone riches! I assure you, there is nothing whatsoever on the Anvil."

"But . . ."

"I think we had best adjourn these proceedings until tomorrow," another of the judges added. "Obviously something has queered the truth spells. Maybe we can get a better fix on this whole mess with a fresh eye and fresh casting on the morrow."

"A fine suggestion. Take her away, lads."

And so the burly prison guards dragged her back to her cell and unchained her, even going so far as to confiscate—the final indignity—the loop of string that held up her pants.

As the door of her cell slammed shut behind them, the baggy garments slithered from her hips and fell in a puddle about her ankles.

14

It was a travesty. That was the only word for it. Pehndon was lying, whatever the judges claimed, and yet she was too angry and—*admit it, Vera*—too frightened to catch him. There must be something she could do, some argument she could muster. But what? It nagged at her like a hidden itch. What, by all the grasshoppers in Gavrone, had she missed?

But the answer didn't come to her then, nor at dinner— a repeat of last night's moldy bread and cheese—and as the moon rose through the narrow slit of her window, bathing the cell in a silvery glow, the guards returned, rechaining her and dragging her upstairs again, this time into a restraining room containing only a rickety table and two battered chairs. Nor did they resecure her pants, but merely left her clutching them with an awkward fist, her wrist straining against the manacles.

Pehndon, waiting in one of the seats, looked up as she approached and waved the guards away. With a last vicious caress, they left her, pushing her into the remaining chair and running their filthy hands up her body, pinching a nipple or buttock as they went. One even had the gall to thrust a hand briefly into her unsecured pants, his finger darting obscenely between her legs; she could feel her flesh crawl.

Varia help her if anyone ever set those boys loose on her.

"Well? What brings you?" Vera spat, turning her attention toward her betrayer as the door slammed shut. "Come to gloat?"

"No, not gloat; just remind you of the futility of what you are trying to do. It's no good, Leonie; you had your chance. You are never going to convince the judges to convict me. You are never going to convince them that I am involved. So will you just be reasonable and let Jason take the fall?"

"Play into your hands, you mean? Go along with your precious scheme?"

"Andorian did hire you."

"Your Andorian."

"The only Andorian. I've got you in a corner, Leonie. Play it my way, and I guarantee I'll get you a commuted sentence. I have influence in the government, after all."

"Then why didn't you offer this before the trial?"

His brows lowered. "You're being foolish, Leonie. I certainly don't want to sacrifice you, but I will if I have to. I've planned this for too long to let any upstart assassin get in my way. Oblige me, and we both win. Cross me, and you die. Think about it." And rising, he summoned the guards, who dragged her back to her noxious cell and locked her within it.

I'll be cursed if I let him get away with this! she seethed in the initial moments of her release, stalking the narrow chamber and sending the rats squealing into the corners and tumbling down the filthy sewer. *Blast him to a thousand planes of anguish if I let him threaten me!*

But when the moon had set and her cell was once again swallowed in blackness, and she began to think more coherently, the whole visit started to strike her as rather odd. If she were truly in a corner, if he were so confident of his success, then why threaten her? Why not simply let the farce of a trial take its course? That he had come at all suggested one thing: there was something she had on him, something that worried him.

It gave her the only hope she had had in days.

If she could just keep teasing at the truth, then perhaps she would find it.

From what she gathered, the judges had spent the morning going over the chamber with a fine-tooth comb, checking the wards and recasting the truth spells. Then came a rigorous period of testing, during which they peppered her with nonsensical queries in an effort to gauge her responses. And when they were finally satisfied that all was in working order, they asked their burning question: "Who hired you?"

"Iaon Pehndon," she said again.

After that, they weren't quite so easy on Pehndon. "What is this?" they demanded. "Have you been lying? Under spell?"

After a considerable amount of badgering, they finally got their answer. No, he hadn't been lying. But, like Vera, he hadn't been telling the whole of the truth either.

"I was involved, yes," he admitted, amid a buzzing incomprehension from the judges, "but I didn't hire her, and I regret that she formed such a mistaken opinion. It was Andorian who hired her."

"And you know this for a fact?"

"Of course. I was there." He heaved a huge sigh, adding with heavy reluctance, "I didn't want to mention it, since, as you know, this whole trial is being mage-cast"—Vera's spirits soared—"but I have, for many years, been a spy in Andorian's operation."

There was more buzzing at that. Eventually one said, "A government Minister? And they trusted you?"

Pehndon shook his head, a faint grin playing about the corners of his mouth. "Actually, they were delighted to have their little 'spy' in the enemy camp. But now?" He shrugged. "My disguise is ended, I suppose. I had hoped not to relate this so that Jason would remain convinced I really *had* switched sides, but . . ." And he raised his hands in helpless surrender, smiling charmingly all the while.

To Vera's disgust, the judges swallowed it whole. "So you witnessed everything?" they said.

"In a sense. I was aware when Jason hired Malle Varis, and I tried to gain whatever knowledge I could of their plans. But, so help me, Jason can be a close-mouthed bastard at times. When I finally understood the scope of their daring, I tried to stop them, but obviously I was too late; the most I could do was apprehend the assassin after the deed was done."

"Then why this absurd story? The rebel alliance a blind? Really, Minister Pehndon, is any of this true?"

"Of course not, Your Honor. The rebel alliance a blind? How ridiculous can you get?"

"Quite. And what of the Anvil, Iaon? What's all this Anvil nonsense?"

"As you say, nonsense. I was simply trying to mislead her."

"For what reason?"

"Just put yourself in my position, if you will. Istarbion was dead, I had just apprehended Jason's assassin. I knew if I could maintain Jason's trust, I might be able to learn something of his plans in the wake of his assassin's capture. And to do that, I had to concoct some kind of story to keep her from mentioning my name at the trial and uncovering my true affiliation. So I fed her the most ridiculous story I could imagine to throw her off. Admittedly, I was under a bit of pressure at the time and my story was more absurd than it might have been, but I never expected that she would actually believe it!"

The two shared an almost conspiratorial chuckle, musing on Vera's gullibility. Swallowing an angry breath, she snapped, "Then why bother, if I wasn't supposed to believe it? Why invent a story at all?"

"Why, simply to add enough doubt that you would leave me out of the picture altogether. The story was *meant*," added emphasis here, "to be believable enough to convince you that you didn't have all the facts but unbelievable enough to make you hesitate to mention it in public, what with all the concomitant ridicule it would bring. Obviously"—he grinned—"I'm a better storyteller than I envisioned!"

Vera scowled. "You're a bastard, is what you are."

"Malle Varis, please. We understand your bitterness, only please do not sully the good name of Minister Pehndon. It was a noble thing he did . . ."

"Noble?" she interrupted. "Noble? He was part of it!"

"So he admitted."

"But not all of it, eh, Pehndon? Not the part that counts." She whirled on the judges. "He says he was part of the rebel alliance? Fine, I'll buy that; he was. But he certainly wasn't the minor part he made himself out to be. He wasn't ignorant of their plans; he was second-in-bloody-command! He knew everything; he was the one who told me about the minstrels' gallery, who helped me to get up there. He even chose the blasted poison!"

"Malle Varis . . ."

"I'm telling you, he was part of it!"

"And what could he possibly have to gain from such an action?"

She thumped her foot against her bonds in a kind of frustration. "I don't know; why don't you ask him?"

"We have."

"Then he's lying!"

"How? He's under a truth spell."

"As am I. So where does that get us?"

"Frankly, Malle Varis, I have no idea. This trial is proving more of a puzzlement that I care to mention. Perhaps we should adjourn again until we can get Andorian in, find out more of the truth behind these allegations? Guards, take her away."

Her last view, as she was dragged from the courtroom, was of Pehndon's face, suffused with a kind of suppressed anger, and she felt a surge of triumph. That should show him; she was not scratching *his* scabrous back! So what if he had come off looking like a hero today? She had forced one confession out of him already; a few more days and he would be singing like a treeful of canaries!

There was no way Iaon Pehndon was besting the Hawk.

That bloody bitch! Pehndon thought irately, stomping around the wardroom of the Nhuras prison later that night, waiting for the guards to escort him to Leonie's chamber. He had tried reason, he had tried bribery; he had asked her nicely—she had simply refused to cooperate. Fine, he was through with asking. There was no way he would let her spout this nonsense any longer.

She had, he reflected, already proved to be far more trouble than she was worth. Almost, he regretted hiring the Guild instead of using his own loyal followers, but at the time the decision had seemed the right one. It would have taken more bloody time and money to train someone to the requisite competence, and time was a commodity he was fast running out of. Fazaquhian had surpassed his wildest expectations; he could barely restrain the man from crowing about his discoveries, and that would be bloody suicide.

Besides, he had been so blasted proud when he had secured the Hawk, as if it were an omen of success. But that was arrogance, pure and simple. Next time he would simply get a lower-ranked assassin: one a little more easily manipulated. And for now . . . Well, he had learned from his mistakes; now it was time for the Hawk to learn from hers.

Admittedly, he was a bit surprised at how far she had been able to bend the truth—either that, or she had a higher pain threshold than anyone had imagined. But no matter; this wouldn't continue any longer. He had her measure now.

He would be testing those thresholds of hers tonight. She had defied him once too often. Someone needed to teach the Hawk a lesson in humility, and he was only too pleased to oblige.

So when the guards arrived, he gestured them curtly toward her cell, indicating that they should follow him inside, and slammed the door behind them. Then he just stood there, arms crossed casually on his chest—feeling the guards shifting like chained bulldogs at his back—and waited for her to look up.

She did: slowly, defiantly, raising steely eyes from the matted curtain of her hair, her lips drawing back in a snarl.

"Well?" Finding me a bit harder to dominate than you thought, Mal Pehndon?"

"I should think, Malle Varis," he responded coldly, "that you are hardly in a position to gloat."

"Indeed? And what more can you do to me than you already have?"

He began to grin, slowly shaking his head. "Malle Varis, you have barely begun to see the limits of my persistence." He was silent for a moment, adding, "Fine help your Guild is now, eh, my Hawk?"

She was silent, her lips pursed in disgust, and the combination of her haughty disdain in the midst of that filthy cell sent a bolt of white-hot anger through him. With a cold and infinite precision, he stepped forward and slapped her hard across the cheek.

Her head snapped back, the sound echoing crisply through the tiny chamber.

Behind him, he could sense the guards shifting restlessly, eagerly—the heat of their desire tickling his neck.

When she looked up, the mark of his hand was imprinted clearly across her face: a violent red welt. Hatred was burning brightly in her eyes. He stepped back casually, leaning against the locked door.

"All right, boys," he said, "take it away," and saw an instant of fear cross her face before the burly guards closed with her.

Letting his eyelids droop and resting the back of his head against the door, he listened as the first hollow thumps of flesh on flesh, the brutal rending of cloth, filled the air and let a faint smile play about his lips.

He didn't need to look. Vision would only spoil the illusion.

This was revenge, nothing less, nothing more.

She tried to fight, but there were too many and too intent on their purpose. Even her most highly scripted moves couldn't best them. They bound her hands and feet and beat her—the blows battering her naked flesh, for her tattered clothes had taken their last rent—her body pressed against the unyielding stone, the rats gnawing avidly on her helpless toes.

A cold knot of anger formed inside her as she twisted to avoid the worst of the hurt, her feet kicking against their bonds to scatter her furry attackers, and determined she would not scream.

She would not give Pehndon that satisfaction.

But when the first of the guards threw her roughly onto the bed and held her face-down against the fusty mattress—the lumpy fabric clotting in her nose and mouth, hindering her desperate attempts to breathe—and ripped down his trousers, driving heedlessly into her exposed flesh, she was obscurely grateful for the bedding which held her to her resolution.

She never did scream—or even so much as gasp—but later, when Pehndon and her attackers had left her, with bruises peppering her body, her ribs battered and her ears ringing, a trickle of blood leaking from a split brow and one of her eyes swollen half shut, semen leaking from more orifices than she cared to mention, she would find the mattress chewed to sodden pieces, the batting curdling like humiliation on her tongue.

But if Pehndon thought she was broken, he was very much mistaken. This had only strengthened her resolve.

Pehndon would pay for his mistakes. That much was certain.

15

The *Crow's Nest* was everything Thibault had threatened and more; Jen had never seen a more disreputable vessel. The decks were filthy, the cabins dilapidated—although roomier than she had expected—and the cargo holds teeming with vermin. Even the mess hall floor was covered in rancid sawdust, all too infrequently replaced, and the substance they served in place of food was even worse: greasy and all but inedible. Thibault, who had never traveled on shipboard before, was instantly laid low by a combination of the provender and the vessel's rolling motion and spent the first few days of the journey confined to his cabin, his face a most unhealthy shade of pale.

"Don't worry, you'll get used to it," Jen assured him, feeling almost guilty for her own robust vigor, but he merely groaned and rolled over, and she knew she had been dismissed.

Nonetheless, her own confinement to quarters to care for her ailing "brother" was in some ways a blessing. Not only was Thibault grateful for the attention (and it amused her to see their roles reversed for once, with herself playing the responsible party) but it also gave Jen the chance to work on her broad peasant accents and haughty demeanor. After a lifetime of making fun of it, she could imitate Thibault's speech with ease, but her efforts had always been a caricature—a mockery of a mockery, she now thought ruefully—and every phrase rang subtly false. When he could, Thibault coached her, but more often than not he was asleep or wracked with nausea, and consequently of little use. So she solved her problems by simply speaking as little as possible, pinching her face into an expression of disdain and making it clear that the few favors she asked of the boisterous sailors were, of necessity, voiced under great duress indeed.

The crew were a simple lot, slightly crude but generally well-meaning, so her imperious behavior instantly drew the lines of battle as if with an iron hand. In response, they seemed to take an almost indecent amount of pleasure in tormenting her, their catcalls and taunts following her down the corridors, their frequent misunderstandings deliberately designed to obfuscate. Secretly, she took great delight in these sessions, and decided that had the situation been different, she and the boys could have been the greatest of friends. Granted, they were coarse and poorly educated, with a somewhat provincial view of the world, but there was nonetheless a certain energy to them that appealed, a ribald sense of humor that made her want to smile.

She spent a good many hours watching them unobserved and had to mask her amusement as they speculated on her sexuality—or lack thereof—in what they no doubt suspected as the privacy of their mess hall. The consensus held that she was a frustrated virgin, and many creative solutions were proposed to remedy the situation; she found them all equally outrageous, and even came up with a few of her own which would doubtless have convulsed the sailors had she related them. The force of their convictions, however, she resented not at all; she would be the first to admit that Malle LeDoux, as Thibault had styled her, was a truly insufferable prig.

Still, her surreptitious observations taught her much, and another advantage of her supposed confinement was that, as she was not expected to be anywhere in particular, she had the freedom to wander the ship from stem to stern, familiarizing herself with every nook and cranny until she likely knew it better than the captain himself. Her finishing school training—of midnight raids and secret assignations—had prepared her far better for a life of duplicity than she had ever imagined, and, like her teachers, no sailor ever caught her where she didn't belong. So she boldly lurked in halls and holds, ears to walls and eyes to keyholes, until the rhythms of the ship and its crew invaded her very blood. She knew when the watches changed, when the various halls and holds were deserted; she knew who most often won the dart or dagger tosses, who killed the most rats, and what the captain's going rate was for the trophy pelts.

Few of the sailors, had they seen her, would have recognized the dark, simply clad specter that haunted their hull as the cold, haughty sister of young Tomas LeDoux.

By the time Thibault's color began to return and he could manage more than a few mouthfuls of the vessel's unpalatable fare, Jen could have navigated the craft blindfolded—and she would have almost regretted curtailing her freedom to accompany Thibault on his first tottery walks about the ship had the Belapharion not been so beautiful. Yet even as she lounged on the decks beneath a high, cerulean sky, listening to the silken slap of waves against the hull and watching the foreign ports glide seductively by, she found herself obscurely missing the shadowed maze of the underdecks, the forbidden byways that had become so familiar to her.

So instead of haunting the ship by day, she took to ghosting about at night, trying her hand at darts and daggers in the deserted mess hall, weaving through barrels and bales in the crowded holds in search of four-footed prey.

"You look tired," Thibault commented one afternoon as they perched on a coil of rope on the quarter deck, out of the way of the bustling sailors. "Haven't you been sleeping well?" His face was puckered with concern, no doubt in memory of his own recent malaise.

"Not . . . exactly," she replied, and he groaned.

"I knew it. I knew we should have waited for another ship. I'm sorry, Jen, is this really too wretched for you?"

"Wretched?" She chuckled. "Not in the least. I told you I was tougher than I looked. Actually, I've rather been enjoying myself."

"Enjoying yourself? Here? How?" He sounded scandalized. "Oh, no. Jen, you haven't been . . ."

"Sleeping with the sailors?" she finished, wrinkling her nose. "Gracious, no. They're good lads, Thib, but even I have my limits!"

"I'm relieved to hear it. So what have you been doing?"

"Shall I show you?"

He surveyed her speculatively. "Do I want to know?"

"Confounds me," she replied cheerfully, "but you haven't got much choice. I was going to show you anyway, now that you're better. Which reminds me," and she

poked him, "didn't I tell you that things would improve?
And did you believe me?"

"Jen . . ."

"No. As usual, you were convinced I was wrong. Or ex-
aggerating." She crossed her arms in mock censure and
regarded him sternly. "When are you ever going to learn,
Thibault?"

"Learn? Learn what?"

"That I am invariably correct."

"Ah, yes, how silly of me. Of course, you're always
right, Jenny."

"And don't you forget it." She laughed, tossing her
head, and winked at him boldly when she was certain
none of the sailors were looking.

"You're incorrigible. So when do we leave?"

"What?"

"On this secret mission of yours."

"Oh, that." She smiled mysteriously. "I'll let you
know."

Which of course she did, rising from her bed in the dark
of night when the third shift had gone on duty and those
from the second were safely ensconced in their bunks.
The weary cook, she knew, would have swiped the last of
his pots and halfheartedly rearranged the sawdust before
retiring, and now the mess hall would be locked in silent
darkness, touched only by the moonlight filtering palely
through the open windows and the soft chittering of the
hungry rats as they scuttled through the rancid flooring in
search of food.

Grinning in the wash of moonlight from her own narrow window, she padded naked to her trunk and eased
open the lid, dressing in a pair of soft, worn trousers and a
light chemise top: garments once gifted to her by Vera
and which accompanied her wherever she went, having
proved themselves useful for almost any range of activity.
A pair of canvas-soled shoes completed the ensemble, and
then she braided her hair into a sensible plait and bound a
bulky sash about her waist before broaching her cabin
door.

A brief survey of the lower decks revealed no activity
other than the peaceful glow of the moonlight dancing on
the Belapharion, the soft breeze creaking in the sails over-

head. Pausing only a moment to savor the scene, she eased out of the shadow of her cabin and crossed to Thibault's, jiggling the door handle lightly. It was locked, as expected. She didn't want to knock for fear of causing a commotion and, besides, she could always use the practice. So drawing a pair of slender picks from the sash at her waist, she inserted them into the lock and twisted. One by one, she could hear the tumblers falling, and scant seconds later the knob yielded to her touch.

Easing the door open, she slipped inside, then let it close softly behind her.

Thibault's cabin was the twin to her own, with a rickety desk on the far wall and his trunk gaping open on the right, a clutter of clothes strewn across its open lip. The bunk, surprisingly generous for such a ragtag affair, lay to the left. Across it, Thibault was sprawled in oblivious slumber, his limbs outstretched in abandon and his face half turned to the pillow, his mouth partially open and vibrating with the gentle buzz of his snores.

Jen masked a grin. He looked so innocent, so boyish in slumber, with his hair tousled and the sheet draped loosely about his waist, but there was nothing remotely childlike about the body that rose from the bed. His chest, covered by only the faintest spray of hair, was lean with muscle and possessed of a ropy, wiry strength despite his bulk that would have done any laborer proud. And it was this, more than anything, that convinced her how her old friend had grown.

"Thibault," she breathed and, when he didn't answer, clamped one hand over his lips and pinched his nose shut. He shuddered awake with a gasp, her palm muffling the sound, and she released his nose, keeping her hand over his mouth until she was certain he would make no further noise. His brown eyes blinked disorientatedly at her, registering her presence, and then he shot upright and she let her hand fall.

"Jen? What . . ." he began, unaware that the sheet had fallen in a puddle about his hips until her amused gaze dropped to his lap and he snatched it back, his cheeks flaming.

"What are you doing?" he said accusingly.

"That secret mission I told you of, remember?" She grinned, lounging against the wall at the foot of his bed.

"But . . . How did you get in? I thought I locked . . ."

"The door?" she finished, waving her picklocks smugly. "And when has that ever stopped me?"

He groaned and sat back, still clutching the sheet firmly about his waist. "What time is it?"

"Sometime after two." She rose fluidly and crossed to his trunk, plucking a pair of pants from the pile and tossing them into his lap. "Up. Get dressed," she instructed, and when he hesitated, she added with a chuckle, "Honestly, Thib, it's not like it's anything I haven't seen before! But if it makes you feel any better . . ." And turning her back, she rummaged in his trunk for a shirt; behind her, she could hear Thibault rising hastily, the slither of fabric as he pulled the garment on.

After a decent interval, she turned to see him standing barefoot in the center of the chamber, looking both confused and irritated, and about as ferocious as a barechested young man could look. "Will that satisfy your modesty," she teased, "or do you want this too?" And she held up a white shirt, waving it tantalizingly before him like a treaty flag.

With a growl, he snatched it from her and pulled it on, remarking as his head emerged from the opening, "You're going to lead some man a pretty dance someday, do you know that?"

"Then it's a good thing I'm remaining single, isn't it?" she countered, rising to her toes and tweaking back a wayward lock of his hair. "Shoes, dagger . . ." She tossed him the requisite items. "Now, let's go."

He donned the shoes and tucked the dagger in his waistband before following her to the door. "Where are we going?" he demanded, but she merely touched a finger to her lips, motioning him to silence.

"Trust me," she breathed, then slipped out into the night, feeling Thibault fall into place behind her. Once again she found herself marveling at the catlike stealth of his tread. How such a big man could move so silently . . . Were it not for the vague touch of his breath at her neck, she would have doubted there was anyone back there at all.

She glided up the steep run of stairs to the upper deck and cracked open the mess hall door. Something behind it shifted, and as she pushed it fully open she found herself

staring into the startled, beady eyes of a wayward rodent;
catching the moonlight, the orbs gleamed momentarily
red. Her hand went almost involuntarily to her dagger,
then eased off. *Later, Jen,* she told herself. *There's plenty
of time for that later.*

Sensing its reprieve, the creature skittered off with a
flick of its tail, leaving the room in silence.

Jen advanced.

There was something strangely surreal about the place
at night, with the beams of moonlight falling through the
narrow windows, locking the jumble of deserted chairs
and tables behind a silvery cage: a confused amalgam of
shadows and light, brushed with a random web of rat
tracks.

"Isn't this the mess hall?" Thibault breathed, his voice
the barest thread of a whisper.

She nodded.

"Jen, I think I've had all the food I can stomach," he
hazarded, and she masked a grin.

"Silly boy, we aren't here to eat."

"What, then?"

"Target practice," she replied, and gestured to a shadowed corner, untouched by the pallid moonlight.

"What? Are we throwing blind?"

In answer, she shook her head, drawing a tiny globe of
magelight from the sash at her waist. These globes were
small and portable, infinitely cheaper than the standard
variety, and burned with a far colder light. Vera kept them
around by the trunkful, and Jen had seen fit to liberate
several dozen before her journey, never knowing when
they might come in handy. So far, they had proved eminently useful in lighting darkened corners and in navigat-
ing the deserted byways of the windowless holds.

"Hullabaloo," she muttered, and grinned as Thibault
eyed her askance, denying any involvement in the choice
of the code word. The globe lit with a frigid, verdant
light, casting eerie shadows on the wall-mounted target.
In the greenish glow, she crossed to a small chest in one
corner, deftly picking its lock and liberating a handful of
darts, which she then passed to Thibault.

"How did you know where those were?" he demanded,
and she chuckled.

"I've been watching. Where do you think I was when

you were sick, and every night thereafter? How many
times do I have to tell you? I keep up my practice!"

In answer, he merely grinned, accepting the handful of
darts and weighing them speculatively. "How far back
should I stand?"

"How far back *can* you stand?"

He measured the distance to the green-washed target
with a judicious eye, then stepped back several paces—
further than Jen herself had gone during her solitary sessions. Then, pausing only long enough to draw a single
breath, he sent all five of the darts winging toward the target in rapid succession.

When the last hollow thunk had died away, there was a
moment of stunned silence.

"But . . ." Jen protested at last.

Thibault arched one eyebrow, his face oddly shadowed
in the lurid half light. "What?" he demanded.

"Well . . . you're better than me!"

And indeed, the missiles were all clustered neatly in the
center of the target, with barely a finger's breadth between them. Even at her best, Jen had never achieved
such a grouping—and certainly not from such a distance.

She frowned as Thibault's soft, cajoling laughter
washed over her.

"Come on, Jenny. Longer arms, longer reach."

But she just shook her head. Obviously she hadn't been
trying hard enough, or setting herself sufficiently exalted
standards. And who could blame her, cooped up in a
finishing school for two ghastly years where no one understood the value of good aim or routine training?

Clearly, it was time for things to change.

So, "Give me those," she commanded as Thibault gathered the darts, and set about the rigorous task of winning
back her title.

16

Blast it, scorch it, relegate it to a thousand pits of flaming torment!

Owen DeVeris pounded his fist against the crowded desktop, sending an avalanche of papers raining to the floor, and threw down the offending missive. It landed face-up in the clutter, its bold, spiky letters winking up at him smugly.

Blast the girl, what could she be thinking? What, by all that was precious, had possessed her?

"Curse her," he cried aloud. "May ten thousand maggots feast upon her limbs. May all her heirs provide her with headaches without surcease!"

Then, feeling somewhat better for his outburst, he dropped his head into his hands and tried to figure out just what to do next.

He should have known that Radineaux girl meant trouble, should have sensed something of her intent in the cold, angry glitter of her eyes. He had had enough exposure to the Radineaux obstinacy from Vera, after all; why should he have expected anything different from her niece? They were a load of pigheaded aristocrats, every last one of them: too bloody independent for their own good.

And now the wretched child had gone rogue on him; her letter had arrived that very morning, confirming it. Oh, not that she claimed that as her goal, of course. She had presented all the requisite arguments—family duty and such-like—but they both knew the truth. Justifications aside, she had gone haring off to Ashkharon on a whim, and now he was left to deal with the consequences.

"I must be getting old," he groaned, digging the heels of his hands into his eyes. "Why me? What did I do to deserve this?"

But there was no answer to his question. And much as he would have liked to crawl under the pile of his displaced papers and curl up beneath them until this crisis was over, he was Guildmaster; it was his duty to provide a solution.

"Curse her," he exclaimed again. Why Vera, and why now? The situation was tense enough with his best assassin gone and his two next best risking their necks in an illegal search-and-rescue without throwing a wild card into the mix. Jenifleur Radineaux was an unknown quantity; there was no telling what she might do, or how she might behave. It was like waving a candle over a pool of fire-oil; one false move, and they'd see the explosion from here.

No, he had to stop her, and that meant the Hound and the Falcon—the Hound and the Falcon who were supposed to be using their time to rescue Vera.

Bloody-minded, poxy aristocrats!

"Vander," he bellowed, raising his head. "Vander!"

"What?" came the sour answer from the doorway. "I was in the middle of something . . ." Then pausing, the mage added, "Hang it, Owen, what have you done to your office? It's a bloody mess in here!" And thumping to his knees, he began to gather the scattered papers.

The Guildmaster sighed heavily. "Thanks, Van, but that's nothing compared to the mess that I'm about to be in."

"And what mess is that?" the mage demanded, restoring the papers to their rightful piles.

"Nothing. Guild business," Owen answered automatically, adding, "Curse it, do you have any idea what this is going to cost me?"

"And in all respects, I suspect," the mage countered knowingly, and the Guildmaster groaned.

"Blast it, yes," he agreed, realizing he was going to have to add a little incentive to Derek and Mark's pot to justify stopping Jen. But still, it would be cheaper and simpler than hiring another operative entirely. There was already one too many cooks in this particular kitchen; adding another would confound him entirely.

"You will let me know when Derek or Mark calls in, won't you?" he added plaintively, and Vander raised an eyebrow.

"I always do, don't I?"

"Indeed. What would I do without you, Van? I'm sorry I interrupted; get back to what you were doing."

The mage grinned and left, abandoning Owen to his reflections.

Blast the girl, she was jeopardizing his entire mission. So why did he still feel a kind of sneaking admiration for her temerity, the same bold decisiveness he had always admired in her aunt?

It simply made no sense.

With his brother at his back, Mark Verhoeven stepped decisively from the gangplank of the *Reggan Sprite* and onto the firmness of the Nhuras docks. Overhead, the sun blazed down through a cloudless sky, scenting the air with dust and dryness, and a vague hint of rotting garbage. The sharp odor of camel dung tickled his nostrils from the line of mangy carry-beasts that lined the poorer quarters of the wharf. Further on, where the big ships docked, would be the carriages, carts, and rickshaws, jostling to ferry passengers into the mazy heart of the city. But here, unwashed bodies bustled about him, the clamor of their musical accents and the creak of carts and barrels all blending into the familiar symphony of commerce.

"Well, here we are," he said cheerfully, as the last of their baggage materialized from the belly of the ship. "And at a considerable savings to Owen."

"Don't remind me." Derek scowled. "If De Veris had to travel in that blasted hold . . ."

"But he didn't, so stop complaining and make yourself useful. Now, do you have any ideas about lodgings?"

Derek's reply came in a copious fit of sneezing.

"Gracious, what's the matter with you now?" Mark demanded.

"I'd forgotten how Nhuras stinks. And I think I'm allergic to the bloody camels."

Mark grinned, clapping a hand to his brother's shoulders. "You do enjoy fussing, don't you? But buck up, boyo; don't forget we will be nicely compensated for any inconvenience we may have suffered—and by Owen's own hand, no less."

"Indeed." His brother brightened. "Six thousand marks . . ."

"If we rescue the Hawk."

Derek waved that aside. "So does this mean we can stay in a decent hotel? Preferably one where the beds don't move?"

"Well, Owen didn't specifically issue an injunction against it, did he?"

"No . . ."

"Then I think it can be arranged."

"Crafty little bugger, aren't you?" Derek said admiringly, and Mark chuckled.

"Always glad to oblige. Now, lodgings?"

"Pirhini Street, I think. Decent quarters, reasonably priced, with several good whorehouses nearby." Derek's eyes twinkled, and Mark shrugged.

"Very well, Pirhini Street it is. Off you go, then. Get us a cart. And not . . ."

"Too expensive, I know. Back in a flash."

Mark shook his head as his brother disappeared, but as usual Derek was as good as his word, returning several minutes later trailed by a good-sized cart. It was, the Falcon reflected, one of the more upscale carts with actual padded seats—but a cart nonetheless. Typical. Derek's one fault, as far as his brother was concerned, was his absolute inflexibility when faced with substandard conditions. Nothing could put him in a foul humor faster than a dirty window or a verminous bed, and he had been absolutely insufferable during their last voyage. Granted, the rough pallets thrown into the close hold were not Mark's conception of ideal quarters, but still . . . Derek had sulked for the whole dreadful two weeks of the voyage, and Mark had come as close to killing his sibling as he ever had.

It was an antique argument between them.

"Why should we have to live like this?" Derek would demand. "We're Guild; we have money now. We can afford better."

"Yes, but as Guild-trained assassins, we have to be able to fit into every walk and frame of life, and sometimes that means disappearing among the faceless lower classes."

"But we spent our whole childhood among the faceless lower classes! Now I want to spend some time among the faceless *upper* classes."

"Haven't you learned yet?" Mark would answer. "The upper classes are *never* faceless."

But still the argument persisted. As the younger sibling, Derek had always felt the privations of the gutter more strongly than his brother—perhaps because he had only heard of the crash that lost the family fortunes and had always yearned for the life he had never experienced. But Mark, who had been born into the heart of a prosperous middle-class shipping family, had no illusions as to the luxuries of their former existence, and moreover had gained an early understanding of the fickleness of fortune. He knew that you merely did what you could to stay alive, because an instant stroke of random fate could change the course of your life forever—whether for good or bad. And often it was no one's fault at all.

No, Mark had been forced to adjust to the cold reality of poverty—the tattered clothes and thin soups, the rancid bales of hay that replaced the feather mattresses, the months of shivering in unheated houses—whereas Derek, who had been brought up in its midst, had never fully accepted the necessity.

Still, at least his brother never harbored grudges. No matter how many stinking ships' holds and vermin-infested hovels Mark forced him into in the course of their assignments, the assurance of a decent bed and lodging always restored him to a sunny good humor. Even now, he was whistling cheerfully as he helped the driver load their trunks onto the bed of the cart, chattering a mile a minute as the promise of Pirhini Street erased the privations of the *Reggan Sprite* without a trace.

"Just arrived, did you?" the driver asked as the brothers clambered onto the unsprung—but padded—seats. Naturally, his comments were addressed to Derek.

"Indeed," Mark's brother responded cheerfully. "Just off the boat. So it's Pirhini Street we want, my good man."

"Ah." The driver winked and tapped his nose, clucking his horse into motion. "A spot of pleasure, eh, lads?"

"Quite. We've been working the vineyards, you know. In Venetzia. Bloody hard work, that. No time for a break once you're going. So we thought we'd come to Ashkharon for a bit, to see if anything amusing was going

on or if there was any work to be had. Heard any rumors?"

Mark masked a grin. He could tell from the glitter in
Derek's eye that their driver was about to get the royal
treatment, but then that was the genius of the Hound. Beneath the voluble flow of chatter, reality tended to get a
bit clouded. His eager, innocent air, his apparent desire to
grace even the most recent acquaintance with his entire
life story as he currently perceived it, meant that very few
actually guessed at the depths of his untruths. The scant
handful of friends who knew of their true profession often
wondered that Derek didn't give up the game in the
course of all his talk, but Mark knew better. Derek would
die rather than give up a secret; not even torture would rip
it from him. But that was largely academic; his ready, ingenuous "confessions" would likely convince even the
most suspicious of inquisitors before the question of inducement even came up.

In fact, he reflected whimsically, should they ever get
caught, their jailers would most likely evict them just to
save their ears the wear and tear.

"So, you're not in town to see the trial?" their driver
asked, and Mark felt a surge of excitement flow through
him, though he moved not a muscle nor altered his languid pose of disinterest. *Brilliant, Derek. Brilliant,* he
thought, and sensed his brother's smug triumph.

But Derek's tone changed not a whit as he answered,
"What trial?"

"Why, the assassin's trial, of course." Their driver was
a font of information, encouraged by Derek's wide-eyed
attention. "First Minister of the government—one Guy Istarbion—was murdered last week, right at the start of his
annual public address. Bloody thing was being magecast
at the time, so everyone was watching. Took a dart right
in the throat, he did. Twitched like a gutted sheep going
down. Green foam on his lips and everything." He nodded. "Quite a show."

"I should say." Derek sounded impressed, though Mark
knew he recognized the poison. They both did, for each of
them now carried a dose—always had, in fact. "Weren't
you scared?"

The driver snorted, swerving his cart around a large
procession of camels. "I've seen worse in the back alleys.

But it made quite a spectacle, I'll grant you that. Whoever planned that job certainly knew what they were about."

As she should, thought Mark. He himself had often been in awe of the Hawk, of the flawless precision of her moves.

"Though, of course, how the assassin managed to get caught is beyond me," the driver added after a moment.

"Caught?" Derek sounded astonished. "They caught him?"

"Her, actually, and yes. Caught her red-handed, with the murder weapon and everything."

"How?" Derek demanded, voicing Mark's next question. He had to shout a little to make himself heard as they skirted the bustling fringes of the bazaar.

The driver shrugged. "Who knows? Luck, perhaps, or a little fast thinking. I heard it was another Minister who got her. But no matter. She's safe behind bars now, and the trial starts tomorrow. Open to the public, or so I've heard. Maybe you should stop by; it could prove a good bit of entertainment."

"We just might, at that. So," Derek added, "how does it feel, being without a First Minister?"

The driver took a corner. "And who says we're without a First Minister? Jhakharta took over the day after Istarbion's death."

Mark tensed. Beside him, Derek asked, "Is that usual?"

"Why shouldn't it be? First Ministers pick their successors, and Istarbion picked Jhakharta."

"So who hired the assassin?"

The driver eyed them askance. "Andorian, they say."

"Andorian?"

"Blazes, don't you know anything? Jason Andorian, leader of the rebel faction. He's been rather vocal about Istarbion lately."

"Oh." Derek grinned. "So what do you think?"

The man shrugged, intent on guiding his beast through a particularly tight turning. "Short cut," he informed them as they entered a narrow alleyway. The cart listed slightly, creaking as the trunks shifted, and when it was straight again he added, "Andorian claims he's innocent, of course, though there's some as say that whether or not he did it, it was a good thing it happened."

"And do you agree?"

The driver shrugged again. "Don't know; haven't given it much thought. Man has a point about the government, though, no denying that. And if Andorian can do a better job running the glass factories, then maybe he deserves a chance." He nodded sagely. "Makes a man grateful he drives a cab, I can tell you." Then slowing his vehicle, he added, "Pirhini Street, gentlemen. Now, where can I drop you?"

"The Four Crowns should do nicely."

"Very well." He pulled up before the requisite establishment, unsurprisingly for Derek the best-kept of its fellows. As the trunks were offloaded and the money changed hands, he added with a surreptitious glance at Mark, "What's the matter with your friend, there? Doesn't he talk?"

"Not often," Derek laughed.

"Don't get much of a chance," Mark added dryly, and the driver grinned.

"Fair enough. Well, enjoy yourselves in Nhuras, gentlemen. You're in the best place for it." He winked. "Maybe I'll even see you at the trial."

Derek smiled. "Maybe you will, at that."

17

"So how long are you planning to keep me incarcerated?" Vera spat, her back pressed against the sweating walls and her arms wrapped, shieldlike, about her body. Not out of defense, though, or misguided modesty; she'd be hanged if she let Pehndon get his jollies from the bruises that bloomed against her naked skin and peppered her ribs and breasts. Rather, her posture was one of pure defiance; it flashed from every out-thrust angle and sparked like fire from her eyes.

No, Iaon Pehndon would have to content himself with the shadowed flesh around her left eye, the ugly purple smear across her right cheek and jaw. She would give him no more satisfaction than that.

And from his expression of undisguised loathing, she knew her ploy had succeeded.

She had been trapped in this dreadful cell for more than a week now—though in the endless, unvarying solitude, she had lost track of the exact count of days. After a while, they all blended into a seamless mélange of scalding noons and frigid nights, interrupted only by the twice-daily meals and the twinges of her healing wounds. She had seen neither Pehndon nor her guards since the night of her assault and there had been no hint that her abortive trial was ever to continue.

Instead there were only the rats, and the four unvarying walls to keep her company. Her captors hadn't even seen fit to provide her with new clothing to replace the garments that had been ripped so forcibly from her.

But so help them if they thought that would stop her. Since the night of the attack, she had maintained a secret vigilance, poised in a state of near flight at all times. Even in sleep—even though the deadly tedium of the waking hours, a hidden part of her remained permanently on edge, waiting for the slightest slip, the tiniest error, that would facilitate escape. Someday, someone would slip up, and Vera would be ready.

It never did to underestimate a Guild-trained assassin, not even one unarmed and apparently beaten. For if anything, her savaging had given her the advantage; now they saw her as the victim, an easy target.

She couldn't wait to prove them wrong.

"Really, how long can it take to secure one lousy rebel leader—and one who is in your employ, no less?" she added, goading her captor, and was rewarded by the sudden flash of anger in his steely gaze.

Fortunately for her continued health, he had left his hired goons outside this time.

"You're proving to be far more trouble that you're worth, do you realize that?" he snapped, and she let her mouth curve in an ironic grin, tossing back the matted and oily strings of her hair.

"Always glad to oblige. So when *does* your mockery of a trial continue?"

Pehndon smiled then, a slickly satisfied expression that made Vera's insides clench. "Continue?" he responded airily. "How can it continue when it hasn't even started yet?"

"What?"

"Haven't you learned never to underestimate Iaon Pehndon? Do you think I'd risk letting you appear in public before I'd determined just how far you were willing to go? Really, Leonie, do you take me for a fool?"

She swallowed. "So this whole trial . . ."

"Was a mockery, yes—just like your hire, just like my rebel alliance. How else do you think I managed to fool the truth spells? By sheer force of will?" He snorted. "You may have been able to bend the truth a little, Malle Varis, but no one can thwart a truth spell that fully unless they have the mage in their control!"

"As you did?"

He inclined his head.

"And the judges?"

"Likewise false. All loyal men in my employ, though I instructed them to run the trial as realistically as possible. No need to invoke your suspicions and pervert the whole charade, after all."

"But . . . why? Great jumping junipers, what reason could you possibly have to propagate such a farce?"

"Why, to test you, of course." He sounded astonished that she had to ask. "As I said, I couldn't risk letting you give up the game to the gullible public. They have to believe this entire travesty exists exactly as I have set it up; the whole future hinges on that fact. I simply cannot afford to be implicated. Your accusations—however nebulous and unfounded I can make them appear—will still add that element of doubt that I cannot afford to risk. So I set you up, to see if there was a chance you would actually remain silent."

"And now that you know there's not? Now that you know I won't rest until I see you and your treacherous plans unveiled?" Her eyes sparkled. "Shall you just abandon the trial?"

Pehndon chuckled. "Hardly. It will go on as scheduled; tomorrow, in fact. That is what I came to tell you. I've already got your substitute ready, and she's prepared to swear up and down that Andorian hired her."

"Under truth spell?" Vera scoffed, but Pehndon seemed unconcerned.

"As far as she knows, it *is* the truth. She trusts me, you see."

"Then she's a bloody fool!"

His mouth tightened, his hand twitching as if he wanted to strike her. She almost wished he would. One provocation, and she would be on him like an avenging lion. Pehndon was a politician, a weakling; she could take him out in a second, beat him to a bloodier pulp than his hired muscle had left her.

Part of her longed for an excuse to try.

A larger part, though, was intensely aware of the locked door, the guards lurking lasciviously on the other side—the unfeasibility of escape. Not to mention that such an attack would utterly destroy any semblance of helplessness she possessed.

Still, her fingers itched for vengeance and for a chance to wipe that smugly gloating expression off his face.

But, "On the contrary," he responded, "she's quite a competent woman, smart enough to give the judges the trial they need. That is, the *real* judges." He paused, then added, "I wonder if you realize just how much trouble you've caused me?"

She spat at his feet, as if clearing a vicious taste from her mouth. "Glad to be of service," she said again, and his eyes narrowed.

"Meddling bitch! But gloat while you can; you won't be alive for long. Once the judges pass down the death sentence—and pass it down they will, I assure you—the switch will be made, and you will be duly executed in her stead. And I, for one, will rejoice at your demise!"

As I will rejoice at yours, she thought bitterly. *Now let's just see which one of us goes first, shall we?* But all she said was, "No doubt. And Andorian? What about your famed rebel leader?"

"After a suitably convincing chase, an admission of guilt, doubtless followed by a public pardon. I'd hate to destroy such a good conspirator."

"Somehow I doubt that. And then?"

"Triumph. The game completed."

"And the rewards reaped?"

"Of course."

"You're a coldhearted bastard, Iaon Pehndon. Has anyone ever told you that?"

"Plenty of times; I consider it a compliment."

"You would."

"Indeed." He raised an eyebrow. "But enough of this pleasant byplay, Malle Varis. Now I'll leave you to contemplate your fate, and I hope you receive some pleasure from it in return for all the grief it's cost me. I'd hate to think that all my efforts had gone in vain."

Behind the hard, contemptuous mask of her face, she felt a mounting panic. Pehndon was dismissing her; how many more chances would she get? How many more times would he be entering her cell to gloat, to lord his superiority over his apparently helpless victim?

A desperate plan began forming, fueled by rage and betrayal—one that required exquisite timing, but which still stood a minute chance of working. As her captor raised his fist to pound against the cell door, summoning the guards to release him, she gathered herself and raised her head.

"Pehndon?"

"Yes?" He half turned, raising a condescending brow. On the other side of the door, she could hear the guards turning the key. Any second now it would open, and the brutes would appear.

She paused, waiting for the moment when the first crack of light appeared from the hallway beyond, and then she spoke, her voice cold and hard as a winter storm. "Don't think you're going to get away with this."

"Oh? And who's going to stop me?"

Time slowed and stuttered as the precision of her control, her training, took over. Through the half-open door, she could see the surly face of the guard who had first raped her appear, melting into her vision like butter in a skillet.

"I am," she replied, feeling the tension drawing out her words like taffy.

Pehndon's face registered amusement but she barely noticed, all her attention focused on the guard in the door. Any second now, and she would be in his line of sight.

"And when will this feat take place?" Pehndon demanded.

The guard met her eyes. Slowly she stood, arching her body until the taut points of her breasts, the ripple of bruises across her ribs and stomach—the thatch of dark hair between her legs, moist with sweat from her ovenlike cell—were all revealed in stark detail, glazed by the golden sheen of the afternoon sun.

She let his gaze register it for a moment, feeling the pull of his incipient lust, and then feigned awareness of his regard, shrinking into herself as if in fear. She could feel his attention falter, then catch, drawn into her control by the twinge of her apparent terror.

For an instant he forgot himself, stepped past the doorway and toward her, his body interposing itself between the door and the wall . . .

It was enough. That instant of distraction had given her an opening and the one shot at escape that she was likely to receive.

"*Now!*" she shouted, in answer to Pehndon's question, and released like a tightly coiled spring.

So help anyone who thought a naked and unarmed assassin wasn't any danger!

Flying across the room, she grabbed the edge of the door and slammed it home, throwing her full weight into the blow. The hard metal edge caught the guard in the face—the very face that had loomed, drooling, over her naked body—and flattened his nose, driving on past and into his piggish skull. The back of his head collided with the rough stone of the jamb, and she felt a certain smug pleasure as she heard the muffled crunch of bone.

She had been killing for most of her life, treating it with

the cool, level composure of a trained professional. She had never really enjoyed it until now.

Moreover, her timing was exquisite, for such was the force of the blow that the door rebounded as if kicked, swinging back in a perfect arc to crash against her captor and send him stumbling. A quick roundhouse kick completed the business, her bare sole connecting with the back of Pehndon's head, dispatching him into unconsciousness. She would have liked to do more—to exact a greater vengeance on his helpless body—but there was no time. The other two guards were already converging on the door, and on the body of their fellow, which wedged it open. If she didn't move soon, they would have the hulking form removed and she would be trapped yet again.

So instead she dived for the open door, past the recumbent form of her downed attacker, and out of the chamber.

Like his companion, the second guard was momentarily distracted by her nakedness; she pushed the advantage home. Flying up from a crouch, she drove the top of her head into his chin, and as he staggered beneath the blow, stunned and incoherent, she grabbed his head and twisted, feeling the satisfying crack as his neck snapped in her hands and his body went limp.

Triumphant, she rose, her hair hanging in wild, dirty tangles, her lips curving in a feral grin . . .

Seeing it, the third guard's nerve broke. He turned and bolted down the corridor, bellowing in rage and fear, but his lumbering steps were no match for Vera's fleet feet. She flew after him, her silent steps barely seeming to touch the ground, her foot flying out at the crucial instant to chop viciously against the back of his knees.

It was almost comical how quickly he folded, his nerveless legs collapsing under him. He began to pitch forward, but she caught him by the collar at the last instant, spun him around and slammed him against the wall, her fists caving his windpipe in and ending his screams as cleanly as if she had opened his throat.

There was something almost merciful about the silence.

Satisfied, she let him fall. They had sent these guards unarmed against her, likely afraid that she would seize their weapons and turn them against their bearers. Never had they guessed that weapons—those hard, artificial tools of mankind—were entirely irrelevant.

Never again would these cretins brutalize an unarmed prisoner. Never again would they violate her or any other with their stinking, prurient lust.

But wary that the guard's alto bellows might have alerted others of his fellows, she dragged the body back to the door of her cell—still jammed with the corpse of her first victim—and pitched it in. The second guard followed his companion inside. Then, with one ear cocked for noises in the corridor, she hastily kicked the first guard the rest of the way into the cell—fumbling the keys off his belt as she did so—and let the door slam shut, masking another surge of satisfaction as she locked Pehndon decisively within.

There would doubtless be a commotion of epic proportions when he awoke to find his pet prisoner missing and himself in her place, surrounded by the bodies of his three dead flunkies. But much as she wished she had the time to leave him a more complete message than that trinity of corpses, Vera was no fool. It was certainly not worth risking her freedom for revenge, and reinforcements might be arriving any second now. She couldn't risk being caught— or letting it seem that anything was amiss in the now silent corridor—until she had had the chance to escape from the outer gates.

Still, she couldn't help wondering what Pehndon would think when he came to and found himself in the midst of her bare-handed murders, when he understood that she could have as easily left him dead as alive.

So, suppressing an incipient grin, she briefly checked the corridor for any signs of the recent commotion, then, satisfied that all was in order, ghosted hastily away, intent on putting whatever distance she could between herself and her cell.

Never mind that she was still naked, that she could already hear the echo of footsteps in the distance. Later, when dark had fallen and Pehndon awoke the prison with his cries, marshaling a search, she would steal clothing from some other guard and slip out in the resultant confusion.

Meanwhile, she would spend the next few hours making herself as invisible as possible without one of Absalom's magic amulets.

18

"So, what now?" Derek asked, folding his hands behind his head and relaxing against the pillows with a sigh. Beneath him, the mattress was soft and stable, the room clean and pleasant if somewhat plain. By mutual consent, they occupied a top-floor chamber: Derek because it avoided any instance of noisy upstairs neighbors and Mark because the multiplicity of stairs discouraged potential snoopers. But it was a highly satisfactory accommodation, either way you sliced it.

Derek grinned over at his brother, his good humor restored. "Pretty smart of me, no, getting all that information from the driver?"

Mark snorted. "Indeed. So any ideas what to do next, my paragon?"

"Attend the trial?"

"Before that, I meant."

"Visit the House of Silken Pleasures?" He let a hopeful note creep into his voice, and Mark chuckled.

"About the Hawk, silly boy."

"Oh." Derek grinned. "I leave that up to your expertise, as always."

"Good lad." His brother ceased riffling through his trunk and looked up. "I suggest we snoop around the bazaar, then, for a start."

"The bazaar? Why the bazaar?"

"You did an exemplary job with the driver, my lad, but there is always more than one fish in the stream. And a little extra information never hurt anyone."

"And you think the bazaar is the best place for it?"

"Well, where would you go if you were a local in search of gossip?"

"The House of Silken Pleasures."

Mark laughed. "Later, later. I promise."

"The taprooms, then."

"At three in the afternoon?"

Derek grinned.

"The bazaar first, the taprooms next, and then . . ." Mark paused, relented. "And *then* the House of Silken Pleasures."

Derek bounced off the bed. "Beauty! Let's do it."

"Now?" His brother smiled, locking his trunk. "Impatient, aren't you?"

"Absolutely. Do you know how long it's been?"

"Yes. Two weeks," Mark responded dryly.

"My point exactly!" And with a bow, Derek gestured his laughing brother from the room.

The Nhuras bazaar was teeming. With the searing midday heat faded from the sky, both merchants and buyers had returned from their siestas, and the market resumed its usual air of frenetic activity. The afternoon sun slanted golden through the canopies and booths, sliding off silk and striking seductive glints from gold, silver, and polished stone. A cacophony of voices hawked their wares. Merchants haggled in flowery, ritualized phrases, and above it all drifted the tantalizing smells of frying meat and spices.

Derek felt his mouth start to water and dragged his protesting brother off in search of sustenance. The problem with Mark, he thought affectionately, was that once he was on a job he was likely to forget all the basics, like food and sleep. If the Falcon were to work alone, he would melt away to skin and bones in no time.

As they headed for the food stalls at the center of the bazaar, where the flames of the open grills flared and died, and droplets of fat from the roasting meats sizzled and hissed in the fires, merchants of all varieties called out to them in seductive voices, offering cloth and jewels, charms and daggers. A scruffy mage, his face half obscured by a smear of scar, even accosted them, saying, "You're searching for a woman, gentlemen, no?"

Derek grinned. "Aren't we all?" he replied cheerfully as they moved on.

At the center of the bazaar, fortified with meat pies in hand, Mark admitted that his brother's idea had not been such a bad one after all. Away from the earnest throngs of merchants and buyers, the conversation flowed at an easier pace, leisurely touching upon the latest gossip. Istarbion's

death and the upcoming trial were mentioned frequently as
the two assassins drifted like ghosts through the crowd,
sampling conversations like tidbits from a tasty buffet.

The sentiments ranged from pro-Istarbion to pro-
Andorian, and while there were some who reviled the rebel
leader as a murderer, there were others who hailed him for
a hero. Some even claimed his innocence, and at one point
Derek found a pamphlet thrust into his unsuspecting hand,
adorned with a sketch of a thin-faced and fiery young man,
the words "Not Guilty!" emblazoned in bold letters above
his head. Leaning against the side of a nearby food stall, he
unfolded the paper and perused the impassioned words.
Then he refolded the pamphlet and went in search of Mark.

He found his brother leaning against a coffee seller's
stall, nodding laconically in counterpoint to the man's
words.

"Ah, there you are," he said as Derek approached.
"Hamish, here, was just telling me about the trial. Apparently it's being held in the main courthouse in Government Square. Holds above five hundred people in the
paying seats and an additional five hundred in the free
galleries—standing room only. And the whole thing will
be magecast out into the square as well."

"Fascinating," Derek responded with a mental groan. A
thousand witnesses in the court, likely twice that number
in the square outside. Hardly an auspicious locale for their
daring rescue. With that many people watching, they'd be
lucky even to get a glimpse of their colleague, let alone
lift a finger toward her liberation.

And from the expression in Mark's eyes, he could tell
that his brother had arrived at much the same conclusion.

"Shall we sit?" he said.

Mark nodded. "Find yourself a table. I'll join you in a
minute." Then turning to Hamish, he added, "Two cof-
fees, my good man."

Derek grinned and sauntered off in search of a seat. He
found one in a shadowed corner, next to a half-oblivious
old man thoughtfully sucking on a hookah. The oldster's
head was tipped up to the canopied sky, his beard trailing
across his chest. A faint whiff of Dreamsmoke rose from
his pipe, trickled lazily from his nostrils, mingling with
the thicker, earthier smell of tobacco.

With a little smile, Derek took one of the seats at the

nearby table, stretching out his long legs and tossing the pamphlet face-down across its top. A few moments later, Mark joined him, bearing two minuscule cups of thick Mepharstan coffee and a plate of sweet, sticky pastry, chopped with honey and nuts. "Compliments of the house," he said, laying down the booty and pushing a cup of coffee across to his brother.

"See? I told you you could be charming if you tried," Derek countered, picking up his cup and sipping the rich, pungent liquid. Then, reaching for a pastry, he slid the pamphlet across to his brother.

"What's this?"

"Conflicting view."

"Don't talk with your mouth full," the Falcon said almost automatically and turned over the leaflet, his brow furrowing in concentration as he began to read.

The Hound leaned back in his chair and smiled somewhat smugly. He loved getting information before his brother did; it made him feel useful.

He waited until Mark looked up with an approving smile. "Good work, Derek. This is getting more complex than I thought." He shook his head, absently drumming his fingers against the tabletop. "Methinks we ought to pay a visit to the government courthouse to see if we need entry for tomorrow's event—not to mention getting the lay of the land. But I also think we'd be well advised, later tonight, to spend a bit of time snooping around the Nhuras prison." He sighed and rubbed his temples. "Somehow I think that may end up being our best shot at garnering those additional four thousand marks."

Government Square was packed, as if in preparation for the morrow's events. Throngs of people drifted about, their voices buzzing with anticipation.

"I'll go see about the courthouse," Mark instructed. "You wait here. Keep an eye on things; charm any strangers in need of charming."

"I hear and obey, O Master." Derek saluted cockily and sauntered over to lean against a nearby column, his back to one of the imposing white stone buildings, letting his eyes scan the crowd. In the distance, he could see the Falcon disappearing into the vast courthouse.

For a while, all seemed normal, and then a commotion broke out at one corner of the square.

"Make way, make way," someone called.

"Traitor!" someone else screamed.

A multiplicity of throats took up the cry, interrupted by shouts of "Savior!" and "Hero!" and "What about Alphonse Jhakharta?"

At the edges of the crowd, a phalanx of figures pushed forward like a human shield, penetrating the ragged mass. Derek craned his neck curiously, but all he could see was the top of a dark head, bobbing at its center.

"Let me past," a man cried, his voice rising easily above the crowd, buzzing with the unmistakable echo of mage amplification. "Hear me speak!"

The phalanx of figures was moving inexorably toward the wide stone steps leading up to the main government building, very close to where Derek himself leaned casually against his column. As they approached, he craned his neck to make out the face of the man in the middle, then groped eagerly for his leaflet.

By all that was precious. Andorian!

Mark, where are you? he thought, sending out a silent call. Not that his brother would hear it, of course, but the connection between the two was such that the one often sensed the other's need. And right now Derek would have given his right arm to have Mark hear this particular magecast.

The rebel leader had ascended the steps, his followers fanning out to either side of him like the petals of an unfolding flower, revealing the slim young man blazing like a coal at their center, clad from head to toe in bloody scarlet. When he spoke, his voice rang authoritatively over the square.

"I stand before you falsely accused! By now, you have all seen or heard of Istarbion's assassination. And judging from your reaction to me, many of you have also heard the rumors that I was involved. Ladies and gentlemen— my very good friends—you have been misinformed. This was, I swear to you, none of my doing; I am innocent of any crime!"

A buzz of disbelief met his words, and under cover of the commotion, Derek saw Mark emerge from the courthouse. His brother stood poised on the broad steps, his probing gaze sweeping the square; Derek raised an arm and Mark hastened toward him, slipping through the crowd as smoothly as an errant breeze.

"My friends, you have all heard me speak," Andorian declaimed, the power of his voice, even in the midst of suspicion, still capable of silencing the masses. "You all know my views, and the strength of my complaints. So what, I ask, do you take me for now, a fool?"

"What's going on?" Mark demanded in an undertone as he reached his brother.

"More alternate views."

"Andorian?"

Derek nodded.

Mark whistled softly, turning his attention to the speaker.

"You have heard my arguments and seen my evidence. You have given me your attention and even your support. So would you abandon me now? Would you do me the discourtesy of assuming I have forsaken you—forsaken all I have ever fought for—merely for the dubious pleasure of pursuing my own private vendettas?

"I repeat, my friends: do you take me for a fool?"

"What I wouldn't give to have that boy under a truth spell," Mark muttered, and Derek chuckled.

"Istarbion was a symptom, not the cause, of the disease that grips our land! Corruption and greed abound throughout the government, not just in the person of Guy Istarbion—though I will admit he was a prime offender."

A reluctant chuckle rippled through the crowd, and Derek could almost feel them sway, poised on the brink of uncertain seduction. "The boy's good," he whispered. "How old do you think he is? Twenty-seven, twenty-eight? Not bad for such a youngster . . ."

Mark shot him an annoyed look. "You had been part of the Guild for almost eight years by the time you were his age."

"Yes, but I didn't have the world in the palm of my hand."

"Nor does he."

"Yet," Derek countered shrewdly.

"The elimination of one man, however heinous he may appear," Andorian thundered, "is no solution to the greater problems that face us. 'What about Jhakharta?'

someone was astute enough to ask me. My point exactly! What about Jhakharta? Eliminate one, my friends, and another rises to his place. What guarantee do I have that Jhakharta will be better than Istarbion? None! What guarantee do I have that he will be worse? Based on experience, much indeed. So why would I betray you in that way, eliminating one risk only to let another, potentially greater, one take its place?"

"He has a point there," Derek observed.

Mark nodded.

"You have heard what they are saying," the rebel leader flared. "They are laying this at my door, and they are out for my blood. Yet why would I risk their wrath and my credibility in such a manner? My goal is to fight for your rights, my friends, to bring down the whole of the government if need be! Why risk my freedom, my life, for one futile strike?"

A rousing cheer met his words, but he held up one hand, restoring instant silence. "Yet think of it the other way around for a minute, if you will. I am a threat to the government. How better to eliminate me—to ensure their own survival—than to pin such a ridiculous charge on me? In short, I am being set up, my friends! So don't buy into their wicked lies and condemn me.

"For remember, if I had not scared someone, badly, they would not now be out for revenge!"

The roar of approval was almost deafening, drowning all sounds of dissension.

"Viva Andorian!"

"Our savior!" rang the cries.

Mark frowned. "This is getting more complicated by the minute. I no longer know whom to believe; I think Owen was right when he said this was no simple assignment."

"So what now?"

Mark grimaced. "I don't know. Talk to Owen, for a start. We promised to contact him when we arrived, and maybe we can pump him for more information. I know he tends to get a bit closemouthed about official business, but . . ."

"Quite. And then?"

"Your entertainment. Followed, I think, by a little reconnoiter of the Nhuras prison."

19

Crouched in the musty straw of her newest cell, trying to ignore the growing chill, Vera watched the day slowly draining from the grated window and waited for Pehndon to wake.

It had been an interminable vigil—the passage of time marked only by the slow fading of the light—but now, in the purplish haze of twilight, she sensed an ending to the tension which gnawed at her innards, making her stomach knot and roil like a nest of twisting serpents.

It had been bad enough earlier, in the first instants of her escape. With the auxiliary guards approaching down the corridor, she had bolted around a corner, intent on flight, when something had held her back. Maybe her training, or maybe just her innate need to know; but whatever it was, it had held her breathless around the bend, her breath sucked in and her ears cocked, listening to the lethargic guards as they scouted the empty hallway. She heard their footsteps pass her cell, double back; then she heard the murmur of their speculative voices.

"See anything wrong, Zharen?"

"No. Prisoner probably had another bloody nightmare, that's all. Hey, is everyone all right in there?"

"Cooee! Anyone home?"

Silence.

In a sudden moment of inspiration, Vera gave out a low sleeper's mumble.

An unpleasant ripple of laughter reached her ears, followed by, "Don't know why they waste our time like this. Come on, Teg, let's get back to the game."

They didn't bother to check the cell, never saw the bodies inside. Instead their footsteps retreated back up the corridor, and Vera let out her breath in a thin trickle of relief. Part of her felt almost sorry for them, knowing their tenure in the prison would be over the minute their laxity was discovered, but she was certainly not about to correct the error.

Nonetheless, the conversation alerted her to the advantages of staying in the vicinity, for that way she would know the instant her escape was discovered. Moreover, should her captors become aware of her flight, they would be likely to scout much farther afield, for no one who was remotely sane would suspect her of going to ground so close to her original cell. In fact, part of her began to wonder about the state of her own sanity as she contemplated the idea.

Of course, it was logical. An empty cell was the last place they'd look, no doubt figuring she'd had enough of incarceration to last her three lifetimes—which, of course, she had. But there was a door, two paces away, and it offered her refuge; she would be foolish to ignore it.

Yet despite all rationalizations, entering that cell, letting the heavy door slam shut behind her, was one of the hardest things she had ever done. Even though she had checked it several times—even though there was no possible way it could lock without a key—there was always the potential of magical seals. Not until she was actually inside, on the wrong end of that dreaded portal, could she be certain the door would ever open again.

As it was, she spent the next several minutes easing it open and shut, just to assure herself that it was indeed possible, and even now she sat with one hand resting lightly on its surface, ready to exit if she heard so much as the faintest whisper of a key brush the lock, or a muttered exhortation.

All it would take was one vigilant guard and she would be right back where she had started.

But so far she had remained undetected, and now night was falling. If she was any judge of her strength, Pehndon would be waking in an hour or two, summoning the guards, and if there was any justice in the world, surely there would be one among them she could waylay. For despite the fact that she held the keys, Pehndon's cell and the three dead, clothed bodies it contained were of no worldly use to her—not if she wanted to convince Pehndon she was still naked and at large. Not to mention that legions of hobgoblins couldn't have convinced her to set foot in that dank hole again.

But as fortune would have it, her chance came sooner, whistling down the hall about an hour past sunset, forcing her into a hasty change of plans.

Rising in silence and peering cautiously through the grate on the door, her face half lost in shadows, she beheld a lone guard striding cheerfully past her lair. He was of medium height and slender—at least compared to Pehndon's hulking bullies—and seemed about as perfect a match as she was likely to get. So, scraping her hair into some semblance of order and donning her most lower-class accent, she pressed her face to the grill and exclaimed loudly, "Oi!"

The guard halted in midwhistle and whirled, his face a study in confusion. With a secret grin, Vera swung open the cell door and sauntered forth in all her glory, launching immediately into an angry tirade.

"What right do you have, leaving me here like this while you go off and . . . oh." She let her voice trail off, then crossed her arms pettishly, her lower lip pouting in annoyance. "You're not Zharen."

"No, I'm . . . that is . . . what are you doing here?" the guard stammered.

She let the pout deepen. "Zharen and Teg, they brought me here. Smuggled me in for a little fun, they said, then off they go and disappear, leaving me ready and waiting with no one to entertain me." She indicated her naked body in disgust. "Now, how's that for courtesy?"

The poor lad flushed a vivid and rather blotchy scarlet, his eyes hopelessly trapped, and she gave a little shimmy which only served to compound the issue.

"Uh . . . do you want me to find them?" he hazarded at last.

"Well, they did pay, but . . ." She pushed one bare toe contemplatively into the floor, which had the added advantage of throwing her body into greater relief, and wriggled for a moment in indecision. Then, looking up with a ingratiating giggle, she let her eyes widen ingenuously. "I have an idea. Why don't *you* keep me company?"

"Me? But, I . . ."

"What's the matter, you shy?"

"No, but . . ."

"Well, then." She flaunted her hips. "We'll have a little party of our own."

The boy swallowed convulsively. "You sure?"

"Why not? I've been paid for; someone should enjoy it. And besides, I hate being ignored. So," she grinned, motioning him toward the door, "come on in, and I'll do you for a treat!"

After only the slightest of hesitations, his eyes nervously scanning the corridor, the guard followed her within. A swift chop to the neck dispatched him into unconsciousness; then, rubbing her palms together, Vera set about the assiduous task of stripping the body.

Unlike his compatriots, this one *was* armed, and she chuckled gleefully to herself as she tested the edge of his dagger against her thumb. Sharp and sweet, with a sheen like rippled silk. Poor innocent though he was, he kept his blades in exemplary condition. His clothing even fit her tolerably well, though the shirt was somewhat baggy and the pants needed to be cinched in a notch or two at the waist. His boots were likewise loose, but a bit of straw jammed in at the toes soon took care of that problem.

She belted on the dagger and surveyed her general appearance. Her lean body was fighting-fit, and the tough leather jerkin that passed for armor nicely concealed the curves of her breasts. Add a little bit of a swagger to her stride and, but for her hair, no one would take her for a woman.

Certainly they would never expect to find her masquerading among her own search party.

Still, a disguise was a disguise, and a necessity a necessity—and though her victim had seen fit to provide her with a rough helmet (really, more of an inverted tin bowl) under which she could tuck her locks, Vera was a perfectionist. There was no telling when a bluff might be called, and hers would be under fairly tight scrutiny. So sacrificing vanity to exigency, she drew her dagger and, with a faint, imperceptible sigh, let the first hank of her long, grey-streaked hair drop to the straw.

"Hey!" Pehndon shouted, his fists hammering an irate staccato against the cell door, his voice a chilly bark of command. "Guards! Is anybody out there? Get me out of here. Now!"

He had wakened face-down in the rancid straw with a heavy weight across his legs and a curious rat nibbling at the toes of his boots. Disgusted, he kicked the creature away, then heaved the burden off his limbs. His head ached intolerably, but he nonetheless couldn't repress a surge of anger as he sat up and examined the bodies of his cellmates. They were dead, and brutally so: one with his head caved in, one with his neck hanging limp and boneless, the third with his windpipe crushed to a bloody pulp. And, more tellingly, the Hawk was gone, and he was incarcerated in her place, her message chillingly clear.

He cursed then, viciously, fluently. So help him, he had underestimated the woman again, and once more she had seized the advantage. Not, of course, that it would make any difference to her trial; he already had her substitute ready, and he could sacrifice his accomplice quite cheerfully if he had to. No matter that she was loyal, that she had followed his every command without question. No matter, even, that she fancied herself in love with him; he'd certainly given her no cause to harbor *that* delusion. No, if the Hawk couldn't be found, his agent would carry out her masquerade to the death, assuming the Hawk's place at the scaffold whether she liked it or not. She was already becoming a bit of a drain, with her constant emotional demands; it would be a relief to be free of her.

And as for the Guild's thrice-cursed assassin, she had cost him too much already. He'd be cursed if he let her get away with another infraction. He'd hunt her into death tonight if necessary, just to make sure she couldn't foil yet another of his carefully laid plans.

So, "Guards!" he called again, renewing his pounding, and was finally rewarded by the sound of footsteps hastening to his aid. "Get me out of here immediately!"

There was a brief scuffle while the key was located, leaving Pehndon fuming behind the door, but eventually the lock was sprung, releasing him, and he looked around him in distaste. It was a ragged collection of guards who had answered his summons and who now stood fidgeting beneath his gaze, clearly hoping to divert his frigid wrath from their own hapless pates.

He stabbed a finger at random, choosing a victim.

"You. Yes, you, on the left. Go and fetch the warden. Now!"

With a squeak of muted terror, the man fled.

"And you, boy. Look at you! What right have you to look so sloppy?" Indeed, the guard's clothing hung on him like rags, his helmet stuck like a kettle atop his head. Granted the guards were somewhat eclectic in their dress, but still . . . There were standards to be maintained. "If you're determined to wear a helmet, then at least make sure you get a proper one. Now, remove that thing at once!"

"Sir?" The lad looked up, startled, with a flash of grey eyes—quickly veiled as Pehndon rapped imperiously on his headgear. Off came the offending article, revealing a crop of lank and greasy black hair, looking for all the world like it had been chopped off in the dark with a razor.

Pehndon suppressed a growl of exasperation. What was it about a crisis that always brought out the idiots? "Can't you even . . . ? Oh, never mind. Go bring me the gate-keepers, and hurry!"

The boy scampered.

Mouth pursed, Pehndon surveyed the rest of his troops. "Round up your fellows and bring them to me. I want every guard in this prison here in ten minutes flat! Understood?"

His barked commands must have carried weight, for shortly thereafter the entire complement of the prison guard, with the exception of the three dead brutes in the cell behind him, stood at attention, shifting restlessly on their feet. Crooking an imperious finger, he brought the gatekeepers forward.

"Has anyone—and I mean *anyone*—left the grounds since you've been on duty?"

They shook their heads sheepishly, denying involvement.

"No, sir," one said.

"We'd have seen 'em," replied the other.

"And you *did* lock the gates behind you when you left?"

They nodded, exhibiting the gate key.

"Well, that's something tangible, at least," Pehndon rejoined sarcastically. "Which means she can't have left the grounds—nor will she be able to without that key of yours. All right, all of you, split up and form teams. Search the prison. She must be here somewhere!"

But an hour later, they had turned up no trace of his assassin. Giving vent to an uncharacteristic fury, Pehndon pounded his fist violently against the wall, bruising his knuckles painfully on the stone.

"Where is she?" he raged, feeling the cracks spidering through his self-control. "She can't have just disappeared!"

"Maybe she got over the walls," suggested one of the guards—the sloppy one—brightly. Somehow the pot had reappeared on his head.

"Nonsense. The walls are unscalable," Pehndon growled. But the rest, inspired by their cohort's example, took up the chorus, gamely suggesting a series of impossible scenarios ranging from tunnels to levitation to sewage shafts, until Pehndon bellowed them into silence.

"Enough! You counted the prisoners?"

"Twice. There were thirteen."

Pehndon nodded. According to the prison records, the tally was correct. So what had happened? How had that blasted woman vanished?

And why couldn't he find her?

There had to be *something* he was missing, he knew that, but he couldn't put a finger on it. All that was left was a subtle, nagging feeling that he was missing some vital clue.

"All right," he finally capitulated. "We'll search the grounds. In the morning I'll hire a mage to do a tracking spell, but in the meantime let's see if we can find any signs of a physical trail. You"—he selected five guards at random from his left—"you go left out of the gate, and you"—five more from the right—"you go right. But please, *try* not to destroy the evidence. Can you manage that?"

They nodded somewhat doubtfully, and he turned to the gatekeepers. "Let them out, then, and try to make sure that no one else escapes." His voice was infinitely weary, but even as his search party went scampering off, he couldn't help adding in a muted bellow, "And, boy, *what did I tell you about that helmet?*"

The guard in question gave a startled bob and snatched the pot off his head before sprinting after his fellows.

Pehndon snorted. "Now, about those prisoners. There were twelve, you said, apart from our escapee?"

"No, thirteen," came the answer, glibly.

"Thirteen. Including the escapee?"

"Of course not. What are we, stupid? Who would count a missing prisoner? Thirteen withou . . ." And the warden's voice trailed off, his face pinching in disbelief as he realized his mistake. Fixating on the number, he had quite forgotten to take into account that one of the prisoners was now missing. There should have been twelve in the cells, and not thirteen.

"You idiots!" Pehndon shrilled. "Didn't you realize that was one too many?" Why had he assumed the guards could make the count? Why had he trusted them?

Why had he not caught the error himself?

He felt a sudden surge of panic, quickly quashed. No matter. Was he not Iaon Pehndon, the supreme planner? Had he not mastered every situation that bitch had thrown at him?

Of course he had, and he could bloody well do it now. There was no way the Hawk was getting the better of him!

A sudden chill swept him—freezing him, hardening his resolve. "She's here, do you understand me?" he said, his voice clipped and taut. "She's hiding in one of those cells, so go and get her!"

But all they found was a groggy and somewhat sheepish guard in an unlocked chamber, who cupped his hands about his genitals and asked plaintively if anyone had seen his clothing.

Among the missing items, it seemed, was a battered tin helmet.

And by then, of course, it was too late; the gates had been opened. The Hawk had disappeared, and her headgear with her.

20

"Well?" Derek demanded. "What now, my genius?"

Mark grimaced. His brother's cheerful whisper trailed through the shadows where they crouched in the lee of a darkened building.

They had contacted Owen that afternoon, and what a bloody waste of money that had been, Mark reflected—especially considering how much the mages had charged for the privilege. The old man had been less than revealing. Worse, he had been positively single-minded; the Falcon had never seen his Guildmaster look so distracted. After absentmindedly confirming their decision to scout the prison, he had offered them yet another assignment: for an extra two thousand marks they were to stop a rogue assassin, and when Mark objected—feeling his burdens grow greater, his resources stretched achingly thin— Owen turned a deaf ear to his protests.

"I need you, Mark. There's no one else I can send at this late date. Someone has to stop the girl!"

"What girl?"

"The Hawk's niece."

Mark paused at that; he hadn't even known the Hawk possessed a family, let alone a niece. "And what is the Hawk's niece doing in Ashkharon?"

"Chasing after her aunt, of course."

"You mean she's Guild-trained?"

"Well, Hawk-trained, at any rate," Owen responded whimsically, and Mark groaned. Just what he needed: some cocky youngster with an assassin complex, who probably knew more tricks of the trade than he did.

"She left less than a day behind you," Owen continued, "so she should be arriving in Nhuras in about a week. There may or may not be a young man with her. Please say you'll take the assignment?"

Privately wondering if he hadn't lost the few remaining shreds of his sanity, the Falcon had reluctantly agreed—which was why he now stood in the shadow of the Nhuras prison hoping he could spring the Hawk before her troublesome niece even became an issue. But the prison loomed like a sepulcher: imposing and impregnable, its high stone walls rising solidly into the darkness, its towers and turrets bristling against the sky. Behind it lapped the black waters of the Belapharion, denying any but a frontal assault, and across the broad courtyard, the massive, iron-strapped gates, flanked by their glowing globes of magelight, seemed to mock at him.

So, "Cursed if I know," he answered in response to Derek's question, and his brother grinned.

"Quite a fortress, isn't it? How many mages do you think they're planning to incarcerate?"

Mark snorted. "Several thousand, by the look of it. Why do I sense that we're about to lose four thousand marks?"

"What? Pessimism? From you?" the Hound teased.

"And do you have any idea how to get inside?" the Falcon countered.

"Nary a one."

"Well, then . . . Wait! What's that?"

Without warning, the vast, iron-bound gates swung ponderously open, spilling a ragged cluster of guards into the empty square. Armed with either torches or hand-held globes of verdant magelight, they hovered before the closing gates for a minute in indecision, then separated into two neat streams, stringing out along the walls. They seemed to be searching for something, their lights bobbing like erratic fireflies, washing the stones a vibrant, mottled chartreuse.

"What the blazes is going on?" the Falcon breathed.

"Cursed if I know," his brother replied. "Routine search, perhaps."

"For what?"

Derek shrugged.

Suddenly one of the lights along the right-hand wall winked out, and a shadowy figure split from the group, ghosting swiftly across the open court and toward the shelter of a nearby alley. Oddly, none of the others appeared to notice, absorbed as they were in surveying the rough paving of the court, the impenetrable walls. The figure darted into the alley's mouth and was swallowed from sight. A moment later, Mark heard a muffled clash, as if a metallic object had hit the rough paving of the cobbled streets.

"By Varia," he whispered, "I think we've just witnessed a jailbreak!"

"The Hawk?" Mark could hear the suppressed excitement in his brother's voice.

"It could be . . ." he began, but no sooner were the words out of his mouth than the prison gates swung open yet again and a new figure emerged, striding across the courtyard with a second cluster of guards hovering anxiously behind him.

"To me," he barked, his authoritative voice snapping back the searchers as if they were on a string. Mark could see him counting the winking lights, heard the volley of curses that erupted when he spotted only nine. "How could you let her escape?" he bellowed. "Which way did she go?"

The remaining guards stared blankly at him.

"Move!" Mark hissed, tugging his brother back into the shadows. "We have to find her before they do!"

But even as he spoke, he heard the bark of the tall man's voice behind him. "Fan out! Catch her!" he commanded, and the clatter of feet filled the court as the guards sprang into action, filtering into the surrounding streets and pounding toward the lurking assassins.

Mark broke into a run—his brother barely a handspan behind him—sprinting toward the alley into which he'd seen the figure disappear. As he turned up it in advance of the guards, his feet tangled in something that looked like a dented bowl, and he scooped it up almost automatically.

It was a battered tin helmet, its inside stained a dark and greasy black.

"What the blazes?" Derek demanded.

But, "No questions now," Mark responded, all too aware of the growing thunder of footsteps behind them. "Run!"

Single-minded, they tore down the alleyway in pursuit of the fleeing Hawk, but between the twisting streets and the relentless net of guards closing behind them, they were eventually driven to ground in the shelter of a broken stairway. There, crouched behind a pile of refuse in a well below street level—with only the rats and one drunken, oblivious old man for company—they listened to the sounds of the searchers go past, their voices echoing through the streets as they called back and forth to each other, retracing their ground.

After a while the voices faded, and then the footsteps. Eventually, when the streets echoed with silence, Derek turned to Mark and whispered, "It's too late now. We've lost her."

His brother sighed. "So much for our four thousand marks. Now all we can hope is that the guards have lost her too."

"You think?"

"There's always a chance. But we'll find out soon enough."

"How so?"

"Obvious, my lad: the trial starts tomorrow. If it's delayed, they've lost her. If not, we may yet have a chance to redeem ourselves!"

The streets were oddly empty at this early hour, the buildings loomed blackly over the twisting alleys, and somehow this was the last thing Vera had expected. It could not be more than two, maybe three, hours past sundown, and yet there was no one about, no convenient crowds for her to lose herself in. Granted, this was not the best of areas—real estate fronting the city prison could not be expected to go at a premium—but still she would have expected some activity, some bustle of life from within the rotting tenements. Yet instead there was nothing but the ragged rasp of her breathing, the ringing of her oversized boots on the cobblestones.

And worse, the boarded windows and shattered bricks seemed to catch and magnify every sound, until she was sure the echoes would draw the guards like a beacon. Even now she could hear the muted sounds of pursuit gaining on her, and that more than anything convinced her she had to go to ground. Running, she was a target; if she stopped and hid, the guards might pass her by. And surely there must be someplace among these winding streets that could shelter a fleeing assassin.

But where? Crudely padlocked doorways blocked the most obvious of escapes, and she was not familiar enough with the area to know the local bolt-holes. She could have picked the locks had she sufficient time, but even her lock picks were gone, confiscated by Pehndon and his conspirators.

Darting through the narrow alleys, pausing every now

and then to gauge the sounds of pursuit, she relied on her own innate sense of direction to keep her on as straight a course as possible, and gradually the darkened streets became more populous, the occasional gleam of candlelight winking palely from the shattered windows.

And it was this that proved her salvation: not the paltry candlelight but rather the small pockets of humanity they betokened—humanity who ate, breathed, bathed, and washed clothing. For as she rounded a corner, she beheld a sagging clothesline secured between the chimney pots of two opposing buildings. Hardly pausing to draw breath, she leaped for the drooping bottom and heard the knots creak and groan as they took her weight. Feeling the almost infinitesimal shift as the right-hand hitch began to give, she whipped her dagger from its sheath and sliced the rope, letting the momentum of the swing carry her partway up the wall of the left-hand building. Then, shifting her grip, she began to climb.

In the second-floor window, by the light of a single candle she saw a mother giving suck to a scrawny infant; the woman gaped at her stupidly as she passed. A floor above, an oblivious whore was entertaining a client, the man grunting and groaning beneath the mask of her indifferent face. Then the lip of the roof was before her. Grabbing it, she swung herself up—and none too soon. Below, she could hear the clatter of the guards going by, the urgent echo of their voices.

She waited a moment, until the footsteps faded, and sliced the rope from its mooring, knotting the resultant length about her waist. Then, launching into a run, she flew for the edge of the roof, letting the momentum carry her over the shadowed gap, landing as agile as a cat on the opposite side.

It was a dark night, the moon only the faintest of slivers in the sky, and the blackness hid her silhouette as she darted among the chimney pots, leaping from building to building as easily as if she ran a flat highway. She let this motion carry her a goodly distance from the searching guards, pausing every time she heard an echo of footsteps from below, then hunkered down in the lee of a roof to wait.

She didn't know how much time elapsed before she moved again—at one point she suspected herself of falling into a light slumber—but by the time she came back to consciousness, the streets were dark and quiet. Reknotting her rope around an overhanging cornice, she slid to the ground and began the painstaking task of weaving her way back toward civilization.

There were no signs of her pursuers as she finally merged into the more populous streets and blended into the nighttime crowds of Nhuras, trying to figure out her next move. Pehndon would carry on his trial without her, that much was certain, but interrupting those proceedings without concrete evidence would be suicide. Her previous judges may have been false, but their reactions to her accusations were likely to have been fairly standard, and if she was to prevail she would need to prove Pehndon's duplicity absolutely.

But how?

Andorian and Jhakharta were both in his pay. She could try to locate them and make them talk.

Or she could go to the Anvil.

Her judges had scoffed at that notion; but her judges, she now knew, were false, and there was something about Pehndon's smugness when he had boasted of it which rang true. So to the Anvil she would go, and when she had all the evidence against him that she could gather, she would return to Nhuras and expose him. Expose him for the traitorous fraud he was, and Andorian and Jhakharta with him.

There was, she reflected, only one problem. She was a marked woman now; she could no longer return to her hotel. And even if she could, all her possessions would likely be gone, seized by Pehndon and his bullies. She had no resources, no money. She had nothing but her wits, the clothes on her back, and the dagger sheathed at her waist. She could contact Owen, get him to forward her an advance, but for that she would need money to bribe the mages. Or she could turn to robbery, living for a while by the fruits of her dagger, until she had enough cash built up to finance an expedition to the desert.

Almost unerringly, her footsteps turned to the bazaar. Even at night there was bound to be ready cash there, and some way for her to garner it. But it was odd to see the place at night, with the merchants' stalls shut down and the bustling livestock gone. The food vendors still plied

their trade, but now there were other things for sale:
Dreamsmoke and curses; whores of all ages, sexes, and
levels of perversion. Men, perfumed with cloying un-
guents—their faces painted and their eyes outlined with
kohl—glided past her with a whisper of silken robes, mur-
muring invitations in low, seductive voices. Women with
whips and fighters' bodies strolled the deserted stalls and
aisles, muscles flexing beneath minuscule halters of
leather and iron. And, no, the livestock were not *all* gone,
Vera noticed after a bit. Some of those were even for sale
as well, and prowling among it all were the rogue assassins and renegade mages, the cutthroats and thieves.

And Absalom, sitting placidly on his blanket in the
shadowed alcove he had made his own, legs crossed and
single eye closed, washed in the dim glow of the lone
magelight he had mounted above his head.

She knelt before him, clearing her throat, and that eye
fluttered open, black as the night above them. He looked
startled for a moment as he took in her warrior's garb, and
then his mouth curved in a grin, revealing those cracked,
stained teeth in the midst of his filthy half beard.

"Ah, it's you," he said. "So tell me, did my amulet
work?"

"I don't know," she answered, in the same level tone.
"They took it from me before I had a chance to test it."

"Unfortunate. But I nonetheless see you are well versed
in the limits of illusory disguise. No amulet can penetrate
the depths of your deception, eh?" he observed, reaching
out his good hand and brushing it lightly against the short,
spiky fringes of her hair. His fingers came away shadowed with a greasy residue, which he exhibited with a
whimsical smile.

"Bootblack," she responded with an answering grin,
grateful again for the small vial she had found in the
guard's pocket, as well as for the presence of that ridiculous helmet, which had distracted Pehndon so effectively
that he had never even seen the face beneath it, still shadowed with his bully's bruises. "Sometimes I've found it's
best to hide in the open," she added.

"Wise of you." Less easily distracted than Pehndon,
Absalom's eye wandered over her hurts. "Someone's led
you a pretty dance, no?"

"Yes, but now it's my turn to lead. Tell me, what are you doing here so late?"

"Waiting for someone: you, I suspect."

"You were expecting me?"

He chuckled, a rusty wheeze. "In a sense." And when she raised an eyebrow, he continued, "You really did quite a horrendous job with your hair."

"I didn't have a mirror," she responded tightly, and he chuckled yet again.

"My secret?" he capitulated. "It's not precognition, if that's what you mean. I didn't know you were coming, but I did know that someone was. I get these flashes, you see—hazy visions, indistinct hints. I had one earlier; I thought about you. It seems I was correct."

"But why?"

"Who knows? They say that when you lose one sense, another grows to take its place. I've often suspected nature of whimsy, though, for it rewarded the loss of half my body with these annoying hints of fate." He paused then, adding, "There's someone looking for you, you know. Two men."

"Describe them," she commanded; and when he had complied, a slow smile curved her lips. "Well, I'll be buggered!" It seemed that Owen, bless the man, had sent the Hound and the Falcon to find her.

"Then you know them?"

"You could say that. If I'm right, then we're colleagues of a sort."

"Guild?"

She grinned. "If you know enough to ask that, then you know I cannot possibly answer."

In reply, his dark eye twinkled. "Never mind. Your lack of answer is response enough. How can I serve you, Domina?"

"My name is Vera, and I have no money. If you help me, you'll have to do it on commission and faith. I will pay you back, of course, but you'll have to front me the cash."

"Not a problem." Rummaging beneath his filthy blanket, he pulled forth a leather satchel and spilled a pile of gold at her feet. "And there's more where that came from," he continued, adding the pouch to the pile. "Will it be sufficient?"

She gaped. "But . . . how?"

He did her the courtesy of not misunderstanding. "I may not reside in the Mages Quarter, but that does not mean my services are unneeded. Besides, the bazaar, the clothes, the dirty blanket . . ." He gestured. "Convinced that I am poor and helpless as well as deformed, people often assume that I am desperate—and therefore likelier to charge them less."

"So you're rich?"

"I am a mage," he answered, as if that explained everything. As, indeed, it probably did.

"You're a scam artist!" she accused, laughing, and he saluted her with his mangled claw. "So you'll help me?"

"What I have is yours."

"Why?"

"Because you are an honorable woman. And because you will pay me back tenfold."

"You know this?"

"I sense it. Why, is it false?"

She laughed, then, all her old confidence restored. "Absalom, I will pay you back twentyfold if I can afford it!"

"So." He looked satisfied. "Shall I help you to find your friends?"

"No, they can wait; I have more important business at hand. What I really need is transportation. How are you at camel dealers?"

"Camel dealers?" His scarred face scrunched in confusion. "What need have you of camel dealers?"

"I need to take a trip—a rather lengthy one, I suspect—across the desert."

"So, camels . . . And a guide as well?"

"Most likely."

"Hmm." He considered. "Not a problem. I know a guide or two who owes me a favor. But why the desert?"

"Because, my faithful mage, we each have a destiny to fulfill—and mine summons me to the Anvil."

"The Anvil? And what, might I ask, is on the Anvil?"

She just grinned. "That, my dear Absalom, is precisely what I intend to discover!"

21

This is a travesty, thought Grahme Tortaluk as he watched the assassin's trial unfolding. He had been sitting here for three days now, in the catbird's seat, and each day brought him closer to an undefined sense of oppression. There she sat in the prisoner's box, calm and composed behind the shimmering curtain of her ward spell, looking—or so he assumed, since he could make out no more than a vague impression of her face behind the heavy restraint—for all the world like she was out for no more than a pleasant afternoon's stroll.

And swearing up and down that Andorian had hired her, without so much as a flicker registering on the truth spells.

It was impossible, that's what it was: patently impossible. Granted, he had never made Andorian swear that same oath under spell, but he trusted the man with everything he did and was. Andorian wouldn't betray him; Andorian wouldn't betray anyone. And especially not if it went against everything he had spent his whole life defending.

No, Tortaluk would swear under a truth spell more potent than this one that Jason was honest, that Jason would never betray the cause and his own rigid set of values.

So what, by all that was precious, was going on? And why did that pure, sky-blue halo above the assassin's head shine as unsullied as a summer day, without the faintest trace of scarlet shadowing her verity? He expected fire and blood and sunset skies, eating an acid hole in the air, and yet all he received was a cerulean as clear and deep as the sun-washed Belapharion, without even a hint of violet to mar its perfection.

Jason, help me, he thought. *I want to save you, but I*

don't know how. I don't know how to penetrate this web of lies and misdirections.

But there was no answer to his plea, only more droning of evidence, drowning his hero beneath an inexorable tide of untruth.

He didn't know how they had managed to stretch the trial out to three days, but somehow they had done it—presenting every conceivable bit of evidence, interviewing every possible witness before putting the assassin herself on the stand—doing their utmost to present the perfect case.

And cursed if they hadn't done it. If Grahme hadn't known better, he would almost have believed their claims himself.

Frightening, that—for him, for Jason, for everyone who had ever paid the slightest heed to their alliance. If someone had wanted them eliminated, they could hardly have chosen a more effective method than this.

"We have heard the evidence," the chief judge was saying, "and we have weighed all the facts. Granted, Malle Varis claims she was hired; granted, there is clear evidence of shared guilt. Nonetheless, that doesn't diminish the reality of the situation. Malle Varis admits to killing Guy Istarbion: a heinous act by anyone's standards. And her claims that she was merely a weapon, like an arrow or a knife, we find pointless—for unlike an insensate object, she has judgment and morals; she has the capacity to say no. She admits to murder, and there is no sophistry that can diminish that one obvious fact. Malle Varis is a murderer, and murder has its price. So we of this court pronounce her guilty, and sentence her to die by hanging, the execution to be carried out at noon tomorrow."

A buzzing broke out at that, and one lone, anguished cry of "No!" which echoed Grahme's desolate thoughts. In her box, the assassin straightened defiantly, tossing back her long, dark hair.

"And as for her accomplice, the noted rebel Jason Andorian, a second trial will commence to determine his guilt in the matter as soon as he is brought in for questioning. To this end, there will be a one-thousand-mark reward for anyone who can either locate him or provide us with information leading to his capture."

Grahme groaned, knowing he would have to rush to

Jason's side the minute the court was adjourned. From
this moment forth, the hunt was on; he could hear it the
eager, greedy voices buzzing around him.

"Then, if there is nothing more to be discussed ..."
And the judge looked pointedly at him, sitting prominently in the First Minister's box. In Jhakharta's seat, no
less. His nominal boss had shown a surprising reluctance
to attend the proceedings, claiming legislative duties that
Tortaluk knew were a sham. So here he was instead, the
official voice of the government. What a laugh. Like there
was anything he could really do to help. Reluctantly, he
shook his head.

The chief judge brought down his gavel with a bang,
sending an ominous echo winging through the high-
vaulted chamber. "Court dismissed," he declared, and that
was that.

"I can't believe this," exclaimed the Falcon in an undertone as he and his brother exited the noisy courtroom, filtering through a pack of speculative, excited gawkers
toward the nearest portal and down the crowded halls,
their conversation muted beneath the press of bodies.
"What a bloody nightmare!"

Derek flushed, still faintly ashamed of the involuntary
cry that had burst from him at the judge's verdict. Death
by hanging, and in under a day—and for the Hawk, no
less! Not surprising that he had shouted his denial like an
undisciplined child; he had felt Mark stiffen in shock
beside him, though he knew his brother was far too self-
contained to react visibly. But neither had his sibling said
anything of his outburst, almost as if his silence had con-
doned it, justified it—made it, in some way, right and
proper.

It was certainly an outrage that had to be expressed by
someone in that cold-blooded crowd, and neither the Falcon nor the Hawk would have done it. In fact, their fellow
assassin had done them proud with the degree of her dignity. She had remained straight-backed and poised, her
voice level and unemotional as she spoke her responses to
the accusing panel of her judges. He only wished that he
could have seen her face behind the obscuring ripple of
the ward spell. He had viewed the Hawk once from a distance, but he had long heard of her adamantine beauty and

regretted that the court could not have seen that visage, shining with all the wondrous composure that rang in every note of her perfect voice.

When they had dropped the ward spell to rechain her and escort her back to her cell, he had tried to catch her eye, to give her some sign that support was here. But she had turned away too quickly, and all he caught was a glimpse of a smooth cheek and a fall of dark hair before the crowds had swallowed her from sight.

"It's a cursed mess," Mark was saying, shoving bodily through the press toward the distant doors and the wash of sunshine and heat pouring in waves from the heart of Government Square. "First we lose her at the jail, and now we have less than a day to redeem ourselves! What have we done lately that fate is so against us?"

Knowing better than to answer a rhetorical question, Derek merely shrugged. "Should we contact Owen, do you think?"

Mark glowered at him. "What, are you insane? Why worry the old man? For that matter, why waste our time on a fool's errand when we have a rescue to plan and less than a day to do it?"

Knowing his brother's anger was directed more at the situation than at himself, Derek just nodded his agreement.

"We'll scout the territory tonight," the Falcon continued. "Plot our routes and weapons. And tomorrow we'll try once more. And if that, too, fails, we'll have plenty of time to figure out how to break the news to Owen."

Derek sighed as they emerged into the square and the river of bodies around them broke and scattered like an errant tide.

"Are you sure this is the best of ideas?" he said.

"And what else would you have us do? Give up?"

"No. But if we do succeed, I'd have Owen double our reward for excessive hazard and danger!"

Mark grinned and clapped him on the shoulder. "If we do succeed, my lad, I daresay Owen will be so pleased that he'll accede to whatever demands you may make."

"In that case, then," the Hound countered whimsically, "I'd better start compiling a list."

"And in the meantime, we need to figure out where the

hanging is taking place, and how exactly we can take full advantage of it."

Jason slammed his fist against the scarred and battered desktop, driving a splinter firmly into the heel of his hand. He could feel the bite of it like a tiny, acid sting, a symbol of his crumbling hold on life.

Even his furniture was turning against him.

"Curse it, Grahme! Not even a hint of scarlet?"

His agent shook his head mournfully, his long face drooping. "Not even a flicker. I'm sorry, Jason. As far as I could tell, she was telling the truth."

"And still swearing I hired her?"

Tortaluk nodded.

"Blast!" He dropped his eyes, picking idly at the thorn in his hand. "I don't understand it, Grahme."

"Nor do I," his companion responded, his voice beaten and helpless.

Even from behind his closed portal, Jason could hear the ominous silence that gripped the warehouse floor, the hushed, funereal voices, the muted, listless footsteps—and this, more than anything, galvanized him.

Hang it, Andorian, this is no time for silly hysterics or melodrama, he told himself sternly. *You're in this situation, now—no help for that—so deal with it!*

One problem at a time, that was the way to do it. Forget the weight of the burden, the length of the journey. One step at a time, one quantum of trouble per diem, that was the secret. After all, who else was there to do it? He was the rebel leader. *So lead them, blast you, Jason!*

Massaging the side of his hand, working the splinter loose from its mooring, he grasped the end of the thorn and tugged. It came away cleanly, a small bead of crimson welling in its place.

Obscurely glad that it hadn't broken off in the wound—that would have been one more omen than he could handle—he looked up with a reassuring grin, sticking the heel of his hand in his mouth and sucking the wound clean.

"Blffmm dss."

"What?"

"Blasted desk," he repeated more clearly, removing the offending appendage from his mouth and waving it in

Grahme's direction. "Oh, sit down, Tortaluk, and do stop hovering. I won't bite. I'm a firm believer in not hassling the messenger. Besides, we're bound to work something out eventually; I'm hardly planning to go out with the bathwater."

The First Minister's right-hand aide took a seat, grinning at his superior in obvious relief. *Back to square one,* Jason thought whimsically.

"Now, Grahme," he instructed. "Let's think about this. That assassin—what was her name, Malle . . . Varis? You say she was telling the truth?"

Tortaluk nodded.

"Or at least the truth as she perceived it," Jason elaborated, steepling his fingers. "But what if someone higher up was lying to her? What if she honestly *did* believe I hired her because someone told her I had? Or, conversely, what if Jason Andorian really did hire her?" He held up a hand, forestalling Grahme's reply. "Not me, but *a* Jason Andorian. How is she to know that it's not *the* Jason Andorian? After all, that is the logical conclusion."

Tortaluk's jaw dropped. "Bollocks! Do you think it's possible?"

"In this case, Grahme, I begin to believe that almost anything is possible."

"Still, that would have to be a pretty elaborate setup, to propagate a disguise of that nature."

"A tribute to my powers of heckling and persuasion, perhaps." Jason grinned ruefully. "Maybe I've finally gotten under somebody's skin. After all, how better to eliminate me?"

Grahme's face lit up. "That's just what I was thinking! At the trial, I mean."

"Indeed." Jason smiled wryly. "And while you were thinking, did you come up with any speculations as to who might be behind it?"

"One or two. Jason," Tortaluk hesitated, his brow furrowing, "do you remember what you were saying about Jhakharta, that someone must be paying him? Well, I think I have an idea who that may be."

"And who is that?"

"Iaon Pehndon."

"*Pehndon?* You mean the one who caught her? Why do you say that?"

"Because of Alphonse. After all his excitement about this new position, not sitting in on the trial seems a bit . . . uncharacteristic. I've never seen him so eager to delegate a public appearance before."

"Out of guilt, perhaps?"

"Or something. But right after Pehndon caught that assassin, I remember him talking to Alphonse, almost as if he were reassuring him. And . . . well, Pehndon was at that trial, and he did seem a lot more intent on the action than just an innocent bystander."

"He did catch the woman, after all."

"Yes, but . . ."

"You think it's more." Tortaluk nodded slowly. "Well, I trust your instincts, Grahme; otherwise, I wouldn't have put you in the center of the opposition." Suddenly Jason grinned. "Good work. At least we have a suspect; now all we need is a reason. So, how do you feel about a little office raid?"

"When? Tonight?" His agent's voice was eager, and Jason smiled.

"No, too much excitement. Let's wait until tomorrow, when the execution is over and our friend Pehndon feels a little safer. And if that doesn't work, we can always apply pressure to Jhakharta. If he's this uneasy now, he may well break in the future. It'll be risky, though."

"You can count on me; you know that."

"Good lad! So, what's the price on my head again?"

"A thousand."

Jason snorted loudly, tipping his chair back and resting his booted feet on the top of his desk. "I must admit, it does smack a bit of desperation. Someone must want me pretty badly."

"At that price," his agent countered, "I reckon *everybody* will be wanting you pretty badly!"

Jason laughed. There was a perfunctory rap on his door, then it swung open to reveal a familiar dark-eyed face.

"Afternoon, Tortaluk. How's the spy business? What were you discussing with such abandon? And what could possibly make anyone want you, Jason?"

"The price on my head," Jason responded with a grin. "Come in, Jeryn; take a seat." He waved his brother into the office. "Sorry the accommodations aren't better. I'm afraid Grahme's got the only decent chair."

Tortaluk made an attempt to rise, but Jeryn waved him back. "Don't be silly, Grahme. I'll be fine over here." And he grinned at Tortaluk with a smile that was an uncanny echo of his brother's. In fact, Jason reflected, he had often been told he shared a remarkable similarity with his younger brother, but he couldn't see it. Beyond the Andorian darkness of their southern blood—the copper skin, mahogany hair, and chocolate eyes—he could see nothing alike about them at all. In his mirror he saw a careworn face, prematurely aged by the pressures of running a rebel alliance, whereas in Jeryn's face he saw nothing but a carefree youth and, every so often, the sullen stubbornness of the younger child—inevitable, he supposed, in an orphan family where the children stuck together beyond the age of separation. To everyone else, he was Jason Andorian, rebel leader and occasional hero; to Jeryn, he was simply an annoying older sibling.

"So, how much *do* they want for your worthless hide?" Jeryn now teased, playing the bad boy darling of the rebel alliance, as Jason had always thought of him, with his usual impudent style. He pulled up a rickety stool from the office's back corner, its legs lashed together with belts of worn leather, and blew a cloud of dust off its seat before plunking himself down. The joints creaked ominously under his weight. "Still trying to kill me, I see."

Jason snorted, and Grahme made another futile attempt to abandon his chair.

"No, really, I'll be fine," Jeryn chuckled, rocking on his seat and causing the thing to creak all the more ominously. "If nothing else, I'll make a pretty crash going down, and distract all your dour flunkies out there. So, you haven't answered my question yet. How much?"

"One thousand," Jason admitted.

Jeryn whistled. "Blazes! I'm almost tempted to turn you in myself. Kidding, Grahme, kidding," he added as Tortaluk's face froze.

Jason threw a wad of paper at his brother's head. "Don't pay any attention to this scoundrel. His bark, as they say, is far worse than his bite. He's really quite civilized once you get to know him."

Jeryn stuck out his tongue in response. "So, what now?"

"I shall have to go underground, I suppose."

Jeryn's nose wrinkled in amusement. "And what outrageous disguise are you planning to use this time?"

Jason grinned. His reputation for outlandish costumes was well known among his fellow rebels, for he had long since learned that a truly eye-catching creation could successfully divert all attention from the person beneath, and his outré tastes in concealment had gotten him undetected through many a crowd in the past few years. But still, in this case, more subtlety was likely required. "I'm not quite sure yet," he temporized, "but I'll think of something."

"No doubt you will. Well, I'll let you boys get on with your conspiring. And Jason?"

"Yes?"

"Next time I see you, I firmly expect not to recognize you."

Jason and Tortaluk exchanged an amused look as he left, then set about the important business of planning their office raid.

22

Jen hadn't expected the voyage to pass so quickly. In fact, she was a bit startled to learn that it would shortly be coming to an end. But Granville had come to Thibault two days earlier, informing him of their arrival—as everyone came to Thibault these days, she thought somewhat pettishly. Unlike Jen, he had developed quite a daytime reputation among the crew and was heartily invited to join all the legitimate dart games and rat hunts (despite the sailors' bitter and somewhat baffled complaints that there were far too few of the latter on board): a fact which either irritated or delighted her, depending on the outcome of their midnight contests. If he won, she felt a sneaking hint of unfairness that he had gotten the extra practice; if she won, she couldn't quite conceal a certain smug triumph for not requiring it.

The fact that Thibault was often required to use his expertise to lose counted not at all; each of them knew that it took as much skill to throw a game convincingly as it did to win it. In fact, had the sailors bothered to keep track, they would have noticed that Thibault, reluctant to gamble with Jenifleur's money, ended up losing precisely as much as he had won—an exercise in mastery that made Jen glow with a certain secret pride.

For competition aside, they were a team—and besides, their challenges were becoming more closely matched by the day.

Over the weeks her nightly practices with Thibault had improved her skills until their abilities became virtually undistinguishable. They practiced with darts until they could each deliver a tightly packed bundle of death straight to the center of the target, and there were times when it was almost impossible to remove the missiles after, so tightly intermingled were their pinions. They also, to aid Thibault, practiced throwing the games and could hit any of the lesser divisions with the same accuracy as they could hit the center.

Knife throws followed, and they would further challenge each other by picking random spots on the wall and target so as not to become too accustomed to a single maneuver. And when that became too easy, they would add variations: running, left-handed, and even blindfolded.

They also practiced tumbling and hand-fighting, and one night when Jen had caught Thibault off guard and thrown him in a particularly ground-shaking fall, they were forced to huddle laughingly in the shadows until the sleepy and somewhat baffled cook had assured himself that nothing was amiss in his now silent kitchen.

Some nights Jen won, and some nights Thibault, but there was never much difference between them. And by the end of the voyage, Jen had to admit that the pull of her secret life had seduced her; she could easily have spent the next several months lost in the role.

Consequently, the prospect of facing the realities of Ashkharon and Vera's capture came as a rather unpleasant surprise, for she had almost forgotten the true purpose of her voyage. But ironically, it was the very role that subsumed her that also saved her, for beneath the guise of the prim Malle LeDoux, no one noticed the sudden hardening of her resolve, the mix of fear and determination that marked her first outing as—*face it, Jen*—rogue assassin.

Nonetheless, she wouldn't have been Jen if she hadn't felt some sort of illicit excitement at the prospect, a nervous eagerness that twisted her guts as she stood on deck with Thibault watching the domes and spires of Nhuras slip into view, glittering hard and golden beneath an implacable sky. An exotic scent of dust and spices seemed to rise from the bustling wharf, riding the drifting breeze to the ship, and Jen's fingers tightened around the rail.

"What are those?" Thibault breathed in awe, pointing a finger at the swell of the aureate domes.

"Mages Quarter, of course," laughed a passing sailor. "Who else would be careless enough to plaster their wealth all over their rooftops rather than keeping it safe in their pockets, where it belongs?"

Jen grinned. "See?" she whispered in an undertone.

"Broadening your horizons. Could you have seen this in Gavrone?" And when he shook his head, she added, "Regretting accompanying me now?"

"Don't know," her companion whispered in return. "Place looks peaceful enough, but I haven't seen you turn it on its head yet."

She kicked him.

"Ow." He grinned. "Watch yourself, *sister*, or you'll cost us another job with your high-and-mighty ways."

Jen snorted. "Gloat while you can, *Tomas*. You'll be back to suhdabhar soon."

He laughed and draped a brotherly arm around her shoulders. "So, any idea what to do once we arrive?" he asked seriously, beneath the companionable cover.

Characteristically she shook him off, though a part of her longed to lean into his comforting strength. "Not a clue," she responded lightly. "I suppose we'll just have to take it as it comes."

"Mmm," he nodded. "Then you'd better go pack, sister mine, seeing as we'll be arriving soon." And he gave her a little push toward her cabin, hastening her along with a playful pat to her rear.

Grinning beneath the outraged scowl of Malle LeDoux, she stalked away and busied herself with tidying her cabin and packing the rest of her possessions, leaving behind her the ultimate coup.

For staked neatly to the bottom of the desk drawer were thirty-five perfect rat pelts: the fruits of her shipboard labors—and incontrovertible proof that there was more to young Tomas LeDoux's haughty sister than any of the sailors had ever imagined.

And someone, she reflected with a grin, was going to make a tidy pile of cash from the captain when he turned them in. It was her own way of compensating the crew for her insufferable behavior as Malle LeDoux.

They disembarked a little before noon, with the sun burning fiercely overhead. Unaccustomed to such heat, Thibault could feel the drops of sweat beading off his brow and sliding down his neck as he advanced across the docks with the trunks balanced heavily on his shoulders. Ahead of him, he watched the subtle transformation as Jen morphed back into the grande dame, the certain confident tilt to her head that indicated she was once more back in her accustomed role.

But nonetheless, she couldn't hide the faint, eager bounce to her step as she moved through the throngs of merchants, sailors, and tourists that clogged the wharf, denied their accustomed siestas by the inevitable pull of the noontime tides. Seeing it, he couldn't suppress a certain shudder of dread, hoping that Vera would still be alive, that Jen's fires would not be quenched. Through no fault of her own, Jen had spent her life getting her way, and Thibault had no idea what would happen should she be denied. Himself, he had had a fair exposure to the vagaries of fate, the struggles of poverty and uncertainty; Jen had no such defenses.

Please, he thought, *let Vera be all right. Let everything go smoothly, and let us get out of Ashkharon with both life and limb intact.*

Turning, Jen grinned at him. "Blazes, but it's hot," she said, snatching her hat from her head and fanning herself with the brim. "You all right with those trunks?" And when he nodded, she added, "There should be carriages up ahead. We'll get one to take us to a good hotel, and then we can figure out what to do from there. But I'll tell you one thing: I can't wait to get out of this traveling costume; it's like wearing a bloody wool blanket!"

He chuckled and dropped one of the trunks, wiping his sleeve across his brow. "Advantages to being a suhdabhar," he countered. "One can dress for relative comfort."

She eyed his lightweight shirt and loose cotton trousers with envy. "Maybe we can both be suhdabhars, then."

"You?" He grinned. "Now wouldn't that be a sight?" Then, shouldering the trunk, he gestured her on, weaving his way across the redolent wharf in her wake.

But he had to admit the exchange cheered him. He perpetually underestimated Jen's toughness. Blueblood aristocrat she might be, raised in the lap of idle luxury, but somehow she never let it affect her. After all, look how well she had adjusted to life aboard that disreputable ship. Maybe she would be able to handle Ashkharon—in all its particulars.

Because, to be perfectly honest, if she didn't, then no one would. Thibault had no illusions as to his own powers of leadership; that was Jen's domain, and always had been. And more than half of his concern for her stemmed from the fact that, should she falter, he would be all but incapable of taking control.

The carriages occupied a smart line along one of the broad avenues running parallel to the wharf, and Jen hailed an open landau, settling herself in the back while Thibault lashed the trunks behind the wheels, then perched beside the driver.

"Where to, Domina?" the man asked, clucking up his matching horses.

"I'm not sure, I'm somewhat new to the area," Jen answered ingenuously, "so I'm rather relying on your directions. Tell me, where are the best hotels for a young lady traveling with her suhdabhar?"

The driver grinned. "Usually around Maltha Square in West Quarter, Domina."

"Then take us to Maltha Square. I'm sure we shall find something suitable there."

"Aye, Domina." The driver nodded companionably at Thibault and turned his steeds toward the heart of the city.

Thibault supposed his wide-eyed stare and unabashed gawking was in character for the naive young suhdabhar he was playing—but even if it weren't, he couldn't have stopped himself. In all his years, he had never seen anything like the exotic Nhuras, had never expected to see anything beyond the fields and forests of Hestia and Gavrone. As a child, he had been fascinated by Vera's tales of foreign lands, had made starry-eyed plans with Jen as to all the countries they would visit when they joined the Guild, but he had never imagined it would become a reality. He had never imagined he would actually sail the Belapharion, land on the desert shores of Ashkharon, rub shoulders with camels and traders and copper-skinned natives. Never imagined he would see the golden domes of the Mages Quarter looming above the sun-baked streets, smell the drying dung of the horses, camels, sheep, and goats which clogged the busy thoroughfares.

"First time in Nhuras?" the driver queried.

Thibault nodded. "Quite a place, isn't it?"

"Oh, you'll get used to it. A few days of heat and drought, and it'll seem more like an annoyance than an exotic paradise. Me, I've been living in Nhuras all my life, and your northern lands of green grass and trees sound more exotic to me than this ruddy oven. So tell me, which country are you from?"

"Hestia. But how did you know that I was from the north?"

"With that skin?" The driver laughed. "You look like a cup of skimmed milk, lad; no other place you could be from! A word of caution, though: watch yourself in this sun. It takes northerners funny sometimes." He sighed then and shook his head. "Hestia. Does it snow there? I've heard about snow . . ."

"Sometimes." Thibault grinned. "But snow, like the desert, is not all it's made out to be. Most of the time it's just cold, wet, and nasty."

The driver chuckled. "You here on business?"

"No, pleasure only. We're on tour."

"One final fling before I'm roped into a 'suitable' marriage," Jen piped up cheerfully from the back.

The driver grinned. "I like you, lad. You'll get on fine in old Nhuras, you and your mistress both. But I envy you, seeing the world at your age. Better than driving a cart through the same bloody streets, I can tell you."

"Mmm." Thibault frowned. "Are they always this crowded?" And indeed, the avenues seemed unseasonably packed with carts, bodies, and rickshaws, all swirling around them like an inexorable tide.

"Not usually, no." They turned a corner and found themselves locked in a jam, the street before them blocked with an unmoving wall of traffic. "Of course, I forgot," the driver added, smacking himself in the forehead. "It's the execution today, over in Central Square."

"What execution?" Jen's voice, high and somewhat panicked, rang out from the back seat, and Thibault felt his insides clench.

"The assassin's execution, of course—the one who killed First Minister Istarbion. I knew I should have taken another route."

"Jen . . ." Thibault began, but she wasn't listening.

"Where is Central Square?"

"Just ahead, Domina, but . . ."

"Wait here," she commanded. "And don't move!"

"Don't think I could," the driver began, but no one was listening. Thibault reached out and made an abortive grab, but it was too late. Jen was out of the carriage and pushing her way through the crowd, her skirts bunched in her fists and her hat falling abandoned down her back.

"Do as she said," Thibault seconded, then leaped out of the carriage after her, pursuing her bobbing head vainly through the press of bodies.

"Jen!" he cried again, reaching out a hand, but his fingers only slipped tantalizingly off her sleeve as she wrenched her arm away.

"No, Thibault, I have to go; that's Vera out there!" she exclaimed without a backward glance, and he could only follow her helplessly through a crowd which cursed and snarled at him as he dove headlong through its ranks.

23

Mark huddled, poised, atop one of the buildings flanking Central Square and watched the crowds gathering below. Somewhere down there was Derek, pressed close to the massive wooden scaffold that dominated the square. Mark tried to pick out his blond head, but if the Hound was doing his job, he would be invisible even to his brother. Instead, Mark's attempt to locate him was merely a desperate clutching at the familiar in the midst of the untenable.

For the odds were hundreds to one—thousands to one—against them. Two Guild assassins against a crowd the size of which the Falcon had not encountered in a long time. Bodies packed the square, pushing and jostling for the best position, and government troops patrolled the streets beyond. They would be lucky to escape with their lives, but they couldn't just abandon the Hawk. Not now, when they had one last chance to save her.

Mark readjusted his grip on his crossbow, wiping sweaty palms against his trousers. Briefly, he checked his collection of metal crossbow quarrels, his more conventional arrows flanked by the familiar curve of his lightweight bow. *One chance,* he told himself. *One cursed chance is all you've got, so you'd better make it a good one!*

The grapple and rope were coiled neatly at his feet, in readiness for his escape. Earlier that morning, when the dawn light was just breaking over the Belapharion, he had let himself partway down the side of the building, unlatching a window two stories below, then resetting it so that a swift blow from his foot would open it and allow him access to the room beyond—a room which he could only hope would be deserted since it faced the street and not the looming gallows.

He'd been up on this roof since late last night, before
the guards had taken up their patrols below. In many
ways, it was a pity he wasn't in a better mood to appreciate the view, for it was lovely indeed—if oddly sinister. It
seemed that all of Nhuras was stretched out at his feet,
from the fantastically glowing domes of the Mages Quarter to the vast smokestacks of the glass factories, vomiting
out fiery gouts against the horizon. It was strange to see
the balance of power so visibly depicted, the contrast between wealth and poverty which had so doomed his fellow assassin. Was it a balance that could ever be
redressed, or was every attempt as destined to failure as
the Hawk's?

Huddled in his cloak throughout the chill hours of the
dark, he had watched the stars glinting brightly overhead
while the globes of magelight winked up from below,
their golden light dancing with shadows and echoing with
the sound of industry as busy workers hammered and
sawed the gallows into place. Every so often he would
peer from the edge of the roof, watching the thing grow
like a sinister, skeletal giant, reaching out to snuff the
Hawk with its rigid, jutting crossbeam.

Shortly before dawn, the workers had vanished, extinguishing the magelights, and the square had been swallowed in a clinging half-light. Creeping to a far corner of
his rooftop, Mark had relieved himself in the shadow of a
wall, then returned to his vigil, eating a cold breakfast of
bread and cheese, followed by a few sips of stale water,
before lowering himself to fix the window.

The soldiers had showed up a few hours later, and he
had since remained frozen in place, watching the viewers
trickle into the square in clumps, then streams, then finally in masses—all forsaking their afternoon siestas for
the privilege of watching a genuine execution.

And, Mark thought grimly, if all went well, they would
be receiving more of an exhibition than they'd bargained
for. According to the plan, he would shoot the hangman
seconds before the execution, leaving Derek to leap up
and liberate the Hawk while he himself would hold back
pursuit and cover the Hound's escape with a rain of arrows. Then he would be off the roof and through the window below, blending back into the crowds before anyone
could stop him.

But even from here, he could see there were a million things that could go wrong.

Why me? Why Derek? he thought desperately. *And why now?* His brother was right: it wasn't worth a mere four thousand marks. Forty would be the fairer price. These were their lives, after all; if it hadn't been a matter of honor, he would have abandoned the project entirely.

No, get a grip, Mark, he told himself. *Panic will get you nowhere, nor will dire predictions. You have a job to do, so do it.* Derek would be down there, depending on his covering fire. He couldn't back out now.

It was this bloody vigil, he decided. If you spent enough time alone on a roof, you could start imagining all nature of things.

He could tell from the sun and the restless murmurs of the waiting crowd that it was nearing noon. The hangman, unaware that his own life was under sentence from above, mounted the platform, tugging on the rope, testing the lever that opened the trapdoor and allowed the body to drop. Then the crowd began to roar, opening a channel as the prisoner was escorted through their ranks.

At the sight, Mark felt a preternatural cool grip him and he became the Falcon once again, the swift and invisible killer swooping down from above.

The Hawk was writhing in her captors' grip, squirming like a greased eel as she struggled to get free. She appeared to be screaming something, her mouth a dark and urgent hole, but he couldn't make out the words above the roaring of the crowds. And soon even that was denied her as the guards gagged and wrestled her closer to the platform. Her frantic struggles increased, her loose, dark hair flying.

Somehow Mark would have expected more dignity from the Hawk—especially considering her uncanny poise at the trial—but then, he supposed, she had never been so close to her own mortality before. He didn't know how he would react were he in a similar position. Maybe he, too, would fight with an equal passion and denial.

They dragged her onto the platform and bound her limbs, looping the noose about her neck.

Mark raised the crossbow and braced it against the cornice of the roof, sighting down the shaft, his finger curling lightly about the trigger.

As the rope touched her skin, the Hawk went still, obviously realizing the futility of further struggle, but even from here he could see the cords standing out like bowstrings in her neck.

Derek, get ready, he willed. *Any minute now . . .*

The guards backed away, swallowed by the crowd, and the hangman approached, begging the ritual forgiveness. Peripherally, Mark was aware of a commotion in the crowd as a woman pushed forward, shouting frantically, but he didn't let it distract him.

The moment was at hand; he wouldn't get a better chance than this.

His finger closed around the trigger, sending the heavy bolt whizzing toward the black-clad hangman. Even as he reloaded, he could see his brother easing toward the edge of the platform.

He raised the crossbow again, aimed . . .

The first quarrel hit, taking the hangman through the back of the neck. He seized, swayed, and began to fall. Derek was advancing into position, one of the guards was starting to move . . .

Mark adjusted the crossbow, released a bolt at the new offender . . .

When chaos struck.

Mark had envisioned many things going wrong, but never this. This was the kind of fluke you gambled your career on, hoping against hope that it would never happen.

The black-clad hangman swayed, tottered. Sensing reprieve, the Hawk started. Alerted, the guard advanced, his trajectory paralleling the Hound's. Mark shot him and he stumbled, going down. His outflung hand caught the descending hangman about the ankles, throwing him off balance. The falling body changed course in midstream. Derek made a furtive grab, but it was too late. The hangman did his job after all, collapsing heavily across the trapdoor lever.

The bottom fell out of the platform and the Hawk descended, jerking to a ghastly halt at the end of her tether.

Mark was dimly aware of an anguished voice shrieking loudly above the crowd as the scene froze into a dreadful tableau: the Hound halfway up the platform, hand extended to catch the falling hangman, the Hawk dangling, twitching, on the end of her rope, the guards converging.

By all that's precious, Mark thought wildly, *I've just killed the Hawk!*

The driver's words had galvanized her. Ignoring Thibault, ignoring the crowds, Jen fought her way forward, clawing through the press of bloodthirsty humanity until she saw the opening of the square before her.

The gallows loomed, but she could make out no more of her aunt than a faraway impression of dark hair and a lithe body, bound into a noose an impossible distance from her. The hangman advanced, demanding forgiveness . . .

No, I don't forgive you, she thought fiercely. *Nor does the Hawk. We both of us curse the day you were born!*

Not that it was the hangman's fault, of course, but she was in no condition to think rationally. That was Vera up there, on the end of that tether.

She was unaware that she was yelling as she fought her way through the crowd.

And then the unspeakable happened: Owen's trained goons fouled up. For they had to be the ones loosing the bolt; her sensitive ears could hear the unmistakable twang of the crossbow above the savage howling of the crowd. For an instant she felt like cheering as the hangman went down, and then her cries changed to a horrified roar as he stumbled across the platform lever and her aunt went plunging to her death.

And there was not a thing she could do to stop it.

In the aftermath, with the guards converging on the platform and raking the rooftops with frantic eyes, she tried to fight her way through to the body, to see her aunt one last time, but the crowds swallowed up the funeral cart before she could even get close.

It was too much. Jhakharta's stomach rebelled. If he hadn't been First Minister, he would have been sick right then and there, and witnesses be hanged. But he was First Minister and he had his dignity to maintain; that was all that kept him from spewing out the foulness curdling his guts before the stunned masses.

He had managed to avoid the trial by dint of lying and a little hard work. While he appreciated his new position and Pehndon's efforts in his behalf, he didn't think he could sit though the travesty of Pehndon's trying the very assassin he had hired with his own paid mage presiding—a gift to the grateful and oblivious court. The hypocrisy of it sickened him.

How quickly would Pehndon turn on him if he ceased to be of use?

So he had dispatched his aide Tortaluk to the trial instead, and he didn't think anyone suspected the real reason behind his absence. After all, he was newly sworn in and had a lot of catching up to do, a lot of adjustment to the rigors of his new position.

Rigors, right. Some rigors. The work was all Pehndon's; he had no desire to interfere. All he had to do was get used to his new life of luxury, and a salary that tripled his previous income, Pehndon's bribes included. Istarbion's house was his: that luxurious estate, that land of green grass and peacocks he had coveted for so long. He had spent the first few weeks of his tenure exploring its grandiose halls and darkened byways, examining the illicit account books and lists of merchants who, for a price, would fulfill his every whim. He frolicked in the halls, nestled in the softness of feathered mattresses, and once—in a fit of childish glee—ran through the grounds in his nightshirt, rolling in the lush, fragrant grass beneath a silvery moon, whooping in glory.

There was a larder to satiate his culinary desires and a harem of willing women to satisfy everything else. It was no wonder Istarbion had become such a butterball; the public would howl if they knew half of what went on behind those imposing white gates!

And now it was his. Alphonse Jhakharta—the poor, backward child mocked in school and in the offices of his esteemed government colleagues, poor, slow Alphonse—had just left them all in the dust. Alphonse Jhakharta was now First Minister, and he offered a reverent thanks daily to Istarbion's pudgy soul for procuring him such a legacy.

He had to remember that now, as he watched Pehndon's assassin swinging at the end of her rope—or rather, not Pehndon's assassin, which made it all the worse. As he watched Ariadne DeBricassart twirling in the heat.

He doubted that any others had noticed—even if they had, on an off chance, invoked their amulets. If they even *had* amulets. Pehndon had been clever, keeping his assassin under ward spell throughout the trial so that her face was obscured behind a haze of force. No one would have suspected that she was not the real killer; not even Jhakharta himself had an inkling. Why cheat, after all?

But something must have happened to the real assassin, for this was not she. Oh, she looked close enough, with her long, dark hair and icy eyes, and those who had noticed a difference—amulet or no—might have merely put it down to the finery of the ball versus the grime of the courtroom and prison.

But not Jhakharta. He didn't even know what impulse had led him to activate his amulet—maybe just an obscure compunction to know what Pehndon was up to. Oh, she looked right enough as they dragged her to the gallows with the illusion of the true assassin laid over her features. But maybe it was something in the quality of her struggles that alerted him—for from his one view of her in the ballroom that night, she had seemed too poised to fight with such a frenzied will, shouting her denial to the heedless skies until the guards had silenced her.

He could still remember the wrenching clarity of her cries, spiraling up through the shimmering heat. "No," she wailed. "I am innocent; you have the wrong person!"

And so he activated the amulet and saw that she was right. The woman the guards were dragging so zealously to the scaffold was none other than Ariadne DeBricassart, rebel daughter of one of the lesser Ministers and one of Pehndon's willing accomplices.

Willing, that is, until now.

But he couldn't speak, couldn't protest, because that would queer the deal. Pehndon would turn on him and he would lose everything: all the luxuries of Istarbion's estate and lifestyle that he had worked so long to achieve.

So he let her hang—let an innocent woman go to the gallows so he could keep his lawn and his peacocks, his stables and willing women. So he could be First Minister.

And for the first time in his insignificant life, he began to wonder if it was really worth the cost.

24

It was a very sober Falcon who entered Jihahnad Park later that evening in search of his brother. They had arranged to meet beneath the statue, and it was with some trepidation that Mark passed through the gates enclosing the tiny patch of fading greenery and palms which lurked like a tapped-out oasis in the middle of the city. The sun was sinking, washing the heroic posture of the long-dead First Minister Armand Jihahn in a golden half-light, burnishing the tall figure that paced beneath it.

And until that figure turned his head and Mark saw the familiar glint of sunlight on blond hair, he hadn't even been certain that his brother still lived.

His heart hammering in a kind of giddy relief, he advanced, saying casually, "So, you made it out, I see."

"No thanks to you," Derek snapped. "Bright blue blazes, Mark, do you think you could have cut it any closer?" And he belied his tart words by sweeping his brother into a massive embrace, drawing startled looks from the passersby as he all but squeezed the breath out of him.

"Good to see you, too," the Falcon said dryly as his brother released him, "and I assure you, nothing that transpired today was by choice. What a ruddy nightmare! Shall we sit?" And he indicated a nearby bench, shadowed beneath a spray of dying palms.

Derek lowered himself onto the seat with a sigh. "Well, you wanted time to break the news to Owen," he said, "and now we've got it, so we'd better start thinking. How the blazes are we going to tell DeVeris that we inadvertently murdered the Hawk?"

"That I murdered the Hawk, you mean. It was none of your doing, Derek. Let me take the blame."

The Hound rounded on him furiously. "Hang it, Mark,

this is no time for your bloody heroics. Are we a team or not?"

"Yes, but . . ."

"Nothing! I'm not a child to be protected anymore, and I'm in this as deeply as you are. I could have broken that hangman's fall, but I didn't; I wasn't fast enough. So whose fault is it now?"

"Derek . . ."

"Curse it, Mark, I'm not going to argue with you! It was a stupid accident, that's all; it could have happened to anyone. It was only our blasted misfortune that it happened to *us*. Now we have to figure out what to do—and we need your brains for that, not your bloody self-flagellation!"

Mark grimaced. It was stupid to underestimate the Hound; every time he did, his brother came up with something new to surprise him. But in some ways he could understand Derek's anger. So, "Sorry. You're right," he said. "How long have you been waiting?"

"Nearly five hours. Where the blazes were you? I thought you were dead!"

"I bloody nearly was. I was locked in a supply closet."

"For five *hours*?"

Mark shrugged and was relieved to see his brother start to smile—a smile which soon developed into a bout of full-bellied laughter. And for the first time in this miserable day, he felt reality lift and click audibly as it settled into its accustomed groove.

It had been a ghastly afternoon. From the minute the guard collapsed, leaving Derek stranded on the platform, Mark knew that his time was limited. Even as he dropped his bow and snatched up the grapple, he could see the guards craning their necks, their frantic gazes sweeping the rooftops, their commanding voices ringing loudly across the babble of the stunned observers. Ducking, he scuttled to the far side of the roof, trying to keep his bobbing head below the cornice, and peered over the edge. In the street below, the guards were marshaling their forces, pouring into the building. Five flights up and they would reach him. The only way was to swing straight out over their heads and hope like fury they never looked up—or at least not in time to do anything about it.

He'd have to abandon his weapons, there was no help

for that. They were on the other side of the roof, too far away to retrieve. He cursed as he hooked the grapple to the cornice and unwound the rope. That was a bloody good bow, and expensive to boot; he didn't know where he would find another as fine.

But, *life or bow, Mark,* he chided himself firmly, measuring out the rope, then launching himself over the edge of the roof.

His coordinated swing took him feetfirst toward the window he had unlatched earlier.

"Heads up," a guard below him shouted. "There he goes!"

An arrow whistled by his ear, and then another. Then his boots went through the window slamming it open in a shower of glass. A startled worker, immune to the lure of the gallows, froze as he entered, her mouth forming a silent *O.* Mark released the rope and rolled, somersaulting through the deadly shards, and sprang to his feet all of two paces from her.

The poor woman never even had a chance. With one heavy hand he dispatched her into dreamland, then scooted out the door and down the hall. With the guards thundering toward him, the stairwell no longer offered escape, at least not in the traditional sense. So instead of darting down into their waiting arms, he went up, scuttling through the fourth floor hallway before going to ground in his closet. It was a typical supply room, lockable only from the outside—unless you happened to be skilled with a pair of picks. Hastily, he dropped the tumblers from the inside and hoped the obvious ruse would confound the guards.

And confound them it had, but it was a near thing. Their speculative voices outside the door had nearly stopped his heart; he had probably waited far longer than necessary before emerging, just to be certain.

"So, how did *you* get out?" he asked his brother, once he had related the tale.

Derek just grinned. "Played the fool, of course. 'I was only trying to help,' " he whined in his best lower-class accent, a vacuous expression on his face. " 'When I saw that man going down, what was I to do but try and grab him?' " He snorted. "As usual, they bought it. Oh, they detained me about an hour for questioning, but they didn't have anything on me and they knew it. Eventually they let me go and I came here. To wait for you."

"Sorry," Mark said again, helplessly.

His brother shrugged. "No help for it. So, shall we contact DeVeris?"

"I'd rather not, but I suppose we have no choice. Curse it, what in all the eighteen fishes are we going to tell him?"

The setting sun struck blinding glints from the golden domes as Mark and Derek passed beneath the arch of the intricately tooled gates and entered the Mages Quarter proper. The high portals cast an attenuated shadow along the street, dappling it in an elaborate pattern of light and shadow, and above them the sky glowed persimmon. A warm wind, scented with hibiscus from the hanging baskets that adorned each lamppost, rustled through the elaborate attire of the patrons who glided past on slippered feet.

As they strolled along the broad avenues, a fleet of lamplighters passed them, whispering mellifluous phrases to the golden globes of magelight mounted on the elegant wrought-iron poles. They flickered into life, casting a warm glow across the rich fronts of houses and Mageries, shops and boutiques—all bearing that same air of quiet, understated opulence which seemed to characterize every Mages Quarter from here to Nordevaria.

Even the paving stones were immaculate, flecked with mica that sparkled and glittered like diamonds beneath the dancing lights. And as the sky slowly deepened, the vibrant personalized displays that characterized each Magerie flickered into life, arching a mottled, glowing rainbow across the domed rooftops.

It was almost as if the bustle and stink of Nhuras were fathoms away, swallowed beneath the mages' touch, leaving none of life's more unsavory details to sully their haven.

"So, where shall we go?" Derek demanded.

"Somewhere inexpensive."

"In the Mages Quarter?" The Hound chuckled. "How about that?"

Mark followed his pointing finger to where a great crystalline dome rose, its joists stitched with winking balls of magelight. During the day, the vast glass panels mounted on the weblike skeleton would doubtless reflect the sky like a hundred mirrors, but now they seemed to trap the light from the arcade below, making the whole structure pulse and glow like some graceful, airborne jellyfish, rising against the dusky, purpling arch of the night.

Running away from either side of the dome were two glassed-in wings, their ceilings arched in delicate counterpoint to the swelling dome, the fanlike curves of their pillared supports bearing a rich crop of magelights depending like fruit from an overladen tree. The whole building could have passed for a greenhouse in colder climes, but here the sides of the arcade were open to the air, and the aisles harbored a bustle of patrons that nonetheless bore resemblance to hothouse flowers for the sheer variety and richness of their garb.

"Looks . . . exotic," Mark hazarded.

"But populous. And set up for precisely the kind of service we desire."

And indeed, glass carrels, their sides lightly frosted, were lined between the curving pillars, each bearing a mounted crystal. A trio of mages in gold-stitched robes of purple, midnight blue, and forest green circulated among the crowd, collecting money and activating links.

"Couldn't be more expensive than the last place we tried," Derek continued reasonably, "and maybe everyone comes here for a reason."

Mark's expression showed what he thought of that notion. This was the Mages Quarter, after all; fair prices were unlikely to be found anywhere within these walls. But this place would undoubtedly do as well—or as poorly—as any other, so he merely bent his steps toward the dome in silence.

As they entered the arcade, the blue-robed mage detached himself from his fellows and approached them, his face frozen in a semblance of haughty contempt.

"Can I help you, sirs?" he sneered, his voice as pinched and disdainful as his expression upon surveying their ragged clothing.

Mark masked a smile. "I rather hope so. Have you any private rooms?"

The mage's white eyebrows shot up into his hairline. "Private *rooms*?" he repeated.

Mark opened his purse, revealing a generous quantity

of copper bits in various denominations, liberally interspersed with the silver one-, five-, and ten-mark pieces
that served as barter for the common man. There was
even—and this seemed to impress the mage no end—a
handful of golden twenties and one rare and tantalizing
golden fifty (thrown in as a tease, for it was a coin only
the very, very rich could carry). The man's manner
thawed noticeably.

"Indeed, sirs, of *course* we have private rooms. If
you'll just follow me . . ."

Exchanging secret grins, Mark and Derek trailed him
from the arcade.

Under the light-stitched arch of the dome, a circular rotunda had been erected, lined with a ring of frosted-glass
booths. Two black-robed mages prowled the circumference, monitoring the shimmering ward spells that masked
the occupied chambers.

Their escort led them to one of the unspelled doors and
swung it open, gesturing them inside.

The ball mounted on this counter was far larger than
those in the outer carrels, and in addition the room
claimed a padded bench, a feature that was absent in the
more public spaces.

"You know the code of the exchange, I take it?" the
mage asked as Derek thumped down on the bench,
stretching his long legs out before him. Mark just nodded.
"Very well, gentlemen. Then let me just activate the
link; you can open the channel once the ward spell goes
into effect. Guaranteed privacy for our most discerning
customers, you know. And where will you be calling
tonight?"

"Hestia. Ceylonde."

The mage's eyes glittered. "Ah, long distance." He
rubbed his hands together, calculating. "That'll be fifty
marks."

Mark counted out the coins with a grimace. It was
cheaper than their previous call, but not by much; he laid
three of the bulky silver tens on the mage's outstretched
palm and then, relenting, a single golden twenty. Their
companion muttered a word and the coins vanished—no
doubt transported to some windowless, doorless vault,
deep underground and accessible only by magic.

Bloody mages.

The man made a brief pass over the ball, which then began to glow with a watery light. "You have ten minutes," he informed them curtly, his ingratiating manner disappearing along with the cash, "though of course you can always terminate before that. Don't forget to wait for the ward spell, and thank you for choosing the Consortium." And then he was gone, stepping over Derek's outstretched legs with a disapproving grunt, the frosted-glass door swinging shut behind him.

The brothers exchanged another grin as Derek drew up his legs. A shimmering curtain descended across the booth, rippling down over the walls and doors, cutting off the muffled clamor from the rotunda beyond as cleanly as if it had never existed.

"Well, I suppose we'd better get this over with," Mark sighed and coded the link. Owen's old operative name—Wolf—opened the Guild's private channel, and Vander's image popped up in the ball.

"Hang on, I'll get him," he said, before Mark could utter a greeting, and disappeared, only to be replaced a few moments later by Owen.

"Mark! What's up?" The Guildmaster seemed almost uncharacteristically hearty, and the Falcon winced. "Is Derek with you?"

"Right here," the Hound answered, swinging the bench around and taking a seat before the ball. Mark took the place beside him, and the two assassins stared at their Guildmaster in silence for a moment.

"Well, what's the matter with you two?" Owen demanded at last. "You look like you've just returned from a funeral."

"In a sense we have," Mark said quietly, and the Guildmaster froze. "I don't know quite how to put this, Owen, but . . ." He took a deep breath. "I think we've killed the Hawk."

There was a long moment of silence, then "You did *what*?" the Guildmaster bellowed.

Derek began to babble. "I swear to you, Owen, it was an accident, there was nothing either of us could do. The crowds were ridiculous, and no one expected that hangman to go down the way he did, and . . ."

"Wait. Hangman? What hangman?"

"At the execution, of course. The Hawk's execution."

"But . . . I don't understand! The Hawk was alive and well three days ago. She spoke to me! She'd gotten herself out of prison . . ."

"Well, they must have recaptured her," Mark said gently, "because the trial went on as scheduled. As did the execution."

The Guildmaster's face crumpled, the color draining from his skin until it resembled nothing so much as dry, faded parchment, stretched tautly over his bones. Mark had never seen him look so old. "You'd better tell me everything," he said at last.

Quietly, Mark related the whole story, from the witnessed jailbreak to the ghastly end, with the Hawk dangling motionless at the end of her rope.

Owen said nothing for a long time. Then, eventually, he seemed to gather his wits, though his voice was dull and listless. "I wish I could tell you it's over," he said, "but I'm afraid it's only going to get worse."

"How so?"

"The Hawk's niece—or had you forgotten?" The Guildmaster sighed heavily. "Oh, it's not your fault, I know that. I'm not blaming you. Far from it; you did everything you could. But I know the family, and that girl is not going to rest once she learns her aunt is gone. She's going to want revenge, and you two will have to stop her. I can't countenance letting this situation get any worse by having some non-Guild operative sabotaging it with her own crazy notions of justice. The Guild is *not* in the business of gratuitous revenge. Find her and stop her. Use whatever means it takes."

"Yes, Owen," Mark said glumly.

"Curse that Pehndon, anyway!" Derek exclaimed loudly into the silence. "If he hadn't caught her . . ."

Owen's head shot up, his skin taking on a hectic flush, his dark eyes glittering. *"What did you say?"*

"I said, Curses on Pehndon," Derek continued, oblivious to the Guildmaster's bark. "We wouldn't even be in this mess if he hadn't . . ."

Mark held up a warning hand, stemming his brother's tirade. His eyes bored into Owen's through the crystal. "Blast it, DeVeris, what do you know about Iaon Pehndon?"

Owen blinked. "What do *you* know?" he countered defensively.

"That he's a government Minister. And that he caught the Hawk."

"A government Minister? You must be mistaken; he's nothing of the kind! He's second-in-command of the bloody rebel alliance, the one who . . ." And the Guildmaster's voice trailed off abruptly.

"The one who what?" Mark demanded ominously.

"The one who hired her," Owen finished in a small voice.

The two men stared at each other in horror for a moment.

"Curse it, Owen, if you'd only told us . . ." Mark began, but he was interrupted by a spate of curses from his voluble Guildmaster.

"Get him," was all Owen said, when he had finished.

"But I thought the Guild wasn't in the business of gratuitous revenge," Mark countered dryly.

"It is now."

25

"Are you certain this is the best of ideas?"

Jen planted her hands on trousered hips and regarded her companion darkly. "We've been through this twenty times already, Thibault, and if you haven't been able to shift me yet, you're certainly not about to do so now!"

He gave what she thought of as one of his long-suffering sighs and desisted, but she could tell from his expression that he was far from happy.

Bugger it. He could be as miserable as he wanted; it wasn't going to alter her resolve. Vera was dead, and it was up to Jen to avenge her.

It didn't matter that she could almost understand his reluctance, had their positions been reversed. The building housing the main government offices looked about as impenetrable as a fortress with its thick stone walls and heavy embrasures, glowing faintly in the dim moonlight. And in a few minutes, she would be dangling, exposed on a line, halfway up its massive sides.

But business was business, she told herself firmly, and revenge was revenge. And since she had wanted to become an assassin so badly, she might as well get used to taking risks.

Earlier that afternoon, consumed with a cold fury in the face of Vera's murder, she had paced the elegant white carpets of her room at the Nhuras Arms, listening as Thibault recited the facts he had gleaned from the establishment's various servants. Istarbion had been assassinated during his annual public address, which was being magecast to the masses, and Minister Iaon Pehndon had captured the assassin—one Leonie Varis. Jen recognized the name as one her aunt had used on occasion—as she was coming out of the upstairs gallery from which the deed was perpetrated.

Minister Pehndon . . .

Her mind spun about the name, weighing it.

"He has to be involved," she snapped at last.

"Who does?"

"Pehndon."

"And how do you figure that?"

"Because he caught her, of course."

Thibault sighed, shifting uncomfortably from his perch on the elegant, gold-clothed chaise. "Jen," he said reasonably, trying to take her hands, "I know you're upset, but . . ."

She shoved him away. "I'm not upset, I'm bloody furious, and don't you dare condescend to me! I know what I'm talking about, Thibault, and I know my aunt. No one could catch Vera unless she wanted them to—or unless they set her up in the first place!"

"What are you saying?"

"I'm saying that Pehndon was likely more than an innocent bystander. I'm saying that he may have been involved. I'm saying that he probably betrayed her!"

"And if he did? What are you going to do about it?"

"Kill him, of course."

Thibault sighed again and rose, moving to the window as if infected with her restlessness. Throwing open the doors to the tiny balcony, he stood there for a moment in silence, his back to her, the gauzy drapes billowing, cloudlike, about his body. Behind him, she could see the palm-lined streets of Maltha Square, the elegant facade of the Desert Lion across the way. His shoulders were bunched with tension.

"Without proof?" he said at last.

"With ample proof, if I can get it."

"And just how do you propose to do that?"

"By breaking into his office, of course."

"Curse it, Jen." He whirled on her furiously. "You don't even know where his office *is*!"

"But I will in an hour."

"How?" he demanded, running his fingers through his hair and regarding her with something akin to desperation.

"By going to the government offices and demanding to speak to him on some pretense or other. I'm a lady of quality; my request won't be denied."

"And then?"

"I'll note which side of the building he's on, and which window is his. And later tonight, I'll scale the walls and do a little office raid."

"Looking for what?"

"Anything to link him to Vera." And she flounced onto the bed, ruffling the pale gold counterpane, and glared back at him defiantly.

There was a moment of silence, then it was Thibault who started pacing. She watched him stomp back and forth and felt a kind of sick dread growing within her. *Please, Thibault,* she thought. *Please . . .*

"Just like that?" he exclaimed at last. "Just break into his office like it was a quiet afternoon's stroll? Curse it, Jen . . ." And he gripped the bedposts, his knuckles white, his dark eyes flashing. "What about the guards? What about the security? Do you think they're just going to let you scale a government building because you *feel* like it?" And he loomed above her, shaking the bed just as she was sure he wanted to shake her, rattling some sense into her silly head. She had never seen him so angry; he was usually so placid and composed, like a sleepy bear. She'd forgotten what bears could be like when roused. "Bright blue blazes, girl, what in all the seven oceans could you be *thinking* about?"

She felt her eyes fill with foolish tears and blinked them away furiously. "Vera," she flared. "And as for the guards, I was rather hoping you could help me with that. But, if needs be, I can do it myself."

"With what?" he retorted and threw up his hands. "I came to Ashkharon to keep you out of bloody trouble, not immerse you farther in it!"

"And what makes you think that you're my bloody keeper?"

"Because, obviously, *someone* has to be!"

Their angry voices must have roused the staff, for at that moment they were interrupted by a tentative tap on the door. "Is everything all right in there, Domina?" someone called through the panels.

"Yes, fine," Jen said tightly, still glaring at Thibault. "Thank you."

There was a brief pause, as if whoever was on the opposite side was weighing her words, debating whether or not to interfere, and then she heard the footsteps retreating, carrying with them a little of her fury. It was almost as if their unknown visitor had punched a tiny hole in her self-righteousness, allowing some of her anger to escape.

She deflated visibly, laying a placating hand on Thibault's wrist; unlike her, he didn't try to shake it off. She could feel the warm breeze from the open window cooling her flushed cheeks. "I'm sorry, Thibault," she said, half determined, half pleading, "but I have to do this. Please try to understand. Vera was everything to me; I'd never be able to forgive myself if I couldn't do this one last thing for her. Something went dreadfully wrong here—I know it did—and I owe it to her to find the truth."

"And punish the offenders?" Thibault sounded infinitely weary, but his fury, like hers, had evaporated.

"Yes, if I can. I know it's stupid, I know it's illegal and I know it's dangerous, but . . ." She looked up briefly and met his eyes, then dropped her gaze. "I have to do it, and I need you, Thibault. I need your help. I don't want to have to do this alone."

She sensed more than saw him reach out for her, his arms offering a comforting haven, but she threw up her hands, eluding him.

"Don't, Thib," she pleaded. "If you're nice to me, I'm going to cry, and I can't afford to cry. I have to be angry, just for a while. Just until all this is over. Now I need to be alone for a bit. Come back in half an hour, if you're willing to help me, and we'll go over to Government Square. But for now . . ." Her voice broke, and she stuffed a fist against her mouth to keep from sobbing. Her hair hung in a curtain before her face, obscuring it, but she sensed that Thibault pulled away.

"I loved her, too, you know, Jen," he said softly as he opened the door. "I'll see you in half an hour." And closed it gently behind him.

She lay there for the next twenty-five minutes, staring up at the pale gold canopy and wondering how she had managed to make such a mess of her life.

They didn't mention the conversation again. When they met later it was all business, and—for Jen—brisk efficiency. But it was better that way; keeping busy occupied her, kept her mind off troublesome topics. It gave her a purpose.

And what she needed more than anything now was a purpose.

Dressed in her most elegant clothes, with Thibault a silent half step behind her, she infiltrated the government offices, posing as a charity worker to gain access to Pehndon. His aide, a rather thin and weaselly young man, took her assumed name and disappeared into Pehndon's office.

She leaned over to Thibault. "Know what side of the building we're on?"

He nodded silently, then moved away hastily as Pehndon's door opened and the aide reappeared, saying, "The Minister will see you now."

Jen nodded and rose. Then, turning as if in afterthought, she added imperiously, "Tomas?"

Thibault bobbed obligingly.

"I shan't be here for long, and it's too hot to walk to our next appointment. Why don't you go down and reserve a rickshaw for me?"

"Yes, Domina." He bobbed again and disappeared, and Jen masked a grin as she entered Pehndon's office.

She disliked the man on sight—he was imperious and coldly handsome—but she wasn't sure how much of that was attributable solely to her suspicions and how much was a genuine reaction to the Minister himself. Maybe it was only her assumed hatred that made his eyes seem as flat and cold as two chips of flint, his face carved of chilly granite. He rose to his lean, impressive height from behind his desk and held out a slim, well-manicured hand. It took all her ability to shake it affably.

"Domme Leonis," he said, apparently oblivious to the irony of the name Jen had chosen, a name which had earned her a sharp glance of reproach from Thibault when she had proffered it to the aide. "How may I help you?"

So she took the seat he offered and outlined her mendacious scheme, describing the supposed charity she represented, which took pledges in support of the factory orphans. She waited long enough to let Thibault reach the street, then rose from her chair as if impassioned by her subject, pacing the room in apparent restlessness as she spoke, treading a circuitous path to the window.

"Those of us who have so much should be generous to those who have so little, and especially those who have as little as these children. Some of them are barely infants, left abandoned by their families. It's so tragic." Reaching her destination, she rested her hands against the sill and stared out onto the square as if in contemplation of the horrors she was relating. Behind her, she was aware of Pehndon rotating in his chair to regard her.

"What with Andorian's constant accusations of government neglect in the running of the factories—nay, *involvement* in their mismanagement," she continued, her eyes scanning the square, "some in our organization thought that a show of government support, of government *contribution,* would be a valuable token of commitment to these people." And she raised a hand idly, as if brushing a stray strand of hair from her face.

Down below, Thibault, sensing her movement, finally caught her eye and nodded once, briefly, in return.

She whirled from the window then, catching Pehndon's hands passionately within her own and momentarily startling him from his almost inhuman composure.

"What can I put you down for, Minister?" she exclaimed, pressing the captured bundle to her bosom.

An almost imperceptible flicker of distaste crossed the Minister's features, but he pulled away with commendable dignity and named a figure.

Generous, considering.

Blood money, she thought whimsically, as she withdrew with expressions of profound gratitude and rejoined Thibault in the square.

"Did you get it?"

He nodded. "Third floor, three from the right."

"Brilliant!"

Which was how she stood here now, in the shadowed hours past midnight, wrapped in cloak and hood and lurking in the lee of the government complex, staring up at Pehndon's window.

It was dark and deserted, as was the rest of the building, the blank glass shining faintly in the pale moonlight. In fact, the only activity in the square came from the few guards who lounged in doorways and patrolled the inner perimeters—to prevent people like her from gaining entry, she supposed.

Well, not tonight. With a faint tug on Thibault's sleeve, she drew him back from the brink of the square and toward the outer streets.

There was, she knew, a similar patrol around the outer perimeter, but with their more limited visibility—as each, of necessity, could see the length of only one street—she knew her chances of avoiding detection were better. So she had chosen to scale the back of the building, at least for the initial ascent. But as there was also a greater chance that the doors rather than the windows would be trip-spelled, she knew it was wisest not to broach Pehndon's door until the last minute—when she was on her way out and thus more likely to escape whatever alarms might be present.

It would be truly tragic to have her mission aborted before it had even begun.

But that, of course, meant entering Pehndon's office though the window—a window which fronted the square and a passel of guards with no visible hindrance to spotting and stopping a rogue assassin dangling above them on a line.

"Are you sure you want to go through with this?" Thibault whispered again as they circled toward the back of the building, carefully avoiding the patrols.

"Of course I'm sure. After all, you probably have the more dangerous part."

"Me?" He sounded incredulous.

"Well, you have to distract the guards. That puts you rather in the line of fire, doesn't it?"

"You're crazy, do you know that?"

"Oh, come on, Thib. I love hanging three stories above the street!"

He just snorted.

She pulled him down a shadowed alley which opened onto the back of the main government building, but he stopped her halfway down its length, his hand on her arm. And when she tilted her head to look up at him, she saw his face still and serious in the pale moonlight. "Are you scared?"

"Of course I'm scared," she responded lightly. "I'm stubborn, not stupid. But I also know that I have to do this." And when he nodded, she added, "But I'm also glad I don't have to do it alone. Thanks again, Thibault."

He just shrugged; she couldn't tell from his expression whether he was flushing. "It's the least I could do. I promised your aunt," and his voice cracked momentarily, "I promised I'd look out for you, and I'd be pretty remiss if I abandoned you now."

"Well," she said, "fortunately we have one or two advantages on our side."

"Such as?"

She pulled two tiny buttons from her sleeve, each mounted with a post and a backing, and handed one to Thibault with a flourish. She followed that by producing two curved bits of wire from her pocket, each with a dangling droplet on one end.

"There, what do you think of that?" she declared, and grinned as Thibault gaped.

"Audio links? Where in tarnation did you get *those*?"

"Vera's box," she responded smugly. "So be careful not to lose them; they cost her a bloody fortune!"

Thibault whistled and hooked the wire around his ear, letting the droplet hang, hidden, just behind his right earlobe. The button he fastened to his cuff. "How does it work?"

"Owen DeVeris sucks eggs."

"*What?*"

"Vera's bizarre sense of humor," she clarified, forcing a smile. "They're on now. Try them if you like." And she hooked her own earpiece on, fastening the button to her collar. "Hear me?" she breathed, turning her head and whispering into her shoulder.

"Yes . . ." His awed voice buzzed tinnily behind her earlobe. Then, as something suddenly seemed to occur to him, he turned and hissed incredulously, "How long have you been picking Vera's locks?"

She grinned at the dual echo of his voice, heard both in real time and in amplification. "Two years," she responded.

"But aren't all the locks on Vera's private boxes booby-trapped?"

"Of course they are. It was blasted difficult, too. Took me five years to learn to disable the bloody things. But once you know how to set a trap, you know how to disarm them—and what Vera didn't teach me I learned through trial and error. 'Raw eggs' turns the volume up, 'boiled eggs' turns it down, and if the thing should fall into enemy hands, 'just kidding' turns it off." And as she said the words, she heard the faint after-echo of her breathing leave her ear.

"Owen DeVeris sucks eggs," Thibault said gamely, returning the unit to life.

She grinned and patted his hand. "That's the spirit. Now, shall we do it?"

26

They left the alley under cover of darkness. On the back steps of the government headquarters, two guards were sharing a smoke and a drink; they looked up as Jen and Thibault approached but had no time to react before the two clubbed them into unconsciousness. Then Thibault dragged the bodies into the alley and set about trussing them while Jen got her grapple and tossed it toward the roof.

It caught over the cornice with the faintest of clicks, and she tugged briefly on the line before shedding her cloak, adjusting the roll of tools about her waist, and mounting the side of the building.

"Looking good." Thibault's voice buzzed encouragingly in her ear. "All clear down here."

She acknowledged this with a grunt as she passed the fourth-floor windows, and shortly thereafter she grasped the cornice and pulled herself over the top.

Before her stretched the flat plain of the rooftop and a vast arch of starry sky.

"I'm up," she whispered, detaching the grapple and reeling up the rope with a silken whisper. "Progressing to the other side now."

"Hearing and following," Thibault acknowledged. "I'm heading for the square. Hang tight."

"Planning on it," she responded. "Planning on it."

She heard his ghost of a chuckle as she wove across the roof at a crouch, then knelt and peered over its opposite side.

The paving stones of the square seemed impossibly far away, though rationally she knew she was no higher than the roof of Vera's manor. But somehow it seemed worse. Maybe it was just the unyielding stone that troubled her; Vera's lush lawn had always had a springy look, despite the fact that it was unlikely to offer any more cushion than these cold flagstones. Or maybe it was simply the knowledge that this time counted, that it was no longer some amusing game.

She swallowed against a sudden knot of nervousness and distracted herself by briefing Thibault.

"Three guards on the central court, and two more in the porticoes of the courthouse. One smoking on the council steps across the way. No one seems to be at the administrative offices. I guess they figure the junior flunkies' papers aren't worth protecting. I can't see if anyone's on the main stairs from here."

"Got you covered," came the whispered reply. "There are two, but they've got their backs to you. With any luck they won't look up, but try not to make any noise going down."

Jen just snorted.

"I'm going to aim for the council," Thibault continued. "I'll try to pull the guards off the courthouse and distract the ones in the courtyard. With any luck, your two will be too riveted to worry about human spiders."

"What are you planning to do, strip?"

She could hear the grin in Thibault's voice. "You never know; I just might."

"You?" she chuckled. "That'll be the day!"

"Nonetheless." His voice echoed in her ears. "You've given me an idea. Look out below; here I come."

She counted three windows from the left edge of the roof and hooked in her grapple, tying one end of the rope to her waist and coiling the remainder on the cornice. Then, sliding the appropriate picks into the outermost pockets of her waist roll, she whispered, "Go!"

A few moments later, the sound of slurred, drunken, and rather off-key singing reached her ears and echoed beneath her lobe as Thibault staggered into the square. He had appropriated the liquor bottle from the back-door guards and had apparently splashed it liberally about his person, for she could see two of the courtyard guards reeling back in disgust, hear their revolted mutters.

"Drunk as a gutter whore."

"Someone get him out of here, all right?"

Thibault just laughed and waved his bottle, the liquid

sloshing loudly through the audio link and giving Jen the sudden, uncanny impression of being on the ocean.

She'd have to warn him about that next time.

He let forth another burst of song, then stopped midway through and launched into an impassioned, if somewhat rambling, tirade.

"See this? See this building?" he slurred, swaying and pointing. "Council hall. Laws made here. Laws!" He snorted in sodden disgust. "What kind of laws, I ask you? What poxy kind of laws?"

Jen hoisted herself silently to the top of the cornice, crouching on its narrow margin and waiting to drop. Below, the two courthouse guards came erect, moving slowly along the colonnade toward Thibault. The three courtyard guards were likewise converging, and the one on the council steps had stubbed out his cigarette and was trying to take Thibault by one wildly waving arm. "Don't take on so," he was saying. "Wouldn't you rather just go home and go to bed?"

Swallowing against another spasm of nervousness, Jen muttered, "Going down now," into the audio link at her shoulder. "So you'd better cursed well keep 'em occupied!"

In response, Thibault's tirade abruptly increased in volume as she eased herself over the edge of the roof and began to drop, lowering herself silently hand over hand down the massive facade.

"What bed?" Thibault declaimed. With her back to him, she was apprised of his progress only by the sound of his voice. "Poxy laws cost me my poxy bed! My poxy house, too. My poxy brother's life."

Fifth floor, and all was well.

"Sir, we appreciate your position, but . . ."

"I piss on your poxy laws," Thibault continued. "I piss on 'em, do you hear me? Piss on 'em!"

"Sir, you can't do that here," one of the scandalized guards was saying.

"Don't tell me what I can do."

Fourth floor . . .

"Sir, put that away right now!"

Jen stiffened. By all that was precious, he wasn't going to . . .

A loud liquid gush suddenly fountained through her ears, and she quashed the beginnings of a hysterical giggle.

"Piss on 'em!" Thibault repeated, suiting deed to phrase.

"Sir, come back here!" called another guard as a patter of frantic footsteps filled her ears, punctuated by Thibault's riotous calls of "Piss on 'em, piss on 'em" and intermittent spurts of liquid washing loudly through her audio link.

In some ways it was profoundly embarrassing, putting her a little closer to Thibault than she was prepared to get, but in other ways she found it absolutely hilarious.

Then Pehndon's window was before her and all thoughts of Thibault vanished into profound silence, almost addictive in the sheer quality of its depth and brilliance, as if the world had suddenly gained an added, and immensely tactile, dimension. She looped the slack of the rope about her waist and tied it in a slipknot, leaning back against its support as she squatted on the narrow ledge and slid out her picks, jimmying the window lock, then easing the frame open. She was vaguely aware of more cries and a muffled thud behind her, accompanied by a shattering of glass and an outraged shout, as if a very large body had suddenly hit the ground.

The audio link released an outraged squeal and then a loud, dreadful grinding that raised the hairs on the back of her neck.

"Curse it, Thibault . . ."

She released the slip of the knot around her waist and tumbled through the window. Then, reaching out, she grasped the trailing rope and flipped the grapple free, catching it in one outstretched hand as it plummeted to earth.

"In," she whispered, easing the window shut. Then, "You okay down there?"

Her words were echoed a moment later by the guards.

"Fine," came the clear-edged whisper into her audio link, and then "Fine, fine," louder, in slurred response to the guards.

"Then get out of there, you great lunk, before they toss you in jail for disturbing the peace. I'm switching off now. And thanks; you engineer a great disturbance. I'll work with you anytime—at least if you promise not to do your private business in my ear anymore!"

"Jen . . ." A frantic whisper.

"You're brilliant. I love you. Just kidding," she added

with a laugh as the link went silent. Then reaching into
the roll at her waist, she pulled forth one of the small
portable globes of magelight, activated it, then picked the
lock on the top drawer of Pehndon's desk and began to
riffle through its contents.

"Evening, Johan. Quiet night?"

"Mmm, one rather obnoxious drunk. Fell on Mikel, but
Adzan and Hadri managed to hustle him off. Otherwise,
nothing to write home about. You're here late, sir."

Tortaluk swallowed against a residual nervousness and
smiled. "Forgot some papers I was supposed to take
home, so I thought I'd just come in and work for a bit. I
promised the First Minister I'd have some figures for him
by morning, and I didn't have a chance to do them today.
Can you disarm the system for a bit so I don't set off all
the bloody alarms?"

"No trouble. Just let me know when you leave so I can
reset it. Blazes, sir, but I can't say I envy you, working at
this hour."

"Believe me, Johan, I don't envy me, either. I shouldn't
be more than an hour, though, so . . ."

Johan waved him forward, and he mounted the stairs,
his footsteps echoing hollowly in the deserted marble
stairwell. The place had an eerie, skeletal feel under the
perpetual glow of the magelights, untenanted by the bustle
of warm flesh which swarmed about it by day like maggots over a rotting corpse. Now the corridors were cool
and deserted, as if long petrified beneath an eon of sun and
sand, untouched by all but the eternal desert. He could almost hear the dry sand blowing.

Nonsense, Grahme, he told himself sternly. *You're letting the pressures of the job get to you. Now get your head
out of the clouds and your mind down to business.*

But still the endless echoes of his footsteps seemed to
ring in his ears like the slow passage of history.

He climbed past his own second-floor office and
emerged into the third floor corridor, which stretched
away in silent seclusion beneath the pale magelight. Even
his breathing seemed to echo unnaturally loudly; he wondered that Johan couldn't hear him, couldn't know that it
wasn't his own office he sought.

But gathering his courage, he paused before Pehndon's

door and took a deep breath before inserting the two twisted bits of wire he had procured earlier into the lock.

He was woefully out of practice, and it took several agonizing seconds before the lock gave and he stepped forward into the unrelenting darkness.

Jen had been in the midst of perusing some very interesting papers indeed when she first heard the footsteps approaching down the corridor. Was it merely a random patrol, or had the faint greenish cast of her magelight, glinting through the darkened window, summoned some curious guard? No matter; silently she eased the floor safe shut and extinguished the light, ghosting to the wall. She pressed herself like a statue against the doorjamb, her heart beating an anxious tattoo as the footsteps paused outside the door and she heard the sound of something being inserted in the lock.

They've found me, she thought in a panic and was about to reactivate her link with Thibault when the sound resolved itself into a fumbled clicking.

Not a key, then; not someone who belonged, but rather a fairly inept thief. And if someone else was raiding Pehndon's office, then this was someone that she very much wanted to meet.

That is, if only she could keep the upper hand.

Slowly she slipped one of her daggers from its sheath and held it poised before her, the blade glinting silver in the faint moonlight. The door swung open, closing over her hiding place, and then retreated again as it was eased silently shut, leaving a man blinking in the darkness, blinded by the light from the corridor beyond.

In the brief moments while his eyes adjusted, she surveyed him keenly. He was tall and lanky, with a long, narrow face and drooping mustache that gave him rather the look of a dyspeptic horse. But there was nonetheless a lively glitter to his eyes that hinted at an unrevealed intelligence.

She grinned and advanced.

Grahme stifled a gasp as he felt the body close behind him, the cold kiss of steel against his throat.

"Who are you?" said a voice, a husky whisper. "What are you doing here?" He could tell neither age nor sex from its muffled tones, but the body against his felt lithe and youthful.

How much do I say? Shall I bluff it out? After all, the fact that his assailant was masked in shadows, threatening him with naked steel, implied that neither of them was quite where he belonged—an impression that was only augmented by the high, rapid pulse that beat against his shoulder.

But nervous or no, his assailant never allowed the knife to waver from its steady press against his jugular, so he decided to gamble with the truth.

"My name's Grahme Tortaluk, and I'm aide to First Minister Alphonse Jhakharta," he responded, his hand easing almost imperceptibly toward his own blade.

"And what are you doing here at this hour?" the sexless voice repeated.

"Searching Pehndon's office."

"Why?"

There was a flurry of movement. He lunged for the hilt of his dagger, only to find the sheath empty beneath his questing fingers.

"Looking for this?" his assailant inquired, waving his appropriated weapon beneath his nose.

"But . . . how?" Grahme began, and could sense the answering grin in that mysterious voice.

"Never mind for now. Just answer the question. What do you want with Iaon Pehndon?"

Grahme deflated. "Information."

"Of what nature?"

"Of a highly sensitive nature. I believe that Pehndon was more involved with the assassin's arrest that he cares to admit; I was looking for proof."

"Why?"

"Because someone I know is curious."

"And who might that be?"

He took a gamble, hoping that an interest in Pehndon betokened support of the rebel alliance. "Jason Andorian," he answered.

To his horror the dagger tightened, making him draw a panicked breath. "*That* traitor? But he *hired* Ve . . . I mean . . . the assassin!"

"No, I swear to you, he's innocent; he's been set up!

That's why I'm here; I'm looking for evidence that could save him."

"And here I thought you worked for the First Minister."

"I do," he admitted.

The dagger eased a fraction. "So you're a double agent? Better. Perhaps we can be of use to each other then. Besides, I want to talk to this Andorian."

"Why? To turn him in?"

The figure laughed and lowered the dagger. "To determine the truth. To pledge him my help if he's innocent. Hullabaloo."

A verdant magelight flared into existence, and he turned with surprise to find himself facing an extraordinarily beautiful young girl who looked to be no more than twenty. She was dressed in a sleeveless shirt and a pair of men's breeches and grinned as she sheathed her dagger, then thrust his appropriated weapon through her belt.

"Since we are both on a quest for the truth," she said— and her voice, though louder, still held its husky undertones—"then maybe we can be of use to each other. Start searching, and tell me what you find."

"And then?"

"Then perhaps we'll pay a visit to this Jason Andorian of yours and see if you're really telling the truth, or if he has you fooled as completely as he does everyone else in this operation."

27

"Curse it, everything's gone!"

"If it was even here in the first place," Mark countered reasonably.

"Of course it was." Derek scowled down at the open floor safe. "You heard what Owen said. Besides, who would go to the trouble of having a hidden safe only to keep it empty? No, I know that man we saw coming out had it."

"Honestly, Derek, what do you mean? He obviously belonged here; he knew the guard."

"Nonetheless. He had a stack of papers with him."

"Probably just his night's work. Really, Derek, you're overreacting."

"And you're being entirely too sanguine," the Hound snapped, frowning at his brother. "What happened to all that natural pessimism of yours?"

"Nothing. But just because I never trust the obvious doesn't mean that I instantly assume the worst. After all, Pehndon does have a home. And until we've searched that, I don't think we should go jumping to *any* conclusions."

Derek snorted and turned away, kicking the safe shut, but he still couldn't help feeling that the whole situation was somehow amiss. They had approached the main government building in the depth of the night, expecting all to be dark and quiet, and instead they had found the main door thrown open in a wash of light and some government flunky lounging casually in the doorway chatting desultorily with the guard. They had intended only to scout the area, but Mark had grabbed his brother, saying, "If the front door's open, it probably means the alarms are off. If we hurry around the back, we can probably pick the locks before they are reset."

"And how do we find Pehndon's office?"

"We'll worry about that once we're inside. Now go!"

Darting into the shadows, Derek followed his brother

around the back of the building, alert for guards, but there were none about. Only a half-seen flicker, like two ghosts, disappearing down the mouth of a nearby alley: two figures—one tall, one less so—gone almost before Derek was certain he'd even perceived them.

"Did you see that?" he demanded.

"See what?" Mark answered abstractedly, already engrossed with the lock.

"Nothing," Derek sighed as the door yielded, and the two assassins slipped inside.

Across the main rotunda, the government worker was finally bidding his adieux, sauntering off with a bulky package tucked under his arm, and the guard was closing the doors. Any minute now he would reset the alarms and they would be trapped. Swiftly, Mark gestured his brother to the right and snuck off himself to the left, both hugging the walls of the rotunda until they had circled around behind their quarry.

"Hsst!" Mark said in a carrying whisper, and Derek saw the guard turn and advance partway back into the rotunda, his attention distracted as Mark popped out of the shadows. Behind him, Derek pounced, knocking the man unconscious as Mark quickly swung the outer door shut.

"There. That should buy us some time," his brother declared as Derek set about gagging and trussing the guard.

"And then?"

Mark grinned. "We split up and begin searching the building. Holler when you find Pehndon's office."

"And how will I know which one's Pehndon's?"

"By the nameplates on the doors, of course. You take that side, I'll take this one."

Derek had to admit that, for a spontaneous plan, it was a fairly good one. With the guard trussed downstairs, the alarms remained off and they had ample time to wander the corridors, searching the doors for Pehndon's name. Derek had covered two and a half corridors before he heard Mark shout, "Found it!"

He hastened to his brother's side and discovered the Falcon hastily picking the locks.

"Let's hope no one was vigilant enough to notice that the alarms were off," Mark whispered, and Derek held his breath as his sibling eased the door open. But no Klaxons wailed and no lights flashed, so they entered the office and began their search.

And an hour later they had still found nothing but meaningless files and empty safes, and Derek was reaching the end of his patience. "Are you sure we've found every hiding place?"

"I think so," Mark returned wearily. "But I suppose it can't hurt to look again."

Mikel paced the silent square, waiting impatiently for the dawn and the end of his shift. It had been another long, deadly night, the tedium interrupted only by the ravings of that oversized drunk and the arrival of the Minister's aide—what was his name, Tortarik? Something like that, anyway—and all he wanted was to go home and sleep.

His leg still ached, courtesy of that blasted drunk—it had twisted painfully when the two went down—and his ribs were bruised from the impact of the man's elbow. He rubbed at the latter with an absentminded grimace. Why him? It simply wasn't fair. No one else had had to suffer the man's inebriation to quite the same degree. And Johan, who was supposed to be his friend, hadn't even bothered to help but had just stood across the square, grinning to split his face.

Mikel scowled over at the Grand Stair, but he didn't see Johan occupying his usual position. Come to think of it, he hadn't seen Johan for a while. And though they all did take the occasional break, they were usually not gone for so long.

Idly, Mikel bent his steps toward his friend's established post.

"Johan? Johan," he called, "where are you, you mangy lout?"

But there was no answer.

"Curse it," he muttered. "He must have found himself some willing back-street wench and didn't even invite me to share."

And then he noticed the alarm plate in the door, which was glowing green instead of red.

"Blast it, Johan, you careless fool, you forgot to turn the sodding thing back on! Must I always be the brains around here?"

With a sour murmur, he rearmed the system and continued his pacing, waiting for the light.

"Well?" Mark said at last.

His brother scowled. "Still nothing. Curse it, Mark . . ."

The place was a mess, with files strewn across the floor and the desk drawers overturned. They had even checked the desk frame for hidden compartments or cubbies, but to no avail. There was not a single incriminating scrap of evidence anywhere within the office.

The Falcon sighed gustily. His Guildmaster wanted revenge; he had never seen the man so adamant. It had taken some long and strenuous arguing—not to mention a clear knowledge of his time limit, with the mages doubtlessly tapping their feet impatiently outside the booth—to win from Owen some admission of restraint.

"You can't just convict the man," he told him. "How would it look if the Guild started eliminating people solely on suspicion? It would destroy everything we've worked for! No, let me at least get some hard evidence first—and then we'll talk prices."

Owen had paused, and for a tricky moment Mark was convinced he wouldn't buy it. Then as the ward spells began draining from the booth, restoring the hubbub from the rotunda beyond, he had nodded once, curtly. "Find what you need and call me," he snapped. "And Mark, I'm . . ."

But Mark never did find out what he was, for at that moment the ball went irretrievably black and, having no desire to pay another fifty marks to discover it, he left the booth with Derek at his heels, feeling a certain smug righteousness at the victory.

But where had it gotten him? With every innocuous paper they discarded, he felt his moral high ground eroding. Before long, DeVeris would make him an offer he couldn't refuse and Pehndon would be dead—evidence or no.

And if it ever got out, the Guild would be finished.

"I just had a dreadful thought," Derek muttered, seeming to echo his brother's depression.

"Which is?"

"When we were coming in, I thought I saw someone leaving. What if that government type was covering for someone, distracting the guard until they could get clear?"

"Covering for whom?" Mark said sharply. "And why didn't you tell me you'd seen something?"

"Because you were busy with the lock. And, besides, I wasn't even sure I had."

"Had what?"

"Seen two figures disappearing down the alley."

"Curse it, Derek . . ." Mark grasped his brother by the shoulders as if to shake him, then abruptly reconsidered. "Well, there's nothing we can do about it now. Are you certain your eyes weren't playing tricks?"

"No, that's just the point; I'm not certain at all. But Mark . . ."

"Yes?"

"Didn't Owen say that the Hawk's niece might be accompanied by a man? Because if I did see anything, then that's precisely what I saw. A man and a woman, disappearing down an alley."

Mark slammed his fist against Pehndon's ravaged desk. "Hang and blast! And by Owen's calculations, she should have arrived by now."

"So what should we do?"

"I suppose we'd better begin by straightening this mess before any zealous aides arrive for their morning shift. And then we'll search Pehndon's house. And if we still don't turn anything up after that, we'll check the docks and try to chase down the Hawk's niece and her companion, as well as figuring out who the blazes that government worker was. With the three of them, we should be able to dig up our missing information—not to mention earning back some of our lost commission on that wretched girl. And just where do you think you're going now?"

"To relieve myself. There must be a facility somewhere in this warren."

"Derek, I wouldn't. Someone might have . . ." Mark began, but it was too late. A piercing wail split the air, accompanied by a frantic strobing of the magelights.

". . . reset the system," he finished wearily, as Derek stared back at him in horror.

"Curse it! What now?"

"Get the blazes out of here," Mark responded dryly.

"Mark, I'm sorry," Derek said weakly, but the Falcon just waved it aside.

"You have that rope?"

"Always."

"Then pick the lock of the door across the way, tie it to the window frame, and hope like fury those guards in the back are still missing. We're going out the window."

"And this mess?"

Mark just shrugged. "So much for subtlety."

Iaon Pehndon awoke to a great commotion as the government guards pounded frantically on his door, bawling his name through the silent streets and no doubt rousing all his well-bred neighbors.

With a panicked start, he sat upright, feeling his heart pounding treacherously in his breast. What had gone wrong now? And, more important, why could no one ever do anything for themselves? Why did they always have to come running to him in a crisis?

With a shaking hand, he pushed back the sheet and sat up, his bare feet thunking to the carpet. He located his slippers by touch in the darkness and stood, fumbling into his dressing gown. Then, pushing back the curtains, he threw open the balcony doors and leaned out over the railings.

"What is it?" he demanded irritably, hushing the frantic figures who scuttled below.

There was a long moment of silence.

"Well?" he prompted.

One of them took a deep, valiant breath and began, "Your pardon, Minister Pehndon, but ... that is ... I mean ..."

"Out with it, man!"

"Well, someone's broken into your office."

There was another moment of silence, then *"What?"* Pehndon exclaimed, his fury echoing down the quiet, palm-lined street.

At his cry, a neighboring window slid open and an irate head poked through, its tousled white hair standing rampant beneath a skewed nightcap. "Blast it, Iaon, what's so all-fired important that you have to wake the entire neighborhood with it?"

"Shut up, Malcolm, it's none of your business," Pehndon retorted. And then to the men in the street: "Wait there, and not another peep out of you! I'll be down in two shakes."

What awaited him in his office was nothing short of chaos. The sun was just cresting the sky, washing the flurry of papers in a mellow, rosy light as he stood in the doorway and felt the anger rise and fill him, flowing into every crack and crevice until he thought he would burst with it. All his carefully organized cabinets gaped open, the files strewn like burst fruit about the floorboards. His desk drawers were all overturned.

It was a violation, but worse than that . . .

A kind of incipient panic filled him.

Curse it, I thought she was dead!

He wasn't even aware he had spoken aloud until one of the guards said brightly, "Who's dead, sir?"

"No one," he barked. "Now get out of here. Get out and leave me alone!"

Startled, the guard sketched a hasty bow and retreated, slamming the door in a manner that clearly indicated pique, but Pehndon didn't care; his mind was too busy spinning over the implications.

Why can't she just go away and leave me alone?

He could have sworn the Hawk was dead. The morning after her jailbreak, he had set his trained mages on her trail and was delighted when they had led him to a body— limp and abandoned in an alley, already beginning to stink in the midmorning heat. The short, rough-cut hair was caked with blood, the face unrecognizable: beaten to a bloody pulp and thick with flies. But despite that, the queasy mages had assured him that this was his quarry, for the trail ran cold at the body and the signature aura was unmistakable.

He should have known she wouldn't have succumbed so easily, wouldn't have ended her days as the random victim of some back-alley hoodlum. But how the hell had she managed it? Those mages weren't lying; he paid them too much for misdirection.

The only solution was that she had bribed one of her own mages to lay a false trail, but he could have sworn she didn't have the cash.

Obviously, she had far more resources than he'd given her credit for, and now she was after him.

Random revenge, or . . .

Dropping to his knees, he began to scramble through the scattered papers, pawing them up in frantic handfuls as he quested for the floor safe and his priceless stash of incriminating documents. But when he finally located the trigger and sprang the lock, he found it empty. Empty!

He should never have stored the blasted things in his office, but he could have sworn the security system would have discouraged even the boldest of thieves. It was certainly better than anything he could have commissioned for his home. No matter that he could afford it; merely installing it in a private residence would have aroused unnecessary suspicion. So he had stored everything here, trusting in the government's paranoia to protect him.

But apparently not even the government was proof against the Hawk.

She had it now; she had everything. And whatever wasn't present, she would undoubtedly discover. It was only a matter of time before she unearthed the whole bloody mess.

Somehow he had to stop her.

But how?

A tentative knock interrupted his reflections. Swiftly shutting the barren safe, he rose to his knees, calling, "Come in."

His gangly aid poked his head through the doorway, his hair sticking up in oily spikes. He was still rubbing the sleep from his eyes. "They woke me, sir. Is there anything I can do?"

"Yes. Clean up this mess. And get me the downstairs guard." The aide duly vanished. "Now, tell me exactly what happened, Johan," Pehndon snapped as the man in question appeared, rubbing his head somewhat sheepishly.

"Can't exactly say," the flustered guard responded. "Tortaluk came in to do some work around one, so I disabled the system, and then he left again around two. I was just about to close the door and reset the system when someone hit me from behind."

"Did you see who?"

Johan shook his head.

"We found him trussed up like a chicken and out cold," one of the other guards put in helpfully, then spluttered into silence at Pehndon's baleful glare.

He whirled on his aide. "Start cleaning. I'm going back to bed. Wake me when Jhakharta gets in; I need to talk to him about this aide of his."

But sleep was impossible. By the time he returned home, he found it in worse condition than his office.

28

After Jen's magelink went silent, Thibault made one or two last slurred protests, then let himself be escorted from the square, but once he was finally out of sight he regained his sober demeanor and glanced ruefully at his skinned palm, which had caught the worst of his fall. He didn't like to think what it must have sounded like to Jen when the magelink went skidding across the cobblestones; the feedback alone had nearly deafened him.

It was a wonder she hadn't fallen off her rope.

He had intended to go down more gracefully, of course, but that blasted guard had to intervene, trying to steady him. The man's lunge knocked Thibault off balance, and the reward for his kindness was to become Thibault's cushion; he could hear the anguished *whuff* as his six-foot-four-inch frame landed on the man.

But now, waiting in the alley behind the main government building with two trussed and unconscious guards huddled at his feet, he found the pain in his palm subsiding to a dull ache as other anxieties surged to the fore.

It had been thirty minutes since he last heard from Jen. What, by all that was precious, was that blasted girl up to?

He almost succumbed to temptation and reactivated the magelink, but a shred of common sense restrained him. So instead he contented himself with pacing the narrow alley and reflecting on what had happened.

How about that closing comment of hers?

Ironically, it seemed the only time he could get Jen to admit her affection was when she was halfway up the side of a building and he was unable to do anything about it—not that she had even meant it anyway.

Bloody aristocrats.

Where in tarnation was she?

After an hour of anxious pacing, he heard one of the

guards give a little moan, as if he were about to wake. Thibault kicked him back into oblivion.

Finally, unable to bear it any longer, he reopened the link. "Jenny?"

"Thib?" She sounded horrified. "Is anything wrong?"

"No, all clear. Is everything all right up there?"

Her voice registered a certain amusement. "Not exactly. There's been a bit of a complication."

"A complication? What sort of complication?"

He could hear the laughter in her voice. "An interesting one. It seems Pehndon had another midnight visitor—who was also intent on the same things we were after."

"Well, you beat him to it, I hope?"

"In a sense." She chuckled. "Actually, we're collaborating. He knows someone I want to meet, and he has a plan to get us out of here safely."

In the background, he could hear a voice saying suspiciously, "Who's that? What's going on? Who are you talking to?" A male voice.

Great. She had doubtless encountered some bold adventurer who would seize her imagination while her partner remained placidly outside. "Are you sure it's wise to trust him?" he couldn't help asking.

But, "Why not?" she responded breezily. "We're on our way down now, so if I'm not with you in five minutes, you'll know he's played me false."

"Who's played you false?" repeated that unknown voice. By his tone, he sounded as apprehensive about Thibault as Thibault was about him. Good.

"No one," she told him, then added, "Just kidding."

The magelink went silent, and Thibault grinned as he sauntered to the mouth of the alley, wondering what her new companion would make of *that* comment. But the man seemed to be true, for a few minutes later Thibault heard the whisper of a window sliding open and the soft chink of a grapple being placed, and Jen emerged onto the ledge, a slim, dark shape in the watery moonlight. She slid to safety, then flipped the grapple loose, her eyes scanning the quiet street as she coiled up the rope.

Thibault grinned. "What happened to the alarms?" he whispered as he moved to join her.

She flew at him, throttling her arms around his neck, the blunted points of the grapple digging awkwardly into his

shoulders. "They turned them off for Grahme," she answered prosaically enough, but her voice was brimming.

He chuckled. "Enjoy yourself?"

"Immeasurably. Oh, Thib, it was quite marvelous! I
knew I had chosen the right profession."

"I'm glad to hear it, I suppose. So who is this Grahme?"

"A government aide—to First Minister Jhakharta, inter-
estingly enough."

"And you let him leave with the papers?" Thibault was
horrified.

She merely grinned and extracted a thin sheaf from the
back of her trousers. "Half the papers," she said. "Every
other page, to be exact. After all, trust goes only so far—
even for me!"

"Well, at least you're showing some sense . . . What?"
he demanded as she held up an imperious hand.

"Quiet. I hear something."

Thibault went instantly still and in the hush discerned
the unmistakable patter of footsteps rounding the side of
the building. "Right. Let's get out of here," he said, seizing her arm and towing her toward the yawning alley. As
the shadows swallowed them, he added, "So where are we
meeting this new conspirator of yours?"

"Two streets back." Then something in his voice must
have alerted her, for she added, "Gracious, Thibault,
you're not *jealous,* are you?"

"Not in the slightest," he lied. "Come, then, let's do it."

Jen had to admit to some doubts about Grahme's sincerity
as he led them through street after street of abandoned
warehouses, dark and shuttered in the small hours before
dawn. And what with Thibault casting her the occasional
wary glance, she began to regret the impulse that had
made her accept this stranger about whom, admittedly,
she knew very little.

Instantly, her mind began concocting the direst of scenarios. Perhaps Pehndon suspected. Perhaps he had realized that her afternoon visit wasn't as innocent as it
appeared. Maybe he had installed Grahme as his spy, to
gain her trust, then dispatch her in some convenient alley.

It struck her forcibly that a body abandoned on these
streets could go undetected for weeks.

But, oddly, what disturbed her more was the thought of

disclosing their eventual destination to her silent partner. For all Thibault knew—for all *she* knew, for that matter—Jason Andorian was the man who had summoned Vera to her demise. Would he assume that Jen was simply out for revenge and try to stop her, or would he rather condemn her for leading them straight into the hands of the betrayer?

That is, if Jason was even involved, which Grahme seemed to swear he wasn't.

Which in turn all depended on whose side Grahme was really on, anyway.

It was a cursed circular argument, and the endless rows of warehouses did nothing to allay her suspicions.

She had managed, for the most part, to hold Thibault off with vague evasions, and now she felt doubly guilty as he followed her unquestioningly into the heart of the wasteland. If she erred this time, would he ever trust her again?

Would they both even be alive to worry about it tomorrow?

But eventually they arrived at their destination: a warehouse indistinguishable from the rest, its vast loading door secured with chains of rusty iron that hadn't been broached in at least two decades.

Unable to restrain himself any longer, Thibault breathed, "Are you sure you know what you're doing?" only to be motioned to silence by their new companion.

"Shh, not a word. Follow me."

Casting a final, doubtful glance at Jen, her partner complied.

The man led them around the side of the building, where a tiny door lurked, half hidden beneath a run of external stairs. Pulling a key from his pocket, he inserted it into the rusty lock. The tumblers fell with a well-oiled smoothness, and he swung the door out on silent hinges, gesturing them inside.

The warehouse floor was washed in the palest of magelight, tinting it a dingy yellow that somehow seemed in keeping with its dilapidated exterior. Yet even Jen could see that the floors were freshly scrubbed, the scattered sticks of furniture shabby but utilitarian. A steep run of stairs, mirroring those on the outer wall, climbed to a tiny office, more brightly lit than the rest of the structure but still apparently deserted.

She was on the verge of uttering some scathing comment when the office door flew open and a new figure pounded heedlessly down the precipitous stairs.

"Grahme!" the stranger exclaimed boyishly. "I heard the key. Did you find any . . ." His voice trailed off, and his feet froze into silence as he caught sight of Jen and her companion.

His eyes narrowed, studying her.

Equally boldly, she stared back, measuring him in turn. He was, she decided, one of the most glorious-looking men she had ever seen. Captured in mid-descent, with his hand on the railing and his foot poised above the subsequent stair, his lean, taut body was arched like a dancer's—or a supple bow just waiting to be drawn. Dark hair and eyes, equally flawless, completed the image, and he had a presence that flowed off him in palpable waves. She didn't see how anyone could be in a room with him and not notice.

In fact, she was amazed that she had missed him behind the mere wood and glass of his enclosure.

She tossed her hair back and said, "Jason Andorian, I presume?"

She could feel Thibault tense beside her.

"I have that honor. And you are?" His voice was crisp, precise, but his eyes met hers with a twinkle, returning boldness for boldness.

She felt drawn to him instantly and just as instantly knew that if her aunt had come to harm, it had not been from the hands of this stranger. She could sense the honor in him, as undeniable as his charisma. Still, the formalities had to be observed. "My name's Jen Ra . . ." she began, before a swift tromp from Thibault's boot brought her to her senses. "Ah, that is, Jenna Rafferty," she amended, "but you can call me Jen. I believe you hired someone I know."

"I did?"

"Quite. The assassin who killed Istarbion."

His face went abruptly sober, the twinkle fading from his eyes. "And you brought her *here*?" he demanded, whirling on Tortaluk.

"I didn't . . . I had . . . that is . . ." the poor man stammered. Jen came to his rescue.

"I didn't exactly tell him that part," she stated coolly.

"Besides, when we met in Pehndon's office, we were both simply concerned with one thing."

"That being?"

"Gathering evidence."

"I see." Jason rearranged his posture on the stairs, resting his elbows against the railing and staring down at her speculatively. "And did you find it?"

"I always find what I'm looking for."

"I see," he said again. Peripherally, she was aware that the lights had come up during this exchange, though she wasn't entirely clear what cues had caused it. "I think we had better talk, then," he continued. "Grahme, bring up two more chairs for my . . . guests."

"I'll help," Thibault offered.

"And this, of course," Jen added blithely, "is my partner and associate . . ."

"Tomas LeDoux," Thibault put in hastily, shooting her a disgusted glance.

She shrugged almost imperceptibly in return, then turned her attention back to Jason.

"I'm innocent, of course," he said, that teasing light reappearing in his eyes.

"Yes. Somehow I'm inclined to believe that." She heard a muffled squawk of protest from Thibault but ignored it, smiling at Jason instead. "Now, if you'll lead the way, I think we have some business to discuss."

He came the rest of the way down and offered his arm. He was taller than she, but not by much. She could see the warm lights dancing in his eyes, the reddish glints in his thick, silky hair. His arm, when she took it, was firm and taut, and the spicy, musky maleness that rose ever so faintly from his pores as he neared made her feel vaguely giddy. She could feel a little spark leap between them as they touched.

Nor, from his expression, was she alone in that perception.

Behind her, she could hear the ghost of a sigh from Thibault as he hefted a chair and followed them up the narrow stairs.

After an hour of discussion, they were still no nearer an answer—though at least they had some of the pieces. The papers that Jen and Grahme had purloined from Pehndon's

office were scattered across Jason's desk, as disarrayed as
they had been when they emerged from Jen's trousers and
Grahme's files in two disparate stacks. There were letters
from one Fazaquhian, detailing some operation in the
desert. There were papers from the local prisons, approving the transfer of prisoners to a labor camp outside
Dheimos. There was even an account book, detailing pay-
offs to unnamed sources—one of which Grahme identified
as Jhakharta by the size and frequency of the . . . dona-
tions.

Another—designated simply "A"—was Jason's personal favorite for his impersonator, although the identity
of the man remained a mystery.

Still, at least this Jen Rafferty, or whatever she chose to
call herself, seemed to be on his side, to believe his
protestations of innocence. And that relieved him more
than he could say—for despite her looks and her somewhat imperious behavior, he could sense a core of steel in
her which attracted him more than any beauty or air of
fine breeding.

She would, he suspected, make a very bad enemy indeed.

She had admitted to being the assassin's niece but had
refused to tie either of them to the Guild. By her evasion,
he suspected that the aunt did belong. And as for Jen herself, some hidden instinct told him she was operating on
the wrong end of the law. Which, in the main, was fine by
him; he was no great supporter of the Guild, believing it
was better to solve your problems rather than simply
eliminating them, and in such a situation, any ally was a
valuable tool, regardless of her affiliation.

The honest truth was that he needed as much help as he
could get, now more than ever, and Jen and her mysterious companion seemed likely to provide that—no matter
what their motivations. Though Grahme, he noticed,
seemed quite self-satisfied now that his ploy had succeeded—his mood compounded, no doubt, by his relief
that his new conspirator had not slaughtered his employer
out of hand.

He had looked vaguely sheepish when Jen gallantly returned his dagger.

Jason chuckled at the memory, then steepled his fingers, regarding his cadre soberly across his desk. "Now,

let's think this over. What do we know? First, that Pehndon is indubitably involved in this mess. Second, that he
has been sending both convicts and large infusions of
cash to a mysterious installment in the desert, somewhere
to the south of Dheimos. For what purpose, we don't
know, but it must be something large, as he has several
mages in his employ. So how do we discover what it is?"

"Well, I should have thought it was obvious," Jen retorted smugly. "There's another crew of convicts scheduled
to leave in a few days; it seems the perfect opportunity. All
we have to do is insert someone into their midst."

"And you don't think an extra body would be noticed?"

"Of course not. Why should it? These aren't valued
workers; they're prisoners. What's one more or less to
them?"

"I suppose you have a point. But who should go?"

"Why, Thibault, of course," she said brightly, gesturing
to the oversized young man who had introduced himself
as Tomas LeDoux.

In response, he groaned deeply, saying, "Jenny . . ."

"Nonsense, Thib, we're among friends here. You have
nothing to hide."

"Nonetheless . . ."

"You're the perfect choice, and you know it. Who else
could infiltrate a press gang? Me? Besides, you were
about to volunteer anyway; I could tell it from your eyes."

Jason felt a sudden flush of jealousy, aware of the enduring history and affection between these two, despite
their obviously disparate backgrounds.

"Granted, but that's hardly the issue," her partner continued placidly, yet with an unmistakable edge to his
voice. "I wasn't referring to the job, Jenny."

"I know precisely what you were referring to, and we'll
discuss that later. For now, we have to concentrate on
how to get you into that crew. Grahme, you have connections in the government. Can you find out where they'll
be leaving from, and when?"

"I can try, but it won't be easy. Pehndon's bound to be
suspicious about anyone sniffing around that particular
pie."

"Then be careful," she said dismissively. "Now, what
shall I do while Thibault's playing convict?"

Jason measured her, feeling again that indefinable

twinge of attraction. "It strikes me," he said slowly, never once dropping eye contact, "that there's a lot to be discovered at home. For one thing, we still don't know the name of the person who impersonated me—if, in fact, anyone did."

"Oh, someone did," Jen assured him. "Despite appearances, my aunt is an honorable woman; if she said a Jason hired her, then a Jason definitely hired her."

"So we have an impostor to unmask. We also need some hard evidence against Pehndon, beyond a bunch of cryptic scribbles."

"Yes." Jen frowned, drumming her fingers against one upraised thigh. Jason found himself mesmerized by the subtle play of flesh on flesh. "Thib, how much money do you think you'll need to finance your trip?"

"Well, the passage out is likely to be free, so maybe . . . I don't know . . . two hundred?"

"I'll give you three. Which means," she paused, calculating, then grinned, her eyes glowing like smoky agates, "I still have more than enough left to bribe the mages. Very well, leave the hard evidence to me."

"And what shall I do?" Jason added.

"Try not to get caught?"

He measured her, then took a calculated risk. "Do you have a place to stay? Somewhere safe, I mean? Because if you're putting yourself in danger for me, I want to know you have somewhere to retreat to, some local bolt-hole where the authorities can't find you."

"And who says I'm putting myself in danger for *you*?" she retorted, though her throaty voice was not quite a rebuke. "My motivations—and my reasons—are my own. But you do have a point, nonetheless. Have you anything to suggest?"

"Well, my place is always free . . ."

He could sense Thibault's answering glower, but it didn't matter. Jen's welcoming smile more than made up for it.

Something told him that it was going to be an interesting few weeks.

29

In the heart of the desert, Vera was having a dickens of a
time trying to talk some sense into Neros Fazaquhian. The
man was like a block of stone, utterly impervious to reason. Nor was she in the most gracious of moods after her
harrowing desert crossing—and certainly in no condition
to suffer fools gladly.

The journey itself had been a nightmare, not so much
for the privations of the desert (in fact, Vera considered
herself rather good at privations) but more for the company it created. Whatever services Absalom had performed for the camel drivers must not have been very
great, for they dismissed the debt as if it were no more
than a casual deed—at least judging by the respect they
paid her.

Or maybe it was simply that they assumed a single
woman, apparently past her prime and traveling alone,
was more than fair game for a little sexual byplay. Vera
considered herself a tolerant person; only when their
coarse gibes had gone beyond the stage of innuendo did
she pull one of her many daggers and threaten to make the
next offender sing soprano. After that, they left her
strictly alone—so much so, in fact, that she had to prepare, and even procure, her own fodder for the evening
meals. Nor did it help that she was a better shot and often
brought down more fresh game than their entire company
combined.

It had led to some rather uncomfortable meals as they
lingered reluctantly on the edges of her campfire, munch-
ing dried strips of meat and fruit and all but drooling at
the smell of fresh-cooked game birds, rabbits, and desert
rodents drifting on the dust-baked air. She supposed she
should have shared, but she was becoming less tolerant in
her old age.

Or maybe just less tolerant, period. Her experience
with Pehndon had soured her. She had spent enough time
as the victim; she was tired of people assuming that because she was older and a woman she was somehow
weaker, less capable of defending herself. Or of simply
looking out for her own best interests.

So she had stubbornly—and probably somewhat spite-
fully—hoarded her food and doubtless strained tensions
between herself and her guides to the breaking point, but
she didn't care. That last leering comment—"Come on,
darlin', you know you want it"—had torn it for her. The
lines of battle were drawn. By the end of the journey, she
would have murdered them all quite cheerfully, and it was
merely a token of her restraint that they made it to
Dheimos unscathed.

In fact, if it hadn't been for the nebulous threats of Absalom's vengeance, they would doubtless have abandoned
her one night to wither under the relentless sun.

Vera let a reluctant smile curve her lips as she remembered. The mage had been a wonder. She still wasn't quite
sure why he had helped her, but she wasn't about to question her good fortune. And she had never met anyone,
other than a fellow Guild member, who was more cold-
blooded about the brutal facts of her profession. When
that scrawny whore attempted to rob her and she had
killed the woman reflexively, it was Absalom who suggested a use for the body. Oblivious to the pulpy mess
mere inches from his fingers, he had even placidly dyed
the woman's freshly cropped hair while Vera pummeled
her features into obscurity. Then he laid the false trail as
calmly as if such activities were an everyday occurrence.

By the time they had abandoned the body in an alley,
Vera's estimation of the scruffy mage had increased tenfold.

By the time he had outfitted her for her journey, it was
up to a hundredfold. So what if his camel drivers were
pigs? A man was entitled one flaw or two in the midst of
such greatness.

It troubled her, sometimes, to think how she was ever
going to repay him. She was racking up debts so fast that
money alone would never settle it.

He had instructed her how to survive in the desert, had
supplied her with robes and veils like those of the desert

natives. He had told her how much fluid to drink, what animals made good eating, and where to find water in an emergency.

She even knew what to slip into a pot to make her guides regret ever waking up.

The desert fascinated her. She had been to Nhuras a time or two—and even to some of the lesser settlements that hovered on its fringes—but she had never ventured so far out into the heart of the inferno. Yet it drew her. There was something almost seductive about the flat, empty spaces, the starched tang of the sterile air, the vast, desolate sweep from horizon to horizon. It comforted her, rendered her anonymous. It reminded her that she was a fighter and a survivor.

But she could see how Pehndon's colleagues would have chuckled at the notion of finding something valuable in this wasteland.

In the beginning, the sandy soil was peppered with plants: hardy, prickly, fleshy growths of an anemic green, lying low to the ground like so much desert flotsam. There were animals, too: small rodents and birds, whistling and clicking to each other in an endless din that had little to do with human interference. But gradually, as the caravan progressed, these tiny pockets of life thinned and disappeared, replaced only by endless stretches of rippling sand that were as alien as they were forbidding. It was a mutable landscape, as impermanent as life, and there was something about it that appealed to Vera's current sensibility.

Or maybe it was just that her own life had recently seemed to take on that same shifting indeterminance.

And then they had reached the Anvil, and even the sand was burnt away until nothing remained but a hard, cracked surface, surmounted by a brittle, glassy sheen. Nothing lived here: not a bug, or a wisp of greenery. This was the ultimate forge, where life was hammered daily into nonexistence; it was no wonder they called it the Anvil of the Sun.

What was more amazing was that Pehndon had managed to find something of value in its environs.

The caravan had left her at the tiny settlement of Dheimos, which boasted a camel stable, one or two rickety houses, and an equally rickety hotel flanking a tiny oasis. There they had sold her their worst-tempered beast for an exorbitant price, assured her of lodging (for who else would wish to stay in such a place?), and abandoned her with marked relief.

She had managed to extract some information from the lackadaisical hotel keeper—who had reluctantly furnished her with a greasy, undercooked meal—bearing testament to a large temporary settlement to the south. No, he didn't know what it was for. No, he didn't really care. They paid him for water, and that was what mattered. Three camels a day arrived to haul it away.

So Vera had merely waited for the caravan to arrive the next morning. The water-haulers gave her sour looks—a more ragged assemblage of criminals she had never seen—but short of attacking, there was nothing they could do to stop her as she trailed them back to camp, her own camel grunting and wheezing like an angry grampus, balking every step of the way.

Elsa Rosa had been right; the things did spit most horrendously.

What first caught her attention as she approached the secret base was the tower rising out of the desert: an impossible conglomeration of crystal tubes and towers and bulging bladders, writhing like a nest of serpents between a skeleton of glowing supports. The four largest conduits must have carried the power, for they glinted bright as any magelight, occasionally shooting showers of sparks from their open tops. More streams of light flowed down the coiling veins, countered by a river of midnight fluid which spiraled up, pooling in connecting bladders before pouring out a graceful tap and into a vast collecting vat. The whole thing pulsed and glowed like some living organ, and Vera would never forget her first glimpse of it by night, spilling its rays across the parched ground, illuminating the vast bowl of the endless sky.

But now a cluster of busy mages swirled about it, chanting incantations, while several more lay collapsed in the shade of a nearby shelter, temporarily exhausted. And beyond that stretched a sea of tents, their once white sides already beginning to dull and fade, as if they were being slowly absorbed into the barren landscape.

The workers, garbed like herself in flowing robes and veils, were divided into clusters: some digging holes, others hammering together the components for what looked like three additional towers, still others sauntering in and out of a mysterious abode building that lurked on the fringe of the settlement.

It was quite an operation that Pehndon had conceived, but to what end?

Eventually someone must have realized that she didn't belong, for a burly ruffian detached himself from the nearest group and approached, squinting up at her through the glare. Below an unruly thatch of wild black hair and a bristling beard, a vicious scar ran across his face, twisting one corner of his mouth into a perpetual grimace.

"Well, what do you want?" he demanded with a rusty leer.

She surveyed him superciliously from her perch on the camel. "What I want," she responded coolly, "is to speak to the person in charge."

Something in her voice must have warned him, for he instantly turned and bellowed, "Boss. Hey, Boss!"

"What is it, Razife?" demanded a weary voice, and another man detached himself from the group. Until then, he had been peering intently into a rather large hole. Vera craned her neck from camelback, but she could see nothing over the heads of the crowd.

"Someone to see you, Boss," the ruffian answered.

"I can see that, Razife, but who is she?"

"How should I know? I'm your foreman, not your bloody social director." And with an insolent grin, Razife sauntered off, leaving Vera with her new companion. He was an older man, dressed in the ubiquitous desert garb, his eyes masked behind two round lenses of lapis-glass. His head was unveiled, revealing a crop of dust-grey hair bound up in a stubby ponytail, and his face was lined with the marks of one who had clearly seen better days.

"Pardon my foreman," he said in that same long-suffering tone, "but I'm afraid he's used to associating with a rather different type of person. Did Pehndon send you?"

"In a sense," she responded, sliding off her camel. It turned and tried to snap at her; she gave it a firm clout to the muzzle in return.

"Dreadful beasts," the man said sympathetically. "I'm Neros Fazaquhian, and I'm glad someone's finally here to supervise my work. It's almost past the stage where I can work effectively alone."

Vera didn't bother to correct the impression. In fact, in a technical sense, it was remarkably accurate. If not to supervise, then she was at least here to check his findings over fairly carefully. "And are things progressing well?" she asked.

"Oh, infinitely. We've passed the biggest hurdle, as you know—the refinement—and are now working with the mages to move the process from the labs to the towers. The process is almost completed, so in a few days we should be ready to begin export. All we need is the go-ahead. Has Pehndon approved it?"

She squinted across at him, wishing she had had the foresight to purchase a pair of lenses similar to his own. "Not . . . exactly," she responded.

He sighed. "Yes, I suppose it was too much to hope for, at least right now. Come to that, I haven't even got my packing crew yet; they should be arriving in a week or so. Well, I suppose you'd better come to my office. It's quite unnaturally bright out here, and you haven't had as much chance to adjust to it as I."

He led the way to the abode building and gestured her inside. Within, a number of workers lurked about long, stone-capped benches; every so often, flares of flames would erupt from their stations, blasting toward the ceiling.

Fazaquhian seemed oblivious to the chaos. He led her to a small, enclosed office, off to one side of the main lab. The cool dark was a relief after the blazing sunlight.

"I don't know how you stand it here," she commented, throwing back her veils and wiping her streaming forehead.

"I don't," he responded wryly, "but the pay is good, and I do enjoy the work. Come, sit. Can I offer you some cold water? It's one of my few perks: mage-cooled refreshment. No alcohol, though; I . . . don't drink."

She noted the hesitation, as well as its cause. He had the look of a man who had been wrung out, then hung up to dry—not a pleasant kind of existence. So, "Water would be lovely," she said, then added, "You work with that, I take it?" pointing to a beaker of the mysterious black liquid, perched atop his cluttered desk.

His face brightened. "Precisely. How much has Pehndon told you?" He handed her the water and pulled up a chair.

"Very little, I'm afraid," she responded, taking a seat in turn. "What is it?"

"Black-naphtha," he replied proudly. "At least, that's what I call it."

"And what does it do?"

So he showed her everything, from the refinement to the burn, and she felt her eyes grow round with wonder. No wonder Pehndon was excited; properly exploited, this stuff could give the mages a genuine run for their money!

She'd be blind not to see the potential.

A world economy, with Ashkharon at its center. And Pehndon, presumably, at its head.

Worth killing for? He evidently thought so.

"Ironic, isn't it?" she said.

"What?"

"That you need the mages to exploit a technology that may shortly put them out of business. I'm surprised they even agreed to it!"

"Oh, Pehndon says that the mages are notoriously shortsighted. And that they'll do almost anything for money." The reverence with which he said the Minister's name made her feel vaguely ill.

"And you? Are you looking forward to besting the mages?"

"Me?" He looked genuinely startled. "No, I'm merely here for the discovery, to regain my credibility. I invented this, you know." And he tapped the two lenses of lapis-glass, now resting atop his dust-colored hair.

"Impressive," she said.

He practically glowed. "Fame goes to man's head, I'm afraid. Once, I had a name for myself, but I gambled it away. Only Pehndon was willing to take that second, vital chance on my future. I owe the man my life."

She surveyed him speculatively over the rim of her glass. Now she knew what Pehndon was hiding. The question that remained was, Could she seduce his tool?

By the end of a long, painful week, she was beginning to suspect that the answer might well be no.

30

Sometimes Mark couldn't determine just how fate perceived him. After their singularly unfruitful attempt at office breaking, it had been almost ridiculously easy to perform a similar feat at Pehndon's home. Sliding out the back windows of the office in the wake of the alarm, they merely had to wait until the guards discovered the wreckage and then simply trail along. The poor dupes had led them straight to Pehndon, and then Pehndon had disappeared, leaving them in possession of his immaculate townhouse.

It couldn't have been more perfect if they had planned it.

And then fortune had abandoned them yet again, for they had tossed the house from stem to stern without finding a scrap more evidence than they had gleaned in the office.

Derek, of course, was convinced they had been preempted, but Mark was simply too tired to care. He had been awake for nearly three days running, and his very consciousness was beginning to unravel. Between his midnight vigil on the rooftop and his inadvertent murder of the Hawk, his frantic worries for his brother's safety, and now *this,* all he really wanted was a bed and a bit of quiet—and about thirty hours of solid oblivion.

He got three before Derek rousted him out again, determined to find the Hawk's niece before too much of the day had elapsed. And, blast it all, his brother was bright and chipper, running on that seemingly infinite well of energy he could apparently tap at will. There were times he might have almost suspected his sibling of being half plant—able to run on sunlight alone—except that the same principle seemed to apply on cloudy days as well as at night. When Derek decided to go without sleep, he simply . . . adjusted, whereas without his proper rest, Mark was left feeling like an overused mop. It was, he reflected, a distinctly annoying characteristic.

But then, Derek had been in bed the night before the execution rather than huddled on a chilly rooftop like some people Mark could mention. Maybe that was the difference.

Or maybe he was simply getting old.

Whatever the case, the day seemed to mock him, possessing as much frantic energy and bustle as his rambunctious sibling. The light danced painfully into his eyes, and the cheery babble of voices seemed to echo through the streets as if mage-enhanced. Even the carts and carriages seemed to bounce along with increased vigor, causing him to remark sourly at one point, "What did they do, replace all the paving stones with boulders? They might as well have added a couple of hammers and a large brass band!"

The Hound chuckled. "Oh, come now, it's not as bad as all that," he said, but it was. When they finally reached the wharf, even the docks were peppy, bouncing lightly on the water, the sun glinting mirror-bright off the lapping waves.

Three more hours of sleep, Mark thought plaintively. *Just three more hours, and I wouldn't be convinced the whole of the world was out to get me.*

But fortunately for their present task, the most critical member of the team was functioning at capacity, striding the rolling docks as if he owned them, engaging the sailors in the seemingly idle patter that was his specialty. Realizing thankfully that he would be less than useful in this current situation—and obliquely admiring Derek for his impossible good humor—Mark took a seat on the edge of the wharf with his back against a piling, closing his eyes and tilting his face toward the sun. The fresh sea air caressed his cheeks, and he took a number of deep, satisfying breaths, hoping that such temporary measures would revive him.

And indeed, when Derek returned triumphantly about a half an hour later, Mark was feeling almost human again—and certainly capable of conducting a discussion with something resembling civility.

"So? What did you discover?"

Derek took a seat beside him, swinging his legs out over

the water and batting at the wavelets with one sandaled toe. "Good news," he grinned. "A woman and her brother docked yesterday afternoon, ostensibly looking for work in Ashkharon. They came in on Granville's trader, the *Crow's Nest,* originating from—you guessed it . . ."

"Grometiere," Mark finished. "And what makes you think they were our pair?"

"Small luggage—one trunk each, according to the sailors—and the woman was apparently a haughty piece, a bit above her station. But more tellingly," and he raised a teasing eyebrow, "they found thirty-five rat pelts secreted in her cabin, all reasonably fresh kills. And the sailors had been wondering where all the vermin had got to."

"Gracious," Mark chuckled. "It seems our Hawk has trained herself a live one. So what now?"

"Well, they were last seen heading toward the carriages, so I say we start questioning the drivers."

Despite his lack of Derek's charms, it was Mark who eventually located their quarry, which made him reflect that at least his presence hadn't been a total loss. The driver in question was a garrulous man who remembered the pair in stunning detail. He had been impressed by the suhdabhar and captivated by the unspoiled charm of the lady herself—and it was that change in status alone that convinced Mark they were on the right track.

The fact that the driver remembered the woman's stunned reaction to the news of the execution—of her flight and subsequent recovery—was merely the final nail in the coffin.

So claiming to be a rather concerned set of cousins, Mark and his brother convinced the driver to drop them at her hotel: the Nhuras Arms in Maltha Square. Derek was beaming eagerly at the prospect of recovering a portion of their lost commission, but Mark was more judicious. And rightly so, for they arrived only to discover that their quarry had absconded. She had, the desk clerk almost gleefully informed them, departed mere minutes ago. They had just missed her. No, she hadn't left a forwarding address. She had mentioned that she was staying with friends. Which friends? Well, that was anyone's guess.

"Hang and blast," Mark muttered as they retreated. He could feel the weight of the day slowly settling back onto his shoulders, a faint headache building up behind his eyes. "This is getting positively ridiculous. How hard can it be to find one bloody female?"

Jhakharta was in his office, scribbling away at some tedious report, when he happened to glance up and see Pehndon seated imperiously across from him, his fingers steepled in a manner that Jhakharta knew meant business.

He started slightly, for he hadn't seen his colleague enter or heard his footsteps—though he supposed the thick, luxurious pile of his carpet would have masked all but the most elephantine of approaches. So, "Gracious, Iaon," he exclaimed, "where did you spring from?" Then, surveying Pehndon more judiciously, he added, "You look a positive mess. Haven't you been sleeping lately?"

Pehndon unclasped his fingers and crossed his legs, settling himself more comfortably in the chair. His raptorlike gaze pinned Jhakharta to his seat, making him feel like some vaguely repulsive insect that had been found in a dusty cellar or crawling beneath some overturned rock. He shifted uncomfortably beneath that killing scrutiny.

"Obviously you haven't heard the news," Iaon said calmly.

Jhakharta flinched. He had come to distrust calm. "What news?"

"Someone broke into my office last night."

"They did?" Then, "Do they know about me?"

Pehndon's mouth twisted. "Hang it, Alphonse, is that all you can think about? No, they don't know about you— at least not specifically; I keep everything in code."

"Oh. Good. I mean, I wouldn't want to have to give up my new position or Istarbion's estate . . ."

Pehndon uttered something that sounded suspiciously like a growl. The morning sun slanted harshly across his features, making them look more chiseled and hard-edged than ever. But, "I think you're missing the point, Alphonse," he said placidly enough. "They have my papers, and while those may not be enough to implicate me per se, with a little diligence that information in the right hands could mean an end to my entire operation."

Jhakharta shrugged. "That's dreadful, of course, Iaon, but still I don't see what it has to do with me. You're the one who handles such problems. What in tarnation am *I* supposed to do about it?"

"Fortunately, nothing directly," Pehndon said dryly. "Otherwise, that could well mean the end of everything right there." Jhakharta felt an angry flush mounting his cheeks, but before he could react, Pehndon added, "However, if I go down, you may be quite sure that you will follow."

"Iaon . . ."

"But, more important, there's a good chance that someone attached to you was involved."

"Attached to *me*?" Jhakharta was horrified. "You don't think *I* was involved, do you? Because I assure you . . ."

Pehndon waved a hand dismissively. "The thought never crossed my mind, Alphonse." And when Jhakharta essayed a relieved smile, he added, "You haven't the intelligence to pull it off. But as for your affiliates. . . . How much do you know about that aide of yours?"

"Tortaluk?" He blinked. "I hadn't really thought about it. You think *he's* involved?"

"That's what I'm trying to determine. He was here last night, you know. He left shortly before the alarms went off."

"So you think he absconded with your papers?"

"Honestly, Alphonse, do pay a little attention for once. I said he left *before* the alarms went off, so obviously he couldn't have activated them."

"Then . . ."

"But he could very well have served as the decoy for whoever did," Pehndon continued patiently, as if explaining to a rather small and stupid child. "He was seen talking to Johan for a while."

"Johan? Who's Johan?"

Pehndon grimaced. "Sometimes, I wonder why I bother," he said to no one in particular. "Johan is—was— one of the night guards. So while that aide of yours was distracting him, someone could have easily slipped in through another entry."

Jhakharta didn't like the way this was heading. That one of his own aides had been a traitor . . . Hastily, he scrambled for anything that could get his aide—and therefore himself—off Pehndon's current hook. So, "That sounds pretty coincidental," he argued. "What makes you certain that Grahme is involved?"

"I'm not certain, that's the entire point. I'm merely trying to determine if there's just cause for suspicion. Honestly, Alphonse, do stop trying to think; your ears are beginning to smoke. Just call your man in here so I can question him."

Jhakharta swallowed heavily and scrambled to do his master's bidding.

In the privacy of his office, which was really more of a glorified cubicle, Grahme Tortaluk stifled a yawn and tried to keep his attention focused on the papers before him. He was attempting to read but kept drifting off, feeling his eyelids grow leaden, his chin begin to sink. His head felt like it had been packed with a combination of sand and wet sawdust.

Not too surprising, considering that he hadn't slept a wink last night. The adrenaline from his midnight raid had kept him wired until well past dawn, and by the time he left Jason's office, it was as easy to go to work as to bed. It wasn't until partway through the morning that the lack of sleep had caught up with him, and now all he wanted to do was put his head down on the blotter and take a nice long nap. But instead he forced his attention back to the page, despite the fact that the letters swam dizzily before his eyes.

"Grahme? Grahme!"

It took him a moment to realize that his nominal boss was calling, his head poking anxiously over the cubicle wall.

"Huh? What? Oh, sorry, sir." Grahme stood hastily and shook off the trailing clouds of his exhaustion, reorganizing his scattered papers with what he hoped was an air of brisk efficiency. Fortunately, Jhakharta wasn't paying any heed to his fumbling; instead, there was a worried frown pinching between his boss' eyes, which suddenly bothered Grahme more than his own lack of attention.

"Sir? What is it?"

"Come into my office for a moment, would you, Grahme?" Jhakharta said, still sounding distracted, and Tortaluk felt a flood of adrenaline pour through him, banishing the last of the cobwebs.

"Certainly, sir. Anything specific you want?" He tried to keep the apprehension from his voice.

"Not per se. That is . . ."

Grahme felt his anxiety grow. Hastily, he scraped together a bunch of papers, clutching them to him like a comforting blanket, and hoped the ruse would hide his shaking hands.

But that was nothing compared to the kick of pure panic that hit him when he beheld Pehndon sitting carelessly in one of Jhakharta's chairs. He could understand how prisoners broke under torture; the minute Alphonse closed the door, he had a formless urge to blurt out the whole sordid story.

It was one of the few times he thanked the heritage that had gifted him with a long, dour face, incapable of expressing more than a kind of vague melancholia.

"Please, take a seat," Jhakharta offered, still sounding somewhat uncomfortable—almost as if he, not Tortaluk, were under judgment. As perhaps he was; it certainly seemed to confirm the connection between the Minister and Pehndon.

"Your name is Tortaluk, Grahme Tortaluk, is it not?" Pehndon demanded, taking control of the conversation as soon as Grahme was seated. At his words, the whole focus of the room seemed to shift, leaving Jhakharta marooned almost awkwardly at its fringes.

"Yes, sir," Grahme confirmed.

"And I understand you were in the building last night?"

"Yes, I was."

"Are you aware of what happened?"

It took all of Grahme's duplicity to say casually, "No, sir. What was that?"

"Someone broke in shortly after you left, set off all the alarms. When the guards came in to investigate, they found my office thoroughly tossed. Since you were known to be in the vicinity, I thought I'd see if you had any ideas as to how this might have happened."

Grahme didn't have to feign his amazement. He and Jen had taken pains to leave the office as pristine as they'd found it, and he knew they hadn't set off any alarms. So what had happened? By all that was precious, had someone *else* had the same idea? He had a sudden hysterical urge to giggle. Pehndon's office must have been as busy as the harbor during spring rush last night! But, "No, sir," he managed to say, with commendable sobriety. "I saw no one else in the vicinity. Unless . . ."

"Yes?"

"Well, I was talking to Johan for a bit while the alarms were off, so I suppose someone could have gotten in while he was distracted."

"There, you see?" Jhakharta declared almost triumphantly. "I told you he wasn't involved!" But his enthusiasm, Grahme suspected, was more for the clearing of his own name than that of his aide.

Pehndon just ignored the First Minister's outburst. "And what, may I ask, were you doing here so late?"

"Why, preparing some figures," Grahme responded ingenuously. "Something the Minister needed by morning."

"And did you prepare them?"

"Indeed I did. I was just about to give these to you, sir," he added, turning to Jhakharta and handing him the sheaf of papers.

"Ah. Is this the work for the Levan report?" Jhakharta exclaimed. "Good lad!"

Pehndon appropriated the stack without so much as a by-your-leave and began flipping meticulously through it—and Grahme heaved a mental sigh of relief, thanking the stars for Jason's foresight. Late last night, with their business concluded, he and his new conspirators had been on the verge of departure when Jason had halted them, saying, "Not so fast; we still have some details to take care of. How are you all at figures?"

"Figures?" Jen had frowned.

"Quite. You see, Grahme promised to get these numbers to Jhakharta in the morning and—thanks in part to you—he now has less than three hours to do them."

So in the wake of their plotting, the four had sat huddled around Jason's desk, rather anticlimactically working Grahme's sums. To his surprise, it was Jen's partner Thibault—or Tomas, or whatever he chose to call himself—who had proved the most useful, scratching down numbers in his neat peasant hand, his rapidity all the more startling for the stolid, unassuming style with which he performed it.

But then maybe it was just that Jen and Jason had other things on their minds; he hadn't missed the occasional heated glances that passed between them.

Nonetheless, when Pehndon finished examining the fruits of their collective labors—copied over this morning in Grahme's own hand—he merely said, "And how do I know he didn't do these yesterday? Or even earlier, for that matter?"

"Because I didn't give him the assignment until close to six last evening," Jhakharta responded, "and then he had to rush out to dinner with one of the junior ministers. There's no other time he could have done it."

Pehndon's mouth pursed, but there didn't seem to be anything more he could say, and Grahme thanked the fates again for that last-minute assignment. Usually he hated such rush jobs—knowing, as he did, that the only reason they were last-minute was because of Jhakharta's own carelessness—but this time it had proved his salvation.

Still, he could tell from the bite of Pehndon's razor-sharp gaze that he was going to have to be doubly careful in future. From here on out, the man would be watching him like a proverbial hawk.

31

In the early hours after dawn, Jen and Thibault quit the rebel headquarters and proceeded to their hotel. Jen was strangely giddy, obviously infected by the success of her endeavor and her meeting with Andorian, but Thibault found himself simply savoring the quiet perfection of the morning. With the evening cool just faded from the sky and the sun still low over the golden domes of the Mages Quarter, the day took on a fresh, springlike balminess, as if all the world were born anew. The light was soft and gentle, and the breeze blew fresh over the Belapharion, scenting the city with the faintest tang of salt. Beneath that lingered the subtler smell of the desert, all sand and prickles. The streets hadn't yet begun to stink.

He took clean, deep lungfuls of the morning air, and intermingled with a residual pique at Jen's behavior was an obscure kind of gratitude. For without her, he would still be in Gavrone, dulled by the daily tedium of the carpenter's trade. Without her, he would never have been able to stroll the quiet streets of Nhuras in the cusp of the morning, admiring the play of light over the Mages domes and listening to the distant lap of the Belapharion. What would it be like to be her partner in truth, striding the world as if it were his playground? Sometimes he couldn't help but wonder if he were crazy for insisting on his life as a carpenter's apprentice. Having been here, in far-off Nhuras, could he ever go back? Or would everything else seem perpetually pale, leached of life by the remembered blaze of the desert sun?

Not to mention that there was something about living at her side which simply seemed right to him—Jason Andorians notwithstanding.

Wryly, he remembered his mindless jealousy of the unseen Grahme Tortaluk, and his profound relief when he

finally viewed the long, woeful face of his rival. Not
Jenny's type at all. He had been totally unprepared for
Andorian—in all respects. He could practically hear the
air sizzling between those two. And then, of course, there
was his profound embarrassment when Jen had twitted
him about his method of distracting the guards. He had
felt himself run hot and cold at once, appalled by the
depth of his daring, simultaneously terrified and elated by
the unexpected intimacy.

Still, he couldn't believe she had accepted Grahme's
offer so blithely, pledging herself to Jason without a
quiver of suspicion—and all based on some nebulous stir-
rings of sexual attraction. That was no reason to trust a
person; there were plenty of good-looking villains. And
less still to risk her partner's life on the basis of her own
overwrought hormones. She had even given him their true
names, or at least an approximation; Vera would have had
a fit were she still alive.

Sometimes he forgot she was only eighteen and fresh
from the schoolroom.

He sighed. Well, it was certainly nothing he could resolve in one day, and they were rapidly approaching the
back borders of Maltha Square. He could tell by the
widening, palm-lined avenues, the increasingly pristine
facades of the slowly expanding houses. Time to get Jen
inside unobserved, clad as she was in her unladylike costume. Besides—and his mind tossed the thought up like a
biscuit—in a month it might all be academic. Jen might
have decided to stay in Ashkharon with the handsome and
fascinating Jason Andorian.

In some ways, he could almost understand the attraction. It wasn't that he was taken by men—or women either; his mind was too consumed by Jen to deal in
abstractions—but there was something undeniably compelling about the rebel leader. Still, someone had to be the
voice of reason; someone had to play the skeptic. And
who better than poor, logical Thibault, with his massive,
peasant feet planted firmly on the ground? Stolid Thibault, who would give all he owned for an ounce of Jen's
native impulsiveness?

How different things looked in the sober light of day.

He became aware of Jen, tugging lightly on his sleeve,

trying to distract the desultory tumble of his thoughts. "Wake up, Thib! Give me a boost."

Looking down into her laughing face, he couldn't help smiling as he clasped his hands and gave her a leg up, keeping watch while she swarmed up the drainpipe, agile as any monkey. Eventually she grasped the bottom of her balcony and swung herself up, vaulting over the rails with the ease of long practice.

She waved puckishly as she disappeared through the bedroom window, and swallowing yet another sigh, he proceeded around to the servants' entrance and his own humbler quarters.

As Jen closed the window behind her, she gave a shiver of sheer excitement and did a small, exultant dance about the chamber. Thibault had been quiet this morning, doubtless annoyed at her peremptory handling of the Jason situation, but she didn't care. Maybe it was purely hormonal, but the thought of spending the next few weeks under Andorian's roof made her quiver in anticipatory glee. Oh, but he was glorious! There was something about him that just made her feel elated. It had been too long since she had last felt this delightful tightening of her senses, as if every one of them was doubly—no, triply—alive.

She grasped one of the bedposts and whirled, flinging herself onto the pristine counterpane and ruffling it into jubilant ridges. Then, seizing one edge, she rolled, wrapping herself in a pale gold cocoon, burying her face in the pillow to muffle her triumphant laughter.

It was in all ways a saving grace: not only for the pleasure of meeting the man himself but also because it gave her something tangible to focus on apart from Vera, something that was of life instead of death, joy instead of despair.

She was in no mood for sleep, so she burned off her excess energy by packing, flinging clothes and cosmetics into her trunk in a tumult. Then, changing from her assassin's garb, she unbound her hair and donned a flowing gown and peignoir before unlocking her door and reversing the Do Not Disturb sign she had placed there so carefully the night before. Finally, tossing back the bedclothes, she jumped beneath the covers and waited.

A quick stab of her finger summoned the maid, and she

ordered breakfast and a bath, also conveying the message that she wished to see her suhdabhar on the double. A few minutes later, while the unsuspecting woman was preparing the tub, a rather rumpled Thibault appeared, yawning prodigiously, his hair tousled as if with sleep. Only the rather wry smile in his mouse-brown eyes as he surveyed her, propped imperiously against her pillows with her hair cascading about her shoulders, conveyed his amused wakefulness.

"What is it, milady?" he demanded, his voice still convincingly thick.

"Sorry to wake you at such an inconvenient hour, Tomas," she returned offhandedly and, seeing his eyes glint, masked her own smile, "but we'll be leaving this morning. As fate would have it, my old friend Domme Lascalle is in town and has kindly agreed to put us up. You remember how her husband always had to travel? Well, oddly enough, here they are; I ran into her in the Mages Quarter last night. They've taken the sweetest house in Dalna Street. Oh, thank you, Rosalie, that will be all; kindly bring my breakfast in half an hour." And dismissing the maid, she added, "What?"

"Nice monologue," Thibault grinned when they were finally alone. "So, how are we planning to get to Jason's unseen?"

"You just leave that to me. As usual, I have a plan."

He rolled his eyes. "Doubtless. What's this?" He was surveying the wreckage of her trunk.

"Oh." She flushed. "I was a little distracted; you might want to ask the maid to repack that. Meanwhile," and she flung back the covers, rising from the bed in a flurry of filmy fabric, "I have a bath awaiting. Go take care of what you have to, and I'll meet you back here in an hour."

She could feel Thibault's eyes on her back as she retreated, closing the bathroom door. Then, shedding robe and gown, she slid into the fragrant water and ducked her head beneath the surface, feeling her hair flow around her like a watery weed.

She was hovering over the remains of her breakfast, fully dressed in an elegant morning gown and brushing out her mage-dried hair, when Thibault reappeared, surveying her with a certain speculative amusement.

"Don't you think that gown's a little conspicuous?" he

said. "After all, Jason hardly lives in the finest part of town."

"Ah, but Domme Lascalle most certainly does," she countered. "Trust me, Thib. I told you I had a plan." And twisting her hair up into a simple chignon, she added, "Is everything ready?"

"Awaiting your pleasure, milady."

"Well, then, let's begone." And standing, she scooped up her reticule, swinging it exuberantly at the end of its string, and preceded him out the door.

Thibault shouldered her trunk, and they descended to the lobby and checked out of the hotel. For the desk clerk's benefit, Jen repeated her nebulous stories about lodging with a friend—this time keeping her references deliberately vague—and when the man offered to call her a rickshaw, she dismissed him, saying, "It's not so far, and such a lovely morning. I rather thought I'd walk. You'll be all right with the luggage, won't you, Tomas?"

Thibault nodded ruefully. She could almost hear his sigh as he shouldered both her trunk and his own, already waiting for him in the hotel lobby.

"Well, then." And so she departed for parts unknown, a little bounce in her step for the beginning of adventure.

She simply wouldn't let herself think of Vera.

Raising her parasol and lifting her skirts above the dusty pavement, she traipsed complacently toward her destination, her nerves singing with an awareness of Jason, Thibault a half step behind her. Two streets from the hotel, he paused, saying, "Isn't that our driver?"

Jen turned, shading her eyes with one upraised hand, and watched as the landau rattled past them. The man on the box did, indeed, seem familiar, but this time he had two gentlemen occupying the conveyance. One, shorter and more delicately built, with a thin, sharp face and dull, dirty-blond hair, was intent on conversation with the driver. The other was a big, bluff golden-haired giant who winked at her boldly; she returned the wink with a grin.

Thibault chuckled. "I wonder if he takes all his fares to Maltha Square? He must have a pretty sweet deal set up with one of the hotel owners."

"Oh, honestly, Thib, do keep your mind on business. We turn here." And she saw his eyes light with comprehension

as they rounded the corner and encountered the looming
bulk of one of Nhuras's public lavatories.

Similar buildings were scattered throughout the city,
divided by both gender and class, as Jen had discovered
yesterday. Luxurious chambers in the front—almost
miniature dayrooms—serviced the rich; small, squalid cu-
bicles in the rear had to serve for the poor.

"Wait for me around the far corner," Jen instructed,
adding wickedly, "I find myself in sudden need of a little
. . . refreshment!"

Thibault chuckled, waiting until she had collapsed her
parasol and stuck it crosswise through the straps of her
trunk before complying. Jen herself strode boldly to the
lavatory door and handed the attendant the requisite fee.
She was shown into a plush room complete with sink,
chaise, and a discreetly disguised commode. There was
also a high, frosted-glass window propped partially open
to admit the sun and breeze but not the curious gaze of
potentially prying eyes.

Jen shut the door, then locked it, stripping off her gown
to reveal the sleeveless shirt and breeches she was wearing underneath. A few minutes later, a bulky bundle was
lowered out the window, followed shortly thereafter by
Jen herself.

Garbed anew, she circled around the back of the facility
and rejoined Thibault, who started for a moment when he
was approached by the young suhhe with shabby clothes
and braided hair, a large bundle bouncing over one shoulder.

"Jen?" He blinked. "Where did you get those clothes?"

"I was wearing them all along."

"Then where's your gown?"

She twirled the bundle by its string.

"But isn't that . . . ?"

"My reticule? Yes. Clever, isn't it? In the compressed
state, it's stuffed with itself; Vera gave it to me." And she
slung it cheerfully across her back. "Now we're delivery
boys."

"Bearing a little bundle for 26 Lhuvhas Street, I take it?"

"Precisely. Now, give me a trunk and let's get going."

He grinned. "What, are you crazy? You can be our
navigator." And he hoisted the trunks once more to his
shoulders. "So lead on, O Bold One."

She did, and Jason himself opened the rickety door in the East Quarter tenement, his face—all but invisible in the darkened entryway—lighting in a sudden grin as he took in their disguises. Jen could feel that deep, velvety gaze sweep across her like a caress before he threw wide the door and gestured them inside.

She grinned. *There, that's trust,* she wanted to say. Thibault had already berated her soundly for giving Jason their names, yet here he was giving them his very address—information that would doubtless go for a rather steep price these days. She shot her companion a triumphant look, but he merely shrugged, readjusting the trunks on his shoulders, as Jason closed the door behind them and lit a candle.

Jen hadn't expected the lack of magelight, but then this street was also poorer than she had envisioned: the gutters overflowed with uncollected filth, the windows were unglazed and boarded. Probably few in this neighborhood could afford the mages' exorbitant services, but surely Jason was better off than that. That he should live here, in this slum, surprised her. But then, these were his people; he would probably be safer among them than anywhere else in Nhuras.

Having assured herself of his reasons, she was thus even more astonished when, instead of leading them into the depths of the house, he ushered them through another door and down a steep flight of stairs.

"The back way," he informed them, with the hint of a grin in that magnificent voice, "and please do pardon the substandard lighting. Here, Thibault, why don't you let me help you with one of those trunks? It can get a bit precipitous down here at times."

In the flickering light of the candle, partially blocked by the bodies of her companions and wavering with myriad shadows, Jen had to pick her way cautiously forward, running her hands along a banister worn cool and smooth from years of groping fingers. Between them, Jason and Thibault each maneuvered an ungainly trunk down the winding stairs—though she was aware that Thibault had given Jason the lighter of the two and he himself retained the one with their various equipment—and finally into a long, sloping tunnel which wound deeply below the houses, its nether end lost in darkness. Every so often, she could see the mouths of connecting tunnels yawning out of the blackness and wondered that the rebel leader didn't lose himself in this subterranean labyrinth. She had always prided herself on her sense of direction, and already she was hopelessly muddled.

Briefly, Thibault turned and shot her his own kind of cynical glance, distorted by the leaping shadows. *So much for trust,* it seemed to say; she quelled an urge to stick out her tongue in return. But eventually they reached their destination: another run of stairs, surmounted by a thick, heavily barred wooden door.

"Sorry again about the misdirection," Jason grinned as he released the locks with the aid of an inaudibly muttered word and blew out the candle, swinging the door wide in a wash of magelight, "but, in my position, one can never be too careful."

32

Jason's true residence was a far cry from the mildewy rooms on Lhuvhas Street. The tunnel door opened onto a cozy kitchen with a huge brick hearth dominating one end and cabinets and counters of a rich, dark wood peppering the rest. Copper pots gleamed brightly against the terra-cotta walls, depending from hooks set into the low ceiling beams, and the air was perfumed with the lingering smells of fried eggs and toast. A capacious sink harbored a clutter of unwashed dishes.

"Breakfast," explained Jason with a smile, letting the trunk slide from his shoulders. Thibault followed suit. "I just finished eating, but I can always make more if anyone's hungry?" He glanced about expectantly, but Thibault just smiled faintly and shook his head.

"We're taken care of, thanks."

"Good. Then let me show you where to leave that trunk. Space is at a bit of a premium here, but I believe we can make do. Jen can have the back bedroom, but I'm afraid we'll have to put you in the common room. There is a daybed in there which is reasonably comfortable."

He sounded almost apologetic, and Thibault found himself struggling against a certain quiet resentment, for the man seemed just too perfect. It was undeniable that his offer of asylum had been directed solely at Jen, yet here he was pretending to worry about accommodations for an unwanted addendum, as if concerned that his hospitality might be viewed as lacking. Though he undoubtedly wished Thibault gone, you would never be able to confirm it from his manner—and that alone made Thibault uneasy, for he simply couldn't conceive of anyone being that genuine.

But, he reminded himself sternly, it was his duty to play the skeptic. Andorian was an unknown quantity;

someone had to stay aloof, to measure and judge, and it certainly wasn't going to be his impulsive partner. It was his function to remain impassive.

At least that was what he kept telling himself.

So, "No, really, don't trouble yourself on my account," he said in as civil a tone as he could manage. "I'll be just fine in the common room." And he watched as those velvet-brown eyes lit with a warmth that made him want to scream. *Stop trying to charm me,* he thought. *I'm not like Jenny. I'm not that gullible or that easily swayed.* The man was just too good, and he couldn't be certain whether that relieved or terrified him.

Looking over at Jen, who was following Jason's every movement with shining eyes, he began to suspect it was very much the latter.

"Come, then," Jason was saying. "I'll give you the three-bit tour. Meanwhile," to Jen, "please make yourself at home. I'm afraid there's not all that much to look at."

"Oh, don't you worry; I'll find something," she said, baring her teeth in what Thibault liked to call her predatory grin—and which usually betokened chaos to follow. Unfortunately, Jason was not aware of the true meaning of that expression, nor that he had unwittingly offered her a challenge. A tiny core of malice kept Thibault silent. After all, the man would have her to himself for several weeks; he had to learn sometime.

Hoisting Jen's trunk, he followed Jason from the kitchen.

The house, though comfortable, was only modestly proportioned—an appropriate dwelling for a middle-class bachelor. A flight of stairs led off the back of the kitchen, climbing to a common room that overlooked a narrow, unidentifiable street through three slim, wood-sashed windows. Running perpendicular to that, on the far wall, was a more modest continuation of the brick kitchen hearth, surrounded by a cluster of furniture that was well kept if somewhat plain. The curtains, now open, were fashioned of a somewhat dusky brocade, and a large red and gold Mepharstan carpet—rather the worse for the wear—adorned the floor. An obvious daybed, several inches shorter than Thibault's own length, was pushed against the wall across from the windows, along with a

clutter of trunks, and on the fourth wall the kitchen stairs
turned and continued up to a second-floor landing.

Jason's room, at the front, contained a large, canopied
bed, with curtains of red and gold to match the downstairs
carpet, a massive wooden armoire, an equally massive
and well-used desk, and an even more minuscule hearth.
Across the landing, a tiny room under the eaves, facing
the back alley, contained nothing more than an iron bed-
stead and a rickety bedside table surmounted by a gabled
window. An equally tiny bath was cemented between the
two.

"Well, that's it," Jason said with a little shrug. "Hardly
impressive, but mine own. You can leave Jen's trunk in
the small room."

Thibault complied. There was barely a handspan of
space between the foot of the bed and the wall, so he left
it pushed parallel to the far end, away from the pillows,
where the door would clunk it on the way out. Jason, he
noticed, seemed oddly ill at ease. Offhandedly, he wondered if part of that apparent discomfort didn't stem from
his awareness of Jen's social status and the knowledge
that she was used to rooms five times this size and ten
times as well furnished. If so, he almost respected the man
for it, but he still didn't know what prompted him to say,
impulsively, "It's great. Jen will love it. But, then, I think
she spent more time in my grandmother's one-room cottage growing up than she did in her aunt's thirty-room
manor."

"Indeed?" The rebel leader's answering grin made him
feel equally odd. He was supposed to be the skeptical one,
curse it, the voice of caution and reason. So why did he
find himself wanting to believe Jason's scam, wanting to
credit that carefully crafted, trust-me persona?

The man was a positive menace.

To cover his confusion, he said, "You live here alone?"

"Yes, quite alone, although Jeryn has his own apart-
ments on the far side of the wall. We subdivided the
house as soon as he reached his majority."

"Jeryn?"

"My brother. But you won't be seeing much of him; he
does enjoy his gadding about." And a wide, affectionate
smile creased the rebel leader's face. "Shall we go back
down?"

The damage was worse than expected, even considering the grin. In the living room, on hands and knees, Jen was rifling through Jason's trunks, hooting when she saw them and gleefully exhibiting a handful of garish robes, hats, and wigs. A truly heinous concoction was perched atop her own cocked head.

"Beautiful," she declared, grinning broadly at Jason. "Which one are you planning to wear today?"

"Jenny!" Thibault exclaimed, trying to keep the residual amusement from his voice. Poor Jason was looking somewhat stunned. "What right do you have to go pawing about through other people's possessions?"

"Nonsense, Thibault, don't be such a prude," she responded airily. "They're only costumes. Besides, locks this flimsy are positively begging to be picked! So, how do I look as a blonde?" And plucking the hat from her head, she replaced it with a ringleted wig, the effect somewhat spoiled by the spill of her long, dark braid.

"Positively ghastly," Jason retorted, recovering his equilibrium. He turned to Thibault, adding softly, "Does she do this often?"

"You have no idea. Sorry. I suppose I should have warned you."

"Never mind, I'll adjust. I have plenty of time to get used to it, after all."

Caught between laughter and a sudden stabbing jealousy, Thibault remained silent.

"You're not really planning to wear any of this, are you?" Jen added.

"And why not? It's served me perfectly well in the past."

"I can imagine. The dignified Jason Andorian would never be caught in public in something like *this*!" And she held up a particularly eye-catching outfit.

Jason grinned. "Ah, yes, one of my favorites; it's gotten me through many a sticky situation. But you're right, of course. At times like this, outrageous will no longer do. With the magnitude of price on my head, I can't afford even a smidgen of attention. I've been wracking my brains for what will serve."

"Then isn't it good you have me along?" she countered cheerfully, bundling Jason's disguises back into his trunk. "Thibault, bring me my box, will you?"

By the time he had retrieved the desired item from the bottom of his trunk—put there to avoid the hotel servants' prying eyes—Jason's possessions had all been packed away. But, being Jen, she soon created a new chaos by upending the box, spilling a welter of jars and vials, ropes and wires, weapons, sheaths, bags, darts and blowpipes, and other such items across the threadbare carpet. Jason's eyes widened as she pawed through the mess at random, nonetheless avoiding all the razor-sharp edges, and eventually retrieved a drawstringed bag slightly larger than the others.

"My disguise kit," she said, waving it smugly. "Now, sit down and close your eyes. This may feel a little strange." And seating herself across from him, tailor-fashion, she proceeded to shake up a flesh-colored bottle, brushing Jason's hair back from his face as comfortably as if she had been doing it all her life. "Oh, and my cosmetic bag, Thib, if you please," she added, without turning around.

He sighed and retreated upstairs. When he returned, Jen had brushed Jason's face with a kind of thin putty, which was already beginning to dry in innumerable wrinkles while still retaining a kind of pallid, rubbery appearance.

"That's amazing! Where did you learn to do that, Jenny?" he demanded, handing her the bulging bag of cosmetics and other female accoutrements which had always vaguely baffled him.

"Vera," she said briskly, rummaging through the satchel and coming up with a brush and a second flesh-colored jar. She unscrewed the cap and proceeded to stroke the liquid atop the putty, restoring it to a more skinlike appearance. He could see Jason wriggling his nose and cheeks tentatively beneath the mask. "Stop that. Keep still." Jen swatted him lightly. To Thibault she added, "Last winter, when you were in Gavrone, I came back on break. There was one week when it was snowing something awful and we couldn't train outside, so I persuaded Vera to teach me this instead. Good, isn't it?"

"Awfully." The color was lighter than Jason's own skin, so she stroked the brush around the edges of the mask and down the smooth lines of his throat. Thibault watched in fascination as she produced still more jars and vials and brushed various shades of brown and tan across Jason's face, sinking his cheeks and eyes into antique pits and jutting his nose aggressively forward. As a finishing touch, she shook a jar of white body powder, smelling faintly of roses, across his hair; he sneezed, shook his head, opened his eyes, and was . . . transformed.

A rather querulous old northerner gazed back at them, only his eyes bright, inquisitive, and youthful within that seamed, withered face.

"Is it . . ." Jason began tentatively, his mouth moving disjointedly beneath the pull of the putty. "I take it it worked?" he added wryly, as he gazed from one face to the other—Jen's triumphant and Thibault's frozen in a kind of openmouthed astonishment.

"Yes, and utterly mage-proof," Jen declared happily. "Look at yourself."

He seemed on the verge of complying when there came an imperious rapping on a door Thibault hadn't noticed before, lurking to the right of the kitchen stairs.

Temporarily forgetting his appearance, Jason rose, saying, "Excuse me," and pulled open the portal to reveal a tiny entry hall—consisting of one door to the street and another to a mirroring residence—and an astonished young man, his features a raw, unfinished copy of Jason's own. His expression, too, was more callow, his manner more self-conscious. This had to be his brother, Jeryn. Thibault felt a moment of sympathy, wondering what it had been like to exist as a perpetually inferior product in the shadow of Jason's brilliance.

"Who?" he stumbled, his voice, too, like Jason's, but again paler, less vital.

Jen was grinning broadly, clearly enjoying her coup.

"Jeryn, it's me," Jason said, grinning in turn.

"Jason?"

"See?" Jen chortled. "I told you it was good. Fools even family members!"

Jeryn paused for a moment, then burst out laughing, his face momentarily transformed into a mirror of Jason's own. "Blast it, Jace, I told you I didn't want to recognize you the next time I saw you, but I didn't mean it literally! Who are these people, and what trauma have they caused that has aged you so prematurely?"

Jason chuckled and threw an affectionate arm around his sibling's shoulders. It was painfully obvious that he loved his brother; what was less obvious was Jeryn's response. There was something almost shuttered about his face that made it very difficult for Thibault to read.

"Come, let me introduce you. My new associates, Jen and Thibault, who were friends of the assassin and are helping me look into the little matter of Istarbion's murder. Jen, Thib, this is my brother, Jeryn."

Jeryn's taut expression lightened into a smile of such heartfelt welcome that Thibault blinked, confounded. He must have imagined that look of reticence, for there was nothing hesitant or shuttered now about Jeryn's outstretched hand, nor his hearty "A pleasure to meet you. I'm glad my brother has someone on his side. Welcome to Ashkharon, both of you. Jace, Grahme's in the office; he needs to talk to you."

"Blast," Jason exclaimed. "It's a workday, so this must be important. Jen, Thibault, why don't you come along? Whatever Grahme has to say, you'll probably want to hear it as well. And . . . oh, I daresay there's no time to undo myself, so I'll just have to carry around my extra years for a while. Thanks, Jeryn." And turning, he bolted down the kitchen stairs, his aged face an amusing contrast to his youthful vitality.

Thibault exchanged a glance with Jen. Then, with a shrug, he followed, leaving Jeryn grinning at the head of the stairs.

Jason couldn't help savoring the expression on Grahme's face as he emerged from the bolt-hole in the basement of the warehouse and entered his office with all his extra years intact. Grahme's already long face lengthened still further, and then he looked suspiciously from Jen to Jason.

"Quite," Jen laughed in that husky, golden voice that already had begun to haunt Jason's mind, reminding him of smoky wine and music. She tossed back her thick, silken plait, and he had a brief memory of her cool, assured fingers stroking the putty across his features; he was glad the mask disguised his sudden flush. "It's all my doing, as you so rightly assumed."

"Better than wigs and hats, eh, Grahme?" Jason added. "Now, take a seat and tell me what happened."

Grahme's face grew even more mournful. But, "Bad news or good?" he said, with that certain twinkle in his eye that Jason knew was his own particular version of a grin.

"Bad, please."

"Very well. Pehndon suspects. Alphonse called me into his office this morning, and there was Pehndon. He proceeded to give me a rather thorough grilling."

"Did he succeed?"

"Not a whit, thanks to your foresight; those figures saved my life. But still, he's suspicious. I spent half of my lunch hour tracing as circuitous a route as I could to your door, making sure I wasn't followed."

"So what's the good news? Why risk Pehndon's watch-dogs to bring me a message?"

Grahme glanced over at Thibault. "Fate is on our side," he declared, and only Jason was aware of the degree of triumph he packed into the innocuous words. He had become adept at reading his colleague over the years of their association. "I know when the prisoners are going out."

"When?" Jen demanded urgently.

"How?" Jason countered, more relevantly.

It was the latter question which Grahme addressed. "Road work," he declared. "They want to repave the main highway. Came to ask the First Minister if there were any large departures scheduled that they had to take into account." He grinned; it made an odd expression on that long, mournful face. "Alphonse immediately went running off to someone—Pehndon, I suspect—and arrived back with the answer that the road work had to wait three days, as there was a sizable convoy leaving from the prison that morning."

"Three days," Jen murmured, looking musingly at Thibault. "Will you be ready? I wonder if we could make you a truly terrifying scar . . ."

Her eyes twinkled, but all he said was, "It would wash off. Or melt. No, we'll simply have to make do with my humble peasant origins."

"Still . . ."

Jason grinned. "Thanks, Grahme. It seems like we'll have a lot to think about over the next few days."

"Primarily," Thibault added dryly, "restraining Jenny."

33

Pehndon frowned irritably and tapped his fingers against the tabletop. It was a quarter past the hour, and already his appointment was late. Not a good sign, especially considering that the man himself had arranged the meeting. In fact, as Pehndon saw it, he was doing his colleague a favor just by being here; the least the man could do in return was be punctual.

Of course, the fellow was doubtless convinced that the favor was his; his hasty note had contained tidings of some urgent news to be related. But as far as Pehndon was concerned, that connection had already served its usefulness and he didn't see how anything further could come of it—at least not for the present. Besides, the alehouses of Raghdon Street, on the borders of the wharf, where the coarse sailors drank themselves into a stupor and the filthy dockside whores plied their trade, were certainly far from his usual fare. The only advantage they offered was anonymity, for no one was likely to recognize a government Minister in his shadowed back booth, barely touched by a watery magelight which was badly in need of recharging.

But then, everything in this establishment could have done with a little spit and polish, not to mention a certain basic attention. The ale alone was a grade below pig swill.

Pehndon fastidiously brushed a fly from the lip of his glass and unfolded the note again:

Meet me, two hours past sunset, at the back booth of the Salty Dog. Urgent news to relate on the subject of a certain local hero—or shall we say soon-to-be transgressor? Won't the people have a fit?—A.

So where was the man?

Perhaps he had given up on the Minister. After all, the

note had been left at one of their secret drop points, a location which Pehndon himself checked only on an irregu-
lar basis. Who knew when the thing had materialized? At
the thought that his associate might have been frequenting
this place for several nights running, waiting for his absent appointment, Pehndon masked a sudden grin.

Seeing it, one of the gutter whores, her breath redolent
with garlic and her mouth missing two of its side teeth,
approached him, bending over with what she doubtless
thought was an alluring shimmy but which in reality sent
a wash of sour sweat wafting across the table. Her stringy
hair hung limply near Pehndon's right elbow.

"Here, love," she drawled, "you look like a lively
one—and cleaner than the usual gents. How about a little
tumble?"

He backed away in revulsion, but she merely sidled
closer, seemingly intent on following him into the narrow
booth.

"What's the matter, mate, don't you like women?"

He was about to utter a scathing comment when a new
figure materialized, patted the whore cheerfully on her
scrawny behind, and thumped onto the opposite bench.

"Now, don't you trouble your head with him, honey.
He's with me."

She snorted knowingly. "Figures. Well, I wish you the
best with him. He's a bit of a snooty toff, if you ask me,
but he seems well heeled enough." And she winked and
tapped her nose suggestively before sliding back into the
crowd.

"There, you see?" Pehndon's new companion grinned.
"You're earning yourself quite a reputation, Iaon."

"Well, it wouldn't have happened if you'd been on
time," the Minister countered sourly. "So what have you
got for me this time, Andorian?"

Jeryn grinned and flagged down a passing waiter, exchanging a handful of marks for a glass of the rancid ale,
which he then swigged in obvious enjoyment.

Pehndon suppressed a shudder. "Well?" he prompted.

"I wouldn't have been late if you'd been here two
nights ago," Jason's brother countered.

"You neglected to date your orders. Besides, I only
picked the thing up this morning."

"Yes, I figured as much."

"So? What have you got for me in recompense for forcing me to wait in such an . . . establishment?" And Pehndon looked about him with distaste, indicating the numerous drunken brawls and staggering patrons, the miasma of poverty and degradation which seemed to hang like a pall beneath the low-beamed ceiling.

"Patience. Live a little, Iaon. You'll love this one, I assure you."

Pehndon measured the man across from him, wondering how anyone could see a resemblance to Jason in his face. The man was an empty-headed pleasure-seeker, nothing more. At least Jason had a vision and a drive, counter though it be to Pehndon's own. Jeryn had nothing; you could see it in every shallow line and feature. Nothing, that is, but a petty, childish need for revenge against a brother who would always be everything that he was not.

Then again, nothing said that Pehndon had to respect his victims; he could merely use them.

"I fail to appreciate your definition of 'living,' " he responded, "but very well. What will I love?"

"Jason's got someone new working for him."

"He does? Who?"

"Don't know precisely, but my gut says they're assassins. All I know is that they're friends of Leonie's and are helping him to look into Istarbion's murder. But I thought you might like to know that there's someone else on the trail."

Pehndon felt a sudden surge of triumph fill him. His information net hadn't failed, then; he still knew how to choose his links. And as for the ramifications . . . well, they were staggering! By all that was precious, he could almost feel the pieces falling into place. Leonie Varis wasn't alive, and the raid on his office was no supernatural visitation or revenge from beyond. The body in the alley had been Leonie's; his mages hadn't led him wrong. She had merely unwittingly made good on her threat. The Guild had sent someone after her, and now they were after him. No problem whatsoever.

He had handled one Guild member already, reputedly their best. He could take on these two easily.

And the fact that the two were now allied with Jason . . . He would bet his next paycheck that he knew exactly where his papers resided: somewhere within the headquarters of the rebel alliance. The only problem was that he had no idea where the real alliance was located.

Tragically, he and Jeryn each had their rules. The man was out to humiliate his brother, to discredit him, but not to kill him. He would play Jason for the assassin, would front the fake alliance, but the one thing he consistently refused to do was give up his brother's location. Maybe he simply didn't trust Pehndon—though Iaon had assured him repeatedly that there would be no trial—or maybe it was the last bastion of decency showing through his selfishness and greed. Ironically, this one stubborn refusal was the sole thing that Pehndon respected about the man. He admired people who stuck to their principles, even if it was pointless.

And Jeryn's refusal was pointless indeed. He was too weak, and Pehndon too good; he knew the man's codewords as if he held the list in his hands. He could turn Jeryn on and off like a magelight. Oh, it was pointless to push him now, of course; it would earn him nothing. And though he knew he could break the man, where was the joy in that? No, better that Jeryn believe his protestations that he meant his brother no harm—although, of course, the trial would go on the minute he laid his hands on Andorian Senior, and the verdict would be death—and continue in his safe assurance that he could be of use.

As, indeed, he could be. If the papers were in Jason's office, who better to retrieve them than his trained seal, Jeryn? He began to grin, feeling the tide of his fortunes reverse again, wafting control back into his hands.

Still, he wouldn't be entirely comfortable until he could once again feel the weight of those papers against his palms. Knowing they were out there, unguarded . . . Too much had been going wrong lately; any snag began to seem like disaster.

So, "Indeed. I *am* most interested to hear it," he said. "It explains a number of mysterious details. You've just earned yourself quite a hefty commission, Andorian."

Jeryn grinned. "How much?"

"Quite equal to what you've received before, I assure you."

"Bollocks! That was easy. Any more information I can supply you with to expand my pockets some more?"

"Not information, precisely, but I do believe I have another job for you. One that will earn out quite handsomely if you succeed."

"Do tell."

Pehndon smiled dryly. Revenging himself on Jason was motive enough, he knew, but the money was an added incentive, wedding Jeryn more firmly to his cause. In all of Nhuras, no one but Jason could be ignorant of the size of his brother's bar bills and gambling debts.

"There are some papers I want you to retrieve," he said. "Papers which are vital to me and which I now believe reside in Jason's possession."

"In Jason's possession? How did they get there?"

"Well, you just said he had two new assassins working for him, did you not?"

"Yes, but . . ."

"Then I take it you didn't hear what happened three nights ago. Honestly, Jeryn, with the whole of the rebel alliance to spy on, you really do know frighteningly little."

"So? Politics bore me," Jeryn countered with an obvious attempt at nonchalance; Pehndon thought the more accurate response would have been: *Politics baffle me. Politics are yet another realm where my brother will forever outdo me.* Oh, yes, he could read Jeryn like a book. "So, are you going to tell me what happened?" Jeryn added somewhat impatiently.

"My office was broken into."

"Indeed." Jeryn's eyes twinkled. "So that's what Grahme and Jason were so excited about."

Pehndon blinked. "Excuse me, but did you say *Grahme?*"

"Yes, Grahme Tortaluk, one of Jason's cronies. I don't know what he does—he's not around all that often—but he does seem closer to my brother than the rest of the alliance combined. They always seem to have their heads together over something."

Pehndon felt like laughing. It wasn't something he did often, but he surrendered to the impulse now, causing Jeryn to stare at him curiously—and that, oddly enough, only made him laugh all the harder. *I knew it, I knew it!* he wanted to shriek.

"What's the matter, Iaon? Are you feeling all right?"

"Never better, I assure you. My dear boy, you are a

wonder—a genuine wonder! Whatever price I quoted, double it. You've just earned it."

Jeryn was still looking baffled. But, "That's part of the problem," he said gamely enough. "You haven't quoted me any price yet."

"Well, then. About those papers. Find them and restore them to me, and I will pay you half the reward on your brother's head. Half again, including the information you have just provided. Is that generous enough for you?"

"Quite. But," Jeryn frowned slightly, "you promised that Jason wouldn't be harmed, at least not physically."

"And you're concerned that the price might rouse the bounty hunters?"

"Well . . ."

"You're quite right; it might. But the question is, do you honestly believe that anyone will be able to find him?"

"I . . . No. But did you really have to make it so high?"

"And what kind of fool would I have looked if I hadn't? Besides, it was the courts that ultimately decided, not me. You just keep your brother out of the streets, and I'll worry about keeping the case out of the courts. The money will be in its usual place in the morning. You can go now. And thank you, Andorian."

Jeryn drained the dregs of his beer and set down his glass, staring at Pehndon for a moment over the rim. Then, shrugging visibly, he nodded. "To a profitable partnership—as usual. See you around, Iaon."

Pehndon watched him leave, a faint half smile playing about his lips. In the corner by the door, two sailors commenced a drunken howling, obviously distressed by the outcome of a dart game. How much louder would they howl if they knew the scale of the game that Pehndon was playing?

Poor innocent Jeryn was out of his league, hindered by residual twinges of guilt, which Pehndon would use—and ruthlessly. It wouldn't be long before Jason was his.

Pehndon took one small but triumphant sip of the revolting ale, saluting the tavern's crass patronage as if in celebration, then stood and stalked from the riotous portals, leaving his drink all but untouched behind him.

Nevertheless, a small, bleak, and almost unacknowledged part of him couldn't help wondering if the game weren't still very far from over.

It was with a certain satisfaction that Jeryn inserted his latchkey into the lock and muttered a drunken password, letting himself into the subdivided establishment he shared with his brother. He had been out late imbibing— spending part of Pehndon's promised profits—and now Jason's side of the house was dark and silent, with only the faintest glow of a banked fire whispering through the ground-floor windows where that giant lay curled on his temporary bed.

He wondered if the dark-haired wench was sharing his brother's, their two bodies entwined in mutual self-admiration, but he dismissed the thought with a snort. His brother was too bloody perfect for anything so crass as fornication.

Not Jeryn, though. He had his women, and his wine. So why was it never enough, never quite sufficient to erase that gap between his brother and himself? All his life it had been Jason, Jason, Jason—the endless and constant refrain. Jason the perfect student; Jason the perfect leader; Jason the all-round perfect creation.

How, eclipsed by the brightness of that light, could anyone have noticed Jeryn—who had tried so hard to be everything his brother was and he so painfully was not?

Eventually he had stopped trying, taking pride in being his brother's opposite. Flighty where his brother was sober; joyful where his brother was serious; extravagant where his brother was parsimonious.

And still they whispered.

Poor Jeryn. Never enough.

Well, he'd had it; he would show them. Iaon Pehndon had opened the way. A few little acts and he would shatter Jason's pedestal like an eggshell, toppling the great hero, proving at last that Jason Andorian was as human and fallible as they or he. That Jason Andorian didn't hold all the answers.

That Jason Andorian couldn't, ultimately, fulfill their dreams.

Sometimes he wondered why it still pained him, why it still even mattered. And the hidden voice that tormented him—that he barely even acknowledged—whispered insidiously in his ear.

Love takes many strange forms, and without love there couldn't be hate. Did he hate Jason, or love him—love him so strongly, so deeply, so enduringly that he ached to follow him, to support him, to believe in him, more than all of Nhuras combined? So that Jeryn could be the center of Jason's world as Jason had always been of Jeryn's?

Sometimes he no longer even knew.

With a weary sigh, he turned from Jason's door and fumbled open his own, stumbling drunkenly up the stairs to collapse across his bed in a dreamless, depthless, blissfully mind-numbing slumber.

34

Three mornings later, in the hazy minutes before dawn, Thibault lurked outside the walls of the Nhuras prison, watching as the line of mangy camels was assembled into a functional caravan. Grunting and protesting, glaring down their supercilious noses, they planted their splayed feet firmly against the cobblestones and refused to be shifted, oblivious to the goads and prods of the handlers who tried to arrange them into something resembling a ragged line. Eventually one, under great duress, would be persuaded to move, and then it would be shackled to the beast before it, much as Thibault was sure the line of prisoners would later be fettered. The lead camels, already bound, rattled their chains and belled their protest to heedless morning.

The loading, likewise, seemed to take an era, and Thibault shifted in the shadows, trying to surreptitiously stir some life into his motionless limbs. His cheek itched and he moved to scratch it, temporarily surprising himself when his fingers encountered the ridged welt of the putty scar which, against his better judgment, Jen had fashioned for him in the small hours of the morning. It was a truly horrendous creation, seamed and puckered, meandering crookedly across his cheek from the edge of his left eye to the bottom corner of his mouth. The slight tug of tension of his lip was supposed to remind him of its presence, but somehow he just kept forgetting.

Nonetheless, it did add a certain recklessness to his appearance, making him look more like some bold desperado than the stolid, loyal peasant he knew himself to be. Sylvaine, were she alive, would doubtless shriek with horror at his appearance, then berate him soundly for capitulating to yet another of "Jenny's whims."

The problem was, he reflected, that "Jenny's whims"

were usually all too accurate, and the scar would certainly add credence to his disguise as a hardened criminal.

Now if he could only remember its presence.

He shifted his position, propping his shoulder against the wall, and reflected on his parting with Jenny. Oddly enough, she had seemed a little misty-eyed as she checked the last of his preparations and retreated to her bed, leaving him with a fierce hug and a kiss, and a firm injunction to come home safely. And with the echo of her footsteps still soft on the stairs, he stared after her in a kind of bemusement, not untouched with a certain nebulous regret. He was used to the transience of Jenny's presence in his life, but somehow this was different. Always before, he had left her with someone: Vera, Sylvaine, even Genevra, but now there was no one left. He could see the bold carriage of her head as she retreated up the stairs, not looking back, and he knew it for a lie.

He could feel her loneliness and confusion spiraling down to him like the threads of some exotic perfume, and he almost followed her up. But instead he retreated into the night and took up his vigil in the shadow of the prison walls.

On the whole, it seemed the least dangerous proposition.

So now he watched as the camels to the front and rear were loaded with baggage and those in between fitted with unsteady platforms that bore only a central divider like an elongated, inverted T. Then the gates swung open, disgorging a cluster of prisoners surrounded by a wary circle of guards. There were about twenty all told, shipped in from various provinces over the course of a month to supplement Nhuras' dwindling supply of native lawbreakers.

Several seemed intent on making a break for it, and in the resultant confusion it was frighteningly simple for Thibault to slip into their midst. He had no luggage save for the fifteen twenty-mark pieces stitched into hollows in his rough, shabby belt, and the four extra tens for emergency which Jen had inserted into the soles of his sandals. Otherwise, like the rest of the crew, he was garbed in ragged, filthy, redolent castoffs which Jen had bargained away from a local beggar; his skin twitched as he contemplated the multiplicity of vermin they might be harboring.

Wouldn't it be just his luck to come home crawling

with lice or fleas, or some other unpleasantness, simply as a product of Jen's brainstorm?

The guards, less than delighted about being forced from routine at such an early hour, began seizing prisoners at random and applying arm and leg irons, then padlocking the trailing chains together, parceling them into ragged groups of four. Thibault was conscripted into a cluster consisting of two other men and one woman. One of the men was a surly, belligerent sort and, though not as tall as Thibault, outmassed him by a goodly margin. He also had a real scar slicing across his nose which was almost as nasty as Thibault's reconstruction. The other, falsely hearty, had the shifty gaze of a professional con man. But of all them, it was the lone woman who scared him most. With her cold, snakelike eyes and quick, furtive movements, she gave the impression that she carried at least a dozen concealed weapons—all of them deadly—though rationally he knew the guards had stripped her clean.

And from the look in her eyes, one of those nonexistent weapons would find its way into the ribs of each of the trio if he stepped even the slightest bit out of line.

Still, Thibault had decided he could probably survive the journey when one of the guards suddenly yelled, "Hai, boys, we've got one too many," almost stopping his heart.

That was it. They would find him and question him and . . .

He got no further with his speculations, for another called back cynically, "Wouldn't you know? I knew that bloody warden couldn't count! Well, put him somewhere; I don't care where. Chain him to the baggage rack if you have to."

Once shackled—with Thibault at the head of his little group and the woman at its foot—they were hustled to one of the waiting camels. There was enough slack on their chains that they could walk with reasonable comfort, and Thibault was further assured that Jen's prediction would come true. After all, as she had so reasonably observed, he was part of a labor force; it wasn't to anyone's benefit to abuse the prisoners such that they couldn't work once they arrived.

As they approached, the camel drivers forced the beasts to kneel—whacking their front legs peremptorily out from under them when other, more traditional, methods failed—and each cluster was then mounted on a platform, two to a side, with their backs to the wooden partitions and their knees dangling over the edges of the boards. This distribution was done regardless of weight or balance, and thus Thibault found the two largest of their quartet, himself and his neighbor, initially positioned on the same side. The platform tilted precariously under their weight, threatening to spill them both headlong onto the paving stones, and when Thibault clutched desperately at the seat back in an attempt to haul himself up, his fingers met the dry, scaly flesh of the woman seated behind him. She hissed at him and, startled, he dropped his hands. The platform swayed again, and the irate guards grumbled as they were forced to unchain and reposition the prisoners, swapping the men so that Thibault now found himself cheek by jowl with the swaggering con artist.

They exchanged rather relieved grins, obviously seeing each other as the least threatening of the quartet.

Still grumbling, the guards closed the circle, securing Thibault's chains to those of the woman still behind him, then fastened the lot to the leads that bound the camels.

"Enjoy it," said one of the guards with a rather nasty snicker. "That'll be your palace for the next eight days."

"Well, at least we'll get pay and a pardon," one of the more waggish prisoners exclaimed from two camels back, "which is more than I can say for you lot. Watch yourselves; we'll be back before you know it."

"Aye, and safely returned to your cages," a second guard chuckled.

"Perhaps, but what fun we'll have until then!"

A ragged cheer went up from the assembled prisoners, and another shouted cheerfully, "Don't forget, we know where you live, Willy!"

The second guard snorted. "Your fine threats don't scare me, Bren; I've seen you in and out of my clutches far too often. Now get this lot out of here. I have better things to do than hanging about all day listening to insults."

Thibault masked a grin, and then the world tilted. There was a sickening lurch as the camel was goosed to its feet and the platform swayed wildly, causing him to clutch at the boards in panic. An anxious moment later, the thing achieved a precarious equilibrium.

"All right, then," the head guard called, gesturing to the caravan drivers. "Move 'em out. And enjoy the journey; I understand the desert's particularly lovely at this time of year."

Jen had been up late, helping with last-minute preparations and fixing Thibault's scar. Oddly, she had felt a certain reluctance to bid him farewell, though the hour was growing late, the house dim and silent, and Jason long since asleep. But at last she had hugged him firmly and dropped a kiss on his unscarred cheek, feeling an uncharacteristic desire to bawl.

"Take care of yourself, and come back safely," she said firmly—almost an order—and then retreated to her tiny chamber beneath the eaves. And there she lay, staring up at the sloping ceiling, feeling the last links to her old life sliding away. With Vera gone, Thibault was all she had. If anything should happen to him now . . .

She suppressed the thought with a shiver and stifled an urge to pad across the hall and into Jason's bed. But that wasn't fair, to burden him with her confusion; he deserved far better than that. Besides, the poor man needed his sleep. He had retired hours earlier, and would doubtless be up with the sun and full of his usual boundless energy.

But since sleep was a long time in coming, when she finally awoke it was well past her usual hour, and the tiny room was steaming in the heat. She threw off her covers and lay for a moment in sweat-drenched sheets, listening to the sounds of the house around her. A perfect quiet filtered through the stairwell, and something about the quality of the silence told her Jason was long gone and she was the sole resident; the note tacked to her door was merely a courtesy detail.

Gone to the office, it read in a bold, decisive hand. *Latchkey's on the kitchen table. I won't bother to say make yourself at home, because I know you'll do so anyway. Have a good day, and don't make any plans for dinner.—J.*

Jen grinned and crumpled the note, pitching it into the common room hearth on her way down to the kitchen. Then, slipping the door key into her pocket, she proceeded to rifle through his stores in search of breakfast,

assembling a hasty meal, then depositing the dirty dishes
in the sink on top of Jason's.

*I'll do them when I get back, and won't that surprise
him,* she thought with a grin, but for now more urgent duties called. With Thibault gone, she could devote her full
attention to getting more concrete evidence on Pehndon,
and that required a trip to the mages. She briefly debated
the merits of changing into one of her more sumptuous
gowns but eventually discarded the idea. Her peasant costume was far more comfortable—especially in this heat—
and besides, it was the quantity of her money which
would impress the mages, not the quality of her finery. So
she slipped a bulging purse into her pack with some other
concealing items, tucked a few more stray weapons about
her person, and set out for the Mages Quarter.

Jason's address proper was somewhere on the boundary
between Port and West Quarters, in a region of quaint re-
spectability populated mostly by up-and-coming merchants and traders. Using the golden domes as her guide,
Jen wove her way placidly through the ever-widening
streets toward the mages' domain, reflecting on the di-
verting display of urban logic which perpetually led to
cities with more than four Quarters. To date, she had
counted at least seven in Nhuras and was certain there
were some she had yet to discover.

Maybe tonight she could get Jason to give her the
guided tour of Nhuras' multiple Quarters; it might prove
an amusing diversion.

Chuckling at the thought of having Jason all to herself
at last, she marched beneath the soaring archway and into
the Mages Quarter, strolling into the first establishment
she encountered and flashing her money. The glint of
marks brought her to the instant attention of the attending
mage, and she fired off a series of pointed questions before sauntering off down the street and repeating the
whole procedure at the next establishment.

After about two hours of strict comparative shopping,
she had narrowed the field to three candidates, all of
whom she felt were equally capable of giving her reasonable, high-quality, and overall discreet service. From that
point, a childish game of chance completed the selection.
She simply sat on a bench with her eyes closed and assigned each mage a color in her mind, based on a mix of

personality and instinct. Then, opening her eyes, she waited for the first passerby whose clothing matched one of her choices.

When a woman breezed by clad all in teal, Jen grinned and rose, returning to the establishment in Wisteria Street. She was ushered back to the mage's sanctum, where she took a seat and regarded the woman with a sober demeanor and the faintest hint of a grin. Then, laying out her money on the table, she crossed her legs and settled down to some serious bargaining.

Elsewhere in the city, some equally serious bargaining was occurring, and for a much more stringent price. Grahme Tortaluk had reported to work as usual and was sitting at his desk shuffling papers when three very hefty men materialized, casting him into an ominous shadow.

"What the bloody blazes . . ." he began, looking up with a start, then—thinking better of it—inquired diplomatically, "What can I do for you, gentlemen?"

"Cooperate, for a start. Failing that, go quietly."

"What?"

Pehndon emerged from behind one of the hulking behemoths, and Grahme felt his heart impact soundly against the roof of his mouth.

"I beg your pardon, sir, but . . . is there a problem?"

"Oh, yes, a most decided problem," Pehndon informed him, with an annoyingly self-righteous smirk. "I didn't quite believe your little story yesterday, and it seems I was correct. One of my sources indicated your involvement in the theft of my papers."

"But . . . He's lying, sir!"

"I think not. Though there are, of course, ways of confirming that. Would you care to repeat that oath under truth spell?"

Grahme hesitated, suddenly unsure if one of the lurking monsters might in fact be a mage, and the spell already in place. After all, mages came in all shapes and sizes, just like regular people, despite the fact that public opinion tended to cast them in a far more glorified light. And while his silence might be suspicious, at least it was better than condemning himself outright.

"Ah, you have chosen the latter course, I see," Pehndon

purred, as Grahme's lips remained stubbornly sealed. "Well, so be it. Take him away, boys."

The bullies grabbed his arms and wrenched them painfully behind his back, binding them firmly before he had even a chance to protest.

Quite frankly, he was still in a state of considerable shock.

Belatedly, he wriggled in their grasp, causing Pehndon to emit a cynical chuckle. "You can't do this," Grahme exclaimed. "You have nothing on me!"

"On the contrary, my dear Grahme, I think you will find that I can do anything I want. Including bunging you in a nice, cozy cell until I have all the evidence I require."

"But . . ."

"Oh, no, Grahme, don't bother to protest; you might get yourself into further trouble." And again he gave that self-righteous grin, which provoked another wriggle out of the trussed Tortaluk. "I assure you, I was not kidding about that witness. With some judicious pressure, he will testify against you—and once he returns my papers, I will have all the evidence I need to stage a nice little trial. By the time I'm finished, not even your precious Andorian will be able to save you."

Grahme's last hope died a slow, messy, and horrible death. They knew about Jason. They knew about his connection to the rebel alliance. They would never let him go now.

Perhaps, he reflected as they dragged him away amid the curious and often gloating stares of his former colleagues, Jen had been right after all. If not with Jason, then Pehndon had another in with the rebel alliance—for this had to have been an inside job. And if that were true, then his former boss was sitting on a very large and very unsteady hole indeed.

That is, if his former boss was even telling the truth.

He hated himself for the niggling suspicion which had suddenly begun to enter his mind.

35

When Jason arrived home that evening, it was with a certain frisson of satisfaction and the tantalizing knowledge that Jen was now in residence. He felt it the moment he turned the key, cracked open the outer door. He could feel her presence like an intimate touch, her own unique scent—not perfume but something subtler and yet wholly Jen—twining in the air, imbuing his entire dwelling with a certain sparkle and vitality. Almost, he had the feeling that he could reach out and touch her despite the walls, that the air carrying his awareness would return those caresses to her as if by magerie. In some ways, it was almost as if she plugged a hole: a Jen-size hole, one he hadn't even known existed. And yet there it was, curved to her contours as if it had been tailor-made, as if it had been lurking there invisibly below the common room ceiling and he had spent his whole life skirting its fringes, brushing it, merely, and never once stumbling into its treacherous embrace.

He was amazed that he had missed it for all these years.

Pocketing his latchkey and tossing his hat to a nearby peg, he closed the door softly behind him and felt the beginnings of a grin curving his features. For even as he was aware of her presence, he was abruptly conscious of another absence, as if something awkward and angular had been removed from his life. Not that he had anything against her partner; in fact, his respect for the man had surprised him. If he hadn't been pledged to Jen, Jason would have welcomed him into the rebel alliance. His instinct for people was seldom wrong, and he knew Thibault was a creature of great integrity. But the man had stood between them like an ungainly bolster: comfortable to lean against, true, but nonetheless a barrier.

In many ways, it was his respect for Thibault that had

kept him from approaching Jen, from welcoming her into his life and his bed with the openhearted candor he had so longed to display.

But no longer. Thibault was gone and Jen remained, and his stomach knotted almost uncomfortably in reminder.

She was precisely where he knew she would be, seated, tailor-fashion, in the center of his worn carpet, surrounded by a welter of gadgets which glinted with the unmistakable aura of magerie. There was a crystal ball and another structure of crystalline rods, like a miniature pipe organ, webbed with glowing conduits; he couldn't even begin to guess at its function. Hovering above her head was a tiny crystal fleck, cut like a diamond, which winked back at him as he entered.

She seemed absorbed in her task but said, alertly enough and without looking up, "Good evening. I remain available for dinner as requested," and, "Actually, you don't look half bad as a blond."

His hand went almost involuntarily to his head, feeling the unfamiliar contours of his wig. Actually, it wasn't a true blond like that ridiculous concoction Jen had unearthed from his trunk, but rather a sun-bleached brown: straight and thick like his own hair, yet different enough to add a certain variance to his appearance. He had bought it the other day on Jen's recommendation, and had raided her cosmetics for powders to lighten his skin and make his eyes glow in their sockets like two tarry pits. When he added a jaunty hat, cocked rakishly over one eye, he barely recognized himself in the mirror.

"Thank you . . . I think. But how did you know? Are you suddenly a mind reader like the mages?"

She turned then and smiled at him, her eyes gleaming like two mossy agates, and he felt his heart invert. "Not precisely, but the mages do have something to do with it, as you so rightly surmised. Come here."

He approached soundlessly, kneeling behind her and peering into the ball over her shoulder. The insides of his thighs grazed her waist and she leaned against him, lining her forearms along his legs and curling her hands about his knees as if she reclined in the most comfortable of armchairs.

He felt himself stir at her touch.

"What?"

She couldn't have been unaware of the feathering movement against her back, but all she said was, "Look. Closer."

He lowered his chin to her shoulder, but his mind couldn't have been further from the crystal. Instead, his whole awareness was seized by the arch of her ear, the fall of her cheek, the curve of her mouth, which tilted up ever so slightly in a smile as she divined his intention. She inclined her head, muttered an unintelligible word, and . . .

It was the sweetest of kisses, as soft and sensuous as the smoky warmth of her voice. Her mouth opened beneath his with an unhurried acceptance that had nothing to do with artifice and yet was nonetheless art. Her cool fingers curved up around his neck, and when he eventually opened his eyes, it was only to see the twin rings of gold that surrounded her umbrous pupils smiling up at him.

"Well? What do you think?" Her voice was soft, throaty.

"About what?"

She ran a finger down his cheek, guiding his gaze to the crystal, where an image of the two of them reposed, he in his wig and she with a delicate tendril of hair escaped from its braid and curling about her cheek. He tilted his head, and the figure in the ball tipped slightly in the other direction, as if they were aligned around a central pivot. Even with the makeup, his skin was dark against her own, but like their reversed positions, there was a certain symmetry to it: his image of coppery skin and lighter hair gazing across at her own copper-haired, ivory-skinned paleness.

They were like a matched set, only negatives.

"Perfect," he said.

"What? Us, or your disguise?"

"Both, actually."

She grinned. "I see you've put my lessons to good use. I particularly like the eyes—very nice shadowing. So where have you been that necessitates such artifice?"

"Out, about. On the streets. Gathering information."

"Find anything good?"

"I might have."

Nonetheless, he had to admit that if it was anonymity

he was seeking, he had failed miserably. Instead of skittering uncomfortably off his surface (an effect which his more outré disguises usually achieved in spades), the eyes of women—and sometimes men—raked him boldly; he had trembled in his proverbial boots until he realized that though they looked, they didn't see. His identity remained a secret; it was only his veneer which drew their attention. So he forced a friendly swagger into his stride and was staggered by the number of invitations he received: to tea and coffee—and sometimes other things entirely—and the friendly openness which surrounded those impromptu sessions he accepted. These were the type of meetings he would never be invited to as the exalted Jason Andorian, the type at which drink and conversation flowed freely and frankly, covering topics from Pehndon to potholes.

It was a welcome reminder of exactly what he was fighting to preserve.

"One does," he said, "Tend to get so caught up in the abstractions that it is hard to remember the reality. It was a good day."

"I'm glad; so was mine. And getting better by the minute . . ."

She kissed him again, and he watched with half an eye as their images in the ball melded and fused, watched as his finger twined in that stray tendril of hair, as her lips trailed down the curve of his neck.

"Rather voyeuristic, isn't it?" she chuckled softly into his collarbone.

He shivered as her tongue traced a line along his skin. "Indeed. But fascinating, nonetheless. How much did you pay for this thing?"

She lifted her head, her bright eyes twinkling. "A pretty fortune, so it's a good thing I'm staying with you and not at some hotel; I'd probably have been destitute otherwise. Not," she added, drowning again in the taste of his skin, "to discount the other advantages . . ."

He inserted a finger under her chin, tilting her gaze up to meet his. Almost without his conscious knowledge, his other hand was unwinding her braid. "You're a bold one, aren't you?"

"What, are you complaining?"

"Varia forfend. Have you always been like this?"

"Since finishing school, anyway." The sudden spill of

hair across his fingertips startled him; she shook back the heavy mane with a grin. "You might be surprised how . . . broadening . . . an education I received in Haarkonis. Thibault's convinced I'm quite the wanton."

There was a moment of silence, as if the mention of her partner had driven a subtle wedge between them, the ghost of the bolster lingering between their bodies.

"So, what are you planning to do with your new acquisitions?" he said eventually, nodding at the spread of her mage-powered apparatus.

"Bug Pehndon's office, of course."

He surveyed the assortment dubiously. "With all that? Won't he be a bit suspicious?"

But, "Silly," she said, "I shan't be using the whole thing. Just the little crystal here." And she indicated the chip, hanging motionless in the air like an expectant bee. "It was split from the ball, you see, so it bears an affinity for its mother crystal even at a distance." And she guided his fingers around to the back of the viewer, where a faint imperfection in the spherical surface matched the dimensions of the hovering splinter. "And what the chips sees, the ball sees," she added proudly.

"And that?" He pointed at the pipe organ.

"Stores it all—for posterity, as it were." She chuckled. "Shall I show you how it works?"

"Not necessary. I'll take your word that it functions. But this is amazing, Jen. I've never seen anything like it."

"Nor should you have. The mage designed it to my specifications."

He whistled, impressed despite himself. "No wonder it cost you a fortune. How long will it remain active?"

"Long enough, I hope, because I can't afford another memory unit once this one's full."

She sounded somewhat sheepish, and he blinked. "Blazes, Jen, that's really putting all your eggs in one basket, isn't it?"

"Well, it's my usual style—or so I've been told—but it really is quite a sturdy basket. So are you sure you don't want to see how it works? It is most phenomenally clever . . ."

He twisted her loose spill of hair about his wrist like a silken rope and shook his head. "No, because that's business, and tonight is for pleasure; I get few enough breaks these days. Now, I promised you dinner and," he stood, releasing her hair and pulling her against him, suddenly aware of thighs that were stiff and trembling from too much squatting, "dinner you shall have. I'm in costume for it, after all. Shall I take you to the best restaurant in Nhuras?"

He was glad she was tall; her eyes were only a few inches below his own. But now they clouded, their teasing glint vanished. "No, Jason, I don't want any fancy meals or exotic cuisine. I'm tired of being the bloody aristocrat . . ."

He silenced her with a kiss, bending his head and swallowing her protest as it emerged. She stiffened for a moment, then swayed against him, and he could feel the lean core of muscle beneath her deceptive softness, her hair flowing in a torrent across his hands and arms. He could have bedded her now: here, on the floor, in the middle of his threadbare carpet, and he knew she would have opened her body to him as warmly and generously and unselfconsciously as she now opened her lips. But it was better to wait, to let the delicious anticipation of dinner draw out the tension between them as they gazed at each other across a softly magelit table, walked home through the balmy cool of the desert evening with the stars winking brightly overhead and the air perfumed with jasmine, hibiscus, and sage from the hanging baskets and fragrant hedgerows along the Promenade. As they listened to the soft lap of the Belapharion beneath their whispered words.

Better by far.

So he merely released her, saying, "Nonsense. I didn't say the *finest* restaurant; I said the *best*. So will you please deign honor me with your humble, middle-class presence?"

She chuckled. "With the utmost of pleasure." And freeing herself, she added, "Let me just get changed," and dashed off, her feet pounding joyously up the stairs.

Jason smiled, went downstairs, and began placidly washing the dishes.

36

The room glowed around them in a warm red embrace as Jen tucked away the last of her meal and laid her napkin aside.

Jason was right, she reflected; this was far from the finest restaurant in Nhuras. The ruby color was flaking delicately off the walls, and the fanciful spattering of gold paint, glittering above them like a tiny firmament, couldn't hide the unmistakable signs of dry rot in the low, dark wood beams. The warren of rooms, each holding no more than five or six diners, stretched in a jumbled subterranean labyrinth, and the maroon tablecloths were stitched with a multiplicity of stains, burns, and meticulously mended rents. Even the watery magelight—while decidedly atmospheric—likely had more to do with economy than ambiance. Hence the necessity for the tiny candles, winking in rough cut-glass holders at the center of each table, preventing the patrons from groping blindly for their dinners.

It was, she decided, all quite phenomenally romantic.

Better yet, the food was as wonderful as Jason had promised: pungent, spicy, and tender in equal measures. She polished off a veritable array of delicacies—from a tangy soup to a sweet, flaky pastry—while Jason smiled indulgently and ordered dish after dish that she couldn't locate on the menu, heaping her plate when she showed signs of flagging. And so she ate, reveling in the myriad of foreign flavors and textures, and all the while they talked. Talked and talked and talked, as if they couldn't get enough of each other's company and history, as if they had to absorb the most minute details of each other's existence.

She told him of Genevra and Favienne, and of her first visit to Vera. Of her first sight of the sturdy peasant lad she would torment until the end of his days.

"He was so serious," she laughed around a mouthful of pilaf laced with shreddings of fruit and delicate, razor-thin slivers of nut. "So big-eyed and lonely and oddly lost that I just couldn't resist teasing him. And he took it so well—so placidly, almost gratefully—that I had to do it again and again and . . ."

Jason chuckled. "So on to eternity."

"Precisely. Poor Thibault; I've led him quite a fear-some dance over the years."

He was silent for a moment, picking idly at a bed of frondlike greens. "You love him quite a lot, don't you?" he said.

"Of course. He's my best friend in all the world. I'd be lost without him." She grinned and speared a piece of the meat, which had a wild, gamy tang beneath the curry; she was somehow convinced it was camel, despite Jason's laughing denials. Popping it into her mouth, she added, "I like to think of him as my conscience, only somehow ex-ternalized."

He groaned. "Wonderful. And now he's left you with me. So how far away is your conscience now?"

"Partway to Dheimos, I imagine. Think you can handle it?"

"I don't know. How much trouble do you usually cause?"

"Oh," her eyes twinkled, "you have no idea!"

He chuckled and passed her a plate, caressing her fin-gers beneath its curving lip. "Here, have some more camel," he offered.

"Don't mind if I do. But I thought you said it wasn't camel."

"It isn't, but you seem to enjoy it more that way. Tell me," he smiled, his eyes black and bottomless as depth-less pools, "do you ever do anything by halves?"

"Not usually." And she watched those eyes widen un-der his ridiculous, sun-streaked wig as she brushed a bold, stockinged foot along the curve of his thigh. Then, to her surprise, he reached beneath the table and captured the straying appendage, his strong fingers almost idly mas-saging her toes, the high, aristocratic arch of her foot.

She felt her temperature slide up a notch, echoing the fires of the peeling walls, and took another sip of her deep, spicy wine.

The best thing about Jason, she reflected, was that he seemed just about as devastated by her as she was by him.

The lift of that marvelous mouth as he smiled, the flare of his perfect nose, the depthless warmth of eyes that could glow as bright as new-minted copper or swallow her in a darkness as profound as a moonless night but which mostly slid against her like smooth, rich velvet—all combined to ignite a slow fever within her. A fever which was reflected by every plane and curve of his brilliant, marvelous face.

I'd die for you, she thought. *But blazes, my dear, I'd far rather die* with *you, as I fully intend to do tonight!*

His gaze mirrored the emotion.

So she told him about her various scrapes and tumbles from grace; about the life of a pampered and somewhat reluctant aristocrat. And he, in turn, told her of his existence: of the father who was one of the junior Ministers, of the government-sponsored schools for the sons and daughters of the ruling classes that he had attended with his younger brother. Of the quaintly elegant parties his mother had hosted for his father's colleagues and of how he, as a precocious seven-year-old, would glide among the earnest knots of civil servants all discussing the government's latest policies.

"I learned diplomacy, as it were, at my father's knee. I was nourished as much by theories of government as I was by my daily bread. How proud he used to be, how amused, when I would pipe up with suggestions in my trilling, childish voice. Jeryn was never interested, or maybe he never had to be. He had his peers and his play and his wild, inventive pranks—I imagine he was much like you in that respect—but I was the shy one, the quiet one, and maybe I needed more approbation.

"He never had any problems with making friends or with belonging; he was always in the midst of some swarm or other, indistinguishable from the rest. But I was ... different, maybe too intelligent for my own good. Adult things always came too easily, and theories of government were, to me, like breathing. I *understood* them, knew how to implement them, almost without conscious thought. It set me apart. Oh, it wasn't that I was unpopular; my peers liked me, respected me—revered me, even—but they never ... I don't know, accepted me, I suppose. I was never one of them. And what little kid wants to live on a pedestal?" He laughed: a wry, almost deprecating chuckle. "Fine story, no?

"But I'm not complaining, not really. It was probably best that I was already half grown up, because I had to

finish the process in a cursed hurry. When I was fourteen
and Jeryn nine, our parents were robbed and murdered in
a back alley for a few paltry marks by some nameless,
faceless factory workers who were furious with the government and at the end of their rope.

"I suppose it's surprising, all things considered, that I
didn't turn against them there and then. But we weren't
rich, and when the will was read, there wasn't enough to
keep my brother and me alive. A few thousand marks and
the house, that was it; without my father's salary, we were
as good as lost. They wanted to send us into the factories
as wards of the state: more cheap, expendable labor for
their underage workforce. And they probably would have,
too, if I hadn't been such a precocious little bastard. For I
went to one of my father's old colleagues and struck a
bargain. One year, I told him. Let me work for one year in
the factories—as management, not labor—and if at the
end of that year I prove unworthy of my duties or incapable of supporting my brother and myself, then we'll
join the workforce—both of us.

"It was a ballsy proposal from a fourteen-year-old
whose voice hadn't even broken, but maybe that was what
made the difference. The man pulled a string or two, more
on a whim, I think, than anything else—a kind of grand,
glorified joke—but I did it. By the end of the year I had
not only earned money, I had saved it; and the factories
seemed happy enough with my work and too quintessen-
tially lazy to bother terminating me and training another.

"And so, logically, by one route or another, I fell into
my current position. Who better? I knew everything those
blasted factories did, every cursed corner they cut, every
worker who died from their negligence and lust for profit.
And but for one stupid quirk of fate, that could have been
me and my brother suffering down there, *dying* down
there. So when I turned twenty, I took my savings and disappeared underground, beginning the movement that led
me to where I am today." He smiled whimsically, adding,
"Back underground and still in hiding."

Jen felt a shiver run through her at the tale, in some ways
like her own but with one notable exception: Vera. Once
again, she breathed a silent thanks to the aunt who had
raised her and loved her, provided her with a stability that
her fragmented family had never possessed. Vera who had

deserved far better than an ignominious public hanging, condemned for a crime that was in no way balanced by the hundreds of small kindnesses shown to two lonely children.

"Blazes, Jason," she said when his tale was finished. "I thought it was bad enough when my mother died—or rather, when my mother was still alive and trying to mold me into the type of offspring she so desired. How did you ever survive it?"

He reached out and took her hand across the table, twining his long, lean fingers with hers, his skin cool and smooth as silk. "I did because I had to. You and I, we're both survivors, Jen. And like you, this is what I've always wanted. Just as scaling walls and raiding files comes as naturally to you as breathing, so leading the oppressed is my métier. I don't regret a thing that's happened. And, on the whole, it's been a good life. The only disadvantage I can see is that I am sometimes forced to go about in disguise while entertaining beautiful women." He grinned, and lifted her fingers briefly to his lips. "You sure you can stand to be seen with a blond?"

"I think you'll find," she answered slowly, "that I can stand to be seen with almost anything. Besides, who's to know?"

She watched him look around the restaurant in bemusement, registering the empty tables. "Touché. I hadn't realized it was so late. Shall we walk?"

"If I can. You were quite correct, you know; if there's a better restaurant in Nhuras, I'd like to try it. You may have to carry me home."

"It would be my pleasure, Domina." And he stood, sweeping her a bow, then held out his arms as if preparing to sweep her literally off her feet.

"Silly," she laughed, tucking her hand through the crook of his arm—then uttered a wordless cry of protest as he dug into one of his pockets and scattered a handful of marks across the table.

"Jason . . ."

"Hush, it's my treat. It's not often I get to squire lapsed members of the aristocracy. Now, one of my favorite things about this restaurant is that it's only a quarter mile from the Promenade. Shall we go?"

The Promenade, as Jen soon discovered, was an area of boardwalk on the seaward side of the Mages Quarter.

There, the cultured opulence had been extended into a public walkway lined on one side with benches, flower-beds, and arching poles of mounted magelights, while on the other a curved wrought-iron fence gave out on the moon-washed and rippled Belapharion.

At this hour, the flagstoned walkway was virtually deserted, and the only sound apart from their slow, measured footsteps was the whisper of the mage-powered sprinklers as they hissed a fine mist of water over the bushes and flowerbeds, scenting the air with a cool, mulchy dampness.

"What a waste," she said, watching as the spray of liquid moistened leaf and stone alike.

"Oh, I don't know," Jason countered idly, sauntering along with his cool fingers interlaced with hers, their joined arms swinging. "Sometimes it is nice to see a patch of greenery in this infernal desert. It may not be anything to you northerners, but we natives appreciate a bit of life—even if it is paid for and provided by the mages." And he reached out with his free hand and broke off a fragrant bloom, tucking it into her hair. "From Nhuras to you," he added. "Compliments of its rebel leader."

"Yes, I always have preferred the rebels." She sighed. "It is beautiful here, isn't it?"

"Yes, it is."

And so it was. The Belapharion rippled and lapped beneath their feet, streaked with a spill of moonlight and the pale, reflected glow of the magelights, and a soft breeze blew off the water, tangling her skirts about her legs and stirring in her unbound hair. The daytime heat had faded, adding a cool, green scent to the air and to the mingled smells of flowers and pungent desert weed from the tiny, mage-watered gardens. Ahead, the sky was black, freckled faintly with stars where the moonlight and magelight couldn't reach, and against it, around a distant curve of the winding shore, a building loomed darkly, all turrets and towers and crenelated walls, like some lost and forgotten castle. To her left, lights twinkled and glowed off the swelling domes of the Mages Quarter, washing them in a vivid, mottled rainbow.

On the near side of the Promenade, the spearlike points of the fence that enclosed the mages' domain peeped above the high hedges, and halfway along its length were two massive gates, now locked, with a faint ripple of force playing about the bars.

"Gracious. It must be late if the Mages Quarter is closed."

"Late indeed," Jason responded, seeming not in the least perturbed by the silent emptiness of the boardwalk or the resonant echoes of their footsteps. Jen wondered if he had his own reasons for assurance or was merely depending on the twin daggers strapped to her calves, the blowpipe and darts secreted in an inner pocket.

It was always safe traveling with an assassin, she reflected, even an unofficial one.

Briefly she paused, leaning against the curving fence on the far side of the walkway with the water to her back, and felt Jason's arm come around her. With her head nestled against his shoulder, she let her eyes scan the glittering domes, washed with the mages' signature fires. One swelled white against the night, like a light-stitched gossamer web stretched over a glowing balloon of crystal and air. Another had flickering ruby fires corkscrewing down its burgundy sides, tipped with golden flames which shifted and glowed in an endless, dizzying dance. Still another swirled blue and green in mottled, changing patterns like the heart of a storm, shot through with silver bolts like miniature lightning. All colors, all patterns, every conceivable combination and structure.

One even glowed a violet so dark as to be almost invisible, capped with eight arched and outreaching indigo spars, each dotted with tiny points of brightest blue, soaring above it like the arms of some oddly inverted octopus.

"Strange," she murmured. "So beautiful, so unreal. So peaceful. You could almost forget there was a city out there, beyond the domes."

Jason sighed and shifted his grip. "Yes, almost. That's the operative word. Look." And he turned her slightly, facing her in the direction from which they had come.

There, behind them, stretched the silent docks where the huge ships moored, their masts bristling against the sky, the sails furled in skeletal bundles. And behind that, the crimson gouts from the chimneys of the glass factories, illuminating the night in belches of lurid smoke and fire.

"That," said Jason softly, "is why I can never forget where I am, or what I am fighting for: the eternal curse of the factories. The mages may try to outshine it in sheer splendor and glory, but for me that is still the brightest and most terrible light in all of Ashkharon. Every time those fires flare, I wonder how many people are dying, how many families are losing their fathers or their mothers, their children."

"Jason . . ."

"Remember that, Jen. Even for assassins, causes don't grow in a vacuum. There is always something to fight for, something *worth* fighting for. The trick is just to discover it."

She turned her head slightly, looking over at her companion—his eyes now black as twin holes to the night, bare inches from her own, his face limned in silver moonlight—and felt a little shiver run through her. Then his hand tangled in her hair and he bent toward her, his lips brushing hers, and she forgot the moment in the mundanity of human passions, the beating of his heart beneath her hands and the hard, urgent press of his body against her own.

"I'm tired of waiting," he said, his voice low and husky, as he released her. "Let's go home."

She agreed wholeheartedly, but couldn't help wondering as she lay beside him later under the high, arched canopy of his bed, with his lean, satin-skinned limbs intertwined with her own and the sheets smelling of sweat and the sweet muskiness of sex, exactly what he'd been referring to—herself or his mission. Or indeed, if the two hadn't become hopelessly muddled, linked by the fires of his twin passions.

For even as he entered her—even as that magnificent body sank into her own, pulling her under like an outflowing tide—she felt a ragged edge of frustration to him that drove him harder or deeper than mere lovemaking, as if he sought a redemption or absolution in her body that she was purely incapable of giving. As if, through the giving of one to the other, he could drive through the barrier of mere flesh to achieve some unattainable goal.

And so, as she clutched with urgent fingers at his slick-smooth body, her nails digging bloodless crescents into his back, and shivered beneath his outflux, she couldn't help feeling that she'd somehow betrayed him by simply being human.

37

Neros Fazaquhian parted the twin canvas flaps at the front
of his dwelling and applied a hesitant eye. Before him
stretched the familiar sea of dust white tents, populated by
the usual riotous cluster of Pehndon's handpicked criminals, and the looming bulk of the second extraction tower,
which had gone up late the previous evening. He waited a
few minutes, but no one seemed to be lingering in one
place or paying undue attention to his residence so, encouraged, he cracked the slit a little wider and poked the
pointed tip of his nose out like a frightened rabbit, all but
scenting the air in his anxiety.

It was beastly hot as usual, and the thin layer of cloth
that sheltered him from the sun was doing less to protect
him by the minute. Already the tiny tent was baking like
an oven, searing the air into a thick, unbreathable mix. Almost it would be better outside, for at least there the air
would be moving; here it hung around him like a pall.
More than anything, he longed for the cool darkness of
his lab, the heavy, shadowed walls of his tiny office, but
to get there he would have to cross several yards of open
space and therefore become a target for that . . . *woman*.

It was patently ridiculous that the leader and brains of
this entire operation should be stuck in his tent like another of the common criminals, afraid to venture out into
the open, but so it was. Every time he even set foot outside, she was on him like a curse, nattering about Pehndon, responsibility, and integrity until he thought his ears
would burst.

It never failed; even when he was convinced that he
was safe—that she was occupied elsewhere or that she
had to eat and sleep *sometime*—one step outside would
spirit her to his side as if by magerie. So, of necessity, he
had taken to lurking in his two private realms—office and

tent—darting from one to the other like a frightened hare when exigency summoned.

Why, he reflected somewhat bitterly, was she pestering *him*? What did *he* matter in the grand scheme of things? He was only trying to do his duty, a duty for which he was being handsomely paid. What did it matter whom she thought Pehndon might have murdered?

He hated himself for the small twinges of conscience which told him it *did* matter; that he was a scientist, not a killer. And if Pehndon was doing what she said he was, the very thought made him feel vaguely nauseous. Once he had prided himself on his integrity and morals—the very qualities she was always harping on about—but that was before he had fallen. That was before Pehndon had invested his personal fortune to lift him out of the gutter.

What of loyalty? Wasn't that a virtue she valued? And loyalty was something he owed to Pehndon, in spades. How could he betray him? That was as much a part of his code as his queasiness in the face of his savior's supposed crimes.

So what if Pehndon had murdered Istarbion—or had hired her to murder Istarbion, which all amounted to the same thing? Where was *her* moral code? Besides, by all reports, Istarbion was no great shakes as First Minister anyway. His loss would hardly devastate the government. No, just as well to let Istarbion go, to let someone else— someone better—fill his place.

"Let him go"—what a ridiculous euphemism.

What was it about sober life that was so complex? Almost, he would have welcomed the fog of alcoholic stupor, in which all decisions, all choices, got reduced to their lowest common denominator and morals were merely a function of necessity. In which "good" became anything that promoted oblivion and "bad" its dreadful opposite.

How much simpler life had been back then.

He sighed and stuck his nose a little further from his shelter, until the round lenses of his lapis-glass spectacles emerged and the blinding glare of the midmorning sun lanced into his eyes, contracting his pupils to pinholes. He rotated his head from side to side, surveying the terrain, then scuttled into the light, beating a hasty path to the lab.

Two steps later, a white clad specter fell in beside him, materializing from around the back of his tent.

"Good morning, Neros," it said cheerfully. "Hot one, isn't it? You slept late this morning."

He whirled on his nemesis, scowling up at that raptor-like face with its short fringes of dark, spiky hair and keen, scrupulous grey eyes. "What do you want from me? Why can't you just leave me alone?" he pleaded, all too aware of his petulant tone.

The woman answered easily enough. "You know precisely what I want, Neros. Have you given any more thought to my proposition?"

"No. Leave me alone. I'm not betraying Pehndon!"

"Why? He's killed one rival already. Who's to say he won't kill you when you cease to be of use?"

"Because he promised . . ."

"Promised what?" she interrupted, her implacable face hardening. "How many promises do you think he's broken to me already?"

There was a note of chilling finality to her voice that sent a sudden shiver of apprehension though him, and looking into that icy, resolute gaze, he had no doubt that she knew whereof she spoke. That kind of hatred didn't grow out of nothing; he could almost see the scars in her eyes. But all he said was, "Stop it. Pehndon saved me!"

"Only so you could destroy yourself again, is that it, Neros? Pehndon's ship is going down. Do you want to go down with it?"

"I owe him my life, curse you!"

"And what kind of life will it be, rotting in one of the government prisons? Or floating face-down in the Belapharion? For once the people and government of Ashkharon learn what your savior's been up to, do you honestly think they'll let any of his associates live?"

Fazaquhian's feet pounded across the hard-baked ground, pocked with treacherous hollows of shifting sand, which threatened to trip and spill him, as if by sheer persistence he could escape her. "I'm not listening," he said.

"Oh, yes, you are. I see you sweating."

"It's the heat," he snapped, desperately mopping his brow with the trailing edge of his sleeve. "It's dire out here, or hadn't you noticed?"

"Don't change the subject."

"I'm not changing the subject. You brought up the . . . Oh, never mind; this is pointless!"

"Pehndon killed Istarbion," she persisted. "And he would have killed me, too, if I hadn't gotten free."

"And whose fault is that?"

"Your revered savior's a murderer, Neros. Do you really think he'll spare you just for auld lang syne if you cross him?"

"No, he'll probably hire you to kill me, just like he did with Istarbion," Fazaquhian snapped, "which is why I'm going to stay safely here, do my job, and *not* cross him."

"And so ally yourself more firmly in his camp? Blast it, Neros, save yourself while you can. Come back to Nhuras and testify against him!"

He threw up his hands. No matter what argument he gave, she always found some way to twist it, to turn his words against him. It was hopeless trying to best her. "I'm not betraying Pehndon," he said stubbornly, "and that's final!"

"Neros . . ."

He knew it was stupid, and he knew it was childish, but sometimes there was nothing left for a man to do. So, "I'm not listening," he said, and stuck both forefingers in his ears. Then he ran the rest of the way to the lab, humming a silly little tune.

He wondered why he still didn't feel any better when he finally reached the sanctuary of his office and sank into his chair, resting his head wearily between his hands.

By morning, Jen felt infinitely better about her relationship with Jason. They had made love three more times over the course of the evening, and gradually the hungry urgency had faded from his caresses. Eventually he had let her just be human—and had seemed content to find her so—and by the time the morning light began to peek through the windows, washing the room in a faint blue glow like the ocean shallows, their movements had altered to a languid sensuality that lacked the depth of their first encounter but also much of its frustration, and Jen found herself oddly contented.

I much prefer being me, she thought as she smiled down at him over their linked bodies, the fall of her hair sweeping across them like a curtain, and his eyes blazed back as dark and rich as old mahogany. In fact, without that ridiculous wig, he was all of a piece, as smooth and carved and polished as living wood. From the copper perfection of his skin to the midnight of his eyes, from the thick, sleek thatch of onyx hair that fell rakishly over his eyes to the silky black brush at his groin, he was perfection, absolute perfection.

When she finally drifted off to sleep a little past dawn, it was in complete satisfaction, with all thoughts of Thibault, Vera, and her mission a thousand miles away. But when she awoke again at midday, with Jason gone and the bed empty beside her, it all came flooding back.

A nice interlude, Jen, she told herself, *but now back to work. You have an aunt to revenge and a friend to rejoin, not to mention a villain to catch.*

She sighed and stretched, flexing her naked body beneath the sheets, then rose and padded downstairs, wrapping her robe around her as she went.

The clutter of her mage-constructed toys remained on the common room carpet where she had left it, and downstairs in the kitchen a once hot breakfast was slowly congealing under a copper cover.

Beside the plate, in a porcelain cup, Jason had balanced the flower he had procured last night. Its crimson head brushed softly against the rim, the profusion of petals already beginning to droop in the heat. Grinning, Jen plucked it forth, shook the water from its base, and tucked it back into her hair. Then she picked up the note resting beneath the cup.

Gone to the office, it read. *Join me if you want; map attached. And have I mentioned lately that you're quite phenomenal?—J.*

Pinned beneath the note was a map of the tunnels, with the route to the warehouse marked out in red.

Here we go, she thought with a smile, and tucked into her breakfast.

With the aid of a single candle and Jason's map, Jen navigated the subterranean labyrinth of the tunnels, pausing every now and then to consult the sketch before continuing. When she finally reached what she assumed was the warehouse bolt-hole, she uttered the password Jason had scribbled on the bottom of the page and was relieved to see the wards releasing. Then, holding the paper to the candle flame, she burned it to a cinder before slipping through the doorway and letting the portal swing shut.

Behind her, she could hear the wards resetting.

She tripped up the stairs to Jason's office and found him seated alone behind his desk. Oblivious to the curious stares at her back, she rapped on the glass and was beckoned inside. With a little smile, he opened his arms and she nestled herself in his lap, but his welcoming kiss was perfunctory, as if his mind was not quite involved in the business at hand.

"What's the matter?" she said, cocking her head and regarding him curiously as she broke the embrace. "No regrets, I trust?"

"Huh? Oh, no. Varia forfend." He shook himself slightly, then grinned with a semblance of his old vitality. "I'm sorry if I seem a bit distracted this morning, but I just received some bad news. I'm afraid Grahme's been taken."

"What?"

"Yes, Pehndon threw him in jail yesterday on suspicion of purloining his papers."

"Without proof?"

"Apparently so."

"But . . . Curse it, Jason, can he do that?"

"Unfortunately, it seems he can. No one's raised much of a fuss, at any rate."

"Blast! And I wanted Grahme to help me plant that bug in Pehndon's office. I guess I'll just have to do it by myself now."

"Jen . . ."

"Don't worry, I'll be fine. I'll just use my old cover, that's all."

He smiled faintly. "You seem awfully unconcerned about Grahme."

"That's because there's little to be concerned about. They're not going to do anything to him until they have you, Jason. He's just the bait."

"You sound awfully certain."

"I am. Look, Pehndon wants you. How better to get at you than to imprison your operative?"

"But how does he know that Grahme was my operative?"

Jen's face sobered, and she thought his question over

with a sinking feeling. "There has to be a spy," she said at last, reaching the unavoidable conclusion. "A spy in your alliance."

He nodded glumly. "That's what I had figured."

She considered for a moment more, then said brightly, "Well, not to worry. With that bug in Pehndon's office, we'll know what he's thinking before he's thinking it. If Grahme's in danger, we'll get him out."

He cocked his head quizzically, obviously amused by her assurance. "And how, exactly do you plan on doing that?"

She just grinned and wrapped her arms around his neck, dropping a playful kiss on the top of his nose. "I have no idea," she admitted, "but I'll figure it out when the time comes. I'm always good at figuring things out."

"Yes, I suppose you are," he said, and since that seemed to be the greatest praise she would get out of him that morning, she rose from his lap and began planning her second assault on Pehndon's office.

38

How hard can it be to find one bloody female?

Mark snorted. The words tormented him. As the days wore on with no sign of the Hawk's niece, he began to more than regret that particular statement—especially since Derek would not let him forget it. Moreover, the answer was quickly becoming apparent: it was cursed difficult. Cursed difficult in a city the size of Nhuras when they had no idea where to even begin looking.

As far as Mark was concerned, when they lost her in that hotel, they lost their sole chance at redemption. For they had no idea what she even *looked* like, other than Derek's vague moonlight impression of long, dark hair and a lithe body. Which, Mark reflected with a grimace, probably matched the description of half the women in Nhuras. But, at Derek's insistence, they had taken to camping across from the main steps of the government complex, trying to avoid the notice of the guards and hoping that she had not concluded the last of her business with Pehndon.

Their mission was far from easy. For one thing, the tedium was deadly and the heat unbearable. And for another, Derek was not exactly inconspicuous, and putting off the vigilant guards became tougher each day. All of Mark's carefully hoarded disguises had been used at least three times each, and it was getting harder and harder to find new combinations.

He sighed gustily and surreptitiously tried to wipe the sweat from his brow with the edge of one flowing sleeve. They were playing pilgrim today, wearing voluminous black robes that enveloped them like cotton sails, but whatever had possessed him to think that was a good idea was currently beyond him. The dark fabric soaked up the heat like a sponge, seeming to trap it in a steaming miasma beneath the drawn-up hoods.

"What is it?" Derek grinned from within his own cowl. Like his brother's, his face was invisible but for the lone curl of chestnut hair which protruded artfully from the flowing cover.

Mark snorted again. It simply wasn't fair. Derek even managed to wear his wigs with style, whereas all he himself resembled was an inverted, funereal mop. "This is getting ridiculous," he said. "How many days have we been lurking here and still no sign of that wretched child?"

"Patience," Derek chuckled. "After all, as you said yourself, 'How hard can it be to find one bloody female?' "

"Oh, do shut up and be constructive for once. We have got to do something about this situation!"

"And what would you suggest? Are you telling me you have any better solutions? Any brilliant new insights?"

"No, but . . ."

"Then I suggest we keep waiting. It may be boring—and beastly hot—but it's our best chance to find this girl, and I, for one, am *not* going to lose another chunk of our commission! Besides . . ." And he paused, his eyes fixed pointedly on the square.

"What?" Mark demanded, shaking his arm. "What do you see?"

"By Varia, I think we've got her!"

"Where?"

"There. Look!"

Derek was practically quivering with excitement. Mark narrowed his eyes and followed his brother's stabbing finger.

The girl was beautiful, no doubt about that; she carried herself with an aristocratic poise and the grace of an acrobat or dancer. Moreover, she matched Derek's vague description. Her long, dark hair was piled on her head in an elegant chignon, and over one shoulder she carried a parasol which matched the formal lines of her green-sprigged white morning gown. An elaborate foil-wrapped package was inserted under one cocked arm.

But what set her apart from the crowd—and from every other aristocrat on Varia—was her preternatural alertness and the way her bright eyes swept the square, almost as if she were searching for something, or maybe just questing for signs of pursuit.

"Well? What do you think?"

Mark's natural caution surged to the fore. "I don't know. What makes you so certain that's our girl?"

"The walk," his brother stated firmly. "I recognize the walk."

"Well, you may be pigheaded at times, but I do tend to trust your instincts. If you say so, we'll tail her when she leaves. But Derek . . ."

"Yes?"

"You'd better be certain about this one."

"I am; believe me. And there's no way she's getting free this time!" Derek's mouth stretched into a grin, and he rubbed his hands together as if polishing the gold that Owen would soon shower into his outstretched palms. "I'll go around the back, just in case she chooses a more discreet exit. Whistle if you see her." And he darted away.

Mark chuckled softly to the ghost of his brother's back. "He's got you where it counts, lad," he said, "right in the pocketbook. Old Owen certainly knew what he was about when he offered that reward."

Pehndon's aide didn't seem in the least suspicious when Jen showed up, sans suhdabhar, on his doorstep, dressed to the hilt as Domme Leonis. Apparently they hadn't connected her with the robbery—which, she reflected, was a very good thing indeed—for skilled as she was at planning, she had no idea what she would do if she were suddenly discovered.

Other, of course, than simply running.

But the ugly little possibility never even raised its head, and the aide just blinked at her as she materialized, saying, "Ah, it's you. Domme . . ."

"Leonis," she gushed, patting his hand. "How sweet; you remembered!"

He flushed. "I take it you want to see the Minister?"

"Just for a teensy moment, if it's not too much bother." And she gave him her most charming smile.

"Then, I'll, uh . . . just go see if he's available."

He backed through Pehndon's doorway and a few moments later emerged, saying, "The Minister will see you now."

To her profound satisfaction, Pehndon appeared a trifle less assured than he had at their previous meeting. His hair was just the slightest bit ruffled, his impeccable collar ever so faintly askew, but his grey eyes met hers as coolly as ever as he said, "Domme Leonis, what a pleasure. To what do I owe this delightful visit?"

To her profound amusement, she had never met anyone who sounded less delighted than Pehndon. "Oh, dear, Minister," she fluttered, "I do hope I'm not interrupting . . ."

He took a noticeable breath and forced a reluctant degree of animation into his voice. "Nonsense. Your pardon if I seem distracted; I was just down at the prison conducting a rather . . . unsatisfactory interview."

She masked a surge of excitement. It had to be Grahme ruffling that almost inhuman composure; what other prisoner would have such an effect? Moreover, judging from Pehndon's faintly distracted air, Tortaluk was in a far from cooperative mood. Jason would be delighted.

"Oh, dear, I am sorry," she cooed mendaciously.

He waved it away. "It is of no significance, Domme Leonis. Merely one of those plagues we Ministers are heir to." But the faint frown between his eyes belied his careless words. "Now, what can I do for you today?"

"Oh, no, Minister Pehndon," she responded with a coy smile. "It is not what you can do for me, but rather what I can do for you. You have been so generous that my organization just wanted to present you with a little token of our gratitude and esteem."

And she drew the package, which she had commissioned at the bazaar earlier that afternoon, out from under her arm. As she passed it across to him, she let the tiny shard of crystal fall invisibly from her sleeve and into her waiting hand.

He raised a quizzical eyebrow at the gift, but she merely smiled and nodded, encouraging him to open it, while her fingers deftly weighed the splinter. Where to place it to achieve a maximal view of the desk and door? As he unwrapped the package, she surveyed the terrain, her heart tripping in an anxious rhythm. If he caught her now . . .

Above the window, she decided, atop the lintel. But could she get it up there while he was still distracted? Letting her cultivated flightiness serve as her cover, she drifted across the room, only to discover that the desired spot was too far above her head. There was no way she could make that reach without discovery.

Still, what was an assassin without a contingency plan?
Silently, she deposited the shard on one corner of the windowsill, saying ingenuously, "Do all Ministers have such
a charming view?"

"Not at all," he answered abstractedly, still tugging at
the intricately knotted ribbon. "Some, I'm afraid, are far
less charming than others."

"What, views or Ministers?" she couldn't resist asking
as she circled back around the desk and resumed her seat.

He looked up with a sharply suspicious glance, as if
weighing her intelligence, and immediately she curved
her lips into an empty-headed smile. He seemed to be satisfied by her expression, for he went back to his unwrap-
ping, peeling the paper back from the polished bronze
plaque, which read:

To Minister Iaon Pehndon
For dedication above and beyond the call of duty.

She was particularly delighted by the wording and
wondered if he would pick up on the subtle irony it en-
coded, but apparently he was arrogant enough to take it at
face value—for not a shred of suspicion crossed his face,
nor did he repeat that raptor-sharp glance. Instead, his lips
curved into a lukewarm smile. "Domme Leonis, this is
. . . most gracious."

He sounded far from touched, and she wondered why
she had the impression that he was secretly delighted by
the gift, if not by the giver. Maybe it was that subtle glitter in his eyes that was not quite gratitude but more . . .
triumph? A certain insufferable smugness?

She smiled hesitantly back. "You do like it, don't
you?" she pleaded.

His smile widened without getting any warmer—almost
a baring of teeth. She wondered if it was just women he
disliked, or humanity in general.

Whatever, it was almost amusing to see him try to
placate her against what was so obviously his natural
inclination.

"Indeed, Domme Leonis, it's quite charming, but you
needn't have gone to all that trouble."

"Honestly, Minister Pehndon," she simpered, reflecting
that he would be even less delighted to know that the

money he had given her had gone straight back into his
possession in the form of the tiny crystal that now reposed
on his windowsill. There was a certain subtle irony to it
which pleased her. "It was the least we could do to repay
your phenomenal generosity. And, I assure you, it was no
trouble at all; we weren't in the least put *out*. We thought
you could hang it *up* on your wall."

She tried to keep the command codes subtle, and he
seemed oblivious enough, for he never noticed the small
shard of crystal that floated out from the edge of the window and up over his shoulder, winking in the noonday
sun. When it had drawn level with the top of the frame,
she added, "Anyway, it's *in* your hands now, and I must
get back *down* to the square; I *left* my suhdabhar waiting
with the carriage. . . . *Stop!*"

His head shot up and he froze, his hand and the plaque
it held arrested bare inches above the desktop. "Excuse
me?" he demanded.

She drew a hasty breath. With the crystal shooting
steadily past the center of the lintel, her inventiveness had
evaporated. She had to halt it before it went spinning off
the other side, forcing her to repeat the entire procedure.
Pehndon's oblivion wouldn't have stood up to that much
abuse. So feigning a nonchalance she didn't feel, she
scrambled to cover her mistake, saying, "That is . . . I
meant . . ." her eyes hurriedly swept the desk, "don't put
it down *there,* Minister—I'm sorry I startled you—but
you were about to crush the . . ."

"What?"

She peered closer, brushing a tentative hand across his
immaculate desktop, and forced a nervous giggle—not
too hard, considering. "Silly me, I thought I saw a . . .
Never mind. I'm afraid my eyes aren't what they used to
be, and I'm too frightfully vain to wear spectacles. What
an awful fool you must think me!"

For a moment he looked suspiciously from her to the
plaque and back. She offered him her most ingenuous
smile and was relieved when he laid the thing aside with a
final probing glance.

"Nonsense, Domme Leonis. It was very kind of you to
protect me from . . . whatever."

She didn't have to feign her answering blush. "It was my
pleasure, Minister. And now I really must be going. Tomas

will be getting anxious." *Or would be,* she thought, *if he were anywhere in the vicinity.*

"Then I shall bid you farewell. And, Domme Leonis," he added, as she was halfway to the door, "do mind those steps on your way down."

Her smile was one of pure relief. "I fully intend to, Minister."

Derek's head shot up as his brother's whistle shot piercingly over the square. Bold or oblivious, she had come out the front, and now the Falcon was after her. Not bothering to hide his grin, the Hound took off at a lope, circling back around the building and entering the square to one side, his eyes scanning the crowd.

The girl—minus her package and with her parasol furled purposefully at her side—strode across the flagstones, her gait brisk but unhurried. He did indeed remember that walk. There was something about it that reminded him of a panther or some other jungle cat, the sleek head held high and the long legs moving in a measured stalk beneath the graceful flow of her formal skirts. She looked neither to the left nor to the right, but exited the square with a cool oblivion, seemingly unaware of Mark's shadow converging on her from the left.

Picking up a parallel course, Derek approached from the right, falling in beside his brother as they entered the winding maze of streets branching off Government Square. At some point during the wait, they had both divested themselves of their costumes, which now reposed in twin packs suspended over their shoulders.

Tossing back his bright blond locks, Derek exchanged a triumphant smile with his sibling. *Finally,* he thought, *something in this whole ghastly mess is about to go correctly!*

39

Jen was so distracted by her gaffe with Pehndon that she almost didn't notice the tail. One minute she was sauntering from the square, berating herself soundly for being such a bloody overconfident idiot—*Vera would never have made such a ghastly mistake*—and the next . . .

An unmistakable beat of footsteps, twin to her own, distinguishable among the bustle by their ghostly synchrony.

No, Jen, she told herself firmly. *You're overwrought. You're upset. You're just imagining things.*

She paused briefly, let her feet break rhythm . . .

There was barely a hesitation before the others stopped too. If she hadn't known better—if she hadn't been trained to recognize such signs or if a part of her hadn't still been alert for pursuit—she could almost have believed them to be the echoes of her own strides, resonating between the narrow buildings.

Quietly she rose to her toes, her full skirts masking the motion. With the sound of her own heels no longer ringing against the pavement, she could hear the pursuit more clearly now. Definitely back there. Definitely . . .

She cocked her head. There was something wrong with that rhythm, something . . .

She executed a sudden complex, unrepeatable jig, her heels and toes flying in a spontaneous dance. The echo broke, flowed dissonantly away from her own rhythm, and then she heard it.

Two. There were *two* of them back there. Bloody shades of oblivion, and here she was leading them straight to Jason!

Well, no more. Turning up a nearby street, she hastily doubled back on her tracks. If she remembered correctly, the bazaar was nearby; surely there was a way she could lose herself in the throngs that bustled among the busy booths. All she had to do was get there in safety and avoid any deserted streets, lest they have her for certain. As she took the corner, she turned her head slightly, trying to catch a glimpse of her pursuers, but one glance alone couldn't sift them from the crowd.

It was a very professionally done tail, she had to give them that. In many ways, it was almost up to Guild standards; Pehndon must be rich as a miser to command such services. But she saw the picture clearly now. The esteemed Minister had suspected her from the very beginning—he must have—and her current gaffe had merely confirmed it. So he had sent his bullies after her, to see where she would lead him.

Thibault was right; she should never have used the name Leonis. It was as bad as waving a red flag before an irate bull.

Curse it, Vera, she thought wildly, *how much more didn't you teach me before you let them kill you?*

At the end of one of the less populous avenues, she deliberately fumbled her parasol, ducking her head beneath her arm as she retrieved it, her eyes frantically tracking the inverted crowd. And then she saw them—two faces, the same as on her last brief survey. And worse, she recognized them. She had been standing on the street beside Thibault, outside the Nhuras Arms, when their carriage had rattled past. The big blond one had even winked at her.

With her heart battering frantically against her ribs, she scooped up the parasol in one sweaty hand and hurried on, taking the ensuing corner so narrowly that she nearly overturned a stout, middle-aged housekeeper on her way from the market. Bracing herself against a nearby wall, the woman survived the encounter, but her basket did not. Caught on the dratted parasol, it swayed and tipped, scattering peaches and turnips and heads of leafy lettuce to be trampled under the feet of the heedless passersby.

Outraged, the woman howled curses after her, but Jen just hurried on—feeling vaguely guilty for her lack of courtesy but unable to stop the increasingly frantic staccato of her heels against the cobbled streets.

Behind her, her pursuers likewise picked up their pace. She must have been nearing the market, for the avenues were growing increasingly populous, and she careened helplessly off the jostling bodies, feeling rather like a dinghy bobbing valiantly against the tide. In one sense it provided her with cover, but it also slowed her pace—and if her pursuers got close enough, the presence or absence of the crowds wouldn't matter. One dagger to her ribs, and she could be spirited straight out of their midst.

She took a corner, and then another, trying the avoid the worst of the masses . . .

And then, as if by magerie, the street ahead of her suddenly drained of people, and she found herself alone with her pursuers in the midst of an odd, empty eddy—as if the bazaar beat with life like some gigantic heart, disgorging clots of humanity in measured, flowing quanta, and she was caught between the tides.

Abandoning all pretense at anonymity, she tried to run, but her skirts tangled in her parasol, almost tripping her. As she lurched to one side, she heard the punctuated belch of a blowpipe and felt the wind of a tiny projectile brush past her left ear. A sudden wave of nausea swept her.

I wasn't trained for this, I'm not ready for this, they're supposed to be tailing me, not killing me! Her mind served up the panicked refrain. For an instant her body froze, and then she gathered her skirts in both hands and began to run, weaving a frantic, erratic path through the narrow street—her parasol unfurled behind her like a lacy shield, dodging projectiles. She was keenly aware of every tiny failed missile that whizzed past or hit the panels of her impromptu buckler; when something took her low in the ribs, she expected to feel the numbing lethargy invade her limbs.

And still she kept running, all the while repeating, *Why did I think this would be fun, why did I think this was a game?*

And then the bazaar was before her, and furling her parasol, she threw herself into the throngs of warm, pungent, sweaty, and miraculously tactile humanity, reveling in its snarls and curses and exclamations of polite surprise. She passed merchants and traders and once a dirty, disheveled mage who tried to grab at her with one deformed claw, and still she ran on, burrowing ever deeper into the heart of the human ocean.

* * *

"Do you see her? Where did she go?" Derek clutched his brother's arm anxiously. "Blast it, I can't believe she picked us up so quickly!" And he craned his head above the sudden swell of humanity, disgorged from a nearby cross street. The blowpipe had disappeared up his sleeve as if by magerie.

Mark grimaced. "I daresay you didn't hit her . . ."

"No, curse it. She dodged those darts like a professional dervish."

The Falcon's mouth twisted ruefully. "Well, don't forget, the Hawk did train her. She's bound to be fairly good."

"Yes, but . . . Tarnation. There she is! She's trying to lose us in the bazaar." And retaining his grip on his sibling's arm, Derek all but towed him into the fringes of the market.

He still couldn't believe their cursed luck. What was it about this woman? She simply had to be living a charmed existence. To have tripped the way she did, evading that first dart—there was no artifice about that; that was fortune, pure and simple. And after that . . . Well, there went the element of surprise, and any subsequent attempts at skill were therefore annihilated. All the Hound could do was fire blindly and hope to blazes his darts actually hit something—primarily, the Hawk's infuriating kin.

Which, of course, they hadn't, and now she was diving into the bazaar like a rabbit gone to ground. Curse it all, there were infinite places she could hide in there, and if they didn't grab her soon . . .

With something suspiciously resembling a growl, the Hound went barreling in after her, toppling merchants and patrons alike, trying vainly to keep her bobbing chestnut head in sight. But rationally, what bothered him most about this encounter was that she had recognized him— and he her. Who would have guessed they'd been so close that day at the hotel and never even known it?

And then a wave of dizziness hit him, and he staggered, momentarily blinded. He tried to shake his head, to toss off the dreadful disorientation, but it was as if his brain had suddenly been stuffed with cotton wool. His sense of direction, keen as any hound's, was instantly inverted, and the many aisles of the bazaar—once straight and true as arrow tracks—became a twisting, winding labyrinth, seeming to change subtly with each passing step.

Five paces in, and he was no longer sure of where he had been, let alone where he was going.

He stopped as suddenly as if he had run into an invisible wall, and a split second later Mark impacted soundly against his back. His sibling was rubbing his forehead, an equally baffled and oddly betrayed expression clouding his eyes.

"What the blazes is happening?"

"Cursed if I know," Derek responded. "Has the world suddenly gone all topsy-turvy on you too?"

The Falcon nodded ruefully.

To their credit, they kept searching the stalls—weaving their way through a profound mental maze—until an hour had elapsed and the fit suddenly passed. One minute there was confusion and a mass of booths that all seemed indistinguishable, wavering beneath a shifting curtain, and the next they found themselves in the midst of a perfectly recognizable bazaar with a curious crowd of spectators regarding them with something suspiciously resembling amusement.

Flushing, and unsure of what they had been doing as they wandered in their confusion, Derek merely flashed their audience a disarming grin before grabbing Mark by the elbow and dragging him unceremoniously from the market.

Jen had gone to ground in a silk-sellers' stall, feigning interest in a large bolt of emerald cloth and a matching shawl when her pursuers passed, their eyes wide and anxious, scanning their surroundings. Draping the cloth about her face, she shrank into the shadows, expecting at any moment to be accosted, but they merely brushed by in silence, seemingly oblivious to her presence, even though their boots had all but grazed the trailing hem of her skirts.

Maybe they hadn't seen her—or had merely taken her for another patron—though she could have sworn that both pairs of eyes had swept her cleanly. Moreover, trackers worth their merit wouldn't have been thrown by a mere scrap of green fabric.

She dropped the shawl in consternation and stepped from her concealment, staring after them as if waiting for her presence to register. But they merely kept walking, weaving somewhat oddly as they scanned the stalls, and she swallowed an absurd impulse to summon them back and demand an explanation.

Her thoughts were interrupted by an impatient tugging on her sleeve and a fulsome voice saying, "Are you planning to buy that, Domina?"

"Huh?" She blinked, then glanced down at the green silk shawl, which was still clutched in one fist. "I'll, uh . . . think about it. Perhaps later." And thrusting the bundle back at the startled merchant, she took off in the opposite direction as fast as her shaking legs would carry her. Not until she was halfway to Jason's and certain that there was no pursuit did she let her frantic steps slow. She leaned against a nearby building to catch her breath and calm her pounding heart. Taking a brief assessment of the situation, she found it worse than expected. The fabric of her sunshade was peppered with tiny thorns, and another was embedded firmly in one of her bodice stays. Pulling them free, she examined the coated tips with a shudder of revulsion, then threw them violently from her.

Talk about luck.

Thibault would kill her if he ever discovered how narrowly she had escaped.

Then, suddenly, she began to grin. Luck, indeed. She had spotted that trail and successfully dodged her pursuers despite an arsenal of weapons. You could avoid a dart, and if they had attacked with knives or daggers, they would have found themselves facing the slender but deadly rapier that formed the core of her parasol. That she was still alive didn't mean she was lucky, it meant she was good: as good as—or better than—they were.

And that, she decided, called for a celebration.

Still, she couldn't help wondering exactly what impulse had driven her so frantically into Jason's arms upon her arrival, making love to him with a passionate, demanding fury as if an army of assassins were on her tail and he was her only salvation. Was it truly a celebration or more like a purging—a frantic affirmation of life in the face of threatened death?

There were, she decided afterward, some things it was probably best not to examine too closely.

40

By the time they reached the camp outside of Dheimos, Thibault had never been so glad to see a tent in all his life. Granted, they had not been abused during the journey—they were part of a workforce, after all, and therefore were expected to arrive in employable condition—but being chained to a camel in the blistering heat, released once every five hours to drink and attend to necessary business, was hardly his idea of a good time. As it was, he soon grew used to the smells of stale sweat and urine, for those who couldn't last the five hours were granted no special favors by the surly caravan drivers.

Moreover, the company was hardly of the finest. Kayla—the woman seated to his rear—uttered no more than five syllables during the entire voyage, and the hulking Raglan seemed to think that civilized conversation consisted of inchoate grunts interspersed with the occasional bawdy comment. Pietr, on the other hand, seemed more than able to make up for his companions' lack by keeping up a steady stream of inconsequential chatter, all centered around himself and his adventures, which kept Thibault torn between laughter and a profound desire to throttle the man. If it hadn't been for the chains he might well have succumbed, but as the days wore on with only the unvarying monotony of the desert for distraction, he began almost to welcome the little man's prattle.

At least it was something to occupy him, and besides, Pietr could be quite informative when he got to outlining the various thefts and scams he'd initiated. Thibault hoarded the information, memorizing some of the choicer tales to relate to Jenny, and made a point of directing Pietr to those particular details instead of the gleeful stories of his more spectacular sexual conquests—which he seemed equally intent on relating and which set Kayla to seething silently at their backs.

Raglan took to calling them the Ladies Sewing Circle and disgustedly advised them to pick up their embroidery along with their gossip, but even he could be induced to relate a few of his own tales upon occasion.

And so the days continued.

At night the camels collapsed to the sand with a minimum of persuasion, and the prisoners were unchained except for one manacle, which was linked to the main caravan chain by a short tether. In this way, they could wander two feet in either direction and bed down in relative comfort, with their bound wrists only moderately strained above their heads. Jutting out two to a side from the beasts' mangy bulk, they were often forced to huddle close for warmth since they lacked the blankets the caravan drivers so gloatingly retained.

The first night out, one of the few female prisoners, feeling distinctly amorous, decided to mount her neighbor. As far as Thibault was concerned, it boded rather badly for the nights ahead, but amid the groans and pants and quite obvious exclamations of envy from those less fortunate, Thibault could clearly hear Kayla's warning growl and Raglan's rather despondent sigh, and he had to mask a chuckle.

Fortunately for his peace of mind, Pietr proved an exemplary companion, merely chuckling as the disgusted drivers surveyed the line. And to their disapproving mutter of "Animals!" he would answer, "I'll wager Kayla agrees with you, lads; isn't that right, my dear?" To which Kayla would growl again, and Thibault would smile silently into the darkness.

And then the Dheimos settlement was before them, and Thibault drew a sharp gasp of wonder at the two glowing towers rising miraculously from the desert, the arrow-straight supports capped by cascading fires, and the skeletal, force-bearing conduits enmeshing an organic symmetry of coiling tubes and bladders. Overall, it resembled nothing so much as a fantastical combination of pipe organ and monster—one midnight black, the other purest pale.

"Criminy," Pietr whispered, "what in the seven vales is *that* monstrosity?"

Craning his head painfully around the seat back for a

look, Raglan added, "That does it. I am not working for those bloody mages!"

"You'll work for whoever we say you do, lad," a new voice chuckled, "and no mistake!"

Thibault tore his eyes from the towers to behold a hulking brute, almost outweighing Raglan for sheer intimidation potential. He had coarse black hair and a bushy beard tufting wildly from his head, and the vicious scar that ran down one cheek pulled half his face into a perpetual grimace. Yet despite this he gave a grin that was both feral and oddly dynamic, and gestured to his companion.

The second man was even larger, and as bald as the first was hirsute. His tiny piggy eyes glinted with malice, and he flexed his broad biceps speculatively.

"All right, you lot, listen up," the first commanded, and his voice, though not loud, nonetheless carried an undeniable authority—if only for the wildness which implied that inattention could be punished as easily by death as anything. As he spoke, the sullen drivers progressed down the line, forcing the camels to their knees and unchaining the prisoners for the final time. "My name's Razife, and if you want to live out the day you'll answer to me. This here's Nasur, and the same applies to him, though he don't often make himself known as . . . vocally as I do." A faint ripple of laughter washed through the prisoners at his words. "Now, you're all here to work off your various crimes, but if you work hard you can get ahead—and pardoned all the faster. I mean, look at me. How many murderers do you know who command a force of this magnitude?"

He grinned again, and Pietr murmured, "So help us."

"What was that, runt?"

"Nothing, nothing." The little con man waved his arms frantically, denying involvement, and the drivers working on his chains cursed him lethargically.

"Good. And don't think, any of you, that just because you're being unchained means you have the freedom to come and go as you please. There's better than a hundred miles of this bloody stuff out there, and you're as like to die as escape. So be warned."

The guard unlatching Thibault's chains snorted. Tentatively, Thibault flexed his hands and feet, reveling in his newfound freedom.

"Now," Razife continued, "this here's the big boss. He assigns the tasks, I just make sure you do 'em. Right?"

"Um, right. Yes. Thank you, Razife."

And a rather rabbity man in faded robes stepped forward, pulling at his ponytail and casting surreptitious glances over his shoulder. When nothing materialized, he continued, "Your, ah, duties here will, um, consist of . . ."

"Ah, *there* you are, Neros. We need to talk!"

The voice was staggeringly familiar and Thibault gasped, feeling the color drain from his face. The man named Neros apparently had the same reaction, for he forgot his speech and froze, sending a wave of titters skittering through his impromptu audience. Thibault hardly noticed. Instead, he was frantically scanning the horizon, hoping against hope that he had heard correctly, that the heat hadn't permanently scrambled his overwrought brain. A slim figure approached, clad in billowing robes, her face masked beneath a welter of veils. When she threw them back, she revealed . . .

"Vera?" he exclaimed, his voice cracking audibly.

She halted in midstride, those familiar grey eyes widening. She blinked once, then, "Thibault?" she exclaimed.

He nodded, barely trusting himself to speak.

"By all the blowfish in the Belapharion . . . What the bloody blazes are you doing *here*?"

He began to grin. It was Vera, all right. But if anyone had told him a month ago that he would fly at his redoubtable neighbor, sweeping her off her feet and swinging her in a joyous, exultant arc beneath a blazing sky, he would have told them to have their heads examined. Yet that is precisely what he proceeded to do, and when he finally released her, he added raggedly, "We thought you were dead!"

She shook him lightly. "And what possible reason would I have to be dead?" she countered with some amusement.

"Because we saw you hang."

Her brows lowered, and she waved impatiently at the caravan drivers who were tugging ineffectually at the back of Thibault's shirt. "Off, all of you." And then, whirling on her former neighbor, she added, "Who saw me hang?"

He flinched. "Jen and I."

"Jen? She's *here*?" And her eyes scanned the assembled

prisoners, her fingers tightening convulsively around his biceps.

"Ouch, Vera." He pried her loose. "No, Jen's back in Nhuras. She dispatched me to Dheimos as her scout."

"On the prison caravan?"

"Yes."

"That being Jen's idea, I take it?"

He nodded, and she threw up her hands. "Blazes! Sometimes I wonder where that girl keeps her brains. A hired caravan would have sufficed, you know."

"I . . ."

"Leonie, do you know this man?" the one she called Neros finally demanded; he had been hovering anxiously over her shoulder, apparently eager to question her.

She turned from Thibault then, and he drew a breath of relief for having avoided the explosion. She had entrusted Jen's safety to him, yet here they were several thousand miles from where she had left them, and firmly enmeshed in the heart of the danger.

"Yes, of course I know him; he's one of my associates. He only came in on the prison convoy because . . . Well, so help me if I know why the bloody blazes he did it, but suffice it to say he's here and undoubtedly comes bearing vital information. Right, Thibault?"

He nodded.

"Then . . ."

"Go and address your recruits, Neros. I'm going to hear this boy's story, and then we're going to talk—and seriously this time. No more of your silly evasions. There is more at stake here than you seem to realize, and now is hardly the time for indecision. Have I made myself clear?"

He nodded reluctantly.

"Good. Come along, then, Thibault. Something tells me you have a powerful lot of explaining to do."

He swallowed convulsively and followed her from the assembly.

She led him to a tent on the outskirts of the camp and seated him on the cushions inside, but instead of the outburst he expected, she merely handed him a waterskin, saying, "Despite everything, it is good to see you."

"And you. Just look at you! What in blazes did you do to your hair, Vera?"

She grimaced and ran a hand somewhat self-consciously through the fringes. "I know. Horrendous, isn't it? But I had to leave something behind at the prison, and it was either that or my life. But what about you? I swear, you must have grown two feet since the last time I saw you. I'm surprised Jen even recognized you! Either Gavrone agrees with you or poor little Sylvaine had giant's blood in her veins."

He smiled whimsically. "More likely the blood. Gavrone's all right, but its . . ."

"Boring? Tedious? Unexciting? I trained you for more than that, Thibault. If nothing else, it seems as though you're finally fulfilling your destiny." He flushed at her dry tone. "But if you don't mind my asking, where in tarnation did you get that hideous scar?"

"Oh, that." He fingered it ruefully; he had momentarily forgotten its presence. Again. "Jen gave it to me."

"*Jen?* What the bloody blazes has that girl been up to now? I leave her alone with you for a few weeks and already . . ."

He chuckled. "Give me some credit, Vera; I did manage to stop her short of mutilation. It's a fake." And he pried up one corner in demonstration.

"Ah. Not bad. However," and grasping the mock scar firmly by one corner, she peeled it swiftly from his face, "your days of disguise are officially ended."

He rubbed the reddened patch ruefully. Her tug had been a little too energetic for comfort. "Are you mad at me, Vera?"

"For what?"

"Letting Jen follow you to Ashkharon."

She sighed gustily. "No, I'm not mad at you. I have no illusions as to the magnitude of Jen's pigheadedness. I'm afraid I've indulged that girl rather frightfully. Besides, if you hadn't come with her, she'd just have come by herself, right?" He nodded. "No, the only one I blame in all this is Owen, for telling her in the first place. He ought to have known better, the old fool. After all, he's had years of exposure to the Radineaux obstinacy!"

He grinned. "You know, it's really good to have you back again, Vera."

"Silly boy, as if Pehndon could have killed me." She

patted his hand. "But tell me, how did you know about Dheimos?"

"Jen figured it out. She said that the only way Pehndon could have caught you was if he betrayed you. So she searched his office and confiscated a rather sizable stack of his private documents. Among which were a number of communiqués from a mysterious labor camp outside of Dheimos."

"So she dispatched you to do her dirty work?"

"Essentially."

She chuckled. "Not bad, for a bunch of beginners. You know, I should have both of your hides for this, but . . . Really, not a bad bit of work. So who has the papers now? Jenny?"

"No, actually. Andorian has them."

"*Jason* Andorian?" Her voice sharpened. "Blazes, Thibault, that's Pehndon's partner!"

He felt his heart plummet—not untinged with a certain odd satisfaction. So it hadn't just been jealousy; his instincts had been correct. He had warned her not to trust Jason, and now . . . A mindless panic flooded him. "We've got to get back, Vera, now! She's living . . . that is . . ."

"Wait! Slow down, Thibault. Who's living where?"

"Jen. Jason." He waved his hands incoherently.

"Jen's living with Jason?" He nodded. "Blast the girl, whatever can she have been thinking? Very well, we'll leave today. But first I want to hear everything you two have been up to, from start to finish, so sit right back down and start talking!"

When he had finished, Vera frowned and tapped her fingers speculatively against one sandaled foot. "Curse it all," she said, "this is getting excessively complicated. Well, we can pretty much assume my life is up for grabs once I return, because there is no possible way Pehndon can let me live knowing he's killed an innocent in my stead. However . . . How much money do you have?"

"Not much. Three hundred."

"Enough to get us lodgings when we return. I have a camel, and we can hire a guide at Dheimos. I've used up most of Absalom's gold, but . . ."

"Excuse me. Absalom?" Thibault looked puzzled. She just grinned.

"It's a long story; I'll explain later. Meanwhile, here's what we'll do. When we get back to Nhuras, you get Jen out of that traitor's clutches—I don't care how you do it; knock her over the head if you have to—and bring her to me. I'll hammer some sense into her. Then you two can get those papers back while I talk to Absalom. If Neros cooperates, we'll have more than enough to implicate both Pehndon and his thrice-cursed accomplice. And then," her eyes twinkled, "we can set about reaping a little justice of our own."

"So we're going back? Today?" Thibault was practically vibrating with impatience.

"Yes, we're going back. But first I have to talk to Neros. Without him . . ." She let her voice trail off, then added, "Wait here and start packing. I won't be a moment."

41

Jen had never been so bored in all her life. And just slightly humiliated, for all her great plans had come to naught and suddenly Jason's comments about baskets and eggs began to rankle. Maybe he was right, maybe she had taken too great a risk, but it should have been a foolproof plan. Foolproof, that is, except for Pehndon, because now it seemed that either he was aware of the bug or too circumspect to conduct his private business in the office—for after more than a week of waiting, nothing had happened.

Nothing, that is, except the daily tedium of a government minister's existence, and that was a lesson she could well have done without. Obliquely, she couldn't help wondering why Jason was so keen on the prospect, if this was all that leadership entailed. It was really all too awful, and finally, after serving as the reluctant audience for a lengthy discussion on public road works and tax readjustments, she decided that something just had to be done.

After all, as Vera had taught her, there was always more than one way to scale a fish—even so cold a one as Pehndon.

For one thing, she didn't really have to be present to survey Pehndon's doings. She could merely set the crystal to record passively, then review her gleanings later each evening. And meanwhile, she could work on him obliquely. She would enact an elaborate charade of spying and collusion, as if she knew something he did not or was planning some outrageous coup, and his agents would report it back to him in faithful detail.

It was all too bloody perfect.

And all too bloody dangerous, another, more sober, part of her acknowledged. She had nearly lost her life the last time she ran up against his men, and now she was deliberately

walking back into their trap. There was no guarantee she
would survive a second encounter, and Thibault would kill
her if he ever found out. In many ways, she was glad he was
miles away and unable to stop her, for a small part of her realized this was one argument she would have gladly lost.
Nor would it have taken much persuasion—which was why
an even smaller part of her yearned for his immediate and
spectacular return.

But nothing ventured, nothing gained, she told herself
sternly, and garbing herself again as Domme Leonis, left
her mage-powered apparatus running in the center of Jason's carpet and headed out for Government Square.

Her heart was hammering frantically as she approached
the borders of the white stone complex, but everything
went better than expected. From the moment she entered
the square, she was aware of Pehndon's two agents tracking her, could feel the hungry, eager press of their eyes.
She knew, as if a string connected them, when the larger
of the two rose to follow her as she headed purposefully
for the Grand Stair; it took every ounce of her courage to
mount it in seeming nonchalance. And more important,
she felt him halt when she entered, settling back into a
waiting posture. For after all, if she had business inside,
she was bound to be occupied for some little while.

Masking a grin at his logical, if completely erroneous,
assumption, she passed beneath the shadowed portal, nodding familiarly to the guard as she advanced. No harm in
making him think she was planning to acquaint herself
with the place over the next few days; in her own
way, she was. Crossing the lobby with the same purpose-
ful, seemingly unhurried strides with which she had entered, she went straight out the back, merging into the
resultant crowd and checking for signs of pursuit. When
she found none, she grinned in secret triumph and returned to Jason's.

Over the next few days she led them an elaborate
dance, and as she became more familiar with the rhythms
of chase and pursuit, her confidence increased until she
felt almost like a child again, leading Thibault through the
depths of the Hestian forests. Where she led, they followed, drawn inexorably into the stink and bustle of
Nhuras. She played a subtle game: popping into their

sight when they faltered, only to dodge them again just when they were convinced they had finally caught her.

Granted, there were some sticky moments, but that was what made it fun. Exciting, exhilarating, at times oddly terrifying, but always fun. She played them like a harp, always ensuring that her missions seemed fraught with a kind of sinister purpose, varying her routes enough that they would be left scratching their heads and thinking, *What could she possibly be up to now?*

Once, convincing a sympathetic shopkeeper that her husband and his brother were after her in the wake of some indiscretion, she persuaded the woman to sell her a blonde wig and let her out the back. And as for what Pehndon's bullies would say to find their trail running cold in a ladies' haberdashery . . . She could only imagine their bafflement and grinned at the thought of the concomitant confusion—and hopefully panic—that the report would instill in their supercilious employer.

Keep them guessing, that was another thing Vera had taught her. Keep them perpetually off balance, and soon the mistakes will start occurring. She watched the crystal's gleanings every night, waiting eagerly for the explosion, and couldn't hide her disappointment when nothing happened. Days passed; her missions grew more elaborate, their destinations more outrageous, and still nothing.

Pehndon must be made of wood, she decided eventually. Or granite.

Or ice.

Even Jason's sympathetic caresses couldn't console her.

Clearly, it was time for stronger measures.

The pursuit that day was long and complex, and though they trod the same streets they had during that initial, panicked attack, Jen had finally learned the proper controls. The trick, she decided, was simply never to become the victim—even if you legitimately were. That first time she had been flustered; she had let them flush her. This time she kept her wits about her, outthinking—outwitting— them at every turn.

Today she had abandoned her parasol and all other accoutrements of the aristocracy and instead was wearing a rather baggy smock dress, clearly designed to represent a genteel lady's idea of "disguise." In truth, the garment

served a far better purpose, for while it suited her to have
her actions viewed as especially clandestine on this particular day, the blousy garment was chosen more for conve-
nience than any real attempt at secrecy. Its main advantage
was its comparative worthlessness; though Jen was not
particularly vain, it would have nonetheless given her a
certain pang to abandon one of her finer gowns in some
seamy back alley, as she fully intended to do with this one.

She had set off close to sunset, about an hour before the
government offices were due to disgorge their nightly
cluster of workers, drawing her two pursuers from off the
courthouse steps, where they had been waiting on that particular afternoon. As they were not expecting her change
of costume, she was forced to be a little more obvious than
she would otherwise have preferred, aping a studied nervousness which she simply no longer felt. But eventually
her panicked flutters and misstarts caught their attention,
and the chase began in earnest.

She led them along the fringes of the bazaar, darting
around corners and into doorways—every so often making
a panicked foray into its midst as if to purchase some nefarious item. Then she would reemerge, anxiously stuffing
air and promise into her voluminous robe. She managed,
by rearranging the angles of her elbows and knees, to create a shifting pattern of bulges beneath the baggy garment,
as if a multitude of hidden pockets were bursting with a
multiplicity of secret items. In fact, only one item reposed
beneath the fabric cover, and that was tucked firmly into
the waistband of the trousers she wore under everything.

When the bell rang the hour, chiming a musical con-
catenation from the distant domes of the Mages Quarter,
she threw her tail. Picking the flimsy lock of a back-garden
gate—which she had observed over the past few days and
thus was aware remained deserted until well after sunset—she slipped within, pulling the door shut behind her
and applying an eager eye to a chink in the wood. Scant
seconds later, her followers tumbled around the corner,
cursing as they viewed the now empty street. They made
one or two abortive passes up the neighboring avenues
and finally came to a reluctant halt almost directly across
from her hiding place.

"Well, what now?" the big blond one demanded in some
irritation.

The other sighed, and Jen held her breath, awaiting the desired answer. "Go home, I guess, curse it. It's too late to keep staking Pehndon's; she's made her appearance for the day." Behind her flimsy barrier, Jen masked a grin. "What do you think she's up to now?"

"Cursed if I know. But Mark . . ."

"Yes?"

"Hasn't it struck you that this whole situation is getting a bit ridiculous?"

"Struck me? Infinitely, many times," the one named Mark growled fitfully. "Come on, Derek, let's call it quits."

They turned their steps away from the garden, and Jen swiftly threw off her smock, revealing the unassuming garb of a scruffy young suhhe, a blond tail unexpectedly depending from her trousers. Swiftly she pulled it free and, bundling up her hair, tugged the wig—done up in an untidy braid—over her own chestnut locks. Then, grabbing two fistfuls of dirt from the tiny garden, she proceeded to anoint both face and hands until a grubby urchin stood within the garden walls, an urchin who grinned fiendishly before easing open the gate and sauntering out after her former pursuers.

Vera would have been the first to admit that her final interview with Fazaquhian had been less than satisfactory. In response to her gimlet stare, he had swallowed nervously several times, then eventually croaked, "What?"

She crossed her ankles. "He did it again, you know, your precious Pehndon."

"Did what?"

"Extinguished another innocent life."

Fazaquhian flinched. But, "How do you know?" he challenged nonetheless.

"Because Thibault told me. There was a trial, Neros, a trial conducted in my name—and in my absence. Oh, he had informed me that he had my substitute all lined up, ready to stand trial in my stead. Some loyal puppet of his, I presume. Only he didn't just try her in my stead; he executed her in it too. There was a public hanging, Neros, witnessed by the masses. Ask anyone."

"I . . ."

"That's a nasty death, you know, dangling from a rope, struggling for breath, feeling your lungs slowly col-

lapse, your spine separate joint by joint. Not the kind of
death you'd wish on an enemy, let alone a trusted conspirator. And yet Pehndon did it without a thought, without a
twinge of conscience, simply because it suited his plans.
So how does that make your savior look now?"

Fazaquhian scowled, and she knew she was pushing too
hard, too fast, yet she no longer had the luxury of time.
She needed Fazaquhian and his testimony, but more than
that she needed to return to Nhuras. The thought of Jen,
alone with those monsters, made her blood run cold. She
would never forget her last sight of Andorian, his hand
resting lightly on Pehndon's shoulder as he waved an
ironic good-bye. Would never forget the smug satisfaction in Pehndon's face when he set his bullies loose on
her, then decorously turned his head. It had been bad
enough for her, and she was a woman grown, with a lifetime of experience behind her; she was no stranger to bru-
tality and violence. But Jen was a child, and when
Genevra had given her only daughter into Vera's protection, it was not to see her abused in such a fashion. If
Pehndon got his hands on Jenifleur . . . No, she had to get
home—and quickly. And if that meant pushing Fazaquhian a little harder than she would ordinarily have
liked, then so be it.

But Fazaquhian was not showing any willingness to be
pushed. In fact, he was being decidedly obstinate. "How
do you know she was a conspirator?" he now demanded.
"How do you know Pehndon sacrificed her without
qualm? She could have been just another criminal, slated
for execution and hanged in your stead. What makes you
so certain it was some nefarious plot?"

"Because he told me. He informed me she was his
tool!"

"Who informed you? Pehndon? And you're trusting his
word? Isn't that precisely what you've spent the past few
weeks trying to convince me *not* to do? So make up your
mind, Leonie or Vera or whatever you're called. Are we
to trust Pehndon or aren't we?"

She shivered. It was the first reasonable sign of logic he
had shown since she'd arrived; it was merely her bad fortune that it was turned against her. That, and the fact that
she had clearly not taken the time to marshal her arguments. There must be something she could say to turn

him, but for the life of her she couldn't think what it might be. It was just what Owen had always told her and she had never heeded, believing herself too well controlled for such advice: Get your emotions out of the equation; assassins think with their heads, not their hearts. Anything else is crippling.

She had never really understood the truth of those words until now.

But because it was Jen's life at stake—Jen's innocence, Jen's simple joy in existence—her brain curdled, and all she could say was, "You can't trust him, curse it! Pehndon is evil, Neros; take my word on it!"

"Why should I? Why should I take your word against his? Why should I take the word of a known *assassin*," he practically spat the epithet, "when it's Pehndon who has given me everything? Pehndon who has raised me from the gutter? What have you ever given me that I should grant you equal trust and loyalty?"

"The truth!" she countered furiously. Emotions, curse it; emotions. *Think, Vera!* "Listen to your instincts, Neros. You know you don't trust the man, deep down where it counts. You know how easily he has manipulated everything, yourself included!" No, no; wrong approach. Logic, not emotions. Logic. "Think, Neros! Why do you believe he chose you when there were other, better scientists available, dry and sober? Altruism? A certain fine feeling for his fellow man?" She snorted. "Be realistic. He chose you for your loyalty. He could have paid for the best; what he did was purchase the most desperate, and therefore the most malleable. It's your gratitude that matters to him, Neros, not your scientific genius—or the lack thereof."

It was a cheap shot and she knew it, but Neros winced. The truth was always painful, she supposed, no matter what the form.

"Listen to me, Neros. Pehndon is not your friend!"

"And what's your blasted hurry all of a sudden? Why has it become so important to convince me? And why now? What's *your* agenda, Leonie or Vera or whoever you are?"

Vera paused for a moment, weighing the question and her answer. For a moment she considered misdirection, then with a mental shrug she threw the whole ugly truth at his feet. Let him do with it as he would. "The name's Vera,

Vera Radineaux, and I'll tell you my bloody agenda—and my bloody hurry. It's because Pehndon had me tortured. Because he had me beaten and raped for daring to tell the truth. And because I learned today that he now has my niece." She saw his face ripple and clench, and continued implacably, "It's all right for me. I'm old; I'm almost forty. I've seen something of the world." Her voice was hard and sarcastic, belying her words. For it was not all right; it never had been. "But my niece—Jen, that's her name. Jenifleur. Her mother died three years back, and she's my ward now—Jen is eighteen. Eighteen, Neros! And Pehndon is *not* going to destroy her life like he tried to destroy mine, not if I can help it! So, as much as I would love your aid in bringing him to justice, if it comes to swaying you or saving her, my choice is clear. That, Neros, is my bloody agenda—and my bloody hurry!"

There was a long moment of silence. Then, "Leonie . . . I mean, Vera . . ." he began, but she cut him off angrily.

"Stuff it. I'm leaving in an hour. If you want to do the right thing, come with me. If not, I wish you joy in the life you have chosen. May you be very happy and very prosperous. And if not, I hope your death will at least be quick and painless, because I honestly don't see how Pehndon can let you live, knowing what you do."

And she rose abruptly, nearly knocking over the stool in her haste to be gone, and stalked out of Fazaquhian's office. Furious with herself for her lack of control, she never bothered to turn and see the expression that graced the scientist's face.

And in all their futile conversation, that may have been her greatest mistake.

42

It was odd, Jeryn decided, sneaking into your own brother's office. Not, of course, that his presence at the rebel headquarters was in any way unusual. Not that he was even really sneaking; he was here as openly as the rest of the alliance. It was only his purpose that was a bit . . . nefarious. But then, he rationalized, he wasn't doing anything illegal. Jason or his agents had stolen those papers from Pehndon; all he was doing was restoring the man's rightful property—undoing the crime, as it were.

So why were his guts knotted into a panicked tangle, his palms damp with random bursts of nervous moisture?

Jason's agents were hardly out in force. A scant half dozen occupied the battered desks, making the high rafters echo with a kind of desolate silence. Too desolate; too silent. Jeryn shifted nervously. A strange thought for one intent on burglary, but there it was. The more people, the more bustle, the more chance of distracting his brother's attention. For, sibling or no, Jeryn had no key to the warehouse door, nor did he know the multiplicity of turnings and codes that governed the underground tunnels. He had simply been too lazy and too uninterested to learn them, and to change that now would seem, at the least, suspicious. So of necessity he had to propagate his theft in the daylight hours, right under the noses of the assembled faithful.

Maybe that was the cause of his anxiety. It was much easier selling information; you never had to steal that, at least not physically. But the papers . . . The thought of everything that could possibly go wrong—including being apprehended by his moralistic brother—made him feel vaguely nauseous.

What would Jason say if he caught him sneaking out the back with all of Pehndon's carefully hoarded documents? It was not a question Jeryn even liked to consider.

Which was why he now wished for a few more sheltering
bodies to serve as decoys, but all of Jason's forces were
doubtless out on the streets, canvassing the workers, proclaiming Jason's innocence. His brother was nothing if
not a blatant opportunist; he always knew when to play
the game.

Obliquely, he wondered what had happened to Grahme.
He hadn't seen Tortaluk around the warehouse in days,
and he had been assiduously present, lounging about in a
bored fashion, awaiting his opportunity. And what made
it all worse was Jason's obvious pleasure in his presence.
Why, this very morning—tousling his brother's hair on
his way from the warehouse floor to the office—the rebel
leader had grinned and said, "It's good to see you around
more, Jeryn. Maybe we'll finally get you interested in this
old business, after all."

It was a teasing sort of comment, and Jeryn was never
quite sure what his brother meant by such remarks, but he
nonetheless flushed an unbecoming shade of magenta in
response.

To which Jason, clearly misinterpreting his confusion,
added, "In any case, I do appreciate the support."

Which, of course, only made it worse.

Jeryn sighed and readjusted his position on the lumpy
couch, finally abandoning the book he had been trying to
read for the past half hour. Rising instead, he decanted a
pungent stream of coffee from the battered tin samovar
into one of the assorted mismatched mugs which had col-
lected about its base. As he gulped down a scalding
mouthful, he surveyed the empty warehouse and had to
mask a certain satisfaction. It hadn't been so long ago that
he had reigned over his own rebel alliance; he wondered
what Pehndon would think if he knew how closely Jeryn
had modeled the copy to the genuine article—from the
lofty upstairs office to the very sofa he now occupied.

Or how he would respond to the fact that the fake alliance lay all of one street over. If you lined it up correctly, you could even see the corner of one from the
doorway of the other.

Right under his bloody nose.

Upstairs, Jason's door swung open, and his brother
emerged, escorting one of his operatives to the head of the
stairs, sending him on his way with a laugh and a hearty

clap to the shoulder. The man grinned back in a silly, be-
sotted sort of way—ridiculous on a grown man. Jeryn
masked a snort. No, better to put an end to this nonsense
before Jason's head swelled so far it exploded.

Leaning out over the balcony rails, Jason caught his
brother's glance, calling down, "You still here?" from his
lofty perch.

"Nothing better to do." Jeryn shrugged, feigning indifference.

"Then get up here and talk to me. I'm about to go
insane! If I hear of one more plot or problem, I shall probably abandon the whole rebellion entirely." One of the
busy workers chuckled. "Oh, and bring me up some coffee, if you would."

Masking a sigh, Jeryn poured a second cup, then
mounted the stairs and handed it to his brother, who took
a deep, relieved gulp and added, "Bless you, Jeryn. Come
in; sit down. Distract me. Blazes, but this whole situation
is running me ragged!"

Jeryn raised a supercilious eyebrow. "A little too much
excitement and a tad too little sleep?" he inquired pointedly.

To his amazement, Jason flushed. "Ah. So you noticed?"

"How could I not? You haven't exactly been subtle,
you know. Besides, those walls we erected are pretty thin.
She's a wild one, isn't she?"

His brother buried his face in his hands, but his eyes
twinkled mischievously from between his splayed fingers.
"Yes, I suppose you could say that," he retorted, and
Jeryn had a sudden, poignant memory of their teenage
years—before Jason had become the center of the rebel
alliance, when his life had still belonged to his sibling.
When they had dissected their baffled adolescent troubles
and discussed their latest conquests in the comforting
dimness of their shared bedroom. *What happened to those
days?* he thought miserably. *Where did everything go
wrong? And why did bloody crusading Jason decide he
had to go save the world?*

"Sorry," his brother added, lowering his fingers; his
eyes were still gleaming. "Consider it payback for all
those many years I was forced to listen to *you* . . ."

Jeryn met his dancing gaze, and abruptly the two of

them burst into gales of conspiratorial laughter. *I miss you, Jason,* he almost said, but before he could act on the formless impulse, a knock came on the office door.

Wiping his streaming eyes, Jason looked up. "What?" he demanded.

One of the workers poked his head around the door-jamb. "Pardon me, Jason; no crisis, but . . . could you come look at something for a moment? I want you to re-view our latest poster campaign."

"Yes, I'll be right down," his brother responded. Then to Jeryn, "Make yourself at home; this shouldn't take long. Then after that . . . maybe we can get lunch or some-thing?" He sounded oddly tentative, and Jeryn shrugged.

"Yes, maybe. Whatever." *Why now, Jason?* he was thinking, even as his heart beat an anxious tattoo. And then his brother departed, leaving Jeryn alone in the of-fice.

By all that was precious . . .

Even as his sibling's feet pounded down the stairs, Jeryn was out of his chair, pulling out drawers and rifling through papers, trying to find Pehndon's purloined docu-ments. At any moment he expected to hear the measured tread of Jason's return, but from the sound of the muted voices on the warehouse floor, some kind of conference was going on: every available worker was clustered around the downstairs desks, commenting and critiquing.

Jeryn tamped down a guilty surge of relief and turned his attention to the desk itself. It was a bargain piece, with no custom-made panels, no hidden compartments. It didn't take him long to find what he was looking for, tacked firmly to the bottom of the uppermost drawer. He pried the envelope free and checked the contents briefly. It was Pehndon's, all right; he would recognize that tight, meticulous hand anywhere. Hastily, he tucked the pack-age down the back of his shirt, then waited a few minutes for his racing pulse to slow.

Fortunately the sheaf was fairly thin and didn't make much of a bulge beneath his clothing as he sauntered back down the stairs.

"Sorry," Jason said distractedly as he passed, without looking up. "This is taking a little longer than I expected."

"Never mind; it's not important."

His brother did look up then, his eyes registering puzzlement and an odd kind of hurt. "You're leaving? But what about our lunch?"

"Another time, maybe," Jeryn responded, as casually as he was able. "I just remembered I have something to do."

It was a flimsy excuse—he knew it—but he could think of nothing better.

Besides, he already felt guilty enough as it was.

Clad this time in a provocative outfit, the blond wig ensconced firmly on her head, Jen peeked around the borders of the government complex, registering the continued presence of her two pursuers. They were seated on the Council steps, scanning the square with resolute eyes.

Perfect.

She slipped back around her corner and trotted happily up the street, certain that she had avoided their detection.

She had followed them home last night, trailing them to a vaguely respectable inn on Pirhini Street, cheek by jowl with some of the more elaborate whorehouses. Lurking in a nearby doorway, she had watched them enter, and was about to circle the premises to see if she could locate their window when the blond one stuck his head out of a top-floor chamber, muttering about the heat and surveying the street below.

Instantly she stooped and made a show of scratching one ankle, then sauntered away with a provocative wiggle of hips guaranteed to disguise her in that particular setting. And apparently they hadn't suspected, for they were back in the square the next morning as usual, leaving their rooms wide open for further exploration.

Using the company kept by the inn as her guide, she garbed herself as one of the seedier strumpets and had a story ready in case the hosteler should stop her. But as it happened he was occupied elsewhere when she entered, and so she was able to slip upstairs unobserved. There were only four doors on the top-floor landing, so it was no trouble to locate the proper portal. Slipping her picklocks from an inner pocket, she threw the bolts and entered, easing the door shut behind her.

It was a neat double room, nothing extravagant but certainly clean and comfortable. A few changes of familiar clothing were scattered about, but what interested her most was the large, iron-bound trunk. The lock was massive and complex, and to a trained eye it fairly bristled with challenge. Grinning, she took a seat before it, laying out her tools, and set to work.

As expected, it was extensively snared; a less suspicious thief would have missed about half the tricks. Even Jen, who had encountered an endless array of traps while picking the locks on Vera's boxes, almost fell victim to one or two. But eventually persistence and a little genuine luck got her through, and she finally eased the lid up, smiling as the contents were revealed.

They were worthy of the Guild, for both the content and the complexity of the barriers that protected them. Weapons and wigs, poisons and penknives. By all that was precious, these had to be Guild outcasts! No reputable agents would work for Pehndon, and some of the potions they carried were available only through the Guild aegis; Jen had been tutored extensively by Vera in such matters and knew what she was looking at.

She rifled through their possessions, trying to find evidence of their contract—or even *contact*—with Pehndon, but could find nothing. She sighed faintly but was hardly discouraged. There were two purposes to this little exercise of hers. One was to gather evidence against the Minister, if she possibly could. The other, and less obvious, was to rile the man still further. To have his assassins—for that they were, no doubt of it now—chasing after her was one thing. But to have their quarry suddenly, and very obviously, turn tail and pursue them was another matter entirely.

And Jen intended to prove definitely that she was now the huntress and not the hunted. So drawing out a note she had penned earlier, she laid it deftly across the topmost layer, then artfully draped a fold of cloth over the box's lip, shut the lid, and painstakingly reset all the locks and traps, leaving that sole scrap of fabric protruding as evidence of her presence.

Whistling happily, she descended the stairs, wishing she could see their faces when they returned and discovered her intrusion. No one who guarded themselves that carefully could be anything less than thoroughly shaken. Looking back later, she therefore considered it a kind of cruel twist of fortune that, in less than five minutes, it was she herself who was stricken literally speechless.

43

Thibault felt an almost terrifying sense of purpose as he arrived back in Nhuras with Vera at his side. Or rather seated at his back, for they were mounted double on the camel—a situation which caused Thibault no small embarrassment. He still hadn't quite shaken his childhood awe of the Hawk, and there was something decidedly undignified about having her perched behind him, clinging like a monkey to his shoulders. She should, he felt, have been mounted in front, but she had been quite adamant on the matter. It was a question of weight distribution, she said, although Thibault couldn't help but wonder if his lead position weren't in part a sort of tacit approval for having followed her halfway around the world—despite specific orders to the contrary.

But whatever the case, he had to admit that it was a somewhat heady feeling, giving him the temporary—and undoubtedly erroneous—impression that he was in control. It was only now, in retrospect, that he could admit how isolated he had felt when Jenny had dispatched him, as though he were being dismissed from the center of the action to some remote corner where he couldn't do any damage. But that hadn't really been true; there *had* been valuable information to be gathered in Nhuras and, more important, he was the one who had located the Hawk.

Not exactly a trivial contribution.

He couldn't wait to see Jenny's face!

So, "You all right back there?" he asked, half turning, as the stench of the city wafted up and assailed him.

His companion chuckled. "This place reeks like a sewer, but I've come to think of it as home. Ah, but revenge will be sweet, Neros or no Neros! Tell Avram to head for the bazaar and we'll settle up there."

Thibault complied, and on the outskirts of the bustling

market, Vera handed over coin and camel, then rubbed her hands in satisfaction as their taciturn guide led away the foul-tempered beast that had served as their transport back to Nhuras. At least, Thibault reflected, the returning leg of the journey had been more comfortable than the outbound one, but—whether he was chained or unchained—the desert was the desert, and he was heartily glad to be free of it.

"Well, what now?" he asked, surveying the bustling throngs of merchants, their cacophonous babble so alien after the weighty silence of the Anvil.

"Lodgings, I think," she responded. "We're going strictly middle class for a while, my lad, so deliver up your hoard." And she tapped cheerfully on his belt buckle.

With a resigned smile, he unhitched the belt and handed it to Vera, holding up his pants with one hand until she passed him a bit of string in return.

"Jen's work?" she asked as she extracted the coins. And when he nodded, she added, "Sometimes that girl amazes me—but don't tell her I said that; she has too high an opinion of herself already. Now, if you don't mind venturing among the whorehouses, Pirhini Street has some decent lodgings."

Predictably, he felt himself flush, and Vera chuckled at his expression. It wasn't that he was prudish, he acknowledged, just . . . repressed. "Thibault, you're a positive treasure," she said. "Very well, Pirhini Street it is."

It was about a ten-minute walk from the bazaar, but Thibault found himself welcoming the respite from the camel's swaying gait. As it was, it took him most of the distance to recover his land legs and rid himself of the feeling that the dusty pavement was tilting precariously beneath him. In fact, so preoccupied was he by the stability that he almost missed the tall blond harlot progressing nonchalantly down the center of Pirhini Street.

He blinked, then reached out an impulsive hand to seize an elbow, swinging the figure around to face him. Almost instantly, he felt the point of a dagger pressing sharply against his belly, and a husky voice exclaimed, "Unhand me at once!"

"Quiet, Jenny, it's me." And he grabbed her wrist, forcing the blade away from his body. "What are you doing here?"

"I might ask the same of you," she responded tartly, the knife disappearing up her sleeve, but when she tilted her head to meet his gaze her eyes were dancing. "Blast it, Thibault, when did you get back?"

He was about to answer when Vera's voice drifted back to them, sharp with familiar reprimand. "Honestly, Thibault, this is no time to be pawing your favorite strumpets. We have work to do."

It would have been almost amusing had the situation been different, but as it was—with Jenny's body a bare handsbreadth from his own—he felt her go rigid with shock, then abruptly limp. Her knees buckled, and she would have fallen had he not hastily gripped her elbow.

"Vera?" Her voice rose, cracked—a raw and painful note. "Curse it, Thibault, if this is some kind of trick . . ."

Much as he tried, he couldn't help the small, triumphant smile which curved his lips as he answered, "No trick, I swear it."

She turned then—slowly, almost fearfully, her hand absently sweeping the blond wig from her head—and when she saw her aunt standing halfway down the street, uttered a joyous cry and launched herself at the woman, practically knocking her from her feet. "Vera! Vera, you're alive!"

"Gracious, my girl, and why shouldn't I be?"

"But . . ."

"What am I doing here? It's a long story, so let's get some lodgings and I'll explain."

They got an upstairs suite at the Twin Palms, consisting of a small sitting room barely large enough for a couch and a fireplace, and a back bedroom with a single, wide bed. Thibault masked a grimace; no question where he'd be sleeping. Almost, he missed Jason's daybed; at least that had been reasonably his size.

Jason. He still shuddered to think how Jen would react to *that* particular news; fortunately Vera hadn't broached the subject yet. Instead, she was sitting calmly on the sofa, quizzing Jen, while the girl was buzzing about the room like a demented butterfly, alighting briefly on various bits of furniture before popping up again, all but rebounding off the walls in her frenzy.

"You came in by ship?" Vera was asking.

"Yes, and a thoroughly disreputable vessel it was, too.

The *Crow's Nest,* but it should have been called the *Rat's Nest . . .*"

"Jenny!"

"Well, it should have; it was crawling with the things. I killed thirty-five on the voyage."

"You did?" This time it was Thibault's turn to sound horrified, and she flashed him a grin.

"You doubt me? But pleasantries aside, Vera, I still don't see why we have to stay here. There's plenty of room at Jason's; we could just as easily lodge there—and at no expense!"

Thibault could see Vera wince. "I don't know quite how to tell you this, Jen," her aunt began, "but . . ."

"We were wrong about Jason," he finished gently—and rather diplomatically, he thought.

Her eyes flashed angrily in response. "What do you mean, wrong?"

Vera rose, moving to where Jen hovered impatiently by the window. Laying a gentle arm around her niece's shoulders, she guided her to the sofa and forced her to sit, saying, "You're young, Jenny; you have a lot to learn. And I don't blame you for being fooled, because he was good. Very good."

"What are you saying?"

"That Jason's in league with Pehndon. I saw him; I went to the headquarters of the rebel alliance when he hired me. And he was there when Pehndon betrayed me, turning me over to the government guards."

Jen erupted from the couch, throwing off her aunt's embrace. "I don't believe you! I know Jason; he's a good man, Vera!"

"Based on what? His looks? Hang it, Jenny . . ."

"It's more than just his looks. Give me some credit! I'm not as ignorant as you seem to think."

"Eighty thousand gryphons on a string, Jen, you're eighteen!"

"And just because you're twenty-one years older means that your impulses are somehow more valuable?"

"Well, of course they are. I've had more time to refine them!"

"An impulse," Jen countered furiously, "is by definition unrefinable!"

Looking from one angry face to the other, Thibault

could feel the tension rising and hastily stepped in, saying softly, "So don't fight about it. Prove it."

Two sets of Radineaux eyes swung blankly toward him, two mouths frozen in mid-retort. It was Jen who recovered faster.

"What do you mean, prove it?" she snapped.

"You know where to find him," he retorted. "Take Vera to the headquarters and see if that's the place she visited, if Jason is really the person who hired her."

"And if he is?"

"Leave him; stay with us."

"You know what your problem is?" she spat. "You're just jealous!"

"Perhaps. But what if I'm not? What if Vera's correct?"

She was silent for a moment, eventually adding, "And what if she's not?"

"A public apology," the Hawk grinned. "And a pledge of undivided support. There. Will that satisfy you?"

Jen just grimaced, looking pointedly between Vera and Thibault. "Everything I have is at Jason's," she challenged eventually, still fighting, and Thibault had to admire her persistence, if not its cause.

He exhaled gustily. "Then remove it. Please, Jen . . ."

She held his eyes for a long, painful moment, then dropped her gaze. "Hang and blast! All right, you win. Come on, Vera, let's do it."

"What, now?"

"Why not? The sooner I know, the better. Besides, if I'm to clear out my possessions, I'll need sufficient time."

Vera shrugged. "So be it. See you in a bit, Thibault."

He wasn't even aware that he was standing until his legs all but collapsed under him. As the door shut behind them, he sank down on the sofa with a shaky breath. By all that was precious, he had handled her; he had actually won an argument with Jen!

Throwing his head back, he began to laugh—slowly at first and then stronger, filling the room with loud, vaguely hysterical peals.

Grahme rotated slowly, surveying the sweating walls of his domain with a certain subtle satisfaction. Not that he liked the view. On the contrary, he hated it—hated everything about it—from the rats that tumbled through the

open sewer to the fist-size bugs that crawled about the
walls, clicking in frustration when they couldn't find the
exit. He despised the stench of the matted straw and his
own overripe waste, loathed the way the narrow window
seemed designed to funnel and intensify the evening cool.
He abhorred the way the blankets rasped against his skin
and detested the humiliation of remaining perpetually
naked, as though he could no longer retain his secret
thoughts when he couldn't even hide his private flesh.

And yet . . .

He had done it; he had bested them. He had beaten
Pehndon at his own bloody game. For as long as he was in
here, and visibly unharmed, he knew that Jason was alive.
They could not risk marking him while the rebel leader
remained at liberty; they needed him too badly as a witness. And that knowledge alone kept him silent throughout all of Pehndon's imprecations, Pehndon's threats,
Pehndon's lies and worthless promises. Like the walls, he
sweated, but he stood; he *endured*.

Sure, there were tortures—hidden, subtle, indescribable
tortures, whose ghastly echoes pervaded his very dreams—
but Jason was alive. And surely it couldn't have been
worse for Ricard when he lost his hand to the vats, seared
off in a mass of molten liquid and flesh. Surely his pain was
as nothing compared to that of the hordes of workers who
daily won themselves similar disfigurements at the hands
of a careless government. No, he would suffer for Jason—
die for Jason—quite gladly, if it would buy his idol some
more time. If it would allow Jason to bring down Pehndon
and his regime in one glorious stroke.

And so he smiled grimly at the impenetrable stone and
pictured the bond between them growing. Strengthening.
Stone did not bleed. Stone did not hurt. Stone did not cry
out. And, most important, stone had no tongue to give
voice to traitorous confessions.

It became his litany.

Pehndon was iron; he would not yield.

Pehndon was fire; he would not crack.

Pehndon was an ocean; he would not erode.

He was stone, and he would survive.

44

Jen felt a certain grim resolution as she led Vera toward the rebel alliance, her joy in the Hawk's reappearance muted by the knowledge of Jason's perfidy. Not that she could even credit it; there had to be some other explanation. Someone must have made a mistake, because the thought that she might have been wrong—that she might have misjudged him—sent a ripple of unease fluttering through her. If that were true, then how could she ever trust herself again? How could she trust anyone? Her instincts were supposed to be reliable. Such things couldn't be learned; either you had them or you didn't. And what sort of future did she hold with the Guild if everything she believed in was so intrinsically flawed?

No, Jason had to be innocent. That was all there was to it.

So why did she feel this sudden, crippling doubt, gripping her with a strength that could wring her dry? But, "Here we are," she said eventually as they reached the warehouse door, hoping against hope that her aunt wouldn't know it.

Vera frowned slightly, surveying the rutted street. "Are you sure? I could have sworn it was . . ."

"What?"

"One street over." Vera shook her head, then caught sight of the flaking green door, chained with its rusty padlocks. "No, never mind; the Anvil must have addled my memory. This is it, after all; I recognize that portal."

With the last of the eagerness dying from her face, Jen eased the side door partly open and applied an eye to the crack. With a queer wrench she recognized Jason, leaning out over the balcony rails, regarding his followers with the very grin that had once played such havoc with her senses. Which it still did, she admitted, even when it was directed elsewhere. Almost reluctantly, she moved aside, yielding the view to Vera.

"That's him there, on the upper landing," she said.

Her aunt nodded, and Jen could read the answer in the slow slump of her shoulders. "Yes, that's him; I'm sorry, Jenny."

"Whatever."

They were halfway back to Pirhini Street before either of them spoke again. Finally, it was Vera who said, "You realize, of course, that now we have to get back those papers?"

"Pehndon's papers?" Jen felt her already black mood growing darker. "Curse it, Vera . . ."

The Hawk laid a gentle hand on her shoulder. "It's not your fault, love; how were you to know?"

"Because I should have guessed, I should have felt it! What kind of an assassin am I if I can't even identify the villains?"

"It it makes any difference, I didn't suspect them myself until they threw me in prison. Sometimes it happens. And how stupid do you think I felt then?"

Jen managed a reluctant smile. "I guess. But everything was going so well, so perfectly, and then . . ."

"What?" Vera sounded concerned.

"Blast it! No wonder I haven't been getting anything out of Pehndon. Jason must have told him about that thrice-cursed bug!"

"What bug?"

So Jen explained, describing everything from her purchase of the equipment to her trailing of the two assassins, and when she finished she was astonished to hear the Hawk's laughter ringing out through the narrow streets.

She raised a disgusted eyebrow. "What now?" she demanded.

"Great bouncing catfish, Jen, do you have any idea whose rooms you have just raided—and whose locks you have so expertly picked?"

"Apparently not," she answered sourly.

"Then let me tell you, my love, that you have just mounted a successful assault against two of the Guild's top operatives: the Hound and the Falcon."

Jen felt her jaw drop and wondered why she had the sudden impression that the sky had just fallen; she felt abruptly dizzy. "But," she managed at last, "if they were Guild, then what were they doing in Pehndon's employ?"

"Silly girl, they weren't in Pehndon's employ; they were in Owen's."

"Owen's? So why were they chasing me?"

"Because, much as I love you, you have been doing something highly illegal—at least in the eyes of the all-seeing Guild. And fond as Owen may be of me personally, he certainly isn't about to let that affect Guild policy!"

That was it; she was finished. There was no way Owen DeVeris would let her join the Guild now. Not after he had paid to have her stopped—or even eliminated. She shuddered and was about to say something more when she suddenly realized that Vera was still chuckling.

"What?" she demanded, in some irritation.

"The Hound and the Falcon. Just wait until Owen hears about this; he'll have a conniption! You didn't take anything, did you?"

"I might have . . ."

"Better and better! You know, I believe he'll have to take you into the Guild just to spare himself the humiliation?"

"You think so?" Her mood abruptly lightened.

"I hope so, at any rate, because—just between you and me, my girl—you've got quite a talent for this!"

"Even though I've been focusing on the wrong targets?"

"Even so. Your impulses were sound enough, no matter what their direction. And no one can be right every single time."

Jen grimaced. One mistake, maybe; that was forgivable. But lately it seemed that she was piling mistake upon mistake, error upon error. Just look at her impulse for Jason. No, talent aside, she was pretty far from perfection.

Suddenly, she didn't feel quite so wonderful.

It had been a wretchedly long day, and now night was falling. Mark uttered a despondent sigh and glanced up at the purpling clouds. The government workers had long since departed, and Pehndon himself had left an hour ago.

And still no sign of that blasted woman.

What, by all that was precious, was she up to now?

"I'm tired," Derek complained eventually. "Let's go home."

"And what if she returns? After all, she's been up to something for days; I don't want to miss anything now."

"Somehow, I don't think you will."

"And whatever leads you to that conclusion?"

"I've been thinking. Call it an instinct, Mark, but I believe she's toying with us. Whatever she's doing, it's aimed at us, not Pehndon."

"You've got to be kidding me!"

"No. I'm telling you, Mark, she's not coming back; she's up to something entirely different. Something that depends on keeping us safely here."

Mark considered this for a moment, then abruptly exploded. "Hang and blast, Derek, if you're right . . ."

"What?"

"We have to get back, now!" And hauling his brother to his feet, Mark set off at a panicked trot.

"Mark, wait. What's the hurry?" Derek panted to keep up.

"Our possessions—what do you think?"

Derek grinned. "You and that bloody trunk . . ."

But Mark was right—or rather, Derek was—for when they returned to their room at the Four Crowns, the first thing he saw was the swatch of fabric protruding from his private box. "Look!" he accused.

Derek followed his pointing finger. "Come on, Mark, are you sure you didn't leave it packed like that?"

Mark scowled at him.

"Right, of course; silly me. You leave something sticking out of *the* trunk?"

Shooting his brother a sour look, Mark squatted and began undoing the locks.

"I told you she was up to something. I told you she was . . ."

"Stuff it," the Falcon retorted. "Has anyone ever told you that you're a lousy winner? Entirely too smug." And he raised the lid.

Derek leaned in, craning his head over his sibling's shoulder. Resting atop the contents was a folded page: pristine and alien amid the colorful clutter. *To Mark and Derek,* it read in a bold, spiky hand.

Mark snatched it up and unfolded the paper.

For once, mercifully, the Hound was silent, obviously shaken by the sudden implications. That was his brother in a nutshell: gloat first, think later.

Together they read the unspoken challenge:

If you think you can stop me, then think again; I am not to be deflected so easily. Pehndon will go down, will pay for his crimes against the Hawk.
—A Friend
P.S.: I deducted the price of a parasol. That business on Nhevon Street has quite ruined my old one.

"So she thinks we're working for Pehndon?" Mark ex-claimed.

"She did what?" Derek cried, almost simultaneously. Predictably, he was rooting through the trunk in search of their purse. Spilling out the coins, he started to count them, then suddenly began to chuckle. "By Varia, she did it; she actually did it!"

"How much?"

"A hundred."

"Bloody expensive parasol," Mark said sourly.

Derek was still chuckling. "What a nerve," he said admiringly. "Now there's a woman after my own heart!"

"I'll try to remember that the next time we encounter her. So, shall we eat?"

"What, aren't you even going to relock the thing?"

Mark just shrugged. "What's the bloody point?"

Jen looked down miserably and pushed a bean around the edges of her plate—an ambulatory bit of dinner. Then, looking up, she met Jason's eyes across the table. They were warm and brown, and as velvet-honest as they had been the first time she had met him.

I trust you even now, she thought. *Even when I know I shouldn't. What's the matter with me?*

"Is something troubling you, love?" he asked, in un-canny echo of her thoughts.

She forced a smile. "No, nothing. It's just that everything is going so slowly. Pehndon, the evidence; Thibault's not even back yet." She choked out the lie.

He reached across the table and took her hand, his fingers entwining with her own. She returned the pressure almost automatically, and despised herself even more for the spark of attraction which still flared between them. It was the hardest thing she had ever done, sitting here across this quiet table with a man her heart still trusted, serving as an exotic kind of bait while, back at his home and office, Thibault was industriously removing every trace of her presence from his life.

She had given her partner explicit instructions: handing over the latchkey, describing how to deactivate and dismantle her mage-powered apparatus, revealing the location of Pehndon's papers. It was almost too easy—except for one annoying detail. She simply couldn't decide whom she hated the most: Jason for deceiving her or herself for allowing it to happen.

Curse you, she thought. *How could you do this to me? How could you do this to me and still make me believe that you didn't?*

He squeezed her fingers lightly, those dark eyes troubled. "Poor Jen. Not only are your investigations going badly, but the rebel leader has become too bloody busy to share in your worries."

You bastard. Don't do this to me! Her wild thoughts presaged a sudden, painful flare of remorse. She would never forget the sight of his face as she'd entered his office that evening: the relieved, almost grateful, smile that lit his features, as if he had transgressed and she, by her very presence, was absolving him. It simply wasn't fair. Why was he making her feel the traitor here?

"Jason . . ." she fumbled, desperately searching for words, for composure.

Sensing her hesitation, he sighed and dropped her fingers. But, "No, love, it's true," he insisted nonetheless. "I know I've been distant lately; and I'm sorry for it. For making you carry this on your own."

"I . . ."

"Jeryn came by again today," he continued, as if she had spoken. "He's been in the office almost every day for a week now, as if he were waiting for something to happen. For me to notice him, I suppose. And I've been too preoccupied to pay him any attention: worried about Grahme, about my organization, about the bloody workers." He grimaced. "This is my brother, Jen. I practically raised him; for years he was all I had. And now something's troubling him, and I was too bloody self-involved to notice until it was too late. Too late!"

"Jason, please don't beat yourself up about this," she begged, mentally adding, *I can't bear it. Were you always this bloody good, or am I just the world's biggest idiot?*

"But don't you see?" he persisted. "I abandoned him when he needed me, and I've never done that before. Never!"

"You can't always be there for everyone, Jason."

"But this is Jeryn; it should be different. It should have *been* different. And then he just . . . left me—dismissed me—as if he no longer needed me. Which was why I was so glad to see you. I was afraid that you had abandoned me too."

His despair was palpable. Jen managed a watery smile, all the while feeling her self-respect sink lower, an obscure anger rising. Either he was very, very good, or she was about to give the killing blow to a man very much in need.

And the ridiculous thing was, she still didn't know which to believe.

45

Thibault sank onto the couch in their tiny suite, resting his feet on a low hassock, and watched the embers of the fire flickering through troubled eyes. Neither Jen nor Vera was back yet, and he didn't know how he was going to break the news, for his mission had been only partially successful. Oh, he had had no trouble liberating Jen's possessions; the two packed trunks now rested neatly against the back wall, and Jen's mage-powered apparatus was safely stowed in a nearby satchel. But when he had progressed to the headquarters of the rebel alliance, his luck had deserted him.

The rebels had been cordial enough, welcoming him back and informing him of Jen and Jason's absence; they had even offered to let him wait in the office. Scarcely able to credit his good fortune, he had proceeded upstairs, and when he was certain they had forgotten his presence, he set to work. Jen had assured him she knew where Jason stored the papers—in an envelope tacked to the bottom of his topmost drawer. But when Thibault looked, he found nothing but the faint ghost of pinholes to mark their former presence. No envelope, no papers. And though he searched the entire office—frantic that Jen and Jason could return at any moment, for how long could she keep up the charade, after all?—it was to no avail.

He couldn't find the documents anywhere.

Eventually, when Jen's acting ability had proved better than his capacity to wait, he returned to their rooms in Pirhini Street. Admittedly her absence troubled him, and not only for her safety; another part of him was frantic that Jason's charm would win the secret from her. She would trust him again, tell him of their suspicions, of Vera's return . . .

As far as Thibault was concerned, the missing papers

were only further proof of the rebel leader's duplicity. He had doubtless returned the things to his mentor the minute Jen had left them in his hands.

He was distracted from his musings by the sound of a key in the lock, and he looked up to see Vera shutting the door behind her. She looked infinitely weary, her short hair ruffled, dark circles under her eyes. But there was nonetheless a composure to her gaze, as if a certain weight had been lifted from her conscience.

"Good evening, Thibault. Any luck?"

"The papers were gone. Everything else went fine."

"Bugger." She threw another log onto the fire and poked up the embers to a respectable glow. "Where did you search?"

"Just the office; I didn't know if I had time to go back and check the house. I didn't know how long Jen would be able to maintain the facade."

"And?"

He grimaced. "She was obviously more successful than I imagined."

"She's still not back, then?"

He shook his head. "And where did you depart to?"

"The Mages Quarter. I couldn't find Absalom at the bazaar, so I decided to use the proper channels to contact Owen."

"And?"

Her mouth twisted. "After he got over his shock at seeing me alive, he was most obliging. A little less than happy to hear about Jen, but impressed despite himself at her progress. I promised him we'd speak to the Hound and the Falcon on the morrow."

"The Hound and the *who*?"

"Jen didn't tell you?" Vera chuckled. "It appears our girl had herself a bit of a run-in with my rescue team in your absence. She broke into their rooms this morning and raided one of their Guild-locked trunks."

Thibault cursed lethargically and dropped his head into his hands.

"Not your fault." Vera leaned over the top of the couch, tousling his hair reassuringly. "You can't keep an eye on the girl all the time. But in retrospect," she added almost conversationally, "it does give me some pause as to the status of my own boxes."

Face still hidden, Thibault masked a groan. "I'm sorry, Vera."

"Blazes." She sounded more amused than anything. "What did she take now?"

"The audio links." And he looked up somewhat sheepishly.

She chuckled. "I always knew there was a reason I didn't have any children. Never mind; no harm done. I mean, they aren't broken, are they?"

"No."

"Then you'd best hang on to them; you never know when you might need them. And tell her when she gets in that I've gone to bed. It's been a long day."

"Right. Good night, then, Vera."

"Good night. Oh, and Thibault?"

"Yes?"

"You've done a good job. I thought you might like to know that."

"Thanks."

His tone was glum, and she must have sensed his hesitation, his lack of conviction, for she laid a gentle hand on his shoulder, saying somewhat unexpectedly, "She's young, Thibault. Give her time. She'll figure it out eventually."

"Figure what out?"

"How much she needs you." And brushing his hair back, she dropped a light kiss on his forehead, leaving Thibault staring into the fire with his face as bright as the flaming embers.

He was still sitting there when Jen returned.

Almost an hour had passed, and she looked somehow drained and deflated as she settled beside him, sighing heavily, and propped her feet up next to his. He glanced obliquely at her, but she seemed disinclined for conversation, so instead he merely raised one inviting arm and to his vast amazement she slid over, pillowing her cheek against his shoulder. Lowering his arm, he just sat and held her until he felt the tension drain from her body.

"You all right, Jenny?" he said at last.

"No. It was dreadful; I hated every minute of it. I still can't believe he's guilty, even though I know he is. So, how did it go with you?"

"I got our possessions out, if that's what you mean."

"And the papers?" He shrugged, prompting a string of curses. "That doesn't look good, does it?" she finished.

"No, I'm afraid not. What took you so long?"

She stiffened. He was afraid she would pull away, but after a moment she relaxed wearily, saying, "I didn't sleep with him, if that's what you're implying. He was just troubled and needed support, someone to listen. Or at least, he was pretending to." She was silent for a moment, then added, "He kept telling me how glad he was to see me, how pleased he was that I hadn't abandoned him."

"Why? Who else has?"

"Grahme, for one; Pehndon arrested him the day after you left. And today he felt like he had betrayed Jeryn. He seemed so hurt and depressed that I couldn't help it; I just let him talk. And, blast it, I even halfway believed him!"

Sensing the raw edge of anguish in her voice, he wisely didn't push the matter, asking only, "So how did you get free?"

"He had to go back to the office. I claimed exhaustion and said I'd meet him at the house. Fine surprise he'll have when he gets home."

"You mean he didn't even try to accompany you?" He heard the baffled condemnation in his voice and winced, but it earned him a watery smile, the first she had conceded all evening.

"You obviously don't know Jason; with him, work always comes first. Not even my dubious charms can distract him."

Thibault grimaced. What was it about Andorian? Even in disgrace, he could still turn her head. "So what are you going to do?" he asked.

She deliberately misunderstood him. "Now? Catch up on Pehndon's doings, I suppose; learn more about the tiresome job of running a country. Now be a love, Thibault, and help me set up. I've got eight hours of policy to review."

Curled up on his common room couch, Jeryn was reading through Pehndon's papers with an increasing sense of unease when he heard a knock on his inner door: Jason, from the characteristic pattern of the pulses. Rising hastily, he shoved the documents under the cushion of a nearby armchair and pulled the portal open to reveal his brother's worried face.

"Jason, what happened?" He feigned concern, oblivion, though he knew perfectly well what was the matter. Jason had discovered the missing papers.

"She's gone. I can't believe it. Did you see her? Did she say anything?"

Jeryn blinked, feeling his face grow blank with incomprehension. This was a different Jason, one he hadn't seen in a long time. His brother's face looked lost and baffled, young, and somehow human. "Excuse me?" he hazarded.

"Jen. She's gone; everything's gone."

By all that was precious! "So that explains it," he managed weakly, and winced as Jason's fingers closed, vicelike, around his shoulders.

"Explains what?" his brother demanded.

When Jeryn had arrived home that evening, after delivering a secret missive to one of Pehndon's many drop points, he had seen a movement behind his brother's windows. The lights had been on too, which was unusual for Jason. Ordinarily he was in his office until later—and especially recently. But it could just as easily have been Jen in there, and Jeryn had paid it no heed until later, when he heard the front door close. Then, peering out though the slitted curtains, he saw a tall man depart, bearing two laden trunks down the shadowy street.

"What? Why didn't you tell me?" Jason accused when he had related the incident.

"Because I figured it was just another of your schemes, and when do you ever tell me what you're up to? Besides," he added bitterly, "when are you ever even home?"

Jason sighed heavily and collapsed into the armchair. Jeryn drew a panicked breath; he could all but hear the papers crinkling under his brother's weight. He desperately entreated whatever fates governed such matters that Jason wouldn't notice anything amiss, for to have him so close . . .

"You know, it's probably all my fault?" Jason admitted at last, heavily. "That she left, I mean. If I hadn't been so bloody self-involved . . ." And he dropped his head into his hands, silent for so long that, despite himself, Jeryn began to worry.

"Jason?" he hazarded at last.

His sibling looked up, his eyes dark and mournful. "Sit down, please, Jeryn. There's something I have to tell you."

With a watery smile, the younger Andorian took a nervous perch on the vacant sofa, wondering what on Varia his brother was up to. He expected the worst: threats and imprecations; hurt and accusations. He certainly never anticipated the humble tone with which Jason said, "I owe you an apology, Jeryn. I'm sorry."

"For . . . for *what*?" Jeryn practically yelped.

"For everything, for all these past few years. I've been so caught up in the rebel alliance that I haven't been able to see what's under my own nose. I've been neglecting the people who need me for the people who, well, who also need me, I suppose—but still, that's no excuse. I haven't been very available, have I?"

"You've been busy, Jason, and worried. Grahme's in prison, the city's in turmoil, and you have a one-thousand-mark reward on your head for a crime you didn't even commit." To his amazement, Jeryn heard the words pouring from his mouth, exonerating his brother for a situation that he had, in the main, created. So why was he now trying to console the man, having spent the past few weeks expertly manipulating him into just such a position?

It was even more disturbing to see Jason's face flare with gratitude, and when his brother reached out to grasp his hand he almost broke down and related the entire sordid truth.

But not quite.

"Thanks, Jeryn," his brother continued, oblivious to his distress, "but that's no excuse. You can't trade one type of caring for another. If you happen to see her, please tell her to come back. And as for you . . . Well, if you want to know about my bloody schemes, then ask me! I never meant to keep you in the dark deliberately; I just figured you weren't interested. After all, you never needed politics the way I did. You never required that kind of acceptance."

"Acceptance?" Jeryn blinked; he couldn't believe he had heard the words aright. Jason, requiring acceptance? Jason not having everything he needed in the adulation of his faithful? "Hang it, Jason . . ."

"Do you have any idea how much I envied you, growing up?" his brother continued, as if he hadn't spoken. "How much I admired your independence, your daring?"

Jeryn felt as if his entire life were collapsing. He could only sit and stare stupidly as Jason rose and grinned rather sheepishly at him. "Well, enough maudlin confessions for one night. Promise you'll tell me if you need anything? And beat me over the head if I don't listen?"

Jeryn nodded dumbly, and when his brother had left, collapsed before the armchair as if he lacked the energy to climb into its distant seat. Throwing off the cushion, he looked down at the pile of papers—slightly bent and crumpled from Jason's body—and wondered how he would ever be able to go through with this.

But Pehndon was waiting, or would be the moment he got the note, and now that he wanted something, he wasn't about to dally when it came to checking the drops. He would be in that tavern as specified tomorrow night, and if Jeryn knew what was good for him, he'd be there too.

After all, he wasn't about to destroy Jason's existence, just his credibility. And look how far a little humility had gotten him already.

The perfect rebel leader had been almost human tonight.

No, it would all be for the best; Jason would come back to him, and . . .

And what of all those others who needed his brother— the workers, the poor—what about them? Would their lives be any better under Pehndon's regime? Or would they suffer as badly in the naphtha refineries as they had in the factories?

He simply no longer even knew.

46

Vera awoke early the next morning and slipped out of bed, looking over at her niece, who slumbered, oblivious, on the far side. Jen's hair was tangled wildly, her face pulled into fretful lines, and Vera felt a moment of profound sympathy. Poor Jen; she could understand Jason's appeal, having so nearly fallen under his spell herself. But the man was a traitor, and Jen would have to learn how to handle betrayal if she wanted to succeed in this crazy life.

Vera could remember caring with that same, all-consuming intensity when she had been younger, but over the years that fire had mellowed, and her assignations now were heralded by a kind of gentle, unassuming pleasure. Better, perhaps, in the long run, but she couldn't help wondering—with an odd twinge of regret—if she weren't sometimes missing more than she had gained.

Almost, she envied Jen her youth and her two-handed grasping at life.

With a rueful grin, she crossed the room and dressed in silence; she hadn't gotten where she was by being impulsive. She was a thirty-nine-year-old assassin—oddity enough in such a profession—and, all in all, it had been a good life. Who else could have traveled so far and so frequently? What other scion of the aristocracy could have wakened in far-off Ashkharon as mistress of her own destiny, not once but on four separate occasions? Not to mention Mepharsta, Venetzia, Konasta . . . No, her life had been a grand one, and as for the sacrifice? Well, one always had to lose something along the way.

Easing open the bedroom door, she poked a cautious nose into the sitting room. A low, rhythmic buzz led her to Thibault, who was curled on the floor by the hearth, a pillow from the couch under his head. In that slack, peaceful face, she could almost see the ghost of the shy

ten-year-old she had once known, not quite lost beneath
the years of growth and maturity.

Dear Thibault. Sylvaine would have been so proud to
see him now.

Suddenly she grinned. By all that was precious, what
had gotten into her this morning, looking back in misty-
eyed reminiscence? If this was the result of having everyone gawk at her as though she'd just arisen from the
grave, she'd soon be doubting her own ability to stay
alive. She was the Hawk, after all; she hadn't gotten to the
top of the Guild hierarchy by being careless. Or even less
than perfectly resourceful. With a little snort, she eased
open the door to their suite and set off for the bazaar.

Soon she would show Pehndon and that traitor of his
what it meant to cross the Guild.

Fortunately, she found the mage ensconced in his usual
alcove this morning. Kneeling before his tatty display, she
grinned and said, "Good morning, Absalom. Where were
you last night? I was looking for you."

"As I was aware." He looked up with a flash of that bottomless black eye, his lips parting to reveal the yellow wreck
of his teeth; there seemed to be the remains of a sandwich in
his matted half-beard. "Unfortunately, I was . . . otherwise
engaged." And when she raised a teasing eyebrow, he added,
"Charming as she is, one does have other clients."

Vera chuckled and folded herself, tailor-fashion, before
him. "Not to mention that there are certain services you
can't perform outside the Quarter, eh, Absalom?"

"Ah," he responded in his old fulsome manner. "I presume you are referring to the Treasuries? Quite so, dear
lady, quite so. Most perceptive." And his one eye
twinkled. "So we have, I take it, come to that little matter
of tenfold repayment?"

"Indeed we have. And I fully intend to make good on
my promise."

His rusty chuckle scraped her ears. "How fortunate."
And reaching beneath his shapeless robe, he drew out a
leather pouch, opening it expectantly.

With an answering grin, she reached into her own
pockets and poured a stream of golden fifties—Absalom's
due and more—into its waiting maw.

He closed the purse with a satisfied smile and secreted
it again beneath his robes. Then, folding both good and

mangled hands into a bundle, he pressed them to his heart
and bowed extravagantly. "Always a pleasure doing business with you."

She raised an eyebrow. "Aren't you even going to
count it?"

"There is no need. So how was your journey? Successful?"

"In its way. But your camel drivers were pigs, my
friend."

He shrugged a careless shoulder. "A surprise? It is en-
demic to the breed."

"My guide back was perfectly civil."

"Ah, but he is only one man, and you were traveling
with a companion. Yet put him in a group with others of
his ilk, and you but one woman? As you say, pigs."

"You could have warned me."

Again the shoulder. "You survived, no?"

"Yes, I survived. And my thanks again, Absalom. Despite everything, you are a genuine miracle worker."

"Well, one does endeavor to please. And speaking of
which, I did perform one other service during your absence which might invoke your gratitude."

"Which was?"

The mage just displayed his crooked smile.

"Blast it, Jen! You never told me . . ."

Jen looked up with a panicked start and frantically motioned her aunt to silence. Scowling like a thundercloud,
Vera loomed in the doorway, but fortunately Jen's mo-
tions stemmed the verbal tirade. In the crystal, she was
keenly aware of Pehndon looking up sharply and saying,
"What was that? Did you hear something?"

His aide shrugged his confusion.

"Two-way transmission?" her aunt mouthed and, when
Jen nodded, threw up her hands. Then, gesturing imperiously, the Hawk motioned her into the hall with a summons that brooked no denial.

Wincing, Jen rose and tiptoed from the room, pulling
the door silently shut behind her. Vera was already seated
on the topmost stair, and Jen took a seat beside her, resting her cheek against the faded paper of the landing wall.

"Where's Thibault?"

"Asleep; I gave him the bed when I woke. Why?" Her
tone was aggrieved. "What have I done wrong now?"

Vera exhaled gustily, then said, "You didn't tell me the Hound and the Falcon chased you through the bazaar. An armed and deadly Hound and Falcon, I might add."

Jen flushed, remembering that nightmarish pursuit; it wasn't exactly something she had wanted her aunt to discover. But, brazening it out, she said, "Actually, I can recall several chases."

"But only one that counted—and don't pretend you don't know what I'm talking about, young lady!"

"Why? I survived, didn't I?"

"With help. Curse it, Jen, didn't you ever wondered how you escaped two Guild-trained assassins so easily?"

"I didn't know they were Guild," Jen hazarded. "Not then."

The Hawk shook her head. "Semantics, my dear; and don't try to change the subject! You got off frighteningly easy, and you know it. Ever wondered why?"

"Because I'm good?"

Vera didn't even dignify that with an answer. "Aren't you even curious how I found out?" she demanded instead.

Jen looked down at her hands, clasped bloodlessly around her ankles. "How?" she asked, in a small voice.

"Your rescuer told me."

"My *rescuer*?"

"Yes, your rescuer. Blast it all, Jen, you *never* open yourself to risks of that sort; that's precisely the way to end up in a custom-built coffin before you've even seen twenty! If you want to live a long and prosperous life within the Guild, you're going to have to do better."

"I . . ."

"No, listen to me, curse it! Absalom, a mage friend of mine who works out of the bazaar, cast a spell of confusion over your pursuers so they wouldn't perceive you. That— and that alone—was the sole reason they missed you!"

"So why help me? And how did he even know who I was?" she countered belligerently, and to her surprise Vera chuckled.

"That's my Jen, always asking the insightful question—even in the midst of an interrogation! To answer your question, my dear, I have no idea; I have ceased to query Absalom's motivations or the source of his mysterious knowledge. But this is no joking matter. You were inordinately careless, and it could have cost you—badly!"

"Nonsense. They wouldn't have hurt me. Not really; not if they were Guild. Not if I was related to you."

"You don't know that. And, besides, what if they hadn't been Guild? As, I might remind you, you initially assumed?"

Jen deflated as she realized how neatly Vera had trapped her. She should have known better than to play polemics with her aunt; the woman chopped logic like a champion. "What am I supposed to say? I'm sorry?"

"No, you're not supposed to say anything; what you're supposed to do is never repeat such careless behavior, ever!" And sliding over on the worn step, Vera settled an arm around Jen's shoulders, tilting her chin up and forcing the girl to meet her eyes. "I don't want to lose you, my dear, and I taught you far better than that. Now, promise me you will never do anything that stupid again."

"I promise."

"Good." And kissing her lightly on the forehead, Vera stood, extended a hand, and pulled her to her feet. "Now, leave a note for Thibault cautioning him to be quiet, for goodness' sake, and let's go speak to the Hound and the Falcon."

Derek was sitting on the courthouse steps, wondering if he'd been foolish to insist on returning—there was a remote chance, after all, that their quarry might reappear—when he abruptly felt two bodies sink down on either side of him, too close for casual contact. Almost automatically he had his own knife out, pressed against the belly of the one to his left while Mark materialized behind the other, and felt in return the twin pricks against his ribs.

"Stalemate," laughed the one he had covered in an assured voice, then added without looking around, "Foolish, Jen; never forget to check your back."

The knives withdrew from his ribs, and he turned to see the flushed face of their former quarry sitting to his right, Mark's dagger pressed to her kidneys. He frowned faintly and glanced at his brother, who merely said, "She's right, you know," though he made no move, Derek noticed, to withdraw his dagger.

The girl's flush only deepened, but all she said was, cocking her head up at her assailant, "Duly noted. So which one are you, the Hound or the Falcon?"

"Jen," her companion cautioned sharply, but nonetheless

with a grin in her voice, "don't you know it's rude to ask a fellow assassin his identity?"

Mark chuckled dryly. "That's all right. With all we've been through, I hardly think we need to stand on ceremony. A pleasure to meet you, young lady." The dagger, at last, withdrew—and following his brother's example, Derek reluctantly moved his own knife off a fraction. "To answer your question, I'm Mark Verhoeven, otherwise known as the Falcon." And taking a seat at her other side, he stuck out a weapon-free hand, which she took solemnly.

"Jen. Jen Radineaux," she offered in return.

Then, leaning across the trio, Mark nodded to the figure on Derek's other side, a faint smile on his narrow lips. "And you must be the Hawk."

Derek gaped. By all that was precious! A broad grin and shrewd grey eyes twinkled back at him, set in a visage as flawless as that to his right. More so, actually, since this was a face mature and lived-in, and profoundly self-assured.

He hastily sheathed his dagger.

"Yes. Vera Radineaux at your service," she said, "but I've been going as Leonie Varis for the duration of this mission, so I suppose you'd better get used to that as well."

"But, I thought . . ."

"Oh, I do wish everyone would stop assuming I'm dead," she retorted with some asperity. "It's decidedly off-putting."

Mark chuckled. "And this intellectual giant is, of course, my brother, Derek. Derek Verhoeven, the Hound."

Derek flushed. To his profound embarrassment, he found himself stammering like a schoolboy in the presence of his longtime hero. When he joined the Guild, the Hawk was already a legend. He had never expected to meet her—and especially not so casually, loitering on the steps of the Nhuras courthouse like some country gawkers. With his own dagger, no less, pressed against her ribs. Blast it!

"I understand my niece has been taking some liberties with your possessions," she was saying. "My sincere apologies. She does tend to get carried away by her own brilliance sometimes."

"Vera!" the girl exclaimed in horror.

Derek gave her a conspiratorial wink, adding cheerfully, "So, does meeting you two like this mean we get to collect our reward from DeVeris?"

The Hawk chuckled. "I'll put in a good word for you. But now that the two of you are in town with—I take it—your primary mission aborted, how would you like to consider a temporary partnership?"

"We'd be delighted, of course," Derek answered.

"Dependent on what we'll be doing," added Mark more practically.

"Nothing more than what you're currently involved in. I need someone to watch Pehndon, to make sure he doesn't leave his office without my knowing about it. If he ventures out, follow him; become his second shadow. Tell me everything he does, everywhere he goes—everyone he so much as speaks to! If all goes according to plan, I am going to spend the next few days making him highly nervous, and he should start making mistakes. Catch him at it."

"And what about what goes on within his office?"

"My niece has that well under control, has had for days. Haven't I told you she's brilliant?" And standing, she beckoned to Jen, who shot Derek a laughing look as she rose, extending her hand.

He took it with alacrity and bowed, his lips brushing her fingers. When he looked up, it was to meet her twinkling, mossy gaze, her smile almost wickedly inviting. A speculative look played across his face even as he felt something hard and cool slip into his palm.

"What's this, then?" he whispered, for her ears alone.

"A small token of my regard. Will I see you later?"

"You can count on it."

And she sauntered off.

Derek uncurled his fingers and suddenly began to laugh.

"What is it?" Mark demanded, peering over his shoulder.

Derek splayed his fingers wider, revealing the two gold fifties winking in his palm. "A repayment of debt, I think. You know, I believe things are finally looking up?"

Mark just grimaced. "It seems to me I've heard that one from you before," he commented. "I'll begin to believe it when I see it."

47

Shifting uncomfortably from foot to foot, Fazaquhian lurked in the Minister's antechamber, wondering exactly what impulse had led him into this situation. The minute Pehndon's aide disappeared, Neros felt himself break into a cold, panicked sweat. This was it; he was committed. But committed to what? Something meaningful or merely something futilely stupid? Suddenly he wished he knew. But no, that was a lie; he had longed for the answer to that particular question since the cursed assassin had left him, her words echoing like a death knell in his ears.

Truth or lies? Had Pehndon killed an innocent woman just for the sake of his agenda, or had the assassin invented the story simply to draw him into her own nefarious schemes? He could still hear the painful truth in her voice, echoing in every tortured note—that last frustrated outburst could not have been a sham—but he owed his life to Pehndon.

How could he choose? How could he be expected to choose?

It simply wasn't fair.

But then, who had ever said that life was fair? Three long years in the gutters had taught him the uselessness of "fair." Still, there had to be something—some deeper quest for truth, perhaps—that had driven him into Dheimos in her wake. And there, among the shanties and tatters of the run-down settlement, he had almost expected the urge to desert him. But it hadn't; not then and not after he had hired a camel and a guide to escort him back to Nhuras. Bustling, odiferous, vital Nhuras, home of his greatest triumphs and his deepest defeats. Nhuras, which pulsed like lifeblood through his veins.

And throughout all that long journey, neither his determination nor the anxiety that fueled it had disappeared.

Why was he doing this? What would he say? But he needed to hear Pehndon's story before he made up his mind. He owed the man that much: a token courtesy before betrayal.

Still, it was odd to stand here in this plush anteroom, feeling the unfamiliar embrace of city clothing after long months in the flowing, desert robes, blinking under a light that seemed dim and watery compared to the blaze of the Anvil's sun. Nervously, he reached up and tugged on his ponytail—the one concession to the desert climate he had stubbornly refused to abandon—all too aware of the tense voices projecting from behind Pehndon's closed portal.

But eventually the door swung open, and a sullenly defiant aide gestured him inside without even a token verbal courtesy. Fazaquhian swallowed nervously and crossed the dreaded threshold, his heart battering frantically against his ribs—as if it longed to evade this foolishness and be free.

He couldn't help wondering if the bloody thing was smarter than he was.

Pehndon, looking his usual implacable self, was standing by the window, his eyes narrowed to cold chips of flinty ice, their expression alone enough to lower the temperature of the room by several degrees. "Curse it, Neros," he barked, "what are you doing in Nhuras? Didn't I tell you to stay put until the export was under way?"

"Yes, but . . . You know I wouldn't have come if it wasn't important, Iaon."

Pehndon snorted. "I shudder to think what constitutes your definition of 'importance,' " he countered, "but very well. What was so vital that you had to disobey a direct order? Another monumental breakthrough that couldn't have been conveyed by letter?"

"No, sir, it's not the project. At least, not directly."

"What, then?"

Neros tugged anxiously on his ponytail again. "Well, an assassin came to see me," he began.

The reaction was spectacular. Pehndon's face went abruptly grey, his white-knuckled hands gripping the edge of his desk. "A *what*?" he exclaimed.

"An assassin, sir. She . . ."

"Then she's *alive*?" The minister collapsed into his seat as if his legs had gone abruptly nerveless. Fazaquhian balled his hands to hide their sudden trembling. *So much for innocence,* he thought unhappily. Pehndon was involved; no denying it. That subtle, shocked emphasis had told him everything.

"So you did want her dead?" he managed.

"Of course I wanted her dead; she killed Istarbion!"

"At your bequest?"

Pehndon's eyes went even colder—if such a thing were indeed possible. "So you obviously believe," he answered.

"Quite frankly, Iaon, I no longer know what to believe."

"I see." Pehndon's expression thawed not a fraction. "So you came here to test me? Blast it, Neros, haven't I given you everything? Haven't I saved you from a living death? And yet after everything I did for you—after all I gave you—you still would believe some upstart *bitch* over me?"

Fazaquhian winced guiltily. "I honestly don't know; that's why I came here. To ask you. I'm confused, Iaon; you have to help me. How long can I continue operating in the dark?"

"For as long as I deem it necessary!" The Minister sounded unaccountably furious. "Curse it, Neros . . ."

"Who died, Iaon? Who hanged?"

"What?"

"Someone hanged on that scaffold, I know that, and clearly it wasn't the real assassin. So who was it?"

"And what makes you so certain someone hanged?"

"Because her associate told me."

"Her associate? What associate? Blast it, Neros, you had better tell me everything!"

So, reluctantly, Fazaquhian did: from the woman's arrival to her associate's entrance. He told Pehndon of her suspicions, and of the story she had concocted—and in the end he saw the truth, swirling sluggishly in the Minister's eyes.

"She's right, isn't she, Iaon?" he accused. "She figured it out. You hired her to kill Istarbion, then tried to eliminate her. And when she escaped, you murdered someone else in her stead so it would look like your plans had succeeded. Why?"

Fazaquhian didn't expect an answer; he certainly never expected to see the faint cracks of panic spidering through

Pehndon's self-control. But, "You of all people should understand the value of what we've located on the Anvil, Neros," the minister said with commendable restraint. "Properly exploited, your black-naphtha"—it was the first time he had formally acknowledged Fazaquhian's name for it—"could break the mages' monopoly forever. It could put Ashkharon at the forefront of the Varian economy."

"I understand, but . . ."

"Who is supposed to be controlling that power, tell me that. Istarbion? Some bleeding-heart fanatic like Jason Andorian? I'm the one with the vision, the one who understands what this could mean to Ashkharon—to all of Varia!" To Fazaquhian's horror, the Minister's voice was high and taut, perilously close to breaking. "If we eliminate all rival factions . . ."

"So that's what this is about? Who gets control?"

"Of course that's what it's about! What else matters?"

"Blast it, Iaon, people have died—innocent people!"

"Innocent?" The Minister practically spat. "Who's innocent?"

"Istarbion, for one."

"That popinjay? He may have been ineffectual, but he was certainly never innocent! I could make your hair curl with some of the stories of his less public escapades."

"Then about the woman who hanged in place of the assassin. What about her?"

"Some random criminal, destined to die in any case."

"Are you certain?"

"Of course I'm bloody certain! Blast it, Neros, this is no time to play the shrinking violet. There are monumental changes brewing in Ashkharon, and you're going to have to choose your side. So what will it be? Will you choose the winning team—and one, incidentally, who raised you from the gutter, who gave you back your dignity and freedom—or will you go cringing off to that whining assassin with your tail between your legs like some whipped cur? Which will it be, Neros?"

"Iaon, I . . ."

The Minister moved abruptly, looming over him. "Make your choice, Neros!"

Fazaquhian found himself transfixed as Pehndon's facade cracked away like a coat of cheap varnish, revealing the ruthless madness blazing at the center of his being.

The minister would never back down now; he had come too far and risked too much. He felt almost sick for having trusted the man, for having believed in him.

He had even admired that poor sod Andorian: Pehndon's so-called fanatic. He had always struck Fazaquhian as one of the few people in Ashkharon courageous enough to stand up for something of value—even if he was fighting Neros' nominal employers, the glassworks.

"I'm sorry, Pehndon," he said at last, "I can't be involved in this anymore. The price is too high. Too many people are dying. Nothing's worth that much of a sacrifice."

"So you think."

"Yes. Yes, I do."

To his amazement, Pehndon scooped a heavy bronze plaque off his desk and hurled it across the room, gouging a trail of paint and plaster from the opposite wall. "Curse that bitch, anyway! None of this would have happened if she hadn't . . ." Then, gathering himself with an obvious effort, he added, "And you're just going to walk out of here, is that it? After all I've done for you? Go crawling to your precious assassin?"

"Yes, Iaon. I'm sorry, but . . ."

"And you think I'm actually going to let you do it?"

The man's hollow laughter brought Fazaquhian's eyes up from their guilty contemplation of the carpet. By all that was precious, those cold grey orbs were actually _burning,_ as if they would ignite the very air. Fazaquhian swallowed heavily. But gathering his courage, he added, "I don't see that you have much choice. Sir."

"Oh, don't I?"

He had never known a man could move that fast. He barely had time to register the flash before he felt the dagger's acid bite across his throat.

And then he knew no more.

"Iaon, I . . . What the blazes is going on?" Jhakharta's horrified squeak echoed through the laden air. It was a simple errand he was running, nothing important. All he needed was a lousy signature. The last thing he'd expected was to see Iaon Pehndon, crouched in the middle of his carpet, a dagger in one hand and a body in the other. A body that smiled at him with a mouth too wide and too ragged to be anything other than a violently opened throat.

A pool of blood was already forming on the immaculate carpet.

The two stared at each other in horror for a moment. It was Iaon who recovered faster, barking, "Get in here, blast it, and shut the door!"

Jhakharta felt the bitter surge of bile in his throat as he hastily complied, sinking into the nearest chair and averting his eyes from the crimson puddle.

As if Jhakharta's weakness had brought the minister strength, Pehndon abruptly straightened, letting the body fall in a limp heap to the floor. "Curse it, Alphonse, show a little backbone. He can't hurt you now."

Jhakharta swallowed. "Who was he?" he said, around an uncomfortable thickness in his throat.

"No one of consequence. A business associate."

"And is this how you always treat your associates?"

"If they cross me, yes."

"Curse it, Iaon . . ."

"What? Do you think I wanted to kill him, that it made me particularly *happy* to do it?"

In fact, that was precisely what Jhakharta did think; he acknowledged it with an uncomfortable shiver.

"Do you think he gave me any choice? He was about to go running straight to Leonie!"

"Leonie?"

"My assassin. Where's your head, Alphonse?"

"I, uh . . . Is she still alive?"

"Yes, and back in Nhuras." Pehndon kicked viciously at the corpse. "But don't pretend you didn't know that, Alphonse; I've seen it in your face."

"Seen? Seen what?"

"That you know the truth about Ariadne DeBricassart."

"Blast it, Iaon, did you have to kill her?"

"Well, someone had to hang. And with my own assassin gone, who better than the woman who played her so convincingly at the trial?"

"But you can't just go about murdering your conspirators, Iaon!"

"Can't I? It seems I've done so rather successfully already. But that's hardly the issue now, is it, Alphonse? I have a body in my office, and we have to get rid of it."

"We? *We?* What happened to the great, all-powerful Iaon Pehndon? Why is it always up to Alphonse Jhakharta when trouble comes calling?"

"Oh, pull yourself together, Alphonse, and do stop sniveling. Ordinarily, I'd sack a couple of guards and claim an assassin snuck past them, but this time I simply don't want the adverse publicity. So we have to lose the body in secret. We'll just prop old Neros in the corner here," he said, suiting words to action, "and you can go fetch the mages. Maybe they can get this infernal stain out of my carpet. And later tonight, when everyone's left, you can get our friend out of here."

"Me? Why me?" Jhakharta winced at the panicked note that had suddenly crept into his voice.

"Because I have a previous engagement; grow up, Alphonse. If you want to play with the big boys, you have to get your hands a little dirty. Or else end up like our poor friend there."

"Why? What did he do?"

"Refused to play. Now, Alphonse, the mages. And make it snappy!"

48

"This tension is killing me. How much longer is this going to continue?" Jen exclaimed anxiously, pacing the tiny chamber.

Vera and Thibault looked up at her outburst. Jen could see a kind of sympathetic agreement on her partner's face, but the Hawk merely regarded her with a certain composed censure. "One of the first things an assassin has to learn," she said calmly, "is how to wait."

Jen exchanged a rueful grimace with Thibault, but she couldn't help adding, "And for how long?"

"You know as well as I do that nothing is going to break until nightfall, so be patient. That pacing of yours is not going to achieve anything except driving Thibault and me to distraction."

With a sigh that was more than half a growl, Jen flung herself down onto the bed next to Thibault, but she knew her aunt was right. Her frantic urging would not hasten the sun across the sky, nor would anything else happen until the concealing cover of darkness descended over the city.

But that still didn't stop it from being the most interminable afternoon of her existence—for an amazing sight had awaited Jen and Vera when they returned from their meeting with Mark and Derek. Jen was still feeling a pleasant buzz of nostalgia, augmented by her confusion about Jason; the speculative way that blond assassin's eyes had lingered sent a little frisson of excitement through her.

Maybe it was time, indeed, to move on.

"So, what did you think of the Hound?" she had asked with a certain deliberate nonchalance as she and her aunt mounted the stairs to their quarters.

"Eager to please. Immensely chagrined if he piddles on your carpet."

"Vera!"

The Hawk just grinned. "He's a good assassin," she said, obviously not fooled by Jen's pose of apparent indifference. But after her disastrous affair with Jason, Jen felt the urge to check out all prospects with her wiser aunt first.

She still couldn't believe her bad judgment. She had trusted the wrong man, lost control of the papers, her crystals were a waste . . . So preoccupied was she by the thought that she almost didn't register the significance of the sight that awaited them as Vera swung open the door to their chamber.

Thibault was awake, crouched on the floor with an urgent finger to his lips, his eyes wide and excited as he pointed at the ball. Jen took in the situation with a jolt. It was happening; things were actually breaking! Instantly she went to her knees, her cheek pressed hard against his shoulder, her urgent breath ruffling his sleeve. Unaware of what she was doing, she gripped his forearm in a tight, imperative fist. She was barely conscious of Vera at her other side, joining the huddle, arms around her protégés as they crowded close to the viewing crystal.

Jen felt like crowing. By all that was precious, her plan had actually worked! Either Jason—against all hope—had neglected to mention the shard's presence to Pehndon or Vera's prediction had been true: stir up the pond enough, and the fish will start to surface. But that he was actually confessing it, admitting everything . . . Anxiously, she checked her recording device, convinced that something had to be wrong, that it couldn't be this perfect, but indeed the crystals were filling with the milky cloudiness that indicated an image stored and retrievable. And in the viewer the revelations were coming fast and furious. (Although, admittedly, she couldn't help a slight surge of jealousy when, at the sight of the timid, ponytailed man called Neros, Thibault leaned around and grinned triumphantly at Vera, who smiled back, raised a thumb, and clasped his hand in victory above Jen's head.)

After Neros' murder and Jhakharta's departure, the three had drifted apart in a slow diffusion, staring at each other with stunned, triumphant eyes. Jen felt an exultant whoop gathering at the back of her throat even as Thibault's brows drew together in a worried frown, his mouth falling open as if he were about to speak. Of all of them, only Vera kept her composure. Abruptly rising, she pulled a key from her pocket and gestured them imperiously to their feet. And when they followed her into the upstairs hallway, she merely crossed the landing in silence and inserted the key into a neighboring door.

"What is this?" Jen demanded, her voice tight and thick around the suppressed whoop.

"Thibault's room," Vera answered calmly enough. "I arranged it with our landlord this morning. So everyone in, and let's discuss this."

As soon as the door had shut behind them, Jen let her cry escape, crowing, "We got him, we got him," all the while bouncing around Thibault like a junior dervish.

But her partner's frown only deepened as, ignoring the manic Jen, he turned to Vera and said, "He killed his own accomplice. Two of them." His voice was filled with a profound disgust.

The Hawk only nodded. "I had wondered how far our Iaon would go in pursuit of his dreams. Now, it seems, we know."

"But . . ."

"It's all very easy to take a stance of moral indignation, Thibault," the Hawk cautioned. "What matters is what you do about it."

Jen felt a certain childish satisfaction in, for once, not being the target of Vera's censure.

"So what would you do?" Vera continued.

There was a long moment of silence.

"Who are you asking?" Thibault inquired eventually, his face slightly flushed.

"Either—both. You two are training to be assassins. So how would you handle this?"

Jen frowned, her brow furrowing. "We have the Hound and the Falcon assigned to Pehndon," she hazarded, "so they should be able to follow him to this mysterious appointment of his. I mean, we can trust them, can't we?"

"What do you think?"

It was Jen's turn to flush. "Yes," she said. "Yes, we can. We'll let them tail Pehndon and report back. And in the meantime . . . someone should go after Jhakharta."

"Good. Why?"

"To pressure him?"

The Hawk shook her head. "Too early; we don't have all the pieces yet. Thibault?"

"To, um, recover the body?" he said.

"Exactly. Why?"

"Further evidence?"

"You don't sound sure of it."

"No, I am. I mean . . . Yes."

"Precisely. Thank you, Thibault. Now, here's how we'll run it. Thibault and I will go after Jhakharta with Absalom. Jen, you'll stay put to keep an eye on the office and also to receive Mark and Derek when they return."

"Why? Because I didn't guess right?" she exclaimed before she had a chance to consider.

Vera's eyes went abruptly cold, and Jen flinched. "I am going to pretend I didn't hear that. This is a job, not some childish game, Jenifleur. There is no place for such foolishness in what we do and my reasons—unlike yours, apparently—are always based on logic, not petty revenge. Now, would anyone care to tell me why I chose as I did?" And though the question was addressed to the room in general, her eyes bored into her niece's.

Swallowing heavily, her face a painful shade of crimson, Jen admitted, "Because I designed the equipment and know how to use it. And because Thibault's bigger and more likely to be of help, or at least more intimidating, should anything go wrong with Jhakharta."

Vera's face softened, and she touched a hand lightly to Jen's cheek. "Good. Sorry to yell at you, love, but you'll have to learn these things eventually. And the sooner the better if I'm going to sponsor you to the Guild."

Jen grinned weakly.

"Now—and this *is* a test—did anything strike either of you two as odd about that conversation?"

Jen surveyed the scuffed floorboards, thinking frantically, but to her amazement it was Thibault who answered, slowly and deliberately, as if unsure of his conclusion. "Jason," he said. "Pehndon told the truth about everything else, so why stick to the lie about Jason? It was almost as if he believed the man was innocent—and genuine."

Jen felt a sudden surge of guilt. In her fury and confusion about the rebel leader, she hadn't even noticed the cues that might have exonerated him. But Thibault, who had never completely trusted the man, had nonetheless seen it without prompting.

And wasn't that a telling situation?

"Precisely. Very good, Thibault."

"But why?" Jen demanded.

"Cursed if I know. Perhaps Pehndon intends to betray and execute yet another of his accomplices. But whatever the case, there is more still to come. You can depend on that."

So here they all sat in Thibault's room—with Jen running across the hall occasionally to check the crystal—waiting for darkness to fall and their plans to come to fruition.

And it would be, Jen decided, not a minute too soon.

Night had descended, and in the back booth of the Salty Dog, Iaon Pehndon fidgeted anxiously with his glass as he waited for his companion to arrive. He would be the first to admit that his nerves were frayed to the breaking point. It had all been such a perfect plan until that woman had arrived. One setup, one betrayal, and two trials: it should have gone off without a hitch. But then that blasted female had escaped and thrown his plans into chaos, forcing him to hang Ariadne DeBricassart and stab poor Neros Fazaquhian. He had never intended to kill anyone except the assassin and that cursed thorn in his side, Jason Andorian. And now the body count was mounting, and everything was dissolving around him.

For one thing, that blasted Grahme Tortaluk refused to cooperate. Pehndon couldn't count how many hours he had haunted the prison, trying to force some kind of a confession. He had tried questioning, he had even risked some undetectable torture, and yet Grahme remained as sealed as an oyster locked stubbornly around a priceless pearl.

And then there was Jhakharta. The man was about to crack; he could sense it. Involving the First Minister in Fazaquhian's murder would have been his last choice, but the blasted man had given him no other option, bursting into his office just as Neros' blood was dripping from his fingers. But someone had to ditch the body while Iaon reclaimed his papers, and besides, the threat of being named an accessory might keep the First Minister, and his intermittent conscience, quiet.

No, Iaon had gone too far to turn back now. He was too close, despite all the multifarious complications thrown in his path.

And now the Hawk was back.

He had to act fast, he knew that. Tonight he would reclaim

his papers, and if he played it right he could crack Jeryn and win the location of the rebel base. Then, by tomorrow morning at the latest, he would have Jason in custody, all ready for the hangman's rope, and there would be nothing that woman could do to stop him. She would have no evidence, nothing to tie him to the string of murders he had propagated—and all in the name of controlling Fazaquhian's black-naphtha.

It was fortunate, he reflected, that the man had finished the bulk of his work before Iaon had been forced to eliminate him.

Abruptly, he turned his thoughts to the meeting with Andorian. He would ransom his soul if need be to secure his papers properly; that floor safe was simply no longer an option. He had an appointment with one of his mages tonight; he had set it up earlier when the man had magically banished the blood from his carpet and cast an obscuration over Neros' body. They would meet at his office later, and he would pledge half his fortune to banish his papers to a realm accessible only by magic. It would be worth it. And besides, once this was over, he could always eliminate the mages.

They knew too bloody much anyway.

He was unaware that he had taken a deep, reflexive sip of his ale until the bitter, rancid taste exploded in his mouth, causing him to splutter and gag.

"Iaon?"

He looked up, half choking, to see a hesitant Jeryn sliding into the booth across from him, and felt obscurely reassured. His spy was close to cracking, too; it wouldn't take much to break him. By tomorrow, Jason would be his, and he would have won the final round.

"Well, what have you got for me?" he said.

Jeryn extracted the papers and slid them across the table. Iaon flipped briefly through the bundle. All there. Good. Perfect. Then, looking back up, he fixed his associate with a gimlet eye. "You looked through them, I take it?"

Jeryn nodded uncomfortably.

"Then you understand what I have at stake, why I need to discredit your brother."

"You want control of the government. And, incidentally, of the naphtha fields."

"Smart lad. You have some of those Andorian brains after all. But something's still troubling you. What is it?"

"I wanted my brother out of the rebel alliance, you know that. But I . . ."

"Yes?"

"Well, I never wanted him *dead*. And quite frankly, I don't see how you can let him live, not knowing what I do now. Alive, he's too much of a threat to your control. Dead . . . Well, he's safe, dead. Promise me, Iaon; promise me you won't kill him."

Pehndon was not about to promise anything of the kind. But what he could say, and did, was, "If the trial's large enough—and public enough—I won't have to kill him. Once everyone knows of his supposed crimes, how far do you think they will trust him? He'll be effectively neutralized. But, on the contrary, if you keep sheltering him, I'll be forced to have him hunted down and eliminated. So don't you see, Jeryn? It's safer for everyone if you turn him in now."

"But . . ."

"What are you saying, that you don't trust me? After all I've done for you?"

He was abruptly aware these were the same words he had used so futilely with Fazaquhian, and they looked to be having no more of an effect on Andorian. What was it with loyalty and gratitude these days?

"Yes, that's precisely what I'm saying. I don't want my brother dead, curse you, Pehndon. I want him back!"

"Turn him in, and I guarantee you'll get him back."

"You once told me no trial. Now you're telling me trial but no death. What'll it be next week, hang it?"

Precisely that, my lad. "This thing won't end without Jason in custody. Give him to me, and within a week you can join your brother in freedom." *Or in death,* he added to himself. But then, who was to say that wasn't its own type of freedom? It was freedom from life, certainly.

"I don't know, Pehndon. I . . ."

"Do you want this to end or don't you?"

He was aware that he was pushing too hard, but he was beyond caring. If the direct approach wouldn't work, there were always other ways, and he needed Jason *tonight*.

So sitting back and crossing his legs beneath the cover of the table, he settled down to breaking Jeryn in earnest.

49

About an hour after Vera and Thibault had left on their secret mission, a stranger entered Pehndon's office—at least, a stranger in the sense that he was unknown to Jen; she hastily clarified that mental point. Otherwise there was nothing unusual about him at all, except that she had never seen anyone so nondescript in her life. Even looking at him in the crystal, her eyes fastened intently on his face, she would have been hard-pressed to describe him in any concrete detail. Average height, average weight, no distinguishing marks or features. Hair-colored hair, flesh-colored flesh, and eyes—not exactly colorless, but nonetheless without color: too dark to be properly blue and too light to be truly brown.

Even his behavior was distressingly indefinable. He walked into the office not as if he owned it but not as if he were unfamiliar with it either. And when he sat he chose the guest chair, deferentially, but nonetheless crossed his legs and settled back as if to make himself comfortable. Nor did he fidget while he waited, but neither did he show any signs of vast patience. He simply was how he was and looked how he looked; Jen could get no nearer the truth than that.

But she did find herself wondering what the blazes he was doing in the office at such an hour, and exactly when Pehndon had arranged to meet him.

She didn't have to wait long to receive her answer. A few minutes later, the Minister himself appeared in the doorway, looking thoroughly and disgustingly pleased with himself, a bundle of papers tucked casually under one arm. Laying these down on the desktop, he took a seat and let his mouth curve into a catlike smile, regarding his companion over steepled fingers.

"Well?" the other said at last, his voice distinctly . . .

voicelike; Jen masked an irate growl. "Why did you summon me down here at this hour?"

"These are my private papers," Pehndon responded, either ignoring the question or coming at it from an amazingly oblique angle. He patted the pile fondly. "I finally got them back from that bastard Andorian; liberated them from the enemy camp, as it were."

Still the masquerade, Jen thought. *But why?*

"I'm glad to hear that, of course," his companion answered, "but what precisely does this have to do with me?"

"I had them hidden in a safe beneath the floorboards," Pehndon continued, still on his original tack, and Jen had the sudden feeling that she was listening to two entirely separate conversations.

"Nice, but not exactly original—or, apparently, very safe," his companion commented.

"Which is where you come in. I'm tired of having people help themselves to my private possessions, and especially when it comes to these papers."

"So you want me to hide them? Conjure them to some location accessible only by magerie?"

Jen felt her spirits plummet. By all that was precious, was she about to lose her only chance to retrieve the documents after so foolishly handing them over to Jason? Blast it; blast him. Blast them all!

"Precisely," Pehndon confirmed, with a smug little nod. "Bury them ten miles deep if you have to, but make sure they are good and hidden—and that only I have the password."

"To retrieve them, you mean?"

"Well, of course. They wouldn't be much bloody good if I couldn't get at them, now would they?"

The mage—for that was what he had to be—regarded the Minister for a moment, then nodded. "Very well, but I'd advise you to choose a phrase you won't be uttering every day. Otherwise, it could prove embarrassing to have the things popping into existence at inappropriate moments."

"Fair enough."

Jen began to grin, prepared to learn the code-word, but Pehndon soon dashed her hopes, adding, "This will be voice-linked as well, I take it? Specific only to me?"

The mage shrugged. "Costs extra."

"But worth it, eh? I mean, what good would it do me if someone else said the phrase and got my papers in return? I mean, if I chose the phrase 'Pehndon is a bloody genius,' for instance, then the first of my supporters to express such sentiments could find him or herself in a potentially awkward situation."

The mage didn't exactly smile—but then he didn't exactly not smile either. "Is that the phrase you want to use? 'Pehndon is a bloody genius'?"

"Why not?" the Minister said, and Jen made a disgusted face at his image in the ball.

"Very well. I'll set the spell. When I'm ready, I'll motion to you, and you say the words; that'll set the trigger. And incidentally, it will also banish the papers for the first time."

Jen's interest was immediately piqued, and for the first time since she had commissioned the setup, she was immeasurably glad for its two-way transmission. Up to this point, she had merely viewed that as an annoying, if inevitable, side-effect, but now it stood a chance of working in her favor. All she had to do was say the phrase in tandem with Pehndon and hope to blazes the magic was sensitive enough to register her presence. Then, at best, she could access the documents herself, and at worst they would be stuck forever in their subterranean vault until she once again joined her voice to Pehndon's.

And while she would obviously prefer the former option, she would far rather have the things safely out of reach than in Pehndon's grubby paws.

So when the mage cast a glowing nimbus around the documents, then motioned to Pehndon, she uttered the objectionable phrase in chorus and watched as the papers winked from existence.

"Is that it?" Pehndon said when the dust had settled—or when the dust would have settled if he'd kept his office anything less than immaculate.

"Yes, quite it. So can I go home now, or do you want to test my spell?"

Jen held her breath.

"Pehndon is a bloody genius," said the Minister, and the papers reappeared in his outstretched hands.

Well, so much for locking them away forever, she

thought ruefully. *At least he's not suspicious.* Now, if only the magic had heard her.

"Brilliant!" the Minister exclaimed, putting down the papers and clasping his hands. "Now all I have to do to banish them is repeat the phrase?"

The mage inclined his head; with the exercise of his powers, he seemed to have gained a faintly supercilious edge.

Pehndon did so, and the papers vanished once again. "Wonderful!"

"Now, if you're done playing with your toy, Minister, we have one more matter to discuss."

"Which is?"

"The payment."

"Ah, yes, of course. How much?"

"Two thousand."

"What?"

"Well, security comes at a price, after all."

"But I don't have that kind of money in my possession! At least not currently."

The mage shrugged again. "Five hundred will do for a deposit. You can pay me the remainder tomorrow."

"And if I don't?"

"I can always undo the spell."

Jen got a certain vicarious pleasure out of watching Pehndon squirm as he fetched his purse and painfully began counting out the five hundred in golden twenties.

"Can I go home now?" the mage added, when the transaction had been completed. An inaudible word later, and the coins had vanished to a realm undoubtedly resembling the one Pehndon had just paid them to access. From his expression, Jen could tell he hoped it was the same one, that a stray mark or two might appear, intermingled with the papers, when he recalled the documents.

Fortunately he didn't try it, but merely said, "We can both go home; it's been a deuced long day," and exited the chamber behind his visitor, extinguishing the mage-lights in his wake.

The ball went abruptly black.

"End record," Jen said softly, then looked around the sitting room of their Twin Palms suite. Neither her aunt nor Thibault had returned yet, and there had been no sign from either Mark or Derek. All was peaceful, only a few vague cries and catcalls echoing up from the street below, their impact muted by the tightly shuttered windows.

No better time than the present.

So taking a single deep breath, Jen said, "Pehndon is a bloody genius," and felt the bundle of papers materialize against her palms with a satisfying solidity.

"Look what I've got. Look what I've found!"

"What? Oh, do stop bouncing around, Jen. It's highly distracting." Vera readjusted her grip on her sagging bundle. "Can you make it around that corner, Thibault?"

Her companion grunted, and maneuvered the remainder of Fazaquhian's hooded body into the sitting room. "So you're sleeping with him tonight, I take it?"

"Call it my penance for forcing you onto the floor last night. Besides, he'll be out here and we'll be in there. Now, help me get him on the settee, and don't step on Jen's toys."

"They are not toys!" Her niece's voice was indignant, and Vera chuckled.

"I know, but in the meantime we need to get Neros settled. Mind lending a hand?"

Jen laid something down on an end table and helped muscle the body into position.

"Good. Thanks. Now . . . Where's Absalom?"

"Right here," the mage answered, materializing around the door frame. Takes my old legs longer to make the climb than it used to."

"Nonsense; you had no problem keeping up before. Jenny, meet Absalom. And Absalom, I believe you're acquainted with my niece, Jenifleur?"

"In a sense."

Jen went red, but took the proffered hand courteously enough. "I understand I . . . uh, owe you some thanks," she said.

Vera grinned; Thibault simply looked puzzled.

"My pleasure is to serve," the mage responded in his usual fulsome fashion, bowing over her outstretched hand.

"Well, I'm grateful to you. Though I still think . . ."

"That you could have escaped on your own?" Absalom finished. "No doubt. But I was there, and the obscuration was a simple one. And as I told your aunt this very evening, why make things more difficult than they have to be?"

Jen raised an amused eyebrow, seemingly untroubled by Absalom's appearance, and Vera was abruptly proud of the girl; Thibault had not been quite so sanguine. "Why? What did she want to do?" she asked.

"Transport the body in disguise. Most inefficient. Better simply to carry it as is and avoid the eyes that would profit from illusion." Absalom shrugged. "And how silly it would seem, to be carrying such a heavy weight of air!"

"But we are no longer carrying it," Vera said firmly. "So . . ." And she gestured to the limp form, swathed in one of Thibault's oversized cloaks, that sagged bloodlessly on their sitting room sofa.

The mage mumbled a word or two, waved his scarred hand, and the body vanished.

"Where did it go?" Jen demanded.

Vera regarded her quizzically. "Nowhere, so I advise you not to try sitting down on that side of the couch. Unless, of course, you relish sitting in a dead man's lap."

Cautiously, Jen poked a finger at the empty air, tracing the contours of the invisible body. "Gracious."

"Quite." Vera settled casually on the sofa's far side, her arm lined along its back as if she embraced poor Neros' nonexistent remains. "Now, you had something to show me?"

Her niece grinned, proffering a bundle of papers.

"What is this?" Vera demanded, flipping through the stack.

"Pehndon's papers."

"Jenny!" Thibault gasped. "How . . ."

"I thought I told you not to leave the hotel!" Vera snapped, cutting him off.

Jen's smile only widened. "I didn't," she said. "Pehndon is a bloody genius."

"Excuse me?" Thibault demanded.

"Where did they go?" Vera added in a panic as the papers abruptly vanished.

"Don't worry. Pehndon is a bloody genius," Jen said again and passed back the resultant bundle. She looked distinctly smug.

It was rare for Vera to find herself at a loss for words, but now she merely regarded her niece in silence. "How?" she demanded at last.

"It's a long story, but let's just say I used the crystal's two-way transmission to my advantage."

"Mmm." Vera nodded speculatively. "Properties which I still haven't had a chance to exploit effectively. Tomorrow, perhaps. Bless you, Jen!"

"I . . ."

"Quite a party here, isn't it?"

All heads whirled at the sound of the new voice. In the open doorway, Derek was grinning unabashedly at Jen.

"You must be Thibault," he added, turning and extending a hand. "And you are?"

"Absalom, at your service."

"My pleasure. I'm Derek Verhoeven, better known as the Hound. And have I got news for you!"

Vera frowned. "Settle down. Where's Mark?"

"Still on Pehndon. It seems our revered Minister was up to some rather shady business this evening. He met a man at the Salty Dog—that's one of the Raghdon Street alehouses, in case you're wondering—and came out looking very pleased with himself, clutching a bundle of papers."

"And the man he met?"

"I followed him home; I know where he lives."

"Then take me there. Thibault, you stay here and wait for Mark. And Absalom . . . Well, who am I to command a mage? Do whatever you bloody please, but first do you think you could see your way clear to recoding these papers so Pehndon can't reclaim them?"

"It would be my pleasure."

"Then you have my profound gratitude—again. Jen, you're with me."

After a token grin, she was pleased to see the girl's expression turn abruptly sober as she checked her daggers and nodded decisively. "Right. Let's do it."

50

Despite Pehndon's insistence, it was the light in Jason's window that broke the last of Jeryn's resolve. He hadn't expected his brother to be at home, let alone to be seated pensively on the common room couch, chin in hand, staring disconsolately at nothing. There was something almost pitiful about that small, forlorn figure, so silent beneath the magelights; Jeryn felt his heart slowly breaking. What was he doing? The longer his brother was isolated from his chosen people—the longer he was kept underground and in disguise—the less he became, as if he were being slowly leached of everything that gave his life meaning.

There was no denying it, Jeryn realized with a pang. Jason did need the rebel alliance; he needed their support, their enthusiasm, their accolades. He fed on that energy as a starving man did on bread, and now Jeryn was taking that away from him. He had wanted . . . Well, who knows what he had wanted? His motivations weren't entirely clear, not even to himself. Pehndon had seen only the hatred, but then a man can see only what he wants to see or what he can reasonably comprehend. And poor, driven Pehndon's finer sentiments had long since withered, twisted from disuse into something that was no longer completely human.

There was hatred, undeniably, but there was more as well: anger, betrayal, love, greed, and pain. He wanted . . . what? Revenge? Payback? Attention? He had wanted his brother back; he had never intended to kill his spirit.

But now, seeing Jason sitting there like that, apart from everything he had once held dear . . . Jason had sacrificed everything for him, had given up his schooling and a long and undoubtedly glorious career to keep Jeryn off the factory floor. Without Jeryn, he could have been a Minister by now—maybe even First Minister. But instead, he had become an outcast: exiled, driven underground, and again—though he didn't yet know it—all for Jeryn.

How much more could he demand?

The ironic thing was that, until this very moment, a part of him had been willing to go along with Pehndon's plans. And if Jason hadn't been sitting there, framed by the curtains, Jeryn might have gone through with it, given up his brother's location, watched him take the spectacular and very public fall. And for what?

I must have been blind, he thought disgustedly. *Why did I never see what was happening? Why did I never even look?* No, it was time for a sacrifice of his own—one long overdue—and if it meant losing Jason forever, then so be it.

Still, opening that door, facing his brother, was the toughest thing he had ever done.

Jason looked up as he approached, his face lighting in surprise and a kind of obscure gratitude. "Jeryn, what are you doing here?"

Hardly thinking now, Jeryn dropped to his knees, resting one cheek against his brother's thigh—much as he had done when he was younger and some childish hurt or perceived affliction had driven him to his sibling for comfort or confession. And, as of old, Jason's hand tangled in his hair, cupping the back of his head. Jeryn felt the prickle of tears in his eyes. Almost, he could imagine that the intervening years had vanished, that the house remained undivided, that Jason had reverted to the sixteen-year-old prodigy of the factory floor and that he was an innocent eleven, regretful of some childish prank or dare.

But how much harder these words were to utter now, and how much more severe. In the old days, Jason had doled out consolation and laughing penances with a liberal hand, binding the physical hurts and soothing the less tangible ones with steaming mugs of chocolate in the fire-lit kitchen; to this day, Jeryn associated that scent with the muted glow of copper pots and the quiet warmth of Jason's voice, exonerating him.

And then they would retire to their shared bedroom, where Jeryn would burrow beneath the covers in security, knowing that Jason would be there to wake him when his frequent night terrors left him sweaty and shaken, uncertain of his future. And how many times, he wondered now, had Jason lain awake at night, gazing at a darkened ceiling and wondering how he would ever manage to keep them alive, while Jeryn had slept heedlessly on? Jason had taken all their burdens, both his own and Jeryn's, and yet had never stopped being able to give—or forgive.

But now?

"What is it, Jeryn?" his brother asked gently.

The words dammed in his throat, but eventually he managed to say, "I need to 'fess, Jason."

"To what? Oh, no. You don't need any more money, do you?" Jason's tone was light, but when Jeryn shook his head miserably, the cajoling levity dropped from his brother's voice. He could feel the change in the shifting tension of his sibling's hand. "What is it, Jeryn? Talk to me." And Jason's fingers tightened in his hair, tipping his head back.

Stubbornly, Jeryn kept his eyes downcast, fixed firmly on the fraying threads of that familiar red-gold carpet. "This is a big one, Jason," he said. "You know when Grahme was taken?"

"Yes?"

"Well, that was my fault."

"What?" Jason's fingers jerked involuntarily, painfully, and Jeryn winced—though not so much from the physical hurt as from the unmitigated horror in his brother's voice.

"You suspected there was a spy in the organization?" Jeryn forced himself to continue. "Well, there was: me." The words came tumbling out. "Pehndon hired me to impersonate you for the assassin. He wanted her to believe that the orders came from you, that Istarbion was being murdered for an 'honorable' cause. So he paid me a lot of money, and I set up another warehouse and played you. She never suspected, believing all along she was working for the real alliance. You even had her converted; she had heard you speak, and . . ." Aware that he was babbling, Jeryn jerked to a painful halt, adding, "She believed in the cause, Jason."

His brother's hand fell from his hair. "But you, apparently, did not—and neither did Pehndon. You used me, and you used my alliance. And how many innocent people have suffered for your scheming?"

Jeryn couldn't answer that one, didn't even try. And, after a moment, his brother continued softly, "No wonder she swore I hired her; she couldn't tell us apart, could she?"

Jeryn shook his head miserably. "She only saw you twice. Once from a distance, and once at . . ."

"The gala?" He could tell from his brother's voice that Jason had made the connection. "The woman in the bronze dress."

He looked up then, to see his sibling gone abruptly pale, pallid patches shifting like curdled cream beneath his skin. His hands hung limply at his sides.

"Why?" he said at last, his voice small and infinitely weary.

"There were gambling debts. I . . ."

"No, Jeryn. *Why?*"

He couldn't meet the sudden, naked look in Jason's eyes. Laying his cheek against his brother's thigh, he pressed his eyes tightly shut and mumbled, "I missed you, Jason. I wanted things to be the way they were, before the alliance. I wanted to prove to you that you needed me as much as I needed you."

"And you think I wasn't aware of that? Wasn't aware every minute of what I was giving up? But it was my choice to make, Jeryn!"

"I know. But we're brothers, Jason; we'd always been together, and then suddenly we weren't. And I hated the alliance for taking you away, hated you for being so inseparable from the alliance."

Jason was silent for a long, agonizing moment. Then, amazingly, he said, "Yes, it is my fault, I suppose. You were always terrified of abandonment, always have been. I should have realized that."

And then Jeryn was suddenly, gloriously angry. "*Your* fault? Blast it, Jason, you did nothing but follow your dreams; I was the one being the selfish, insufferable pig!"

"But still. The price of that dream . . ."

"Was nothing, *is* nothing. Hang it, Jason, stop trying to take the bloody weight of the world on your shoulders. This is my blasted problem, not yours!"

"I assure you, I have no burning desire to play the martyr . . ."

"You know your trouble?" Jeryn interrupted rudely. "You're too bloody perfect!"

There was a long moment of silence. "Love and hate, eh?" Jason said eventually. He smiled weakly. "Let me tell you, right now I feel very far from perfect. I mean, I

never even suspected that my own brother would betray
me." Stark and brutal, the words sliced between them like
a razor—the cut so clean and exacting that it was several
seconds before Jeryn felt the flaring pain. "So what made
you come to me now?"

"Pehndon," he faltered. "I never meant to hurt you—
well, maybe I did, but never . . . I just wanted to shatter
your pedestal, make you as bloody human as the rest of
us, but Pehndon wants to kill you. Oh, he never said it in
as many words, but I know he does. In all the time I
worked for him, I never—and you have to believe me, Jason!—I never gave up the location of this house nor the
headquarters of the real alliance; I never let him catch
you. But tonight . . . he pushed me so hard that I almost
broke, I almost gave you up, and that scares me; it scares
me more than anything. It was never what I intended."

Jason stood so abruptly that Jeryn tumbled back on the
carpet, stunned and uncertain. He could almost scent the
acrid tang of his brother's fury, and it terrified him.
Should that pent-up rage be unleashed against him . . .

But, "Curse that coldhearted bastard to perdition!" his
brother bellowed. "How dare he try to use you, use *me,* in
such a fashion—to turn my own brother against me!"

"Jason, where are you going?"

"To tell bloody Pehndon to get the blazes out of your
life—and mine!"

"No!" Jeryn gripped the leg of the sofa as if it were a
lifeline. "You can't; I've spent the past few weeks trying
to keep him away from you! You can't just turn yourself
in to him!"

"And how many guards do you think he'll have posted
around his bedroom door?" his brother responded scornfully.

"You mean . . . face him at home? You know where he
lives?"

Jason smiled bitterly. "I always make it a policy to
know as much about my enemies as possible," he said.
"Providing, of course, that I know who they are." And the
door slammed shut behind him.

Jeryn clutched at the chair leg blindly, maddened by
the thoughts that whirled like a maelstrom through
his head. He had thought he'd lost Jason long ago; it
was only now that he realized how horribly, dreadfully,

mind-numbingly wrong he had been. For even now, in the face of his terrible revelation, Jason was still fighting for him, still protecting him.

By all that was precious, that knowledge hurt worse than losing him.

Which was why, when the door opened again, he said, "Jason . . ." tentatively, pleadingly, only to have the words die on his lips as he stared up into an implacable, well-remembered, wrenchingly chilling face. For an instant he thought it was an apparition, until the thing pointed a finger at him and said, in a kind of muted horror, "You!"

He could only nod disconsolately.

Jen's spirits sank lower with every step as she followed Vera and Derek through the nighttime streets of Nhuras, and the feeling only intensified as the streets grew more familiar, the neighborhood unmistakable.

She groaned involuntarily.

"Are you all right?" Derek asked softly, peering down at her in concern.

She managed a watery smile. "Yes. It's just that . . ."

"You know where we're going," Vera concluded. It wasn't exactly a question, but Jen nodded anyway. "I was afraid of that. Jason's?"

"If that house on the right is our destination."

"Just so," Derek responded, seeming to sense his companion's despair. "Shall I wait outside?"

"It might be better. Come, then, Jen, let's get this over with."

Trailing into the house in Vera's wake, suddenly reluctant to face the traitorous rebel who had played her like a finely tuned instrument—and whose guilt she still couldn't quite believe—Jen instead fetched up hard against her aunt's back as the woman came to an abrupt halt in the doorway. She heard the Hawk's searing accusation, and said, "What is it? What's the matter?"

"Would you kindly tell me who *that* is?" her aunt demanded.

Jen craned her neck around the Hawk's rigid body, her eyebrows soaring in puzzlement. "Jeryn?" she said. "What are you doing here?"

"Jeryn? Who's Jeryn?"

"Jason's brother. And . . ."

"The very Andorian who hired me," the Hawk continued, pouncing and dragging the younger Andorian up into the light like so much terrified prey. "Admit it, blast it! That was you, wasn't it?" And she gave him a ruthless shake.

Abruptly Jen felt as though she had been immersed in ice. Her lips were cold, sluggish; she could barely force them to frame the words. "What are you saying?"

"I'm saying that the Jason Andorian who hired me is this one here! The other one—the real one, I suppose—was like enough from a distance. Like enough to be his *brother*." And she slammed Jeryn against the wall, her forearm pressed hard into his windpipe. "But I never forget a face, and this was the one I met!"

Looking back on that moment, Jen would be forever ashamed of her reaction, for instead of rejoicing in her lover's innocence, her instant thought was one of smug triumph and a certain loathsome justification: *I was right; my instincts were correct!* Almost immediately she regretted it, but the knowledge was there; she had cared more about her own judgment than Jason's guilt—or lack thereof.

And it was that knowledge that made her exclaim, more sharply than she intended, "Jeryn. You didn't!"

He nodded miserably, croaking, "I'm sorry," and with a growl Vera released him, flinging him back toward the sofa, where he huddled forlornly, a sudden spill of tears trickling lamely down his cheeks.

"I'm sorry, Jen," Vera admitted. "You were right, and I was wrong. And that was why Pehndon kept referring to Jason and his rebel alliance as though they were real. Because they were; because they are—and always have been—a threat that needed eliminating. And you," she whirled on Jeryn. "You were Pehndon's little tool, making sure it all happened. Your own brother! Have you seen the conditions in the factories? In the streets? Do you have any idea what he was fighting for and how much it meant? Do you realize what will happen to those thousands of workers who depended on your brother if Pehndon succeeds?"

Jen had never expected to see herself as the voice of reason—and especially not where the Hawk was concerned, but now she laid a light hand on her aunt's arm, saying, "Vera . . ."

"Kill me if you must," Jeryn seconded miserably, "I certainly deserve it. Only . . ."

"Yes?"

"Help Jason. Find him, save him. I'm afraid that something will go wrong, that someone will recognize him, take him. That's an awfully big reward, after all, and he did go tearing out of here without any cover."

"And where might Jason be tearing to that he's in need of saving?" Vera asked coldly. "Or in need of finding?"

"He was on his way to see Pehndon."

"Pehndon?" Jen yelped. "How could he be so bloody stupid?"

Jeryn flinched visibly. "Well, he said he was going to Pehndon's house, that there wouldn't be guards on his bedroom . . ."

"And you let him do it?" Vera rejoined. "Knowing Pehndon? Of course there will be bloody guards! And he'll be bloody taken! And do you know what that means?"

Jeryn paled.

"Precisely! Blast it, Jen, we have to go after him; we have to stop him before he reaches Pehndon's. But how? How can we go after him if we don't know where he's *going*?"

Jeryn looked abruptly puzzled. "You don't know where he lives?"

"No. Why? Do you?"

"No, but . . . If you don't know where he lives, then how did you search his house?"

"What? I didn't search his house! Jen?"

She shook her head.

"Well, someone did," Jeryn insisted. "And he was awfully upset about it."

"Great goldfish of perdition: Derek! Come on, Jen, and hurry. We haven't got much time!"

With a sudden sinking feeling, Jen hurried out after the Hawk. Their priorities were clear. First they had to rescue Andorian. Apologies could come later—if they succeeded.

51

"We would like to like to see First Minister Jhakharta, please."

The aide blinked nervously, surveying the crowd before him. Thibault supposed they did look rather intimidating. Vera stood in the lead, her head cocked imperiously as she made her demands, her eyes doubtlessly cold as two chips of grey ice. Arrayed behind her in staggered ranks were the rest of the party: Jen to her left, looking resolute in her assassin's garb, and the Falcon to her right, with the largest remaining members of the quintet flanking their respective partners.

From the chill of Vera's regard to the looming bulk of Thibault and the Hound, it wasn't surprising that the aide was looking a little discomfited. He swallowed audibly. "Do you, um . . . have an appointment?" he stammered.

"We don't need an appointment. The Minister will see us."

Thibault had to give the poor aide some credit for persisting in the face of such incredible odds. "I'm afraid I really can't help you," he faltered, but nonetheless with a core of desperate resolution. "The Minister is extremely busy; I can't let just anyone in to see him."

"I don't like this one," Jen commented to no one in particular. "Grahme was better, much more gracious and charming."

The nameless aide went scarlet.

"I think you'll find the Minister really *will* see us," Vera continued, as if Jen hadn't spoken. "Just tell him we're here to see him about Neros Fazaquhian."

"Neros Fazaquhian? Who's he?"

"Never you mind who he is; just relay the message. And if that doesn't work, you can always throw in the name of Ariadne DeBricassart."

The aide's eyes widened. "Ariadne DeBricassart? You know her? Rumor has it she's been missing. The Minister's beside himself!"

"The Minister? Which Minister?" Jen demanded.

The man met her eyes uncomfortably, yet with a faint note of surprise in his voice as he responded, "Minister DeBricassart, of course. Her father."

Thibault gasped. By all that was precious, no wonder Vera was worried about Pehndon if this was the length to which he would go, murdering a colleague's daughter in the name of the cause! And from Vera's expression, he could tell the news was a surprise to her as well—although she did seem a little less shocked by it than he was.

"Well, I know of her, at any rate," she temporized. "Now, go and tell the Minister we're here."

"And what names shall I give?" the poor aide demanded, obviously making one last desperate attempt to attach some semblance of normality to the situation.

"Never mind the names. Just go!"

He fled, returning a few moments later to say, "The Minister will see you now."

He was the only one who seemed amazed by the announcement.

Jhakharta, when they entered, was ensconced behind a huge mahogany desk, but instead of using the prop to its full effect, he had more the look of a man trying to hide behind its shielding bulk. His face was so pale he could have been cut straight out of the whitewashed walls, and his hands shook visibly as he gestured them within.

"Malle . . . Varis?" he faltered. "What can I do for you today?"

Vera, as before, was in the lead, and now she settled down in the chair across from him, crossing her legs casually while her compatriots fell into rank behind her. Jhakharta flinched visibly and, if possible, went even paler as Thibault and Derek closed the formation.

"Ah, so you recognize me," Vera purred. "It's been a while, has it not? I don't believe I've seen you since the trial. The first trial, that is."

Jhakharta began to sweat, wiping the edge of one sleeve across his brow. "I . . . that is . . . Pehndon said you were alive."

"I know I heard him."

"*What?*"

From the corner of his eye, Thibault could see Vera's grin curling unpleasantly, and he didn't blame Jhakharta for his skittishness. No matter how many times she had berated him, he had never seen her look so deadly—or so dangerous—as now.

Briefly he glanced over at Jen, who was regarding her aunt in undisguised admiration. *Blast it,* he thought somewhat sourly, *she would be. Is that what it takes to impress her?* For all his size, Thibault knew he was the least threatening member of their party, for he was the one Jhakharta's appealing gaze kept sliding to when he couldn't meet the chilling stares of the others.

"But more important," Vera was saying, "you knew I was alive because you knew he didn't kill me. You knew who it was that he did kill instead: Ariadne DeBricassart."

Something in Jhakharta snapped. Thibault could see the tension drain out of his limbs, leaving him draped bonelessly in his chair. "I . . . It wasn't my fault." He started to babble. "I didn't even know what he had planned until it was too late. And even once I had realized, there was nothing I could do to stop it. She had already been hanged."

"No, she hadn't; I can see it in your face. You could have stayed the execution, you could have saved her, but you didn't. You chose not to take the risk. Or were you simply afraid that, if you did, you would be the next one at the end of Pehndon's rope?"

Jhakharta twisted his hands in silence, while the tension stretched out as long and thick as his carpet. Then eventually he blurted, "What is it you want from me?"

"From you? Nothing; I already have what I need. But you're an honorable man, Jhakharta, if somewhat weak-willed. I can sense the decency lurking somewhere under that pitiful facade. I know you want to do the right thing, but you simply aren't sure how to go about it. Isn't that right?"

"I . . ."

"Yes, you are clearly in accord; I can see that now. So I am here to offer you a choice: your one last chance at redemption, as it were. Your precious conspirator, Iaon Pehndon, is going down. Either you can help us or you can sink with him. Your choice."

"What do you mean, help you?"

"It's quite simple." Vera checked off the points on her fingers. "First, order the release of Pehndon's prisoners—by which I mean Grahme Tortaluk and Jason Andorian; you have the authority to effect it. Second, cancel Andorian's scheduled trial and execution. Third, admit publicly to your own involvement in this matter and denounce Pehndon for Istarbion's killer. And Ariadne DeBricassart's as well, I presume."

Jhakharta was looking a little stunned. Thibault didn't blame him; he was feeling a little stunned himself. He would never forget the moment when Vera and Jen had come bursting into their hotel room with the news that Jason was innocent and Jeryn the betrayer. Thibault, who had become accustomed to viewing Jen as the poor deceived—and had, he realized, developed a rather smugly pitying attitude about it—had felt his world rock down to its very foundations. That Jen had been right and he had been wrong was something he was totally unprepared to contemplate. After all, how could he possibly function as an assassin and Jen's partner if he became blindly jealous—and blindly suspicious—of every man she took up with? For there would, he knew, be many, and if he were as quick to condemn them as he was to condemn Jason . . .

It was all too awful to contemplate. How could Jen ever trust him—provided she even let him work with her again? And until that moment, he hadn't realized how seriously he had been considering that prospect—relying on it, even. He had hardly spoken to her all day, afraid of seeing just such a rejection in those mossy eyes.

He hadn't so much as glanced at her when, as they progressed toward Government Square that morning, the announcement had been magecast through the streets that Jason Andorian had been apprehended and was awaiting trial in two days. Not that the news came as any surprise; Vera had related it the night before. After quitting Jason's abode, she and Jen had trailed Derek to Pehndon's, only to find the place deserted and the Minister gone. From there they had dashed vainly to the prison, only to see Pehndon emerging alone and triumphant. Jason, it seemed, was safely incarcerated, and now Pehndon was wasting no time in condemning him.

"What do you think I am, stupid?" Jhakharta demanded, finally recovering his powers of speech. "What kind of a choice is that? Release the prisoners, publicly confess? What's my other option?"

"Nothing."

"So there is no other option? But I thought you said I had a choice!"

"And so you do." Vera's voice was deadly. "Nothing *is* your other option. Do nothing; say nothing. Take no action."

"And that's supposed to be a choice?" Jhakharta snorted. "To jeopardize everything I've worked for or simply sit back and reap the rewards in silence? You honestly call that a *choice*? Either you must think me phenomenally stupid or you place a far higher value on my morality than you should!"

"What I think," Vera countered softly, "is that you don't fully understand your options. Oh, you have the first part down clearly enough. I'll grant you that. But the second? Let me tell you what will happen if you do nothing. If that trial continues, Pehndon's guilt and your involvement will be revealed to the Ashkharon public in livid and thorough detail. Nothing, I assure you, will be omitted."

"And how can you prove it?" Jhakharta's voice was scornful. "Who will believe your claims over mine, or Minister Pehndon's?"

"Very good, Alphonse." Vera applauded slowly. "You are showing more brains than most people give you credit for. Now I know what you have, so let me tell you what I possess. Item one: a certain stack of papers from Pehndon's private stores. He worked quite hard last night to regain them, but to no avail. Item two: a recording of a conversation between yourself and Minister Pehndon which occurred yesterday afternoon, in which Pehndon confesses his crimes and admits not only to the killing of Guy Istarbion but also to Ariadne DeBricassart's hanging. Item three: Neros Fazaquhian. You know who Neros Fazaquhian is, Alphonse?"

The First Minister shook his head: a jerky, overly hasty denial.

"Actually," Vera continued implacably, "I think you do. But just to remind you, Neros Fazaquhian is the scientist from the Dheimos naphtha refineries whom Pehndon murdered in his office yesterday. Which, by the way, we also have on crystal."

"But, I . . ."

"Eliminated the body? Not quite. You see, we followed you, my associate and I." And she cocked her head at Thibault, who straightened and bowed—and suddenly, in Jhakharta's eyes, became far less benign. "After you—abandoned it, shall we say?—we retrieved it. It is currently in my sitting room, under disguise, but it can be unveiled if necessary. Along with a recording of you removing it from Pehndon's office."

"You're bluffing!"

"I may be. But then, I may not. And do you really want to take that chance?"

Thibault could feel Jhakharta's eyes slide from one to another, weighing them all in turn. He could feel Jen's fierce excitement, blazing like an open flame.

"Your choice, of course," Vera continued. "You have two days to decide. But consider this. If we go public with our information, we will reveal everything. If you, however, choose to reveal the facts, you can disguise them as you wish—so long as Pehndon is proclaimed guilty and Andorian exonerated. Consider that, if you will."

Jhakharta was silent for a long, painful moment. Then, "Who are you?" he whispered at last.

"People with whom it is wisest not to trifle. But if you want names . . . The Hawk. The Hound. The Falcon."

"The Cloak. And the Dagger," Jen finished firmly.

Thibault shot her an oblique look, and her eyes twinkled back.

"Guild? All five of you?" Jhakharta swallowed heavily.

"Quite. Though, of course, we shall all deny it strenuously if asked. We will leave you now. I trust you will do the right thing, First Minister."

After they had left, Jhakharta sat for a long time in silence, replaying the threats and implications in his mind. The right thing; they trusted him to do the right thing. But what, by all that was precious, *was* the right thing?

At present, Alphonse Jhakharta had absolutely no idea.

He let about an hour elapse while he reflected, weighing every possibility, measuring every angle.

But in the end, he did what he always did when reality got to be too much for him.

He went running to Iaon Pehndon.

52

"They said *what?*" Pehndon thundered, and watched as Jhakharta winced. The First Minister was standing nervously before his desk, twisting his hands in an ecstasy of indecision, one toe repeatedly scraping the carpet like a schoolboy.

"That they know everything," he said. "That they'll reveal it all unless we go public and confess."

Pehndon snorted. "And where's the advantage in that, Alphonse? Not much of a choice they give us. Revelation, confession, what difference?"

"The difference, I gather," Jhakharta said almost wryly, "is that in the latter case we get to pick what story we reveal."

"Then," Pehndon chuckled, "I propose to stick with my original yarn, proclaiming Andorian's guilt."

Jhakharta shook his head. "Not an option."

"What do you mean, not an option?"

"They were most adamant on that point. Andorian has to go free. And you and I have to proclaim our involvement."

"Or you have to proclaim mine, eh, Alphonse? For why else do you think they came to you alone?" Jhakharta was silent. "There were five, you said? And all Guild?"

"So I presume."

Pehndon grunted. Not a good situation; very far from ideal. Two he had expected, two he could deal with. But five? That blasted Leonie Varis had made good on her threat. They had sent the Guild after him in force. And now they were trying to turn Jhakharta against him.

Bloody bastards!

Bloody fools—as if Alphonse Jhakharta would turn so easily. Not that he was intrinsically loyal. Pehndon had no illusions on that account. But his figurehead Minister was

too simpleminded to think for himself; it was one of the
reasons that Iaon had selected him. And, for all their
plans, the bloody Guild had never figured that into their
schemes; they had obviously never imagined that
Jhakharta would go running to Pehndon and reveal all.

"Well, Alphonse?" he said at last, leaning back in his
chair and steepling his fingers expectantly. "What do you
plan to do about this?"

"Me? But, I . . ."

"They did come to you, after all."

"Yes, but . . ."

"You felt the need to come running to me. Still. Come
now, Alphonse, you must have one original thought in
that head of yours."

"I . . . Couldn't we concoct some story that clears Andorian while throwing our own involvement into question?"

"And how would you go about doing that?"

"I don't know," the First Minister exclaimed in some
desperation. "That's why I came to you!"

"And it was obviously a good impulse, since it seems
that I'm the only one who can still function around here!
Honestly, Alphonse, the whole idea is to hang Andorian,
not to clear him. Even now, we must keep that goal firmly
in mind."

"But how? They have . . ."

"What? Haven't you been around long enough to recognize an obvious bluff? They have nothing! When has
anyone been around to plant a bug?"

"The night your office was vandalized?"

"Remember, I had the whole place cleaned, and the
mages were there to do a thorough sweep. If there had
been anything, they'd have found it. And as for my papers, I assure you they are in a place where no one but
myself can reach them. I got them back from Andorian
last night."

"When you apprehended him?"

"Not . . . exactly." Pehndon let a slightly superior smile
play over his features. He was still riding high from the
success of that venture; it had been part of his plan all
along. Jason was an honorable man, and you could read
that type like a book. If Jeryn had given up his brother, so
much the better, but there had always been a chance that
he would crack and tell all; it was a risk you took when

working with flawed material. But if Pehndon pushed hard enough, and Jeryn's guilt was particularly wrenching, what an anguished scene that telling would be! And in the face of such suffering, how could an honorable man like Andorian not come running to what he deemed the responsible party, stuffed with righteous indignation?

And so it had been. The man's puerile anger, his blank look of puzzlement when the guards had converged, had been nothing short of a pleasure.

Who would have believed a seasoned leader could be so criminally stupid?

Of course, it was a minor inconvenience that Jeryn would not be standing in for his brother at the trial, spouting off facile lies, but then there were always other ways around that problem—as he had proved so effectively with Ariadne. There were always willing substitutes, and he wouldn't even have to kill this one in the end. No, he had the technique down to an art form by now.

Which was why his reaction to Jhakharta's news stemmed more from irritation than genuine concern. As if mindless threats could stop him, now that he had Jason in custody and was so close to his goals. Not to mention that, at the price he had paid, he was cursed well going to finish this business for once and all! "I tell you," he repeated, "they have nothing!"

"Indeed?"

The new voice startled them, seeming to come from the very air, hanging in a disembodied limbo above their heads. Pehndon frowned. "Did you say something?"

Jhakharta's eyes widened frantically. "I thought you did!"

"Actually, it was neither of you."

"Excuse me?"

"Come now, don't you recognize my voice, Iaon? You've had enough opportunity to hear it over the past few weeks."

Pehndon felt his face grow pale. "Leonie?"

"Right in one. Very good, Pehndon. Now are you convinced we are telling the truth?"

"Where . . ." He began to search the air frantically.

"Oh, you needn't bother looking. I am quite far away," she assured him calmly. "Physically, at any rate. I am merely speaking to you courtesy of the two-way transmission of our little crystal link. It is quite present, and it has been used to make many recordings. Including one of this very conversation."

He leaped mindlessly to his feet, shouting, "Curse you, where? How?" He was dimly aware of Jhakharta, shrinking from his anger.

"What, didn't you like my plaque?" said a new voice mournfully, its teasing tone likewise staggeringly familiar.

"Domme Leonis?" he snarled, making the connection at last. Blast it, how could he have been so stupid? He was as bad as bloody Alphonse. The name alone should have alerted him.

"Quite, and I do hope you appreciated my gift."

Actually, he had; he had found the sentiments surprisingly apt. But now he cursed vividly and tore across the room, snatching up the plaque, which still lay on the floor where he had hurled it. It wasn't ordinarily like him to leave such a mess, but then he'd been busy, and a fallen plaque was hardly top priority.

Or at least, it hadn't been until now.

The disembodied voices let him search the thing frantically for several minutes before the one he knew as Domme Leonis said, "Wrong, actually. The plaque is entirely what it seems."

"And the bug?"

"Follow my voice, Pehndon." That was Leonie again, and he felt his face flaming, his mouth pursed into irate lines, as he tracked the blistering trail of her imprecations to its source: the tiny crystal balanced innocently atop his window frame. Alphonse watched in wide-eyed consternation as he snatched it down and threw it to the floor, raising one foot.

Yet even as he brought down his heel, fully intent on grinding the thing into perdition, Leonie's tinny, disembodied voice drifted up to his ears once more.

"The crystal may have reached the end of its usefulness, Pehndon, but so have you. If you value your life, you'd better not plan on going out tonight . . ."

His heel descended viciously upon the crystal, smashing it into a million fragments of dust and mocking laughter.

And then there was silence.

A long silence.

"Pehndon is a bloody genius," he said at last, dryly, hopelessly.

As expected, there was no response, no flurry of papers to assure him. It was true; they had everything.

The words seemed as fitting an epitaph as any.

"What do you intend to do about it?" Jhakharta said eventually. Pehndon had all but forgotten his presence.

"Ignore it, of course," he replied, with more nonchalance than he felt. Close; he had been so close! "The question is, Alphonse, what do *you* intend to do about it?"

He could tell from the man's expression as he scuttled hastily from the office that he had just been betrayed.

He wondered why he didn't feel anything other than a cold, uncaring numbness.

When First Minister Alphonse Jhakharta reached his office, he bolted the door securely behind him and hurried behind the comforting bulk of his desk. He knew he had been hiding behind it far too often, but he no longer cared. Its solidity reassured him, and soon there would be no more hiding from anything.

With shaking hands, he pulled out a pen and paper and uncapped his inkstand. Then, with his tongue protruding from between his teeth, he began to think as he had never thought before.

Eventually, he set pen to paper and began to write with a fierce, single-minded determination.

He had made up his mind at last, and it felt astonishingly liberating.

Could one positive act make up for a lifetime of neglect? He certainly hoped so, because he was gambling everything he owned on that certainty.

It was fully dark by the time Pehndon left his office. He didn't know what he had done before that moment: perhaps he'd sat and stared idly at the pile of crystal dust under his feet, the symbol of his shattered dreams. Or perhaps he had endlessly and silently repeated his mantra—Pehndon is a bloody genius, Pehndon is a bloody genius—as if by saying it he could make it so. But whatever he had done, it had meant nothing against the magnitude of what awaited him out there in the darkness.

He hadn't clipped her pinions, after all. He had merely trimmed away the dead material so she could come back bigger, stronger, more ferocious. He had created a monster—

not only in her but in himself. He saw that now, saw the darkness in his own heart as clearly as that which lay outside his windows. In grasping for something perverted, he had become perverted himself, a twisted parody of a human. He'd wanted power; he had gained condemnation. And now the game was at an end. The final hand had been played, the final curtain rung down. And he had achieved . . .

Nothing.

Quietly he eased open the window and leaned out into the night. The breeze swept across him like a mother's hand, warm and forgiving; the air smelled of hibiscus and sage. Beyond the bounded formality of Government Square, silent and classic in the looming shadows, the lights of Nhuras winked back at him with all the power of the mages. But instead of mocking him, they seemed oddly peaceful, and somehow beautiful, as he stood at this very casement where Domme Leonis had once stood and pretended to admire the view.

Illusion, all of it; illusion. He would never again stand at this window, see the sparkle of lights on the horizon, listen to the distant lapping of the Belapharion beneath the muted rumble of the city. Never again see, like a ghost at the edges of his vision, the taunting gouts of fiery smoke from the vast chimneys of the glass manufactories. It might as well be a carefully constructed image, as fleeting and evanescent as the fires that danced over the domes of the Mages Quarter, for all the good it did him.

Eventually he closed the window and summoned his guards. They were merely a formality, he knew, but he summoned them anyway, for the small moment of comfort they would provide him between the door and death.

Three steps beyond the borders of Government Square, the first fell lifeless onto the silent streets. A moment later, and the second fell as well. He barely felt his own doom—the tiny pinprick at the base of his neck—before the darkness claimed him, too.

He opened his eyes onto blackness, touched only with the faintest glow of magelight. But as his consciousness slowly returned, he saw above him the vast sweep of the desert sky, stitched with the scintillating glimmer of the summer stars. His cheek was pressed to a paving stone which glinted with mica like the firmament it echoed, and beyond him lapped the inky wash of the Belapharion. Playing over those dark waters was a subtle array of shifting lights and colors, like airy spirits dancing in a liquid ballroom. Blue and purple and acid green, they glowed like no colors known to nature, and it was then that he knew.

He pushed himself slowly onto one elbow, feeling his reality tip and sway with the remnants of the drug. His voice, when he spoke, felt thick and unwieldy. "I'm still alive, then?"

"Of course. It would be too easy otherwise." And Leonie Varis stepped into his view, tall and commanding in the reflected magelight. He wondered how he had ever thought her a lad, even with the shorn hair. That lean, implacable face had a woman's beauty, and a woman's fiery pride.

"What happened to the guards? They're not . . ."

"Dead? No. Merely asleep, as you were. Even now they should be rousing, wondering what happened to their precious master."

He was surprised to find himself oddly relieved, as if, after all this killing, he suddenly cared about the fate of two inconsequential servants. He hadn't even known their proper names. "And what did?" he said. "Why have you kept me alive? And why have you brought me here?"

She reached down one lean hand, pulling him to his feet, and waited until he had taken a shaky grasp on the curved railing, leaning into its comforting strength, before speaking again. "It seemed appropriate to show you before you died all that you had sought to destroy—and all that will live on after you are gone." And the same hand that had helped him now gestured with a fluid, deadly grace.

The Promenade stretched out in both directions, as deserted as the night. The gates to the Mages Quarter were locked and glimmering with a deadly fire, coursing in ghostly pulses up and down the scrollwork bars. Beyond the high hedges—the wrought-iron lamp posts with their suspended balls of aureate flame, the redolence of flower and shrub—the mages' domes glowed in their signature colors, symbol of all he had tried to break and couldn't.

"Someday," she said softly, "they may be humbled—but not by you, or by your methods. Someday, someone who cares may ensure that the mages take their proper place: as another tool of mankind, nothing more. Much as you and I are tools."

"You? A tool?"

She chuckled faintly. "Ah, yes, Pehndon, of the finest kind. For I, you see, cut out society's cankers."

"Like me?"

"Just so."

"Who are you?"

"You want a name?" She smiled, soft and deadly in the magelight. "Vera. Viera Radineaux. And that is the real one."

"An aristocrat?"

She nodded.

"But why? I mean, why choose a life of secrets and cunning?"

"Because not all of us desire to rule."

"So you are going to kill me?"

He had no hope of getting an answer other than he did: the slow, deliberate inclination of her head. He didn't even know why he had asked, except . . . He needed an answer, if only to let him know in what manner he would end his days.

"How?" he demanded.

She met his eyes calmly, and he masked an incipient shiver. "There was a part of me," she admitted, "that wanted to pay you back wound for wound, and bruise for bruise. As you brutalized me, so should I brutalize you. But then I realized that in doing so I would become no better than you, and I am more than that, Iaon Pehndon. Much, much more."

It was right; it was fitting. He acknowledged that even as he saw the silver flash of her dagger, felt the pain blooming between his ribs, driving up toward his heart as quick and mercilessly as a serpent's strike. His last memories were of himself falling, cresting the curving arc of the wrought-iron bars, sinking into the warm, liquid embrace of the eternal Belapharion.

And then he felt no more.

53

"As you are all no doubt aware, the trial of Jason Andorian was to begin tomorrow. That will not be occurring."

The hush that settled over Government Square was audible, and almost frightening in its intensity. The place was packed to capacity, with both protesters and the curious masses who had later flocked to hear the promised announcement. And with almost a thousand bodies pressed in cheek by jowl—and who knew how many more overflowing into the nearby streets—the potential for violence was almost unprecedented. But then, since the moment of Jason's capture the word had gone out, and over the course of hours the assorted workers and poor had arrived: first in trickles, then in bunches, camping before the Grand Stair and clotting up the arteries around the government buildings. When night fell they remained, pressed close together for warmth, and throughout the dark hours still more appeared. By morning they were some nine hundred strong, bearing banners and placards—often misspelled or poorly lettered but nonetheless universal in their sentiments—stinking of the streets and casual neglect.

It was rumored that in their absence the factories had all but shut down, running on the bare minimum of salvageable crews.

Until this point, a reasonable stalemate had reigned as workers and spectators alike awaited the judgment from on high, but with the advent of the magecast words, Thibault could feel the tension pleat and buckle, swelling to engulf the silent square. If Jason's execution were summarily announced, without even the courtesy of an intervening trial, Nhuras would be in flames before the night was out.

But that wouldn't happen. Of all the bloodthirsty or

horrified viewers now huddled motionless beneath the crystalline screens, only he and his band were aware of the true nature of the revelation. He surveyed them with a certain bemused affection: Vera, straight and proud, the ragged edge of emotion gone from her expression until she seemed as deep and calm as a woodland pool. Jenifleur, whimsically wearing her blond wig for no particular reason that Thibault could fathom, her arm looped casually about the Hound's waist. Derek, grinning broadly, his sky-blue eyes dancing as he surveyed the proceedings. Mark, looking satisfied in his own particular, knife-faced fashion.

Crushed into the periphery of the anxious crowd, they alone knew that the swelling tension would not explode into violence; they alone surveyed the proceedings with a certain quiet pleasure. They had all been prepared for several outcomes to their little drama, but the one that actually occurred had surpassed them all.

"To explain the—shall I say, rather unusual?—events of the previous evening," the nameless minister continued on the screen, "I would like to present you with Mal Grahme Tortaluk, aide to the former First Minister Alphonse Jhakharta."

An undeniable buzz went up at that, shattering the reigning silence. Jhakharta's death, late the previous evening, had not been widely publicized. In fact, Thibault had gotten the news only this morning, as dawn's light was breaking over the horizon; until then, he had been as ignorant as the masses.

He began to chuckle softly, and Jen poked him furiously.

Up on the screen, Grahme's image had replaced that of the unknown Minister. He looked serene and self-assured, his long, sober face showing no traces of his enforced confinement, nor of the ravages of his secret torture. Thibault felt a sudden pride, that he had been involved in this; that he had helped, in however minor a capacity, to bring this man to his current position, nodding benevolently down at the breathless crowd.

"This morning," he said, his voice deep and level, "I arrived at work to discover a shocking situation: First Minister Alphonse Jhakharta was dead, and by his own hand; the mages have determined that he hanged himself shortly after midnight. As for his reason, it appears that for several years all has not been well in our government—and late last night the situation reached a crisis. In apparent remorse for his own, unwitting involvement in these events, the First Minister took his own life, leaving behind him this document. It is thus, with great regret, that I now relate to you the First Minister's final words:

People of Ashkharon, it is to my profound dismay that I have recently uncovered the truth behind the events which have so shaken our country. I am referring, of course, to the shocking public slaughter of former First Minister Guy Istarbion, and the trial which subsequently determined Jason Andorian to be the responsible party. In fact, the truth is a lot more sordid—and a great deal more complex.

First, there never was any assassin, and the guilty party was—and always has been—our own Minister Iaon Pehndon. Far from catching the supposed assassin, I have recently discovered that the Minister performed the execution by himself, and then set about apprehending one of his accomplices to present the public with a tangible scapegoat. That accomplice, in full accord with Pehndon, later stood in at the assassin's trial and spouted forth the elaborate lie which the two of them had concocted. That accomplice, without her prior knowledge or consent, was then subsequently hanged to prevent her from revealing her involvement—after Pehndon had promised to substitute a common criminal in her place.

That accomplice, as some of you may have determined, was none other than Ariadne DeBricassart, who, as many of you are aware, has been missing for several weeks. It is therefore with great regret that I inform you of the location of her body, which is buried in the thieves' grave outside the city—although I am certain it shall be moved to the familial vault as soon as it can be recovered.

And as for Jason Andorian, he was—and always has been—as innocent as he claimed. Pehndon's nefarious schemes originated from his desire to control the government, and to that end he murdered Guy Istarbion, who would certainly have never chosen him as successor. Then, while subsequently charming the next First Minister—myself—into granting him the position, he set about eliminating what he saw as the only real threat to his

*power: Jason Andorian. By framing him for the murder—
and subsequently hanging him for its execution—the path
would then be clear for Pehndon's unchallenged succession.*

*You can thus understand the profound horror with
which I learned these facts and realized the extent to
which I had unwittingly become involved in so many innocent deaths. As both my position and my honor have been
severely compromised, I see no solution other than to offer myself up as the final victim in this dreadful charade.
With my death, Pehndon's guilt becomes public, and my
position passes to the only man in Ashkharon who is worthy to possess it. It is thus with great joy and, I hope,
much atonement, that I present you with your next First
Minister. As recompense for the indignities he has suffered during my administration, I name Jason Andorian
my successor and wish him long life and every success in
his chosen profession.*

At the words, a cry of such profound elation surged
through the gathered crowd that Thibault blinked back a
sudden tear. He had never expected to be so strongly affected by his rival's triumph, but he knew it was no less
than the man deserved. His own irrational prejudices
aside, Jason was a good man—and with the jubilant
shouts of the workers ringing in his ears, he let slide the
last remaining threads of his resentment and with a genuine and honest pleasure turned to accept Jenny's embrace.

A festival atmosphere seemed to have gripped the
square as banners and placards were hurled exuberantly
into the air, raining heedlessly down on the gathered public. Releasing Jenny, Thibault found himself grabbed and
embraced by at least a dozen strangers and, caught up in
the excitement, returned the favors with equal fervor. As
did every member of his little group, whooping and pum-
meling their neighbors with shining eyes, their mouths
stretched wide with delight.

When the furor had subsided, Grahme continued levelly, but nonetheless with a certain twinkle in his eyes for
his hero's successes, "I need not tell you that we have
tried to reach Iaon Pehndon for comment, but it seems
that the Minister is unavailable. Any information as to his
whereabouts would, of course, be greatly appreciated."

As one, their little group turned to look pointedly at Vera, who just smiled enigmatically. If she knew what had happened to the erstwhile Minister, she was not telling—though her absence last night, for the space of several hours, spoke silent volumes.

"But meanwhile," Grahme continued, "it is with the greatest of pleasure that I give you your new First Minister, Jason Andorian." And as he stepped back, the former rebel leader stepped forward, smiling down at the cheering crowd. What must it be like, Thibault thought wistfully, to command that much love, that much respect? He looked over at Jen, whose face was glowing.

"That's my boy," she said proudly.

Up on the massive screen, Andorian spread his arms as if embracing his reverent followers. "My people," he said. "I promise that you shall never regret Jhakharta's decision, and I hope that you can find it in your hearts to forgive him his many trespasses."

Jason's head was still reeling in the wake of the magecast as he retired to his new office with Grahme in tow. The past few days had taken on the odd, disjointed quality of a dream, and he still couldn't quite believe the reality of a life which delivered him from nightmare into *this*. One minute, it seemed, he had been betrayed by Jeryn and thrust ignominiously into prison, and the next—just when he was certain his life was over, that he had failed the final test—the door to his cell had swung open, revealing the haggard face of Alphonse Jhakharta, gesturing him out of oblivion.

At first he hadn't even trusted the Minister, convinced it was some ingenious form of mental torture designed exclusively to break him, but then he had seen Grahme Tortaluk, standing in the dimly lit stone hallway. His agent's face was ragged and strained, and yet his smile shone out with a serenity that Jason had never seen before in his ally.

"What is the meaning of this?" he had asked in a wondering tone, not completely certain whether he meant his release or his agent's new composure.

"It's over, Jason. It's finished," Grahme had answered, which, in retrospect, he decided seemed to serve equally well for both. It wasn't until later that he had learned of the hidden tortures, the many attempts to force a confession, which Pehndon had employed so ruthlessly. But for Grahme, the miracle was to come out the victor, unbroken.

But still, staring at Jhakharta across that prison hallway, he had never imagined that, bare hours later, he would have inherited the mantle of First Minister. He hadn't even suspected it when, a little before midnight, Jhakharta escorted them back to Grahme's old office and made them wait, a guard posted at his own door, while he "wrapped up the last of this dreadful affair." An hour later, with no sign from the Minister, Jason and Grahme persuaded the baffled guard to break down the door and so found Jhakharta twirling from the chandelier, his last words in a neat package on his blotter.

From there, it was a flurry of government protocol and frenzy as the mages were called in to verify the First Minister's demise and wishes, while the hastily assembled Ministers met in Council to prepare for the coming magecast. It was only by sheer luck that Jen and Vera had been watching the square, waiting for the outcome of Alphonse's decision, and thus were apprised of the news.

But now, in the wake of the chaos, Jason flopped down in the First Minister's chair and propped his feet up on the gleaming desktop, grinning over at his companion.

"You did a fine job there," he teased. "Swallowing all those lies certainly took some doing."

Grahme's lips quirked ruefully. "He certainly engineered that one right enough; came out smelling fresh as bloody roses! You know, I think it's the first time I've seen him show any intelligence?"

"Well, hopefully we'll have a few more brains around the office in future; I still can't believe he did that! You know, every Minister in Ashkharon is going to hate me for not going through the proper hoops and channels?"

"Nonsense. They'll love you," Grahme insisted loyally. "How could they not?"

Jason raised an eyebrow and reflected on the scene at the prison. "Tell the Hawk that I'm finally doing the right thing," Jhakharta had said, and it seemed that, with the words, the First Minister had finally gained some peace—or at least a certain measure of assurance.

"Well," he said whimsically, "I'm certainly going to need loyal people around me. So I hope you're used to be-

ing the First Minister's aide by now, because you are
most certainly going to retain the position."

"I am?"

"Of course; who else could I possibly choose? You've
supported me unflinchingly and without question. You've
even gone to jail for me! Who better to serve as my wiser
half?"

As the jubilant crowds finally began to disperse, Jen
looked over at her companions. "Well, we did it," she
said. "We evened the score, restored the powers of good."

The Hawk chuckled. "Indeed we did. And I would like
to thank each and every one of you for your efforts. This
could never have happened without you."

"Yes, it could," Mark countered dryly, "but thanks anyway. It's always nice to feel appreciated."

They all laughed at that, but Jen felt a sudden twinge of
regret as she realized that it was, indeed, all over. This
whole adventure had been the most exciting event of her
entire life, and now it was finished. The camaraderie she
felt with these great assassins would doubtless fade, and
Thibault would return to his life in Gavrone. And as for
herself . . .

She sighed despondently, and Vera cast her a sidelong
glance.

"You enjoyed that, didn't you?"

"Eminently."

"Well, maybe you'll get to repeat it then. What do you
say, boys? Put in a good word for her with Owen?"

The Hound smiled broadly and winked. "Of course.
Mark?"

"I'll say anything you want, providing someone's paying me," the Falcon retorted.

"And here I thought I was supposed to be the merce-
nary one!"

"Well," Vera temporized, "if DeVeris doesn't provide
the requisite compensation, then I will. Gratitude has to
be expressed somehow, after all."

"So, what now?" Thibault demanded.

"Venture home, I suppose. I'll book us a ship."

54

It was a sober group that met on the wharf two mornings later to say their final adieux—all of the principal players, Jason thought ruefully, at least, those who were still alive. Vera, who had started it, and whom he had only recently come to know; the Hound and the Falcon; Jenifleur and Thibault; Jeryn and Grahme. The day seemed subdued as his mood as he gazed regretfully at Jen and thought of all that could have been and wasn't. He had never expected her to stay, but he had . . . hoped. He had, he realized over the past, precious few days that they had let themselves again become lovers, constructed a picture of her which he now knew was false: a subtle reflection of his own desires bounced off the mirror of her inscrutable surface.

But then, Jen was a creature of smoke and illusion; already he had seen the measuring looks she cast at that blond-haired assassin. Obscurely, he felt a moment of pity for Thibault, as well as a tiny surge of envy. For while the man might never be Jenny's, Jen would always be his—and that was more than the rest of them could say, the usurping Hound included.

Reaching out, he drew her aside, twining his hand in hers one last time. Her aunt had, Jen informed him, booked passage on the *Belapharion Traveler*; already he could see the ship looming menacingly above them, waiting to carry her away forever. But determined to inject a note of levity into their parting, he said softly, "I'll never forget my first sight of you, on your hands and knees, pawing through my private trunks."

She grinned, unrepentant, and gave his hand a gentle squeeze. "Well, I told you I'd find something interesting—as indeed I did. You do understand, don't you? Why I have to leave?"

"Oddly enough, I do. And I wish you every happiness in the life you have chosen."

"As I do you. And if, in your exalted position as First Minister, you ever find yourself in need of Guild services, don't hesitate to call me. I'll be discreet—and I'll even be willing to do you for free!"

"I'd be honored, of course, but what makes you think the Guild will even take you?"

He was only teasing and she knew it, but nonetheless she answered him soberly. "Because you once told me that ruling countries was for you like scaling buildings was for me. Well, you have what you wanted; it's my turn now. And desires like that cannot be thwarted."

"Some of them can," he answered softly, a fragment of betrayal still clouding his voice.

She shook her head slowly. "No, that's not desire. Temporary obsession, maybe, but you'll understand the difference in time. It would never have worked between us because we both need to come first, and with each other we never would."

"But . . ."

She laid a gentle finger on his lips. "No, you know I'm right. But it doesn't mean I won't miss you, or remember you fondly forever. I will."

"I know. I'll miss you, too." And leaning down, he kissed her one last time, feeling the sweet, open generosity of her lips beneath his and secretly knowing in his heart that she was right.

About everything.

He drew away then, turning to the rest of her party. "Nice to meet you all, however belatedly," he said. "And my thanks again for everything you did."

The Hound and the Falcon took his hand, but Vera just grinned. A day ago, Pehndon's body had been found floating face-down in the Belapharion, too waterlogged and decayed for the mages to determine the identity of his killer. The public had speculated wildly, of course, but no one would really ever know. And Jason was certainly not about to give the game away, even if it meant carrying the secret to his grave.

"Our pleasure," she said. "And now the guilty have paid—all save one. What about him?" And she pointed resolutely at Jeryn. "He sold me off to Pehndon; he tried to sell you. Shouldn't he pay a price as well?"

Jason saw his brother wince, and felt the hardening of his own resolve. Oddly enough, until this moment, he hadn't been completely certain of what he meant to do himself. But now his sibling's expression, combined with his own reaction to Vera's pronouncement, illuminated his path like a beacon.

"No," he said softly.

"What?"

"You heard me. No. There will be no more retribution. My brother has suffered enough for me already."

"So you're planning to do nothing?"

"Not precisely."

"What, then?"

"Give him the management of the naphtha fields, if he'll have it. With Fazaquhian gone, Varia knows we'll need a good man in control."

Jeryn gasped, and Jason laid a hand lightly on his sibling's arm. The shining, awed expression in his brother's eyes told him everything he wanted to know.

He would never fear for Jeryn again.

"But he betrayed you," she persisted. "Why do this?"

"Because he is my brother, after all. What better reason do you need?"

She smiled then, and he knew that he had passed her test. "It's rare to see a ruler who actually deserves the honor," she said, and finally extended her hand. He took it warmly. "I'm honored to call you an ally."

"A friend, I hope, and the honor's mine."

"Come, then," she grinned. "Time and tide wait for no man—or woman either—and Captain Black is as eager as they."

In the flurry of more general good-byes, Jason drew Thibault aside. "I'm sorry we didn't get off to a better start," he said. "Had things been different, I would have welcomed you into my organization and been honored to call you friend."

"Thank you. That means a lot, I think—and I'm only sorry it took me so long to realize it."

"So you don't hate me?"

Jen's partner shook his head ruefully. "You're a good man, Jason Andorian, and I know that someday you'll find a woman who deserves you. After all," and he smiled faintly, "Pehndon can't have killed off all the Ministers' daughters."

"Yes, but whether they'll marry an upstart impostor remains to be seen. Nonetheless, I thank you—and wish you the best of luck with your own condition."

"Is it that obvious."

"To everyone but Jen."

"Hurry up, Thib," the woman in question called from halfway up the gangplank, "or I'll be forced to leave you behind, and you'll never see your precious Gavrone again!"

The two men exchanged an amused look, and then Thibault followed his nemesis onto the ship.

About an hour after the *Belapharion Traveler* had quit the harbor and tacked into the open waters off the Ashkharon coast, Vera received a summons to the captain's cabin.

She obeyed with alacrity, grinning as Kharman Black bowed over her hand and kissed it, closing the door behind her. His bluff black eyes twinkled as of old, and she felt the same familiar flutter run up her spine. Oh, but it was good to be getting home; she had been in the desert for far too long. In fact, the only thing she would really regret was leaving Absalom; that scruffy mage had gotten under her skin somehow. She had gone to the bazaar that very morning to bid him farewell, pressing his good hand firmly and simultaneously gifting him with an additional five hundred marks from sheer gratitude and affection. He had cracked his crooked grin and slipped the booty under his robe, commenting, "I have said it before, and I will say it again. It is a constant pleasure doing business with you."

"And with you, Absalom. So if you should ever find yourself in need of advancement, just come to Ceylonde; you know where to find me. There's always a place for you in my employ."

His rusty chuckle had scraped her ears one last time. "I might just do that," he said.

He probably wouldn't, but the offer had cheered her anyway.

Now, however, Kharman Black was grinning provocatively, and she let her thoughts return to the present with a tangible shiver. "Imagine the coincidence," he teased, "that I should be in Ashkharon just as you are looking to leave. It is truly most delightful."

"It is, indeed."

"And, I might add, I feel quite justified, now."

"You do? Why?"

"You recall my prediction that I could never see you as a teacher? Well, now it seems that I was correct. What have you been doing to yourself, Leonie?" And his hands, as calloused and gentle as she remembered, caressed the short fringes of her hair.

"It's a long story." She smiled.

"It's a long voyage."

"Then maybe I might just tell you, someday. But for now, suffice it to say that the teaching did *not* work out. And, as chance would have it, I happened to meet up with the delightful young lady I boarded with, who is traveling with her husband, brother-in-law, and their suhdabhar. They were kind enough to take me in and, as it happens, Elinore and I discovered that we were distant cousins. Now isn't that a remarkable thing?"

"Quite, though I admit I can see the resemblance. How fortunate, then, that your voyage wasn't ruined."

"Most fortunate."

His bearded face was very near hers now, creased with salt and sun and gleaming with a familiar anticipation. "But I am also glad you are no longer alone in the world," he added, his voice dropping to a low caress. "So all turned out for the best, eh, Leonie?"

"And getting better by the minute."

His eyes twinkled as she closed the distance between them.

Jen and Thibault were leaning against the shipboard rail, watching the shadow of Ashkharon slide into the horizon, when they saw Vera slip into the captain's cabin.

"She plays the ingenue quite effectively, doesn't she?" Thibault commented.

Jen just grinned. "The woman's a master, no matter what she does. That Black's a lucky man."

Predictably, Thibault flushed, but he said gamely enough, "Well, now we've got Vera settled. So what about you?"

In response, he saw her eyes almost unconsciously seek out the tall form of the Hound, who was lounging on the upper decks; he watched the tiny, expectant smile that curved her lips. Not only was she traveling back to Hestia with the man but he was also masquerading as her husband. Meaning, of course, that they were sharing a cabin, and no doubt where that would be leading.

Briefly, Thibault wondered if he would ever get used to her profligate ways.

"What about me?" she said in response, not quite able to hide her amusement.

"Don't you regret leaving Jason, not even a little?"

She sobered, obviously knowing it was an answer he desired and not her usual flippery. "Of course I do; but the affair was over, fond of him as I will always be. Besides, it lasted longer than most of my flings."

"So that's all it was, then? A fling?"

"I suppose." She wrinkled her nose. "If I was looking for a husband, I would have had a Season and married. But I'm not, thank goodness, so I won't. And what a relief that is!"

It was her constant refrain, but now, for the first time, he was beginning to believe her. Jason had been a man worthy of love, worthy of great sacrifice. And that she had left him for the superficial charms of the Hound—whose fancy was as desultory as her own—was, to him, the most telling sign of how little it had actually mattered.

So, "You really do love all this cloak and dagger stuff, don't you?" he said, and she grinned.

"I live for it. And you?"

He shrugged.

"I once said," she persisted, "that when all this was over, I would ask you a certain question and demand an honest answer. Do you remember?"

He nodded ruefully. He remembered all too well; the question had haunted him throughout the journey. But even as he acknowledged this, he realized that he had also never expected her to ask again, convinced she would have weaned herself from requiring his protection, his companionship.

"Well, that time is now," she continued instead. "The adventure is definitely ended, and I want an honest answer. Do you really think you can go back to Gavrone after all we've seen and done?"

He was silent for a long time, then slowly shook his

head, his gaze fastened on the rolling waves. "No. And you knew it, didn't you?"

He could sense the twinkle in her eyes without even looking. "I suspected it; I hoped it, even. We make a good team, Thibault."

He did raise his head then and met her gaze. There was a pleading there, but a kind of joy as well, and it was then that he knew. She might never need him as he wanted to be needed, but she did—in her own small way—depend on him. And for Jen, he realized suddenly, that kind of dependence was more enduring than all her "flings" stuck end to end. Because he demanded nothing, required nothing but that she simply be free and be herself, she was able to give him more than all her lovers combined with their hidden strings and ties and secret burdens. And though she might never be in love with him, she did love him—and maybe that would be enough.

"Yes," he said.

"What?"

"Yes. We do make a good team."

"Then you'll do it?"

He bowed to the inevitable with a grin. "If the Guild will have us."

"Of course they'll have us! Oh, and Thibault, but this is going to be fun! A life of endless adventure and excitement, with no silly Seasons or society! Am I going to scandalize you horribly?"

"Most likely."

"Poor Thibault. But you'll survive. All you really need is a thorough understanding of the profligate upper classes!"

He cast a rueful glance at the captain's cabin. "You know," he said, "I think I'm beginning to get the picture?"

His new partner chuckled. "You know," she responded, "I think you actually might be?"

EPILOGUE

"Well?"

"Well, what?"

Jen looked around at the assembled faces.

"Do we get it?" she said at last, impatiently.

Her aunt grinned. "I told you she was blunt."

The Guildmaster folded his hands. He looked both more benign and more threatening than he had in the crystal, with his probing eyes and swollen fingers. Though when they had first entered the Guild's more public offices, he had jumped to his feet with a smile of genuine welcome and folded the indomitable Hawk into a hearty embrace.

"Welcome, my dear; it's good to have you back!"

"Honestly, Owen, as if you stood in any danger of losing me," she had responded with some asperity. But when she met her Guildmaster's eyes, a certain weighty communication had passed between them. Jen could recognize its import if not its specific content.

Still, Owen's enthusiastic greeting gave her hope, and she let her mouth curve into an expectant smile as he turned to face her—and then instantly felt the expression congeal, falling from her face in sodden chunks as the full force of his resolute gaze assailed her. "So," he said coldly, "this is our enterprising young rogue."

Vera crossed the sky-blue carpet and took a seat in one of the silver-grey brocaded armchairs, regarding her Guildmaster steadily as he returned to his post behind the polished desk. To Jen, it seemed that a silent, deadly battering of wills was occurring, and she fluffed her skirts nervously, readjusting her dagger in its wrist sheath as she looked to Thibault for some sort of reassurance.

It was not forthcoming. Instead, her partner was staring around in undisguised wonder, taking in everything from the high molded ceiling dripping with its massive three-tiered crystal-and-magelight chandelier to the wide, sashed windows which overlooked the courtyard of one of the smaller colleges of Ceylonde University.

It seemed strangely deserted until Jen remembered that it was still high summer and that the hordes of students hadn't yet descended for the fall. In many ways, she found it hard to credit that barely three months had elapsed since she had quit Haarkonis; already it felt like a lifetime, or several. But back in Hestia the grass was still lush and green, the flowers still blooming, perfuming the air with a heady fragrance—and if the sun felt paler than the desert's burning rays, then the sticky heat of the air gave no doubt as to the reality of the season.

She fanned herself surreptitiously while she awaited Owen's decision.

"Well?" Vera said at last, shifting her unspoken contest with the Guildmaster onto the verbal plane.

"She was not operating under the Guild aegis—or under Guild rules," he returned. "And you know the policy on that as well as I do!"

"Ah, but she was Guild-trained and would have petitioned for entry given time. If she had even *had* time."

Owen just snorted.

"Nor," Vera added, "could I have survived this without her. She was of invaluable assistance."

"So the Hound and the Falcon have informed me. If I didn't know better, I'd suspect a conspiracy. Or, perhaps, bribery."

"Bribery? Nonsense. What need has the Hound or the Falcon of my money? I understand they were compensated quite handsomely for their efforts already."

"I do take care of my own," he said somewhat stiffly.

"And by all rights that includes her. She is, in a sense, your professional grandchild. And since when is the Guild in the habit of turning down truly talented and gifted individuals?"

"Which she is?"

"She is a Radineaux, after all."

Jen had held her breath as the Guildmaster's relentless gaze swept her from head to foot, and tried not to let her nervousness show.

"So you want to join the Guild?" he demanded, his tone unforgiving. His eyes annihilated her.

But, "Me and my partner both," she managed, with reasonable composure.

"I wasn't asking your partner, young lady. I was asking you. Do you want it?"

"More than anything."

"Mmm. And you?" He trained his killing gaze on Thibault, who shifted uncomfortably and inserted a finger into his collar. Jen and Vera had bought him the finery two days previously, but in many ways he seemed as overawed by the clothes as he did at the prospect of living under Vera's roof, and had begged them repeatedly to be allowed to return to his comfortable guise as suhdabhar.

"I . . . think so, sir. Yes," he now responded.

The Guildmaster glanced over at Vera. "This one's the voice of reason, I take it?" And when she nodded, he added, "Do you think you can control your partner, lad?"

Thibault frowned. "It's not a question of control," he retorted, his voice seeming to gain assurance as he warmed to his subject. Jen could have applauded. "I would no more try to control her than I would tie my own hands behind my back during a fight. We are partners, equals—her weaknesses are my strengths and my failings, her successes. Sir," he added hastily.

Owen nodded, then rested his gnarled hands against his desk. He seemed to be waiting for something, which had prompted Jen's imperious outburst.

"Do you get it? Do you *get* it?" he now chuckled in response. "My dear young lady, as your aunt so wisely pointed out, I'd be foolish to turn down such dedication and"—he nodded at Thibault—"levelheadedness. Not to mention the honor of having another Radineaux in my employ. But first, you do, of course, realize what this means? What you must give up, what sacrifices you must make?"

Jen nodded soberly, followed an instant later by Thibault.

"And you will, of course, both require more training in Guild etiquette and methodology—not to belittle the Hawk's excellent tuition, of course. This will require certain classes at the University, and for that you must remain in Ceylonde. Will that be a problem?"

Thibault shook his head. He looked a little dazed. Doubtless he had never considered that the University connection meant he would be enrolling in an institution that cost the best families in Hestia a pretty fortune to attend. Truth to tell, Jen had never really considered the true practicality of the cover herself until now.

"Well, it's bound to be more interesting than Haarkonis," she added. "And at least this means an end to that silly Season!"

"Ah, yes, the Season." Owen's eyes turned speculative. "It is, of course, the perfect cover. And the perfect way to make connections. By all means, Vera, proceed with this proposed Season."

Jen felt her jaw drop, heard Thibault masking a sudden chuckle. By all that was precious . . . "I won't do it!" she flared.

"Oh, yes, you will, if your Guildmaster orders it. That's the price of your admission, my dear; I expect you to develop the connection and use it wisely. Now, do we have a deal?"

And he stuck out one gnarled, arthritic hand.

She regarded it in silence for a moment, then abruptly began to grin, proffering her own in return. "I suppose one can't have everything," she said. "Very well, you have a bargain. Thibault?"

Her partner solemnly shook the Guildmaster's hand in turn.

"Good." Vera regarded the pair of them with a certain maternal satisfaction. "We'll close up the house in Nova Castria and live in town until the Season finishes. I shall hate it, of course, but there it is. Thibault, you'll be . . ."

"The suhdabhar. Please, Vera; I've had enough of this silly masquerade."

"Very well, if it'll make you happy."

"It will."

"Then I think we have reached a very satisfactory conclusion."

"I'll formalize your membership tonight," Owen added, "and you can sign the registry on the morrow. Now, what names have you chosen?"

"The Cloak and the Dagger," Jen said promptly.

Thibault blinked and eyed her askance. "You were *serious*?" he said.

ANVIL OF THE SUN

"Entirely."

"But you don't think that's a little . . ."

"What?"

"Well, clichéd?"

She grinned. "One should never avoid a cliché simply because it *is* a cliché. Besides, it fits."

"I suppose." He measured her in silence for a moment, then threw up his hands. "Very well, you win. As usual."

Owen chuckled. "So which one is the Cloak and which the Dagger?"

Jen just smiled impudently in response. "Honestly, do you really have to ask?"

As soon as their newest recruits left the office, Owen glanced across at Vera and let himself relax for what felt like the first time in a millennium. "Well, that does it. Quite an adventure we've had since the last time I saw you."

She smiled rather ruefully, adding, "Yes, it does feel like an eon, doesn't it?"

"Are you all right?" he asked. "Honestly?"

"Yes. The scars will heal."

"I know. It's always hard when you start feeling your mortality, your vulnerability. Pehndon?"

"He's dead."

"A good death?"

For the first time since he had known her, she seemed to deflate, sagging just slightly in her chair. "The frightening thing, Owen, is that it almost wasn't. I have never been so close to forgetting what it means to be Guild. I let my emotions get involved, and it scares me how close I came to wanting revenge."

He sighed. "It was a near thing, wasn't it? Your being here at all, I mean."

"There were times when I certainly thought so."

He masked a shudder. "I remember; it happened once to me. But you're only human, Vera . . ."

"Yes, well." She smiled wryly. "I got over it."

"What?"

"Being human."

He chuckled briefly, then sobered, adding, "Any time you want out, you know . . ."

But, as expected, she dismissed this with a snort, saying,

"Nonsense, Owen, I wouldn't want to force you into retirement yet again; once is enough for any assassin. Besides, there's still some life in the old girl yet."

"You are a constant solace to me, Vera, do you know that? And considering that, for once, you're actually dressed for the occasion . . ." He pushed himself away from the desk and held out one arm. "Dinner at Menot's, at the Guild's expense?"

She looked from him to the magelights pointedly and raised an eyebrow.

"No, I assure you, no tricks this time. Besides, I had them recoded again."

"I shudder," she said and took his arm. "But never mind; I'll figure it out in time. Shall we go?"

"Indeed." Then surveying the tasteful splendor of his public office, he smiled in reflection. "You know," he said, "there are times when I feel positively ancient? Still, at least something good has come of all this. Your pair are quite a team, are they not?"

She glowed proudly—much the same sentiment he felt when surveying her own accomplishments. "That they are. But Owen . . ."

"Yes?"

"Sometimes I wonder if I haven't done the world a very great disservice."

"Created a monster, you mean?" He chuckled. "Well, as for that, my dear, I'm afraid only time will tell."

Don't miss this exciting preview of Jen and Thibault's continuing adventures in *Bridge of Valor*.

"I still can't believe you are making me do this; the whole concept is positively dire!" And Jen scowled fitfully at her image in the mirror and, by proxy, at the reflected glory of the room behind her.

There was no denying that Vera's city dwellings were a good sight grander than her country manor, from the high, plasterwork ceilings to the thick, Mepharstan carpets: dusky rose and cream in this particular room, entwined with vines and stylized roses. At the left-hand wall, stood a mahogany armoire, inlaid with opaline flecks of mother-of-pearl and bursting with gowns. At the right-hand wall, loomed the bed, its cherrywood pillars rising to a canopy of the finest Savill lace, its thick feather mattress bearing a froth of snowy pillows and linens. It was patently ridiculous. Even the magelights rested in silver sconces, glimmering from behind cut-crystal shades, which refracted the glow into a million lucid planes until the very air seemed to shimmer and dance, striking rainbows from every hard-edged surface.

Jen let her frown deepen, her eyes wandering from the gilt scrollwork that edged the mirror to her reflection, and from thence to the image of the delicate blonde who hovered over her right shoulder, curling tongs in hand, patiently transforming Jen's chestnut mane into a series of sleek, controlled coils.

"Ow," Jen added, more for form than substance, as the girl pulled loose the tongs and released yet another springy curl.

But unlike every other well-trained lady's maid of Jen's acquaintance, Elia Dumont merely smiled and widened her cornflower eyes in mock horror, casting a shrewd yet knowing look at her current victim. No protestations, no apologies. No worried "Domina-did-I-hurt-you?"s. But then Elia Dumont was no ordinary maid. Instead, she was one of Vera's pet creations, part of her handpicked cadre of loyal staff. For as a top-flight assassin in the Hestian Guild, Viera Radineaux was one of the highest paid artisans in all Varia, and there was not one of her servants who didn't share the bounty.

Of course, as the Hawk, her identity was supposed to remain a strict secret, so even having servants at all was considered something of a risk. But Vera had her own brilliant system whereby—in return for loyalty, discretion, and five years of required service—her employees would leave wealthy enough to purchase a mansion even grander than the one in which they had served. It was, as she phrased it, a calculated risk—one breach of trust and she would be in danger of losing her livelihood, not to mention her life—but it also was a gamble which had, to date, paid off quite handsomely. Maybe it was just that her servants appreciated their freedom. Other operatives were known to purchase their helpers' discretion by means of the mages' often brutal silencing spells. Or maybe it was the prestige of having a secret that stilled their tongues, leaving them to bask in the reflected mystery of their employer's double life. Or then again, maybe it was Vera's innate charm and charisma that won their hearts and therefore their loyalty.

Or maybe, Jen reflected with a certain, cynical assurance, it was merely Vera's inherent good judgment when it came to measuring the character of her future employees.

Whichever, the secret remained safe. Which was why Jen could now turn to her aunt and remark pointedly, "It simply isn't fair!"

Vera grinned. She was lounging on the bed: a vibrant splash of color against the snowy sheets. But all she said was, with annoying calm, "For one thing, I'm not making you; Owen is—which is a different thing entirely. And for another, it wouldn't be so dire if you'd just relax and enjoy it."

"*Enjoy* it?" Jen retorted. "That's easy for you to say; you're on assignment! I'm the one who has to suffer through the frivolous prattle of a bunch of mindless aristocrats, without even the advantage of any external distractions."

Vera chuckled and smoothed the folds of her gown. She was resplendent in plum satin, the rich, dark fabric perfectly complemented by black lace and piping and glints of golden stitchery. Her dark hair was coiled atop her head, and a faceted gold-and-crystal necklace and matching drop earrings completed the ensemble, glittering against her still-tanned skin like shards of winter ice. She looked phenomenal—and worse, Jen was keenly aware that the right-hand earring housed, as its master crystal, a recording device similar to that which she had used on Pehndon only a few blissful months earlier.

In truth, she wasn't sure what made her more miserable: that her aunt was on Guild assignment while she was forced to wait less than patiently for her first commission, or that Vera, as a matron, was allowed to wear the dark, vivid colors which so complemented their mutual coloring instead of the insipid pastels and virginal whites which Jen was reduced to as a debutante of the thrice-cursed Season.

It simply wasn't fair.

Jenifleur Radineaux—whose lifetime ambition was to be known only as the Dagger—masked a growl and tossed her head, making Elia lose her grip on the curling tongs.

"Jen," her aunt exclaimed severely, "behave yourself! Elia, pay her no heed—and you have my full permission to bodily restrain her if she tries to act up again!"

Jen masked a reluctant grin. In the mirror, Elia smiled, then bent to retrieve her implement. "I just might, at that," she said, her voice brimming with mischief, and Jen subsided as the girl once again began wielding her tongs with an expert hand.

With her wide sky-blue eyes and damask cheeks, her shining waves of golden hair pulled back in a classic twist, Elia had the kind of delicate beauty that could have passed for royalty in disguise. She should have been going to the ball instead of Jen. Her porcelain poise and doll-like features would have certainly looked better in the pastel hues that made Jen either look sallow or so riotously colored by comparison that she appeared almost vulgar.

For one, shining moment, Jen hated her aunt's servant with a passion.

"Honestly, Jenny," Vera was saying, "I don't know why you're making such a fuss about this. It strikes me that the Season is exactly the sort of occasion you should be reveling in. Making wittily cutting remarks under the polite guise of conversation, having roomfuls of eligible men willing to swim oceans for your favors. . . . Where's your sense of adventure?"

"I—"

"After all," the Hawk added, "it's not like you have to marry any of them; we designed your cover specifically to prevent that."

Jen felt her lips twitch in a sudden grin as she thought of her fictitious fiancé, whose presumed existence was supposed to keep the crowds of suitors at bay. Actually, her aunt was right; given the proper motivation, this whole situation was ripe with possibilities—not to mention potential liaisons such as she had enjoyed in her schooldays. Only . . .

"Sometimes I wonder," Vera continued ruthlessly, "if it's really the Season you object to, or rather the fact that you were forced into it without volition?"

Jen gasped, whirling to stare accusingly at her mentor. "Vera!" she exclaimed.

"Well?" Her aunt smiled unrepentantly. "It's true, isn't it?"

Suddenly, Jen began to grin again. "In a sense, I suppose."

"So?"

She shrugged, turning back to the mirror. Actually, it was more than just rebellion—though admittedly that was a part of it. Rather, she didn't feel that she *could* act up— at least, not yet. Owen had forced her into this position so she could be accepted by the aristocracy; so that the Guild would have a hand, as it were, in the enemy camp. And as long as she had to play by those rules, had to fit into the mix, she had to conform to society's strictures: those silly posturings that kept her tongue reined in and dressed her in insipid hues. That kept her simpering and mindless like all the other little painted birds, dutifully chirping out the acceptable phrases.

It galled her beyond belief.

In fact, the only time she felt really free these days was at the University, clad in her anonymous black robes with

Thibault at her side, absorbing the details of poisons, weaponry, and world leadership. So, "Do you realize that I missed my Theories of Government class for this?" she countered instead.

Her aunt was unconcerned. "So? Thibault will take notes for you—as usual."

"Yes. Dear Thibault. Now, if Owen could only get us a job. Or at least if you'd let me help you with yours . . ."

The Hawk grinned. "Don't you remember what happened the last time you tried to help me with my job? You nearly got us both killed, my girl!"

Jen chuckled. Her aunt was teasing, of course—to a degree. They both had nearly died in Ashkharon, though not through any fault of Jenifleur's amateur bumbling or Vera's lack of attention. It was, rather, the ruthless ministrations of Minister Iaon Pehndon that had nearly brought them both to their doom. Determined to seize the reins of power, Pehndon had had Vera raped and beaten, imprisoned. He had even tried to have her executed, but she had outwitted him there and in several subsequent encounters. Eventually, she had even effected his death—or so Jen assumed. She had never gotten a clear answer from her aunt on that, one way or the other.

"Besides," the Hawk added, "there's nothing you can do to help. Tonight I am merely adding the finishing touches to a job I have been working for the past few months. A job, I might add, that had I the connections in society you are currently developing, I could have completed several weeks back."

Jen snorted, unimpressed. "And what about a job of my own?"

"Patience, Jenny, patience. Owen will give you an assignment when he feels you're ready. There, now what do you think of that?" Vera added as Elia stepped back triumphantly to display her handiwork.

Jen cocked her head, surveying her image critically. Slowly, she was learning to bend the rules. Though her current gown was a dusky rose—a shade deemed socially acceptable for young, unmarried women—she had managed to find a fabric overlaid with a faint sheen of copper, so that the material rippled and flowed in shimmering waves, like a fall of liquid metal. Her hair, still streaked with gold from the burning rays of Ashkharon's sun, was gathered in a long fall of coiled ringlets, each sleek and perfect as a seal's pelt, and her jewelry was the twin to her aunt's—only without the more esoteric characteristics, and fashioned of rose quartz rather than diamond and mage-crystal.

The largest of the faceted pink stones lay perfectly nestled in the hollow between her collarbones.

"Not bad," she admitted, smoothing her shimmering skirt and adjusting the floating scallops of the neckline that scooped low off her shoulders. Maybe tonight she would start pushing those other limits as well, trying to add a bit of her natural outrageousness to her repertoire as social neophyte. "Not bad, indeed."

"Not bad?" queried a new voice cheerfully. "You look beautiful as always, Jenny. Good evening, Vera. Great work, Elia."

Jen swirled about with delight as her partner came striding into the room, still clad in his academic robes. He was bluff with the wind and the nighttime cool, his cheeks flushed and a faint chill seeming to emanate from the folds of his garment, infusing the close, perfumed air with the crisp scent of fall. As usual, his prodigious height and broad peasant shoulders seemed to dominate the room, making an odd mockery of the delicate feminine vanities like lace counterpanes and ivory-silk divans.

Jumping up, she dropped a kiss on the hinge of his jaw and tugged at his elbow, dislodging the leather-bound folder tucked under one arm. "Did you take notes?" she demanded. And, "What did Professor Garradon cover today?" She began flipping though his neatly lettered pages.

"Good evening, Thibault," Vera said, rising. Out of the corner of her eye, Jen was aware of Thibault staggering, feigning awe at her appearance, and masked a grin. Their adventures in Ashkharon had been good for one person, at least. Her best friend and partner was finally starting to come out of his self-imposed shell of class-consciousness and accept the exalted Radineauxs as equals.

About bloody time, too.

"Do you need me for anything more?" Elia inquired. "Or shall I leave you to your scholarly pursuits."

"Scholarly pursuits, please." Jen grinned, her gaze still fastened to the papers. "Don't you think, Vera?"

"Indeed. You're free to go, Elia, my dear. In fact, take the evening off. Enjoy yourself."

"Many thanks."

"And from me, too," Jen added again, glancing up briefly. "Great work, Elia."

"My pleasure."

When their audience had left, Vera turned to Thibault with a knowing smile. "Well?" she demanded. "What did Owen say?"

"How did you know?" Thibault demanded.

Jen dropped the papers, her study forgotten. She wanted to ask the same question.

"He told you, didn't he?"

Vera shook her head. "He didn't need to; your face reveals everything. You're about to burst, my lad, so out with it. Is it a job?"

He started to grin maniacally.

Jen found herself bouncing uncontrollably on her toes, practically vibrating in her impatience. "He did it? He found us a job?"

Thibault nodded solemnly.

"A Cloak and Dagger job? No Hawk?"

"Jenny—"

"No offense, Vera, but ... Answer me, blast you, Thibault! Cloak and Dagger only?"

He nodded again, and handed her a card. "Compliments of the Guildmaster," he said.

She took it and examined it. "What the *blazes*?"

"What does it say?" That was Vera, being practical.

Jen frowned over the embossed letters. "It says," and she stumbled over the unfamiliar name. " 'Ruairi—Roo-ah-*eer*-ee?—NaBlaine, Lord of Valor's Rest, Docent of Clan NaBlaine, South Morne, Arrhyndon.' What is this? Is he our contact?"

Vera nimbly lifted the card from her fingers and examined it. "Sit down, Thibault," she said at last. "I think you'd better tell us everything."

With a sudden, broad grin, he complied.

The Roc Frequent Readers Club
BUY TWO ROC BOOKS AND GET
ONE SF/FANTASY NOVEL FREE!

Check the free title you wish to receive (subject to availability):

☐ **DR. DIMENSION:**
Masters of Spacetime
**John DeChancie
and David Bischoff**
0-451-45354-9/$4.99 ($5.99 in Canada)

☐ **EARTHDAWN #2:**
Mother Speaks
Christopher Kubasik
0-451-45297-6/$4.99 ($5.99 in Canada)

☐ **EARTHDAWN #4:**
Prophecy
Greg Gorden
0-451-45347-6/$4.99 ($5.99 in Canada)

☐ **HUMILITY GARDEN**
Felicity Savage
0-451-45398-0/$4.99 ($5.99 in Canada)

☐ **THE DARK TIDE:**
**Book One of the *Iron Tower*
Trilogy**
Dennis L. McKiernan
0-451-45102-3/$4.50 ($5.95 in Canada)

☐ **SHADOWS OF DOOM:**
**Book Two of the *Iron Tower*
Trilogy**
Dennis L. McKiernan
0-451-45103-1/$4.50 ($5.95 in Canada)

☐ **THE DARKEST DAY:**
**Book Three of the *Iron Tower*
Trilogy**
Dennis L. McKiernan
0-451-45083-3/$4.50 ($5.95 in Canada)

☐ **PRIMAVERA**
Francesca Lia Block
0-451-45323-9/$4.50 ($5.50 in Canada)

☐ **THE STALK**
Janet and Chris Morris
0-451-45307-7/$4.99 ($5.99 in Canada)

☐ **TRAITORS**
Kristine Kathryn Rusch
0-451-45415-4/$4.99 ($5.99 in Canada)

☐ **TRIUMPH OF THE DRAGON**
Robin Wayne Bailey
0-451-45437-5/$4.99 ($5.99 in Canada)

To get your FREE Roc book, send in this coupon (original or photocopy), proof of purchase (original sales receipt(s) for two Roc books & a copy of the books' UPC numbers) plus $2.00 for postage and handling to:

**ROC FREQUENT READERS CLUB
Penguin USA • Mass Market
375 Hudson Street, New York, NY 10014**

NAME _____

ADDRESS _____

CITY_____STATE_____ZIP_____

**If you want to receive a Roc newsletter,
please check box ☐**

Roc Books

Photo by Jim Shi

ANNE LESLEY GROELL

is a native New Yorker who received a B.A. in Biology from Yale, then went on to the University of California at Irvine, where she did graduate research and undergraduate teaching. After earning an M.S. in Developmental Biology, she returned to New York to become an editor and writer. The sequel to *Anvil of the Sun* will be published by Roc in 1997.

SHADOW WARRIORS

Born to an aristocratic family, Jenifleur boasts a lady's breeding and education. But the soaring heart that pumps her blue blood yearns for more dangerous pursuits, and her life's passion has always been to follow in her aunt Vera's footsteps—to become an operative of the dark and powerful Assassins' Guild. And now she is getting that chance, for better or for worse. Because Vera has taken a very perilous assignment in the far-off sands of Ashkharon…and is in desperate need of help.

Enlisting the aid of her stalwart friend Thibault, Jenifleur embarks upon an epic journey to rescue her beloved and mysterious aunt. But the young and eager duo are soon in way over their heads—for the two intrepid adventurers are going where even the Assassins' Guild itself is powerless to save them….

"An engaging, high-spirited romp through a world full of color and excitement."
—Paula Volsky, author of *The Wolf of Winter*

ISBN 0-451-45544-4

45544

0 99769 00599 9